Goodbye Emily

Michael Murphy

D0920144

NEW YORK

VIRGINIA

Goodbye Emily
by Michael Murphy

ISBN 9781938467219

Published by

 köehlerbooks™
an imprint of Morgan James Publishing

5 Penn Plaza, 23rd floor
c/o Morgan James Publishing
New York, NY 10001
212-574-7939
www.koehlerbooks.com

Publisher
John Köehler

Executive Editor
Joe Coccaro

 In an effort to support local communities, raise awareness and funds, Morgan James Publishing donates a percentage of all book sales for the life of each book to Habitat for Humanity Peninsula and Greater Williamsburg.
Get involved today, visit www.MorganJamesBuilds.com

Woodstock

Organizers of the festival planned for 50,000 attendees outside of Woodstock, New York where Bob Dylan and other performers lived. They hoped to raise enough money to create a music studio. They secured a location in nearby Wallkill, New York, printed tickets and began to get the word out.

Then things went wrong. Wallkill residents voted to withdraw the permit forcing organizers to find a new site with just weeks before the scheduled event. Fortunately, they found Max Yasgur's farm, and Dylan never played Woodstock.

1

My life changed forever the night I drank the last of my bourbon. Two blocks from home, I entered The Library, once the top tavern in Milton, Pennsylvania. I climbed on a stool at the end of the bar, tuning out the one-liners, high-fives and lame pickup lines of my fellow patrons. I just wanted a drink. Maybe two.

I signaled the bartender. "Bourbon on the rocks." No water to dilute the alcohol.

Time changed everything, including one's favorite bar. In the sixties and seventies, students and faculty from the nearby college hung out and debated war, Watergate, disarmament and nuclear power while classic rock played in the background. Now I had to tolerate Lady Gaga.

The bartender, in his twenties, wore a starched long-sleeve maroon shirt with a glossy "Librarian" button pinned to his black vest. He slid a napkin in front of me and studied my face. "Professor Ellington?"

That's me. Professor—former professor—Walter Fitzgerald Ellington. Close friends, back when I had friends, called me Sparky.

He set the drink in front of me, apparently determined to strike up a conversation I hoped to avoid.

"You let your hair grow since the bastards forced you to take early retirement."

"No one forced me out. I retired a year ago to write the great American novel."

"How's that worked out?"

This kid was either charmingly droll or a complete smart ass. I lifted the glass in a mock silent toast and swallowed half the booze.

He wiped down the counter with a white towel as if the bar paid him for each swipe.

"Last night the dude who *didn't* force you out, Chancellor Warfield, and his co-conspirator who took your place, Professor Blake, came in. They shared a booth, and Blake didn't look happy."

"I really don't care."

I vowed not to think about those two self-indulgent, backstabbing bureaucrats again. I'd moved on. I sipped the bourbon as if I enjoyed the taste while he prattled on about taking my Nineteenth Century English Lit class. I caught something I never expected to hear.

"You presented each lecture like a Broadway show, full of passion and emotion. All you needed was music."

"I get that a lot."

No one ever compared my lectures to theater before. Unless he majored in mixology, my instruction and Milton College hadn't done his career much good.

"Bob." He shook my hand. "Bob Windsor."

A long rambling belch came from the poolroom behind me. A blustery, beer-bellied truck-driver type lumbered from the room and stuffed a handful of bills into his jeans pocket. He wore a greasy green Transcontinental Transport T-shirt and carried an empty pitcher of beer. His shaved head, shirt and thick toad-like body reminded me of Shrek, without the ogre's charm. To my great relief, he chose a stool at the other end of the bar.

I came to drink, not to judge, but when Shrek cursed a perceived lack of service with a reference to Windsor's mother, I muttered to myself, *Man is thy most awful instrument.*

The bartender chuckled. "William Wordsworth."

"What grade did I give you?"

"B plus."

"Perhaps I misjudged you, Windsor. You obviously deserved an A."

I finished the drink, and the young man brought me another. Shrek slid the pitcher toward the bartender, who filled it with draft beer and handed the pitcher back. The ogre took a long gulp from the pitcher then wiped his mouth with the back of a catcher's mitt of a hand. He focused his attention on two college-age girls, a blonde and a redhead at a nearby table, who sipped fruity drinks with tiny umbrellas. The man made wet kissing noises to the redhead as she popped a cherry stem into her mouth and tried to tie it into a knot with her tongue.

The girls wore jeans and T-shirts and only a hint of makeup. Even I could tell they hadn't come to the bar to be hit on. They didn't hide their annoyance with the intoxicated trucker. As his grunts and gestures grew vulgar, their annoyance changed to alarm. The blonde's face flushed and the redhead covered her eyes with one hand.

The co-eds reminded me of my daughter, Cloe, when she was in college. They were nice girls who wanted to enjoy a relaxing drink and not be bothered by a pig like Shrek. I nursed my drink, determined to mind my own business.

The bartender had to see the ashen faces of fear on the girls, but he wasn't exactly the bouncer type.

The blonde grabbed her purse. "Let's go."

"Terrific idea." Shrek climbed off his stool. "I'll walk you to your dorm, Sweet Thing."

Enough! I couldn't tolerate the man's treatment of the girls another minute. I slid the half-full glass of bourbon away, slapped a twenty on the counter and climbed off the barstool.

Over thirty years as a college professor, I often diffused tension-filled situations, and I could do it again. Retirement hadn't dulled my skills that much.

Shrek, while imposing and prison-tough, didn't present much of a challenge. His acne and two missing teeth grew more apparent as I approached. A meth-addict alarm sounded in my head. Shrek gave me the once-over.

"What's your freakin' problem?"

"No problem."

I planned to distract the man long enough to allow the girls to slip out the door.

"Why don't you go back to your cardboard box in the alley and curl up with a bottle of Boone's Farm, you longhaired old freak?"

The Philistine was indeed a most awful instrument.

"You look familiar. I thought perhaps you'd taken a class of mine at Milton College."

"You're a professor? Well, Professor Buttinsky, I'm talking to these bitches."

The bar chatter quieted as people at nearby tables paid attention to our conversation. I caught the blonde's attention and nodded toward the front door.

She winked at me and tugged on her friend's arm. The redhead didn't move. She appeared more interested in watching the drama between Shrek and me.

I took a deep breath. Perhaps I overestimated my ability to outwit this man. Bourbon might have clouded my judgment.

"First off, I don't think the young ladies appreciate being referred to as bitches, and second ..."

The brute slammed a club-like hand against my chest. I stumbled backward, bounced off a table and landed in an empty booth. The bartender grabbed a cell phone and made a quick call.

I regained my feet and a modicum of dignity. It occurred to me, perhaps too late, that sixty-year-old retired college professors shouldn't get into barroom brawls, especially with men half their age and twice their size. I shook my head and flashed a pathetic grin.

A pulsing vein looked ready to burst from Shrek's forehead.

"What are you laughing at, old man?"

I straightened the jacket I valued so much, and my fingers touched a ripped pocket.

"Son-of-a-bitch. Emily gave me this."

Shrek laughed. "Tell whoever Emily is to spring for a new one."

"She's dead, Shrek!"

Several patrons gasped and retreated to the poolroom. The quiet of the bar resembled a library. Katy Perry's "I Kissed a Girl" sounded like someone had turned the volume up all the way.

The two girls slipped out the front door, causing Shrek to bellow like a UFC cage fighter.

"Now look what you made them do, you miserable old fuck."

Shrek slammed a punch to my jaw, busting my lip and jolting my skull like a mule kick. I spun backward and knocked over a barstool. Air burst from my lungs as I fell to the floor. I cracked the back of my head against the tile.

I could barely see through a white flash of agony. I spit blood that landed on Shrek's boots.

The big man let out a Sasquatch roar and stomped a black leather boot onto my ribs.

A wave of nausea shot from my stomach. I struggled to breathe. I tried to suck in air but only managed to squeak like my dog's chew toys.

"Who's laughing now?"

With a crazed cackle, Shrek grabbed my jacket collar and raised a fist for another blow.

A muffled siren pierced through the haze and my ringing ears.

"This is your lucky day, Professor."

Shrek dropped me like a sack of compost. My head smacked the floor again, and he hawked a loogie. An egg white-like glob landed on my cheek and slid down into my ear.

I struggled to lift my head. The room spun like it had the first anniversary after Emily died, when I polished off an entire Jim Beam bottle. The bartender's voice sounded far off as he told me to stay down. The lights dimmed, and the bar's blurry sights and fuzzy sounds faded to black.

♫♫♫♫

My vision and hearing returned. I was in the backseat of a Volkswagen Beetle crowded with sleeping bags and empty fast-food containers.

I coughed from the stink of cigarette smoke. A peace symbol swung on a chain that hung from the rearview mirror, and a sign printed in white shoe polish on the back window read "Woodstock or Bust!"

My two best friends in the world sat up front. Buck Jamison, in a jungle camouflage T-shirt, biceps bulging, sat behind the wheel smoking a Marlboro. He waved to a bitchin' blonde in a pickup bed sharing a doobie with a girl who could have been her twin.

Josh Channing rode shotgun, studying a Woodstock program as if he discovered secret plans to the next moon launch. The geeky but brilliant music guru, in a blue tie-dyed T-shirt, was lead singer in our three-person garage band, The Buck Naked Band.

We were stuck in a monumental traffic jam barely crawling along as rainclouds threatened overhead. In spite of the traffic, I couldn't contain my joy when we neared a green "Welcome to Monticello, New York" sign. Next stop: Bethel, New York. Woodstock!

I rubbed my hands together with the same excitement I felt at age six when my parents took me to a supermarket opening to see the late actor George Reeves in his Superman costume.

Josh pointed to a "Welcome Hippies" sign in a small grocery store's front window. Buck whipped the car into a crowded parking lot. He double-parked behind a psychedelic Volkswagen bus and held out one hand. "Give me some bread, man."

We slapped bills into Buck's palm. He stuffed the money into his wallet, flashed us the fake ID, and went inside the market to buy beer and eats.

Josh and I climbed out of the cramped car and stretched our legs. He grabbed change from his pocket and dropped coins into a pay phone outside the front door.

"Tell me you're not calling your mom." He deserved a wet willy. I slipped my finger in my mouth then stuck it in his ear.

Josh rubbed his ear, turned his back to me and dialed. In two weeks, he and I would be freshmen roommates at Penn State. When we told his mom about the road trip to Woodstock, she preached a long-winded sermon explaining why God would punish those in attendance.

Josh waited for his mother to answer and flashed me a quizzical look. "What?"

I answered with a jerk-off motion.

Josh cleared his throat. "Mom, it's me." Pause. Longer pause. "Woodstock." For the next two minutes, he leaned his head against his hand. He listened to what I was sure was another lecture about the devil's music.

I couldn't bear to watch the verbal abuse of my friend, so I plopped down on a bench on the other side of the door. I checked out a parade of hot-looking girls in bell-bottom jeans and braless shirts. They drifted through the line of traffic hitching rides on motorcycles or cars that barely crept forward.

Josh dropped more change into the phone and continued to listen then cupped a hand over the speaker. "I'm grounded."

I burst out laughing. "Dork!"

"It's not like that at all, Mom. The festival is organized, safe ..." A college girl in bell-bottoms and a pink tube top strolled by and ruffled Josh's hair. "... friendly." Pause. "No, Mom. No drugs."

Buck came from the store carrying a single paper sack. "The shelves are practically empty, man." He tossed me the bag like he was throwing a touchdown pass.

"No beer?" I peered inside the bag. "Prunes. Seriously, where'd you stash the real stuff?"

"That's all they had, moron, and I coldcocked a nerd for the last package."

"Never send a jock to do a man's job."

"Fuck you." Buck dropped down on the bench beside me. "Prunes provide nutrition, which your skinny ass could use."

"Prunes give you the shits. You ever shit in a Porta John?"

Buck nodded toward Josh, still trying to reassure his mother. "What's with the douchebag?"

"He's grounded."

Buck shook his head then gazed off in the distance. He even ignored the fine-looking ladies all around. He wasn't going off to college. The government had plans for Buck. A month after graduation, he received a draft notice in the mail.

He couldn't hide that boot camp weighed heavily on his mind. "You okay?"

Buck lit a cigarette and stared down at his boots. "Just thinking this will be the last roadtrip for the three amigos."

"We've got plenty of trips ahead of us."

We both knew it would be our last trip, certainly as carefree teenagers. Life was about to change for us. Innocence lost. Responsibilities gained.

"I'll be okay." He blew out a plume of smoke and nodded toward Josh. "Worry about *him*."

Josh looked at us and made a yakking gesture with one hand. "Call you tomorrow, Mom. Love you, too."

Buck shouted, "I love your mom too, Josh. At least I did last weekend when she dropped by the garage and asked me to lube her chassis."

Josh covered the phone's mouthpiece, flipped Buck the bird and slammed the phone into the cradle. "Why do I let her push my buttons?"

At the car, I clapped him on the shoulder. "Was that a rhetorical question, because if you'd really like to know, I'd be happy to explain."

Stocked only with our meager supply of prunes, we climbed into the faded blue Volkswagen with the candy apple red peace symbol Buck painted on the hood. The three of us gave the car encouragement. The Beetle coughed then started.

Josh applauded then peered into the sack. "Where's the damn beer?"

We crept along toward the concert billed as Three Days of Peace and Music. Three miles outside of Bethel, traffic stopped. The road became a parking lot. When the heap overheated, Buck shut off the ignition and glanced over his shoulder at me. "What do you think?"

Most everyone climbed from their cars and headed in the direction of the festival. I wanted to hoof it. "Let's walk."

Buck didn't appear enthusiastic about abandoning his car. He studied a foldout map. "Are you serious? It's four miles as the crow flies."

"Fuck the crows." Josh snatched the map from Buck and tossed it out the window.

Buck slipped the bug into neutral. We climbed out and pushed the car to the side of the road. We grabbed our stuff and joined the procession walking west toward the festival.

A day earlier, we left the safety of our Milton, Pennsylvania, hometown to embark on a roadtrip of epic expectations. Three recent high school graduates, friends since second grade, we each managed to scrape together the eighteen bucks for a three-day ticket. With a few extra dollars stuffed into our pockets, one change of clothes and sleeping bags, we came for the music, but more importantly, to lay claim to our independence. At least I had.

We hiked more than two miles in the August heat and humidity. In Bethel, locals stood on their lawns as the parade of mostly freaks walked by. Locals waved and offered encouragement. A woman handed us paper cups of lemonade with ice and wouldn't take any money.

Refreshed, our trek continued. Campsites filled the woods on both sides of the road as we neared the festival. At the site, giant speaker towers sprouted from the rolling farmland. We stepped across downed chain-link fences. No one collected tickets.

Buck ripped his ticket into tiny pieces. "Could've used the money to buy weed."

We followed the crowd toward the sound of rock music and paused at the crest of the hill. A canopy sat atop a massive wooden stage at the bottom of a gigantic amphitheater. I stood in silent awe of the rolling ocean of heads. I wanted to freeze the moment in time. "Isn't this great?"

"Yup." Buck hefted the sleeping bag over one shoulder and sniffed the dense air. "Three days of peace, pot and pussy."

A performer I didn't know sang on stage, repeating the word "freedom," over and over. "Who's that?"

"Richie Havens." Josh scanned the program. "He's not supposed to be on yet."

With a parade of people still behind us, we made our way down the hill seeking space to set our sleeping bags. I searched for a place near a stand of speakers, and froze when I spotted the most beautiful girl ever. For a moment, my heart stopped.

She wore a form-fitting cotton shirt and white shorts, the blonde surfer girl type with legs that started at her shoulders and ended in leather sandals. Beside her was a skinny hippie girl with short dark hair and tinted glasses. The blonde twirled a flower in her hair.

"Hey, guys, how 'bout there?" I pointed to a gap in the throng and made my way through the crowd. I dropped my bag twenty yards from the girl of my dreams and her hippie friend.

Josh settled in beside me while I tried to make eye contact with the blonde.

Buck tossed his bag onto the ground and followed my gaze. "Dibs on the blonde chick."

"Why do you get first dibs?"

"I'm off to boot camp next week, that's why."

Damn, Buck. A couple hundred thousand braless babes and our high school's ladies' man sets his sights on the girl of my dreams. I shot Buck a hot, fevered stare. "She's not a piece of meat."

♪♪♪♪♪

"Who's not a piece of meat?" My daughter. Images of the blonde and Richie Havens shimmered and faded away. I hadn't dreamed of Woodstock in years and desperately wanted to cling to day one and relive the moment Emily and I first met. I let out a groan.

"You okay, Dad?"

I opened my eyes. I was in a dimly lit hospital with a heart monitor beeping behind me. A patient on the other side of a teal curtain hacked a smoker's cough. I was in a flowered gown. This had to be the ER.

A stab of pain jolted my heart over the faded Woodstock images. The events at The Library came into focus, and I realized the throbbing in my chest was the exact spot where Shrek stomped on my ribs.

Cloe stood beside the bed. Worry lines creased her forehead, but she looked as pretty as her mother did at that age. She blinked away welling tears. "Dad?"

"Why's the lighting so dim?"

She brushed a shock of hair from my eyes. "You've had a concussion. They said soft light lessens the effects."

The clock on the wall read a quarter after midnight. I lost two hours. "Where are my clothes?"

"In a bag under the bed."

I took stock of my injuries. I touched my swollen lip then moved my jaw. It ached but didn't feel broken. I took a breath and winced as pain shot across my ribs. I pressed against my chest.

My daughter gripped the bedrail. "Chest pains again?"

"I got kicked in the ribs."

Cloe pulled a chair alongside the bed and sat. "They told me you were in a bar fight. Tell me that's not true."

"Wasn't much of a fight. I didn't even get in one good punch."

She chuckled. "A college professor, my father, in a barroom brawl."

"In pursuit of a noble cause." The two maidens escaped the ogre's evil intentions.

"If Mom were here, she'd quote Gandhi—an uncompromising opponent of violent methods even to serve the noblest of causes."

Emily wasn't here. "Gandhi would have slugged this jerk if given half a chance."

The curtain opened and an unsettlingly young doctor entered. Thirty-something, close to Cloe's age, he wore a stethoscope around his neck like a piece of jewelry. I'd have preferred someone old enough to have graduated from medical school.

He wore a fashionable five-o'clock shadow on his tan face, the look of a *Grey's Anatomy* doctor. Doctor McDreamy showed an immediate interest in my eligible daughter. "You must be the patient's daughter. Ms. ..."

"Miss," I corrected. Few of my daughter's boyfriends ever met her high standards to merit a long-term relationship. Perhaps the young doctor would prove to be the exception.

Cloe recognized my matchmaking mode and shot me an irritated squint. She shook the doctor's hand. "Cloe Ellington."

"She's a lawyer. A public defender." *How noble is that, Doctor?*

"I'm Doctor Malone." The nametag on his white coat read "David Malone, MD."

Under normal conditions, I wouldn't accept a doctor who ignored me. However, with his less than subtle interest in my daughter and no ring on his left hand, I experienced a flicker of hope this one might break through the thick veneer of her career.

"Is my father alright?" Cloe appeared oblivious to the doctor's good looks.

"As long as he stays out of barroom brawls." He grinned.

Stays out of barroom brawls. Good one, Doc.

Dr. Malone shifted his attention to me. "Mr. Ellington, you sustained a mild concussion."

"I'm fine now."

He came closer, shined a penlight in one eye then the other. Why would they keep my area dimly lit then shine a blinding lightsaber into my eyes?

"So you're what, a neurologist?"

"Cardiologist. Have you experienced chest pains?"

Besides an ogre stomping my ribcage? "I wouldn't exactly—"

"Dad's had chest pains off and on the past two years after Mom died. They've gotten worse the last few months."

Squealer.

The doctor listened to my chest with his stethoscope. He studied the monitor and made a note in the chart.

"Grief is how we recover from a loss, but after two years we'd expect to see evidence of healing from the emotional pain."

So now he was a shrink. This wasn't going well. "I lost more than a wife, Doctor. She was my best friend."

"I lost a mother." Cloe blinked away tears.

The doctor placed the stethoscope around his neck. "Have you ever heard the term *stress cardiomyopathy*?"

"I heard about the condition in a deposition. I should've realized." Cloe looked more comfortable with a medical/legal conversation.

"Hello!" I struggled to sit up in bed and winced from tender ribs. "Remember me?"

Doctor Malone snickered. "Mr. Ellington, in our Dr. Oz generation, the popular name for what I suspect you have is *broken heart syndrome*."

Was he serious? A syndrome for a broken heart? "So you cure broken hearts?"

"I treat the symptoms. It's up to you to find the cure."

"You still get paid, right?"

"After Mom died, Dad developed all the classic warning signs."

I braced myself. The good doctor and I were about to hear a list of my shortcomings, at least those my daughter knew about.

"Dad used to be outgoing and witty. Now he's grumpy and keeps to himself. He no longer takes pride in his appearance. He's a mess, and so is the house. He eats mostly junk food, and he drinks too much."

"I don't drink too much, just what I need."

"Then there's mom's urn."

"What about the urn?"

"He keeps it on the coffee table along with the television remote …"

Where she'll be close every day. "What do you suggest, a shrine?"

"… usually next to a bottle of whiskey."

"Not funny." Cloe let out a sigh. "While the urn's sat on the coffee table for two years, you know what's on the mantel? A damn baseball."

Dr. Malone took on the look of a physician anticipating something significant enough to enter onto a patient's chart. "A baseball."

I hoped he was a sports fan. "Autographed by Mickey Mantle." My wife's favorite ballplayer. The ball was a cherished gift from Emily.

The doctor chuckled. "A Mantle on the mantel."

Emily humor. She placed it there years ago.

"You want to tell him the rest, Dad, or should I?"

"I thought we had attorney-client privilege." I cursed myself for running out of bourbon.

Cloe continued as I knew she would. She was concerned for me, so I cut her some slack. "Ten months after Mom died, Milton College forced Dad into retirement. He never sees his two best friends from high school anymore."

Doctor Malone's brow furrowed with concern. "You recently turned sixty."

"What's your point?" He made turning sixty sound like the biggest tragedy of all. The doctor's initial charm had worn off.

"The things your daughter mentioned, we call them life stressors. One thing I suggest to my patients is to write down each item and keep the list where you'll look at your problems every day so you can begin to confront them. You may not get your friends, or your job back, but as you come to terms with each one, your condition should improve. Will you do that, Mr. Ellington?"

"If I say yes, can I leave?"

He made a quick entry into the chart. "We'll get you admitted and run a few tests to be safe. We have to be sure of the extent of your concussion and see whether there's been damage to your heart. You seem like an educated man."

"Dad's a college professor."

"Was."

"We can schedule a battery of tests for first thing in the morning." The doctor checked the chart and smiled. "Your blood work shows when you came in you were legally intoxicated. If the tests check out, we'll have you out of here tomorrow in time for happy hour."

I didn't like his use of the word *battery*, but Dr. Malone possessed a sense of humor and charm, traits that might bode well for Cloe.

"I won't stay."

"Yes, you will, Dad."

Behind the curtain, the patient in the next bed sounded like he just hawked up a lung. I was healthy before they brought me in but wouldn't be by the time I left.

"Lady's alone." I pictured my dog pacing the house and whining.

Cloe patted my hand. "I'll stop by and make sure she's alright."

The doctor snapped the chart closed. "I think we have a plan. Any questions?" Without letting me respond, he gave a passable Jim Carrey imitation. "Alrighty then." He winked at Cloe, pulled aside the curtain and went in search of another victim.

I'll never get out of this hospital. With decent insurance, doctors could justify a never-ending series of tests, most painful and/or humiliating. At my age, I'd never leave with all the body parts I possessed when I arrived. Broken heart syndrome indeed.

"The doctor's being thorough."

"In case you missed his first name, it's David."

Cloe let out a breathless sigh. "Mrs. David Malone. Mrs. Doctor David Malone. I wonder what his sign is, or his favorite meal."

Before I could compliment her sarcasm, the curtain slid open and Dr. Malone poked his head inside. "Sorry to bother you, Mr. Ellington, but I need to know whether you have an allergy to iodine, so I can schedule a scan."

Cloe's face flushed crimson.

I shook my head no.

"Great." He smiled at Cloe. "I'm a Scorpio and my favorite meal is shrimp scampi." With a charming grin, he left and pulled the curtain closed.

Cloe fanned herself with one hand. "I haven't been this embarrassed since high school."

"On you, it's refreshing."

Cloe managed to laugh at herself. "He was cute, wasn't he?"

At least she noticed. The day wasn't a complete disaster after all. "Go home and get some rest, but please check on Lady."

Cloe kissed my cheek. "Maybe what happened tonight is a good thing. At least we'll find out what's wrong with your heart."

"I knew before tonight I had a broken heart. I just didn't realize it had a clinical name."

"This is nothing to joke about." Cloe ripped a tissue from a box on the table beside the bed and wiped moist eyes. "I lost Mom two years ago. I can't lose you."

I held her hand. "You're not going to lose me."

"You have to take this seriously."

"I will, honey. I'll make the list like the doctor suggested."

"Promise?"

"I promise." I struggled with how much to admit to my daughter, to myself. I felt a flicker of chest pain different from the barroom bruise. "I haven't handled the past two years well. I know that. Your mother's illness came up just after we found out what's wrong with Josh."

"You should go visit him."

She was right. I tried to summon the courage several times but never got farther than the front steps. "Don't worry about me."

"You know I do." She dropped the tissue into a trash can beside the bed. She grabbed her purse to go.

I had one more thing she needed to hear. Something I needed to say, and it wouldn't be easy. "You're all I have left."

Cloe squeezed my hand. "You're wrong about that. You have a lot to live for. You just haven't realized it yet." With a wistful smile, she slipped through the curtain and left.

I ignored the man in the next bed who began to snore and reflected on the events that brought me to the hospital. Shrek played a minor role.

Most of my life, I was the luckiest man alive. I loved my wife to the moon and back, and she loved me even more. I adored my daughter and remained close to my best friends, Josh and Buck. I relished the role of respected professor at Milton College. For more than thirty years, I taught students things they didn't know, and I learned from them. Life was perfect, until Emily's cancer. Then it all fell apart.

I had nothing left except Cloe, Lady and booze to take away the pain and help me sleep. Life had spun out of control, and as painful as it was to admit, I had no idea how to get it back.

The patient in the next bed continued his phlegm-clearing even in his sleep. The hospital wasn't doing him much good.

I climbed from the bed and winced from my aches and pains and a tug against my chest hairs by the heart monitor sensors. The wheels on the monitor squeaked as I moved it closer to the patient in the next bed. I peeked through the curtains to make sure the man was still asleep. I ripped off my sensors and stuck them to his chest.

His eyes blinked open. "Who are you?"

"A ... a volunteer. Go back to sleep."

His eyes fluttered closed.

The monitor barely missed a beat. With a satisfied chuckle, I retrieved my clothes from beneath the bed. I tossed the hospital gown into the corner and changed.

Even with the tear in my Steelers jacket I felt better already. I poked my head out the curtains. While nurses and doctors tended to really sick people, I followed the signs, left through the main entrance and made my great escape from the ER.

I took my health seriously, but it was *my* health. I didn't need a wisecracking doctor and a battery of tests to mend my broken heart. I stuffed both hands in my jacket against the chilly early morning and began the long walk home to Lady.

2

In spite of August's heat and stifling humidity, I sat with my blue Penn State windbreaker at my side as heavy gray clouds threatened Woodstock. Like most everyone, Buck and Josh appeared oblivious to the prospect of a storm as Richie Havens belted out a Freedom encore. Josh's head bobbed to the music, and he sang along, lost in the performance. Buck played drums on a soft drink can with two pencils he bummed from a hippie couple who seemed more than happy to share whatever they had.

Havens finished to rousing cheers which flowed over the amphitheater. A man climbed onto the awning-covered stage and announced the festival, with a crowd of more than four hundred thousand, was now the third largest city in the state of New York. *Far-out.*

Buck and Josh watched the next act take the stage while the blonde girl of my dreams laughed as her hippy friend stuck a daisy into her short black hair and stuck out her tongue. The blonde didn't know I existed, but I'd find a way to change that. The beauty's shoulder-length hair swayed to the music, and her friend met my gaze with a smirk.

I flashed the college-stud smile I practiced all summer. The flower child whispered to her blonde friend then, to my surprise, dusted off her jeans and headed our way.

She wore a green tie-dyed shirt and Haight-Ashbury rose-tinted glasses—the hippie look. Thin, maybe five two, she squeezed into a space next to me without difficulty.

Buck and Josh greeted her with halfhearted nods. They focused on the stage, immersed in the performance.

"Looks like your two buds came for the music, and you're here to get laid."

I organized the roadtrip as a rite of passage for three friends facing huge changes in their lives. If I got laid, so much the better. "I'm on a quest for independence."

"Aren't we all. Got any weed?"

I shook my head.

She sniffed the air. "Everyone has weed. What kind of eats did you bring?"

I tossed her the paper sack. "Prunes."

"You're messing with me, aren't you?" She peered inside the bag and giggled. "No weed and the only food you brought was this lame bag of prunes. You guys aren't getting laid. Not this weekend."

Buck set down the pencil drumsticks and checked her out. He lit a Marlboro, took a long puff and offered her one.

"Gross, Ringo."

He took another drag. "So, you'll smoke grass, but not tobacco, is that what I'm hearing?"

"Cigarette smoking is a nasty, teeth-staining habit and it causes cancer."

Buck blew a smoke ring toward her. "That hasn't been proven." With the cigarette in his mouth, he resumed his drumming.

"Hey, don't let science stop you." She ripped open the bag of prunes and tried one. She made a face and swallowed.

She thumbed toward her hot blonde friend and smiled. "If you're interested, you should offer her weed, at least something better than prunes. You're interested, right?"

Were my intentions so obvious? "Maybe."

"Got a name, Slim?"

"Walter ... Walt."

"Nice to meet you, Walter Walt."

She checked out Josh. "What do they call you? Red? Freckles?"

I smiled. "That's Josh. The Marlboro Man is Buck."

Josh gave the girl a once-over then bummed a cigarette from Buck. "Only teachers and his grandma still call him Walt. Even his parents refer to him as Sparky. His old man tagged him with the name."

The hippie girl cocked her head. "I give. How'd you get pegged with Sparky?"

Buck snorted laughter. "He almost burnt down his parents' house learning to smoke cigarettes."

She gave Buck a playful punch on the arm. "That's one way to quit."

"He accidently dropped a lit cigarette into a backyard shed that contained a gasoline can. Whoosh!" Josh made an exploding gesture with both hands.

My best friends enjoyed embellishing the story over the years. To relive the experience at a festival of peace and joy pissed me off.

Some tall, skinny freak, with a scraggly beard and a jungle camouflage jacket, approached my dream girl. He sat beside her and edged closer, like a vulture circling an innocent rabbit.

The three of us hadn't eaten since we devoured a dozen stale doughnuts several hours earlier. If I scored some decent food, I could offer the fox something a whole lot better than prunes.

I peered up at the rainclouds, snatched my windbreaker and scrambled to my feet.

Buck crushed out his cigarette. "You splittin'?"

"I'm off to score some eats."

"Excellent, but you'll get lost by yourself." Josh started to rise.

"You can't come. You're grounded."

"I'll go." The girl held out a hand to me. "I'll show you the food booths by the woods."

Shit! Wrong girl. I offered my hand and helped her to her feet.

She nodded to her blonde friend, who waved back. She didn't let go of my hand as we made our way through the sea of hippies and straights.

Weed's sweet tangy aroma hung above the farm. Everyone seemed to share food, water, whatever. They dug the music, smoked pot and passed around jugs of wine—young people pushing boundaries like young people always did. This would be one hell of a three-day party.

My hippie companion, as if she read my mind, squeezed my hand. "The adventure begins, Sparky."

I held her gaze and something unexpected passed between us. Not exactly the girl of my dreams, but with gentle features, she was definitely cute. She had a quirky sense of humor, and her soft hand was comfortable in mine.

For the first time, I noticed her silver peace symbol necklace and heart-shaped earrings. A peace and love kind of girl, probably named Rainbow or Moonbeam. "You didn't tell me your name."

She cocked her head and smiled, showing a dimple I hadn't noticed before. "I'm Emily."

♪♪♪♪

Emily's image vanished as the doorbell rang. *No!* I bolted upright in bed and pain shot through my body. Lady scrambled to the front door and barked at the intruder.

I gathered my bearings, steadied myself and eased both legs over the side of the bed. I struggled to rise. A lower back spasm yanked me back onto the mattress. The effects from the altercation at The Library added to my normal morning aches and pains. I clamped my eyes shut from the most painful hurt, the loss of Emily's image when she first told me her name.

I arched my spine and stretched. My joints cracked like dice rattling in a Yahtzee cup.

The doorbell rang again and set off another round of Lady's barking.

"Stop with the doorbell, damn it!" I made a mental note to disconnect the bell. Anyone who rang my bell wasn't welcome inside anyway.

I made it to my feet, slipped into a flannel robe and shuffled toward the front door. In the kitchen, I stubbed my toe on a Jim Beam bottle. "Son-of-a-bitch!"

The bottle spun across the tile floor, collided with Lady's bowl and spilled water onto unopened newspapers stacked in the corner.

The knife-like pain in my toe hurt worse than Shrek's punch to my jaw. I limped to the living room, gave Lady the sit command and pulled open the door. Dr. Malone stood on the welcome mat looking none too happy. I stepped aside to let him in. "Think I broke my toe."

He entered the room carrying a black bag like physicians used before I was born. "Your big toe?"

"The one next to it."

"That's not a serious problem."

To him maybe. I closed the door. "I didn't know doctors still made house calls."

Lady, to my surprise, didn't display her usual friendly behavior when she met someone new. She sniffed the black bag then backed toward the kitchen.

"Careful, Lady, I bet he has a thermometer in there."

The dog disappeared down the hallway then peered around the corner at the doctor.

"I'm not a vet, girl." He smiled at Lady.

A specialist making a house call couldn't be good news. Maybe he discovered some previously undetected medical condition. I braced for the worst.

"I'm not here on my own volition. My med-mal carrier insisted I get you to sign a release." The doctor displayed none of the humor he demonstrated in the hospital. Apparently, his charm had been for Cloe's benefit.

"Where do I sign?"

"As long as I'm here, let me take a look."

I limped to the couch, dropped to the cushion and held up my foot.

Dr. Malone snapped open his bag and removed a penlight. He ignored my toe and flashed a light in one eye, then the other. "How's the headache?"

My head throbbed less than my toe. "Gone."

"Any ringing in your ears or hearing problems?"

"What?" I cupped one ear.

Dr. Malone registered a flicker of a smile. He took my pulse and blood pressure without comment. Apparently satisfied, he stuffed the instruments into his bag.

"I called your daughter this morning and informed her of your great escape."

"A regular Steve McQueen."

Cloe would be more upset than the doctor. I dreaded her lecture, but at least the handsome doctor called my eligible daughter.

The doctor gazed around the room. There was an empty pizza container, a pair of old tennis shoes I hadn't worn in a year, a half dozen balled up socks, a bowl with dried cereal and a white crust of milk stuck to the bottom. No doubt, he noted the untidiness in my chart he'd send to his malpractice carrier.

He peered at all the crap in the kitchen. "Your daughter may have exaggerated your lack of housekeeping skills."

I knew sarcasm when I heard it.

He nodded toward the coffee table. "That must be the shrine.

How did you and Emily meet?"

"A little place called Yasgur's farm."

Dr. Malone raised an eyebrow. "Woodstock."

"Four years later, the summer after I graduated from Penn State, Emily and I married. We lived happily ever after for thirty-six years." Until the death do us part thing.

I rubbed my forehead and pictured Emily and me, hand in hand, as we weaved our way through the crowd in search of food.

"Something's bothering you. I can tell. I'm a doctor."

"My toe's broken."

Frustration flickered across Dr. Malone's face. "No more joking. I suspect you have a medical condition, if left untreated, will deteriorate the fibers in your heart until the muscle no longer works. If we catch and treat the condition in time, it's reversible, but you have to confront the unresolved issues in your life. If you haven't made your list of life stressors, I suggest you get started."

The words sank in. He was right. "I'll call your office for an appointment."

"I checked before I left. We can fit you in this afternoon around three."

"This afternoon?"

"This afternoon."

I shrugged. "I'll be there."

"Good." He handed me the release and a pen. I signed the form and gave it back. He stuffed the release into his black bag and made his way to the door. He paused as if he'd forgotten something. "What's the deal with your daughter?"

"Deal?"

"A woman that ho ... attractive and intelligent must be seeing someone."

The house call now made sense. The doctor's appearance on my doorstep wasn't an errand to please his insurance carrier or to check up on me. He dropped by because he had the hots for my daughter.

"I don't think there's anyone special at the moment." I didn't want him to think she was the type to wait around for him to call. "There have been plenty of men ... I don't mean plenty. I mean ..."

The doctor laughed.

I made Cloe sound like a slut. "I meant to say there isn't anyone special in Cloe's life right now. Her career comes first, as I'm sure yours does with you."

"See you this afternoon, Mr. Ellington." He shook my hand and went outside. He drove off in a blue Miata, not quite the chick magnet I expected.

Lady bounded into the room, wagging her tail, celebrating the doctor's departure. She followed me down the hall to my office.

The red light flashing on the answering machine looked like Cloe's blink. I braced myself against my daughter's lecture about why I shouldn't have left the ER. The voice wasn't Cloe's.

"Professor Ellington, this is Victoria Jenkins, Dr. Warfield's administrative assistant ..."

I hit delete without listening to the rest. I had no interest in talking to the bastard who abruptly ended my career—or his secretary.

A whiteboard with a plot outline that never went anywhere hung on the wall. I planned to chronicle the adventures of a charming college professor in the second half of the twentieth century, but I came to realize my life experiences would hardly interest readers.

I wouldn't give up on writing a novel, but for now, I focused on my health. I erased the words and picked up a green marker to write the list I promised Cloe I'd make. I accepted my heart condition could be fatal. I wasn't ready for a death sentence quite yet.

At the top of the board, I wrote "Emily." Beneath her name, I added "Josh." Beneath that, "career." At the bottom of the list, I wrote "Buck Jamison."

I studied the board. I didn't know if I was dying of a broken heart, but I was certain I'd neglected people once very close to me. I didn't know how to begin to come to terms with Josh's condition, but I could face Buck. I had to find out why he didn't come to Emily's funeral. Then I could move on and erase his name from the list. One down, three issues to go.

A tinkling sound came from the hall. Lady stood in the doorway wagging her tail with her leash in her mouth.

I left her alone most of the night. I owed her a trip. "Let's go for a drive."

Forty miles from home, Lady and I neared the township of Lawrenceville, Pennsylvania. Buck's Garage was a former service station badly in need of a fresh coat of paint. I parked my BMW between a late model yellow Mustang convertible and a '57 Chevy with a red glossy paint job and orange flames on the front fenders.

I shut off the ignition and remained seated while Lady gazed patiently out the window. I hadn't seen Buck in years, but I called him the day after Emily passed. He assured me he'd be at the funeral. He never showed, and we hadn't spoken since. I never excused the snub.

I pictured myself crossing Buck's name off the whiteboard. I drove forty miles, not to rekindle a friendship or find whether he'd turned his life around. I came all this way to deal with a health issue. How self-centered could I be?

A stab of pain rose in my chest. I stroked Lady's golden fur. "I can't do this to Buck."

Lady whined.

We both jumped when a hand rapped on the driver's window. I rolled down the window.

A man in greasy overalls with "Tony" stenciled above the pocket wiped his oily hands on a blue towel. "Can I help you?"

Too late to back out now without coming across as some kind of stalker. "Buck around?"

Tony nodded toward the open bay. Buck stood beneath a salt-damaged purple sedan jacked up on a hoist.

"Thanks." I climbed from the car with Lady on the leash.

Tony popped open the hood to Buck's towing truck and removed the air filter as Lady and I waited at the entrance to the bay.

The air, thick with humidity, reeked of oil, gasoline and automotive paint. In oil-stained overalls, with gray hair tied in a ponytail, Buck held a pneumatic gun in his right hand. On his arm was the Scout Dog tattoo—Buck's Vietnam Platoon, the 58th Infantry. He returned from a second tour with the tattoo, shrapnel in one knee and other wounds I suspected he never revealed to anyone.

Buck looked thinner, more fit than I remembered. The pneumatic gun whirled as he worked. He set down the tool, wrestled the shock absorber loose and laid the strut at his feet. He glanced up and grinned. "Well, fuck me Sunday."

"Buck."

He removed a gray rag from his back pocket and wiped both hands. "Sparky."

I met him halfway, and we shook hands.

Buck ran a hand over Lady's head. "Who's this?"

"Lady."

She held her paw up to Buck.

He laughed and shook her paw. "Nice dog."

"You busy?"

"Not too busy for an old friend and a pretty girl." He clapped Lady on her side. "I could use a drink, how about you?"

"I guess." Ten in the morning was too early for booze, even for me.

"Hey, Tony, take a break," Buck called.

"Almost finished." Tony didn't look up from the tow truck's engine. "It's your truck, but if you keep her under eighty, she'll last longer."

"The man's a working machine." Instead of grabbing beer as I expected, Buck plucked two bottles of a cloudy red-tinted drink from a cooler and tossed me one. "Pomegranate white tea, filled with antioxidants and other shit that can help with cancer, heart problems, even erectile dysfunction."

"Erectile dysfunction? It won't go into effect while I'm drinking the stuff, will it?" I unscrewed the cap, tried a sip and shuddered. "I wouldn't feed this to my neighbor's cat."

"It's an acquired taste." Buck took a long gulp. "Man, you and I are at an age when our body parts that should be soft, harden and the parts that are supposed to be hard, soften." He took a long swallow.

Tony slammed the tow truck's hood, climbed behind the wheel and started the engine. He gunned the accelerator a few times, then closed the driver's door and backed it up. "I'll take her for a test, Mr. Jamison."

Buck chuckled as his mechanic drove away. "I always look around for my dad whenever anyone calls me Mr. Jamison."

The door to the office in back opened, and a hot-bodied redhead half Buck's age stepped out. Candy apple-red nail polish matched Angelina Jolie lips. She wore a diamond studded nose ring, stiletto heels and a red leather halter-top. She tugged car keys from the snug pocket of Daisy Duke shorts.

She acted as if Lady and I weren't there. She pressed her toned body against Buck and kissed him, her teeth nipping his lower lip. "Mamma's gotta dance, baby. Be back around six."

"Ashley, this is my old friend, Sparky."

"Sparky, yeah." She gave me a quick hug and a whiff of sweet perfume. "My man talks about you all the time."

Buck flashed a sheepish smile.

"Don't you boys get into any trouble. On the day shift I won't make enough cash for bail money." Shapely hips and the stilettos set a rhythm as she strutted toward the yellow Mustang. She climbed into the convertible, showing off half her left butt cheek and a tattoo that read "Spank Here." She blew Buck a kiss as she drove off.

I tried not to smile. "I didn't know Amish girls could drive."

Buck let out a bellowing laugh. He set two folding chairs in the shade close to a squeaky evaporative cooler that did little but stir the humidity and circulate automotive fumes. Lady finished her exploration and plopped down in front of the cooler. Buck and I sat and watched morning traffic.

"How long have you and Ashley been together?"

"Together? A couple sleepovers a week is hardly together, but she's started to worry me. Six months ago, she changed her stage name to 'Bambi.' Now all her coworkers and friends call us Buck and Bambi and laugh like the joke's on me."

"Whatever happened to that Jamaican girl?" Five years ago, Emily and I ran into Buck and another much younger, exotic woman.

"Tanya, the massage therapist. My lower back misses her. Three years ago, she drove my Silverado to the bait shop to pick up a carton of cigarettes and never came back. *Ces't la vie* said the old folks ..." He held out his hand.

"... goes to show you never can tell." I slapped his palm.

"Chuck Berry. That man understood women."

"Now we're the old folks."

"That we are, Sparky. That we are."

I downed more tea, shocked I kept it down. Why did healthy food taste like crap? "Why didn't you ever settle down with one woman?"

"Why would I want to do that?" He stared at me as if I'd lost my mind. "Love is for saps. The concept sells records, perfume, lingerie and Valentine's Day cards."

I cringed at his skepticism.

"You and Emily were the exception, of course." Buck finished the tea drink and let out a rambling belch. He tossed the empty bottle into a trash barrel in the corner as if shooting baskets. "It's good, and it counts!"

I missed our friendship. So far, the visit seemed like old times, two buddies catching up. Still, we both knew we'd talk about Josh and eventually why Buck hadn't come to Emily's funeral.

"You never did accept my advice about women. Remember back in junior high how I gave you pointers on how to get into Becky

Lynne Wilson's pants? You said she wasn't that kind of girl."

"We were in eighth grade."

Buck rolled his eyes. "Then I guess she became that kind of girl in one year. The summer after our freshman year. We did it in the backseat of her old man's station wagon."

I couldn't tell whether Buck's story about Becky Lynn was true or whether he just wanted to make a point.

"I hear you retired."

"They fired me."

"Cocksuckers! I didn't think a professor could get canned. What about tenure and shit like that?"

"They have their ways. Reorganization. I'd have little to do but sit around all day and feel sorry for myself."

"How do you spend your days now?"

Sitting around all day and feeling sorry for myself.

Buck thumbed toward the back of the garage. "Let me show you my daily reminder that life's worth living."

I dropped the half-empty bottle into the trash barrel.

He led me to the back and removed a canvas tarp to reveal a vintage Harley with polished chrome and glossy black paint. "I might have overstated my denial about love earlier." He slapped the bike's leather seat. "I *love* my Harley."

For a moment, neither of us talked. I'd put off the purpose of my visit long enough. "Buck, why didn't you come to Emily's funeral?"

He avoided eye contact, climbed onto the Harley and grabbed the handlebars as if he wanted to ride away and never look back.

"I couldn't bear to think of a world without Emily or see you in the pain I knew you'd be suffering."

"I still can't bear the thought of her gone, Buck, but I was there." I pounded my fist against my thigh.

"We all were. Josh and even his crazy ass mother made it along with a couple hundred more whose lives Emily touched." Everyone except Buck.

Buck clamped his eyes shut. "I experienced a lot of death in Nam, some men close to me and some men I killed in ways that still wake me up at night."

The pain in Buck's face softened the resentment I'd carried for two years. My voice cracked with guilt. "You don't have to go there."

"Of course I do, but that's not why I didn't come to Emily's funeral." He let out a ragged sigh. "I haven't been to a funeral in almost twenty years. My sergeant in the fifty-eighth came back from Nam more fucked up than me. For the next twenty years, he spent more time in jails than out. You want to hear how he bought it? He fucking froze to death on a tenement doorstep in Washington, DC."

"I'm sorry."

"Sorry? Everyone's always sorry after something like this happens, but no one's willing to help people when they really need it." He let out a sigh.

"Sounds like a good guy."

"You won't find his name on the black marble memorial, 'cause he didn't die in Nam. He was a casualty of the war just the same. Government gave him a seventeen-gun salute 'cause sarge was a fucking hero with a medal in a box somewhere to prove it. Soldiers in blue shiny uniforms and brass buttons folded up a brand new flag. They handed the Stars and Stripes to his miserable excuse for an old man, who wasn't there when his son needed help and understanding the most."

Like I wasn't there for Buck when he came home. I was too busy finishing college, settling down with Emily and starting a career in academia. "You don't have to explain."

"Fuck you. You asked, goddamn it, so I'll finish this. I survived my sergeant's funeral and got drunk. I stayed drunk more than two years. Only way I tapered off the booze was to pop pills and snort blow."

Buck's descent into drug use was no secret, but this was the first time he ever talked to me about his demons. If this was what confronting my life stressors would be like, no wonder I kept them buried. I should've stayed home. "How'd you come clean?"

"Woke up one day in a St. Louis alley covered in puke and piss. I crawled to the sidewalk while people passed by like I was nothin'. Then a cop came by and drove me to a VA hospital. If they hadn't taken me in, I'd be dead." His eyes welled with tears. "I was in rehab a month when they told me they'd done all they could. I found a liquor store, intending to celebrate by downing a bottle of Jack Daniels. Instead, I called a friend who wired me enough money to come home." He paused, waiting for me to ask. "I can tell from your face you don't know who sent me the money."

Not me. Why hadn't Buck called me for the money he needed to save his life?

"Josh?"

"I called Emily."

"Emily?" I couldn't believe she never told me.

"I made her promise not to say anything." Buck's face twisted in pain. "She kept me from living in back alleys and going back to drugs. I paid her back, but I owed her a lot more than the money. Emily saved my life."

Buck wiped away tears, but more filled his eyes. His voice cracked.

"I've been sober for ten years, thanks to Emily. After you called to tell me she passed on, I wanted to go, but I was scared shitless. Afraid I'd get wasted again. It would kill me this time, Sparky." Tears slid down his face. "That's why I didn't go, why I didn't send flowers, why I fucking never called to say I'm sorry." He sobbed.

Lady ran to his side. She rested a paw against his leg and whined.

I threw both arms around Buck. His body slumped, and I held him as he wept against my shoulder. I stayed angry with him for two years because it never occurred to me he might have struggled with his own pain over Emily's death. When did I become such a self-centered prick? I suspected it was a long time ago, and I just never realized it until now. "I'm the one who's sorry."

Buck's sobs subsided. "I think I'm going to puke."

I let go and stepped back. "Not on your Harley."

A smile curled from the corner of his mouth. He wiped his eyes on the gray rag then blew his nose. He petted Lady. "I'll be okay."

The phone on the wall rang Buck climbed off the Harley.

"That's life's way of telling me enough with the fucking self-pity."

I had to leave, not for my sake, but for Buck's. I pulled my keys from my pocket, desperate to end the visit that caused my friend so much grief.

Buck followed Lady and me to my BMW. I opened the passenger door and Lady climbed in. I nodded to the red Chevy. "This your work?"

He looked better in the midday sun. He managed a smile. "I'm an artist. You should let me paint flames on your BMW." He let out a laugh.

I gave him another hug then climbed in my car. With all the pain I brought, I doubted I'd ever see him again.

"Wait a second." Buck brought a shaky hand to his forehead. "I haven't seen Josh since they diagnosed the Alzheimer's. Let's go see him."

Our visit had been painful for Buck and me. After witnessing his fragile emotional state, I suspected he'd have more trouble seeing Josh.

"Maybe it's best to remember him the way he was."

Buck stared into the distance a moment then shook his head. "No, Sparky. It's not."

He was right. I'd put off visiting Josh long enough. Maybe Buck needed to confront his life stressors. "How about tomorrow at ten?"

"Sure. If you're still in the same house, I'll come by and we'll ride together."

"Deal." I doubted Buck would come by in the morning, any more than he showed at Emily's funeral, but if he didn't, now I'd understand.

"I'm glad you came by."

"Same here." Through the open window, I shook Buck's hand. I held the clasp and stared a moment in case we never saw each other again. For a brief moment, we were carefree high school kids again, instead of men in our sixties with painful memories we kept buried.

I drove back to Milton, picturing the pain I'd caused by forcing Buck to look back on memories he'd buried. He'd been sober for ten years. I drank enough to realize it didn't take much to send a person with substance abuse issues plunging back into a hell from where they might never recover.

What had I done? I pounded on the steering wheel.

I jeopardized his sobriety, his life, so I could deal with my health issues. If anything happened to Buck, I'd never forgive myself. I had to make sure he didn't fall off the wagon.

3

By the time Lady and I returned home, I finished beating myself up over causing Buck so much pain. I vowed never to put him in that position again.

I poured myself a drink but left it on the counter when I remembered my exam with Dr. Malone. The light blinked on the answering machine. By now, Cloe must have learned about my flight from the ER.

I wouldn't put off the inevitable. I pressed play on the answering machine and braced myself against my daughter's lecture about why I shouldn't have left the ER. The voice wasn't Cloe's.

"Professor Ellington, this is Doctor Warfield. I'd like to stop by..."

I hit delete without listening to the rest. First Warfield's secretary then the snake himself. I had no interest in talking to the bastard who abruptly ended my career.

Two hours of an intake interview, blood work and an exhausting treadmill test took my mind off Buck's meltdown. Dr. Malone reviewed the results behind a clean and orderly desk while I finished a bottle of water. I tossed the plastic container into a trash can next to the door.

The doctor, with a look of skepticism, glanced up from the chart. "You have two to four helpings of grains each day?"

"Hops and malt. They're grains, right? One or two beers a day."

"That doesn't count."

I sat in a chair in front of his desk. The diplomas on the wall revealed he graduated from the University of Pennsylvania's medical school. Penn Med, as folks in Pennsylvania called it, was one of the best in the country.

A framed photo on a credenza behind the doctor caught my eye. A young boy, maybe five, in a T-ball uniform posed with a baseball bat over one shoulder. "Your son?"

Dr. Malone picked up the picture. "Aiden. He's going to be a gifted athlete."

"Like his dad?"

"I played baseball and basketball in high school. You?"

I shook my head. "Back then I was known more as an athletic supporter."

The doctor smiled and set the picture back on the credenza.

"Is Aiden here, in Milton?"

"He lives with his mother in Philly."

"Must be tough."

"Let's talk about your results." He closed the chart and clasped his hands on the desk. "I'll get right to the point. You have early indications of stress cardiomyopathy."

"Broken heart syndrome."

"I prefer the clinical name. The condition is causing your chest pains."

"I thought they were panic attacks."

"You have a potentially fatal heart condition. Stress cardiomyopathy causes weakness in the heart muscle."

He explained as simply as he could that large amounts of stress hormones, adrenaline and norepinephrine released into the bloodstream eventually stun the heart, causing chest pain and shortness of breath. The remedy: reduce these hormones entering your blood by reducing your stress.

"Make sense?"

The doctor wisely appealed to me with academic logic. The symptoms had occurred more frequently the past two months. Self-medicating with bourbon hadn't helped.

"To reduce stress I have to confront the items on my list."

"You got it. The good news is the condition is reversible. It appears we've caught yours in time."

"I'm guessing there are all sorts of drugs available to treat this."

"Medication will lessen the chances of a heart attack. I'll prescribe vasodilators to open up blood vessels and diuretics to eliminate excess fluid. Drugs alone won't solve the problem." He glanced at the wedding ring I still wore. "Tell me about Emily."

Before today, I hadn't opened up about my loss of Emily, not even to Cloe when she needed to talk about her feelings. Where to begin? Small details came to mind.

"She was comfortable in jeans around the house, or a gown at a faculty ball. She took in stray dogs. Her favorite incense was Sandalwood—"

"I'm sure she loved long slow strolls on the beach, but if I'm going to understand you as a patient, I need you to open up to what you've kept inside since she passed away. Try again."

I let out a deep breath. "What impressed me the most about Emily when we first met was her love for her parents." I struggled to keep my voice from quivering. "She loved her students, she loved life, and ... she loved me." I choked back a sob.

Dr. Malone waited for me to recover then grabbed my file. "Let's take a walk."

We made our way down the hospital corridor. The cardiac unit contained some of the sickest looking people I'd ever seen. "There's no evidence of permanent heart muscle deterioration, but to reverse the damage, you'll have to confront the issues you've ignored the past couple of years. It won't be easy."

Through a door labeled "smoker's lounge," we entered an outdoor patio made from red brick pavers with pots, flowers, ornamental trees and a stone fountain. We sat on a cement bench watching a woman in her twenties pushing a very sick man in a wheelchair. They stopped beside the fountain.

"This used to be a smoker's lounge, but after the hospital banned smoking, the cardiac unit took it over. Patients like to come out here instead of being cooped up in their rooms."

A portable oxygen canister, hanging behind the wheelchair, connected to a mask around the sick patient's nose. With paper-thin pale skin, his head hung, as if lifting it would be an effort.

The young woman, his daughter no doubt, patted his hand. That could be Cloe and me in a few years. I couldn't let that happen.

"A patient of yours?"

"He's on the list for a heart transplant."

Dr. Malone brought me here to show how I might end up if I didn't take my health seriously. At least he hadn't taken me to the morgue.

"Your condition is the result of a number of factors. There's genetics." He read from my file folder. "Both your parents died before age seventy-five. You need to examine what led you to this point and focus on addressing those issues. If your condition doesn't improve, the next step is an angiogram, where we insert a needle in a large vein in your groin ..."

I held up my hand. "I'll do whatever I can to keep that from happening."

"Glad to hear that. You have to change your nutrition. I'll give you a list of heart healthy foods, and you'll need to exercise regularly. I want you to keep a daily journal of everything you eat and drink along with any structured exercise."

I needed to eat better and exercise, but keeping a daily journal sounded like it would take some getting used to. "Diet and exercise. That's it?"

"Diet, exercise and drugs will help, but these things won't reverse your condition. To prevent stress hormones from wreaking further havoc with your heart, you'll have to address what brought you here."

"My BMW?"

Barely a flicker of a smile. "Your daughter identified four issues you've had to deal with."

"I made the list. It's on a whiteboard in my home office."

"Great. Today I've added a fifth. You've been diagnosed with a potentially fatal illness."

The ink on the whiteboard had barely dried. Now I had to add another item. "I thought you were supposed to fix my problems, not add to them."

"I've treated patients with three or four events in a couple of years, never five. Take some time to think about each one and what you can do to lessen the stress these items cause you."

I told him I reconnected with Buck and about our plans to visit Josh. I didn't tell him the damage I'd caused my friend. "It was ... painful."

He smiled. "I said it wouldn't be easy."

"If I don't deal with these issues ..."

Dr. Malone locked eyes with me. "If you don't, statistics tell us you'll be dead in three years."

Dead in three years?

The man in the wheelchair and his daughter apparently overheard. They glanced at me with looks of pity. Imagine that, a man in a wheelchair needing a heart transplant feeling sorry for me.

Dr. Malone's cell phone chirped. He checked the message and rose. "Emergency. No doubt a patient who didn't take my advice."

The streetlight blinked on as I returned home. I parked in the garage and stepped from my reliable BMW sedan. Cloe on her cell phone sat on the porch with Lady at her feet. She snapped the phone shut as I closed the garage door and climbed the porch steps. "You want to tell me why you checked yourself out of the hospital?"

I kissed her cheek and ruffled Lady's fur. "I thought outpatient would work better. Just got back from my checkup."

I sat beside Cloe in one of the two white wicker chairs Emily picked up at an antique store. "Good news. My condition is reversible. I need to change my diet and I need to exercise. Other than that, everything is perfect."

Cloe raised a skeptical eyebrow.

"I can do this, I can." To my dismay, my daughter removed a lighter and a pack of Winstons from her suit jacket and lit a cigarette.

"When did you start smoking again?"

She blew out a plume of smoke. "Dad, I received a job offer in Virginia."

The weight of ten Shreks stomped on my chest. Logic told me she wasn't abandoning me, but I couldn't shake a sense of impending loss. Dr. Malone would call the news another life stressor, a sixth item for the whiteboard.

I couldn't display my concern. "That's wonderful. I assume this would be a good career move."

Cloe stared at the lighter, turning it over and over as if searching for a secret compartment. "I'd work for the Justice Department in Arlington. Much higher salary, more responsibilities. Politically, it's a terrific opportunity, but ..."

"But?"

She stared at me a moment. "The timing isn't right."

My daughter's eyes couldn't hide her concern over my health. I'd never forgive myself if she turned down a dream job because I neglected my health.

I'd miss her deeply, but Cloe needed to live life for herself, not for me. Before we married, her mother and I lived apart for more than four years. We made it work. "Arlington's less than three hundred miles. Besides, with the Internet and Skype, we'd still see each other."

Smoke curled from the cigarette she barely smoked. Cloe swallowed hard. "Geography never separated us, Dad. You keep your distance even when we're in the same room. You bottle up pain inside until ... until it affects your health."

"I have a plan. I'll get rid of all the junk food in the house, use the treadmill every day, walk Lady—"

"Listen to you. You sound like a college professor preparing a syllabus. Change isn't easy." My daughter inherited her temper from me. "You can't just analyze a situation and conclude life is worth living again. Letting go is a process you haven't even started."

I had started. "I visited Buck today. He and I are going to visit Josh tomorrow."

Cloe's mouth dropped. "I'm so proud of you."

"I can change. I know it won't be easy. When do you have to make a decision about this job?"

"I'm supposed to let them know by Monday."

Six days. Less than a week remained to convince my daughter I'd put the pain of losing Emily behind me.

Her cell phone rang again. She glanced at the caller ID but didn't answer. "I'm late for a meeting."

"A meeting at this hour? How many hours do you work?"

"As many as I have to."

She crushed out the cigarette beneath her shoe. She retrieved and field-stripped the butt, allowing tobacco flecks to drift across the lawn. She stuck the filter into her pocket like a good smoking environmentalist should.

Lady and I walked Cloe to her car. I tried not to imagine life with her hundreds of miles away. I was grateful the darkness hid my feelings.

"Your mother would want you to take the job."

Cloe wiped her eyes. "I know." She unlocked her car, sat behind the wheel and flashed a smile. "That was Dr. Malone on the phone when you drove up."

Excellent! "What did he say?"

"He said you were committed to improving your health."

"There you go. Did you talk about anything else?"

Cloe let out an exaggerated sigh. "Why do you insist on seeing me married?"

"I don't want you to be married. I want you to be happy."

Cloe smiled. "You know the saying, a woman without a man is

like a fish without a bicycle."

Although I laughed, I wanted my daughter to find someone who'd make her as happy as Emily made me. "I figured if you and Dr. Malone got together, I'd get a discount on medical care. I know a good-looking auto mechanic, too. Either one would save me considerable cash now I'm retired on a fixed income."

Cloe shook her head and pulled the door closed. She started the car and rolled down the window.

"I'm going to be fine, Cloe. Take the job. You need to move on with your life."

"I've got a week to think it over." Through the open window, she patted my hand like I used to pat hers. "I'm feeling much better about your health now you're under the care of ..." She paused for dramatic effect as she'd done during closing arguments of a trial. "... David."

Cloe winked and backed out of the drive.

David, not Dr. Malone. I pumped my fist and climbed the porch steps. Dr. Malone, David, Dave, Davey. Honey, pass the remote?

The day was about to end far better than it began. I'd taken steps to move on with my life. I'd visited Buck and had my heart checked. I could adjust to Cloe's moving away and felt confident I'd be able to persuade her to accept the job. I just had to convince her I could move forward and wouldn't dwell on the past.

I shut off the lights and went to bed. Lady curled up on her blanket in the corner. Cautiously optimistic about the future for the first time in two years, I drifted to sleep. I didn't expect to dream about Woodstock.

♫♫♫♫

Emily and I, hand in hand, made our way toward the food booths through the sea of freaks and straights. I hoped the threatening rainclouds would produce a shower that would dissipate the oppressive humidity.

Between acts, the cicadas hummed in the warm evening air. In spite of five hundred thousand people crammed over thirty-five acres, everyone seemed consumed with community. A dozen girls sat in a circle holding sacks of carnations. They fashioned flower halos and handed them out.

We passed a girl in an orange sundress blowing soap bubbles

though a plastic ring. She took a drag on a cigarette and blew a smoke-filled bubble that slowly rose until it exploded overhead in a silent puff of smoke.

Woodstock wasn't just a collection of hippies. As Sweetwater sang a gospel sounding song "Why Oh Why," a redheaded kid in a short-sleeve dress shirt, wearing Barry Goldwater black-rimmed glasses, danced. Emily and I paused to watch his James Brown moves. We joined everyone around him cheering and applauding when the song ended. The kid took a bow and collapsed with exhaustion, a broad smile across his face.

Emily took my hand again. We no longer held hands just to make our way through the crowd.

I worried when no lines existed at the concession stands. A tall man in a red Afro with a blank gaze stood inside an empty food booth and sipped wine from a bottle. He broke the news to us. Everything had been sold or given away hours earlier. He didn't know when or if more would arrive.

The man handed us the half-full bottle of red wine and walked toward the pond alongside the festival. He dropped his clothes along the way and strolled into the water naked. Behavior outrageous anywhere else was hardly noticed here.

We sat beside an abandoned booth and shared the wine. Emily described life on a farm outside of Bethel. She laughed that I pegged her as a California hippie.

She took a gulp of wine and handed me the bottle. I told her about living in Milton and my liberal activist parents. I explained about Josh and Buck. How we'd been friends since we were kids. How we formed The Buck Naked Band our sophomore year.

"Why do you only have three people in your band?" When I shrugged, she tried not to laugh but failed. "No one else wanted to join did they?"

"Maybe."

Emily described her occasional frustration having a knockout best friend, the most popular girl in high school. Crystal's well-off parents owned a bar in Bethel. "Why'd you come to Woodstock?"

"Buck reports to boot camp next week."

Emily took a long swallow. Her hand trembled as she handed me the bottle. Tears shimmered in her eyes. "My brother's in Nam."

"I'm sorry."

After a solemn moment, Emily changed the mood. "What will

you major in at Penn State?"

"English Lit."

"Are you serious?" She gave me a playful shove.

The wine gave me a buzz. I wasn't much of a drinker. "Shakespeare and Christopher Marlowe were the rock stars of their time. Even the queen was a groupie. She had the hots for Sir Walter Raleigh. Back then, literature was the only media. Years from now, students will major in the works of Bob Dylan. I don't want people to forget about classic authors any more than I'd want them to forget about Dylan or Jimi Hendrix."

Emily smiled and shook her head. I'd probably just convinced her I was some major dork. Maybe not. She scooted closer and leaned her head against my shoulder. "Crystal and I only purchased one-day tickets."

"Tickets don't mean anything."

"They do to our parents. We promised we'd be home by morning."

My stomach dropped. I looked toward the stage so she couldn't see my disappointment. Tim Hardin was in the middle of "If I Was a Carpenter." Sadly ironic, the lyrics were about a couple's future.

We were just getting to know each other. I liked this girl, and she liked me. I rubbed the back of my neck and wondered what I could do to change her mind.

"You okay?"

"Don't leave tomorrow."

"Sparky ..." I couldn't read her expression. She took a final gulp of wine and emptied the bottle. Plucking the flower from her hair, she set it in the bottle and proudly displayed the improvised vase. She obviously didn't want to talk about tomorrow.

Country Joe McDonald took the stage. He grabbed the microphone and shouted, "Give me an F!"

A half million answered, "F!"

"Give me a U!"

Emily and I joined in the response. "U!"

"Give me a C!"

"C!"

"Give me a K!"

"K!"

"What's that spell?"

The crowd shouted, "Fuck!"

"What's that spell?"

"Fuck!"

"What's that spell?"

"Fuck!"

The outrageous cheer kept me from thinking about Emily leaving.

Emily cocked her head. "The F-word isn't an obscenity. A war that's killed tens of thousands of Americans for no good reason, that's an obscenity."

I couldn't agree more. After the cheer, Country Joe sang his antiwar song "Feel Like I'm Fixing to Die Rag," better known as "Next Stop Vietnam."

Emily and I sang along. The crowd cheered louder than for any song so far. Country Joe McDonald helped prove music could shape our politics. Like so many of my generation, I considered the Vietnam War a tragic mistake. The song reminded me how music evolved in the last few years into a powerful peace movement tool. No doubt, it wouldn't be the last antiwar song sung at Woodstock, but no one would do it better than Country Joe McDonald.

Raindrops fell. Emily giggled and pulled me to my feet. "I think you're drunk."

"I think you're cute."

We held our hands toward the sky as the rain sprinkled down in a welcome cooling mist. The mist turned into sheets of rain. I removed the windbreaker and held it over our heads. I drew Emily close and enjoyed her damp body against mine.

Many in the crowd scattered to the shelter of tents and cars in the camping area at the farm's edge. More sought cover near the speaker towers, which swayed in the storm's wind and downpour.

"We should go back."

Emily took several steps in a different direction, toward the stage. She stopped and held out a hand to me as the flower painted on her cheek slid down her face in wet yellow streaks. "You can go back, or you can come with me."

The Walter part of me wanted to return to the comfort of my friends. The Sparky part took Emily's hand and went with her.

As more people sought cover in cars and tents in the campground, we made our way closer to the stage where Ravi Shankar played the twangy sitar, protected from the rain by the large canvas canopy. Less than fifty feet from the stage, we found room behind a couple sheltered by a yellow tarp.

The storm transformed the grassy pasture closest to the stage into a soggy mud pit. I grabbed a cardboard box people trampled in the exodus from the stage and stomped it flat.

The cardboard offered protection from the mud. With a perfect view of Ravi Shankar, Emily and I huddled close, stretching the windbreaker over our heads.

A young woman in braids and a leather bandana poked her head out from the tarp in front of us. She handed us a folded tarp. "Our friends never showed. Stay dry." She gave us an unlit joint, a matchbook and a cold hot dog wrapped in brown paper.

"Thanks."

The woman flashed us a peace sign. "We're all in this together, man."

Emily and I draped the tarp over our heads. Our clothes were soaked, but for now the canvas protected us from the deluge. I stuffed the hot dog into my jacket for later.

Beneath our improvised tent, Emily examined the joint as if seeing one for the first time. "Now might be a good time to mention I've never smoked grass."

Buck, Josh and I discovered pot the summer before our senior year. "Don't take a big drag the first time." I tried to display my cool worldly ways. "Just a small one and hold in the smoke as long as possible."

"Be careful with these." Emily slapped the matchbook into my hand. "I wouldn't want you to catch the stage on fire, Sparky."

I lit the joint and took a hit. I held in the smoke a couple of beats then slowly let it out. I handed her the joint. "Nice shit."

Emily tugged on one earlobe. "I tried a Marlboro once and almost puked."

"Puking is not allowed. Small drag."

She raised the joint to her mouth and took a puff. A wisp of smoke curled from her lips.

I stifled a smile. "You have to inhale."

Emily tried again. With a look of renewed determination, she held in the smoke, maybe too long. Her eyes grew round. Smoke burst from her mouth in a retching cough. "Gross."

She handed me the joint, covered her mouth and coughed. Her face reddened.

"Smoking is an acquired skill." I patted her back, trying not to laugh. Smoke hovered beneath the tarp. "Just breathe in and you'll get high."

"I don't think I'm a smoker."

I took another hit and began to feel a slight buzz. I offered her the joint.

To my surprise, Emily snatched the joint, took a puff and held the smoke in. She slowly let it out and grinned. Another puff and she handed it back and locked eyes with me. "Wine, pot, rock 'n' roll. What's next, Sparky?"

I didn't know what might happen next. I finished the joint and crushed the small end on my muddy shoe. I breathed in the secondhand smoke. "Feel any different?"

The would-be pot smoker gazed at me with a dreamy expression. She lifted the tarp. We peered through the steady rain. On stage, Ravi Shankar continued to strum the big sitar. The music resonated with a mystical quality, unlike other instruments.

A tear slid down Emily's face, then another.

I slipped my arm around her. "What's wrong?"

"His music makes me think of Gandhi." She blinked away the tears. "Gandhi led to King and the Kennedys and now all four are dead from assassins' bullets. We're left with Nixon. This goddamn war could go on for years, taking people like my brother and Buck." She buried her head against my chest.

I tried to comfort her in spite of my own despair. Her brother, Buck and probably a lot more here might be killed or maimed over there. This festival of peace and love wouldn't save them.

I wrapped my arms around her. She felt soft and comfortable and excitingly close.

She looked at me with doe-like eyes. She intertwined her fingers in mine. The rain fell harder as I leaned toward her. Our lips touched and gently lingered in our first kiss.

The storm pelted the tarp. The Indian music continued. All sounds vanished. The only sound was her breathing and the beating of my heat.

My skin tingled. My palms were moist from the excitement of a first kiss. The softness of her body pressed against mine, our two heartbeats. I finally opened my eyes, and she opened hers. I wiped a tear from her cheek.

I lay back on the wet cardboard. Emily set her head against my chest. Beneath the tarp, we were alone among a half million. I had to convince her to stay.

She smiled at me. "I can hear your heart beating."

♪♪♪♪

I snapped awake and grabbed my chest. I still felt the glow of our kiss. Rain spattered against the bedroom window. I fought back tears of reality. I was home. Emily was gone.

The kiss seemed more than a mere dream. I had experienced my first kiss with Emily a second time, but resurrecting the moment offered no comfort, just overpowering loss and pain.

The sheets were damp from cold sweat. A tight clamping ache gripped my chest. I squeezed the bed sheets against the pain. Any second, I expected my heart to explode. I tried to control my breathing, but the pain intensified, worse than any previous episode.

I wasn't ready to die. I reached for the phone, but the agony proved too overpowering to move.

In the corner, Lady whined. The foot of the bed moved. She jumped onto the bed and crawled toward me. She lay beside me, set her nose on my chest and licked my face.

I stroked the dog, and she ever so gently touched my chin with her paw. In a moment, the pounding in my heart eased and the pain subsided. Minutes later, it had nearly vanished.

Rain-filtered light from a street lamp flickered through the bedroom window. The dog stared in my eyes. I stroked her fur and we fell asleep.

I awoke determined to confront my problems. I fed Lady and headed for my home office. I added two items to the whiteboard: Broken Heart Syndrome and Cloe's Job Offer. Today I planned to focus on Josh and convince Cloe I could take care of my health.

Lady deserved a walk, and I needed the exercise. She fetched her leash, and I took her around the block. She left no scent undiscovered.

We returned home to a strange car in my driveway. Chancellor Warfield climbed from his Lexus. Lady tensed.

A bureaucrat, not an academic, Warfield was twenty years younger than I. He unbuttoned his Armani suit coat and loosened his silk tie.

The man who earned his academic belt-tightening credentials wore Italian shoes and a designer belt that probably cost more than my first car. Lady growled and strained against her leash. Warfield held up both hands.

"I understand why you ignored my calls. I hoped enough time had passed so we might have a pleasant conversation."

I couldn't recall any pleasant conversations with the control freak. Why did he think we'd have one now?

"Five minutes is all I ask."

Compelled by curiosity, I put Lady inside then gestured toward one of the two porch chairs.

Warfield climbed the steps, a hint of triumph in his eyes. We sat in chairs without exchanging a handshake.

During the past year, often at the bottom of a Jim Beam bottle,

I imagined what I might say if I ever faced this man again. At least I possessed home field advantage. I waited for his opening gambit.

The bean counter with narrow birdlike eyes and thin lips flashed a smile as if posing for a photographer. "You're looking well, Professor."

First, I didn't look well. I'd settled into an aging hippie look. Second, I was no professor thanks to this arrogant windbag.

"I didn't expect you to start with bullshit."

"Ah, yes, you always were a get-to-the-point person." He cleared his throat.

Throwing me out on my ass was one of the first moves he made after taking over as chancellor at Milton College.

By replacing me and others with cheaper help, along with other cost-cutting moves, Warfield became the darling of the Milton College Board.

Warfield was chancellor for an institution that thrived for over one hundred fifty years before he arrived. In just a few months, he ran it like a fast food franchise.

"Looking back, I realize I should have handled your separation from our institution with greater ... dignity."

"Dignity? You fired a twenty-five year professor by e-mail. In your defense, you flagged the message urgent."

Adding further insult, the bastard replaced me with someone I considered a trusted friend and fellow member of the Milton Faculty Jazz Review, Timothy Blake. I regretted the breakup of our group almost as much as the loss of my career.

Warfield took a deep breath. "I'm here to offer my sincere apology."

I couldn't take the presence of my nemesis a minute longer.

"Apology accepted. Unless there's something else, I have an appointment."

Warfield didn't budge. "There is something else. I have to replace Professor Blake. I want to offer you your previous position."

My old job? Had I heard right? I pictured the word "career" on the whiteboard. I wasn't certain what I wanted to do with the rest of my life, but a return to Milton College hadn't been an option.

"In spite of my abrupt departure, I've adjusted well. Retirement has allowed me to do what I put off for years."

My mind raced. I was under the treatment of a cardiologist in part because I hadn't adjusted to retirement, in part because of him.

How could he think I'd ever consider returning under his leadership, a man to whom I held no respect? Again, curiosity won out.

"Professor Blake was a friend of mine. May I ask why you need to make a change?"

"Let's just say professional differences."

Blake probably got caught with his pants down with another faculty member or student.

"How did I go from being, and here I'm quoting from your e-mail, 'part of the problem with Milton College in the twenty-first century,' to a solution? Your e-mail also mentioned my department had the highest cost-to-student ratio of any department at Milton." I held up my index finger. "I'm number one."

"The board hired me to slash costs and ensure the survival of the college. However, since you left, I've come to realize you possess assets that are hard to quantify."

"My charm, my wit, my God, man—"

"I'm prepared to offer a two-year contract with a ten percent raise."

I hadn't become a professor to make a buck. I wanted to make a difference in a few people's lives. I could still do that and perhaps regain that portion of my life, but not at any price. "Why me? You must have plenty of options."

"Frankly, Professor, of all the changes I made, I received the most strident objections from students and faculty regarding your dismissal. You have many friends at Milton College."

I do?

"The board thinks you'd make an excellent choice, and I'm in complete agreement."

Someone on the board, perhaps a majority, backed Warfield into a corner. Knowing this wasn't his idea almost made the offer tempting.

"I'd want autonomy ... control over the budget and curriculum."

Warfield clenched his jaw and nodded. Inside his mouth, he must be grinding his teeth.

"And I'll need some time to think it over."

A motorcycle rumbled down the street. To my surprise, Buck rode his Harley into my driveway. He spun a one eighty, leaving a black tire mark on the drive. He killed the engine, pulled off his helmet and pumped a gloved fist in the air.

Chancellor Warfield stood. "The offer is good for ten days.

Please give it every consideration."

"I'll send you my answer ... by e-mail."

"Touché." Warfield smiled and held out his hand.

I hesitated. A quote from Dutch botanist Paul Boese came to mind, "Forgiveness does not change the past, but it does enlarge the future."

I shook Chancellor Warfield's hand, but forgiveness? Not hardly. Even if it meant another item I could cross off the whiteboard. Not yet.

Warfield climbed down the porch steps and headed for the Lexus. He gave Buck a wide berth, like he might be a Hells Angel, climbed inside his car and drove off.

I greeted Buck in the driveway.

In jeans and a black leather jacket, he nodded toward the departing Lexus. "Who's the stiff?"

"My former boss."

"The fuck who canned you? I would have guessed IRS agent."

Buck climbed off his bike and gave me a man hug. "Bet you didn't think I'd show, did you?"

"The possibility crossed my mind." Buck appeared to have buried his dark melancholy from a day earlier. I hoped his mood wouldn't darken when he observed the changes caused by Josh's Alzheimer's. I opened the garage door and gestured toward my BMW.

"Anyone can ride in a Beemer." He slapped the saddle on the bike. "How long has it been since you've ridden on a Harley?"

I laughed at the offer, as I should have laughed at Warfield's.

"Come on, let's go visit Josh." He climbed on the bike.

I tried to think of an excuse not to ride on Buck's Harley. I peered at the thick clouds. "It looks like rain."

"What's a little rain to a couple Woodstock survivors? Besides, it's not going to rain. The shrapnel in my knee never lies."

"I don't have a helmet."

"You have a thick skull."

I ran out of excuses. I hadn't been on a bike in years. Against my better judgment, I closed the garage door, climbed behind Buck and clutched the strap on the seat.

Buck flashed me a Jack Nicholson grin, pulled on his helmet and cranked the Harley. The engine thundered as we sped off burning rubber.

The wind whipped through my hair. What a sight we must be, a couple of aging hippies on a Harley—a senior version of Easy Rider. I shouted in his ear, "You know what we look like?"

"A couple of old friends having a good time?" Buck pointed to two blonde hot bodies walking toward us on the sidewalk. "Hold on, Professor." He shifted to neutral.

"Don't!" I gripped the leather strap as tightly as I could.

Buck gunned the engine, popped the clutch and yanked on the handlebars. I held on as we popped a wheelie, the front wheel rising off the pavement. With a rebel yell, "Yeehah!" he flashed the girls a peace sign as we passed by.

I pressed against my sternum to keep my pounding heart from bursting through my chest until Buck eased the front tire onto the pavement. I had almost recovered by the time we rode into the nursing home parking lot.

He pulled into a disabled parking space, locked the front brakes, sliding the rear tire and leaving a streak of rubber on the pavement.

I jumped off the bike, dizzy as if I rode an extreme roller coaster ride. I set both hands on my knees and caught my breath.

"Don't be offended if I walk home."

Buck laughed. "When's the last time you had so much fun?"

He climbed off the bike, tugged off his helmet and pointed to the disabled sign.

"I have a permit because of my knee."

The sign reminded me Buck's disability went deeper than the shrapnel in his leg.

In front of the Sunrise Assisted Living Center, I gazed up at the red brick building soothingly landscaped with lush green shrubs except for one small plant with curled and shriveled leaves. A plant dying from neglect was hardly good advertising for such a facility.

Inside we approached an attractive woman with glasses seated behind the reception desk. Mid-thirties with short brown hair, she wore little makeup but had a welcoming smile. Her employee badge read "Phoebe Russell, Nurse's Aide." Buck checked her out as I suspected he might.

"You're the prettiest thing I've seen all day."

The woman blushed. "May I help you?"

He winked at her. "I'm sure you could."

Phoebe giggled.

I shook my head at Buck's behavior. Still the ladies' man.

"We're here to see Josh Channing."

"Oh, that's wonderful. Your friend doesn't get many visitors. Have you been in before?" Phoebe slid a visitor's log toward Buck. After he signed, she picked up the log and smiled before handing it to me. "We don't require you to leave a phone number."

Buck shrugged. "I figured if I gave you mine, you might give me yours." He tapped his signature on the log. "In case you can't tell from my handwriting, that's Buck ... with a B."

I signed and returned the log. "Josh doesn't get many visitors?"

"His mother comes by once a week."

"His mother!" Buck shook his head. "I'd have thought she would have died from perpetual meanness years ago."

Phoebe nodded. "She can be difficult, but she drops by a few times a week to read to him."

"The Bible, I bet."

"The Bible can be a comfort, Mr.—" Phoebe glanced at the log. "Ellington.

The Bible hadn't comforted me during Emily's illness or after she was gone.

Phoebe gave me a to-each-his-own shrug. "Have you seen Josh recently?"

"Neither of us have."

"Let me tell you about his Alzheimer's."

She explained about Josh as she walked us to the unit's closed door. I shamed myself for my lack of knowledge of my friend's condition. I knew all about cancer, but the word "Alzheimer's" terrified me.

"Alzheimer's has seven stages. Josh is in stage five. He often acts confused about where he is. Most of the time he doesn't recognize people he's known all his life, so be prepared. He might act differently than you remember, but inside he's still your friend."

She entered a code into a keypad on the wall. One of the double doors slid open. She followed us inside and led us to the nurses' station. A sense of despair hovered over the Alzheimer's unit.

Phoebe's smile vanished.

A gray-haired nurse, with the posture of someone who worked too hard, sat behind the nurses' station with a stack of Medicare forms.

Phoebe approached her with obvious apprehension. "Nurse Crawford, you're still here."

"Try not to act so thrilled."

"This is Mr. Ellington and Buck ..."

"Jamison," Buck smiled. "Call me Buck."

"They're here to see Josh Channing."

The nurse checked us both out then gestured to Phoebe.

"Mrs. Wilcox had an accident. Better get a mop and bucket."

Phoebe sighed and retrieved a bucket and mop from a supply closet behind the nurses' station. On the way down the hall, she stuck out her tongue at the nurse.

With her back to Phoebe, Nurse Crawford peered at me over the top of her glasses. "She's making a face, isn't she?"

I never was a good liar, so I avoided the question. "Phoebe appears to be very compassionate toward the residents."

"Compassion don't clean bedpans. Your friend's in the dayroom." She answered a ringing phone and pointed to a large room with a television on across the corridor.

In the dayroom, a white-haired woman sat in front of the television watching *Little House on the Prairie* with the intensity of a juror listening to closing arguments at a high-profile murder case. She wore a terrycloth robe, fuzzy slippers and a blue pillbox hat Jackie Kennedy popularized during Camelot.

Josh sat by himself in one of the chairs along the far wall. He picked at a thread from the cuff of his green pullover sweater. On the outside, he hadn't changed much since the last time I saw him at Emily's funeral.

He avoided looking at us as we approached. His heel tapped nervously beneath the chair.

I stood in front of him, no clue what to say.

"Hi, buddy." Buck sat beside him. "He's Sparky. I'm Buck."

Josh's eyes darted between Buck and me. "Nice to meet you, Buck ... Sparky."

Buck looked less disturbed than I feared over seeing Josh.

"We went to school together. We took a roadtrip to Woodstock."

"Woodstock?"

The question sent a stab of regret into my chest. I sat on Josh's other side.

"You like it here?"

He scanned the room and lowered his voice, making sure no one else could hear.

"I tried to run away."

Buck raised an eyebrow. "Why?"

He ignored the question and pointed toward the keypad by the security door. "I know the code." As Phoebe entered the room, Josh put a finger to his lips. "Shhhh."

A woman carried a Yorkshire terrier into the room. She set the dog on an elderly man's lap and kissed his cheek. She smiled when the old man petted the dog.

Josh stared at the Yorkie. "I have a dog. She likes to chase tennis balls. Her name is Buttons."

Buck and I looked at each other. Buttons was Josh's dog when we were kids. The sweet old girl died of kidney failure a week after we returned from Woodstock.

"Do you have a dog?"

"I do. Her name is Lady." Lady would enjoy Josh and the other residents. She'd been a therapy dog when Emily was in hospice. I wasn't much help, but Lady made her final days more pleasant.

Josh went back to picking threads from the sleeve of his sweater.

My heart ached for the loss of precious memories, particularly high school, The Buck Naked Band, Woodstock. Josh was best man at my wedding. I was best man at his. I helped him through the pain of his divorce.

What good was I to him now? To Josh, I was a total stranger. I should've been there when he first dealt with the disease, but I was more concerned with my own pain, dealing with Emily's illness.

Buck's eyebrows narrowed.

"Are you okay, Sparky?"

Coming here was a mistake. My breathing grew shallow and my heart cramped. I wiped sweat from my brow and began to wheeze.

"I think I need some fresh air."

The chest pain spread as I approached Phoebe, who knelt beside the woman with the pillbox hat.

"Your room is cleaned, Mrs. Wilcox."

"Thank you, dear. Now bring me the papers to grade. Report cards are due next week, you know."

"I'll get them later." Phoebe stood. "Are you okay, Mr. Ellington? Can I get you some water?"

I nodded.

Phoebe opened a refrigerator behind the nurses' station and grabbed a bottle of water.

A young man in a blue jumpsuit and red scarf wheeled in a keyboard and set the instrument in the middle of the room. He beamed and clapped his hands. "Time for music therapy, everyone." The music therapist's enthusiasm made Richard Simmons seem like a slacker.

Buck met my gaze and shook his head.

Nurse Crawford entered with half a dozen residents in tow. She snapped off the television.

"No, no!" Mrs. Wilcox pointed to the screen. "The little girl is lost in a snowstorm."

"Her pa will find her."

The music therapist set up chairs facing the keyboard. Everyone took a seat, except Josh.

"Josh doesn't like music." Phoebe handed me the water. "It's not easy seeing a loved one the first time this way. It gets easier."

I thanked her for the water. "I need some fresh air."

She walked me to the door and punched in a code. The door slid open.

I stepped through and held the door open a moment.

"Is Josh happy here?"

Phoebe let out a sigh. "We do the best we can, but with government cutbacks, we depend more and more on family and friends to keep their loved ones happy. They bring pets, DVDs, even play music sometimes. I hope you'll come back."

Outside, I unscrewed the cap from the bottle and took a sip of water. I walked down the steps and stood beside the small, withered shrub. I poured the rest of the water around the plant then picked off a few dead leaves. All it needed was water and a little TLC, like the patients inside.

I tossed the bottle into a trash can beside the front door and wiped sweat from the back of my neck with my handkerchief. My chest pains had subsided. I grabbed my wallet from my pocket and sat on the steps. I stared at Emily's picture taken before the cancer.

Emily had her father's determination, her mother's compassion and the same sweet innocence I discovered at Woodstock. She'd barely changed from the day we met, except for a few strands of gray in her hair. I kissed the picture. "I'm sorry. I tried. I really tried."

Seeing Josh this way had been nearly as horrible as watching Emily fade. I worried about Buck's reaction, but I should have worried about my own.

It was more than the Alzheimer's. In spite of people like Phoebe who cared, Josh wasn't happy. What could I do?

Buck came out and sat beside me as I slipped my wallet into my pocket.

"You missed a rousing rendition of "You Light Up My Life.""

"Someone should sing songs from the residents' youth, some classic rock 'n roll."

"Funny you should say that."

I cocked my head. "Why's that funny?"

"Rock 'n roll. Phoebe thinks it's a great idea. Even that drill sergeant nurse said it was okay."

"What's the great idea?"

"You and I come back tomorrow and play some of the old Buck Naked Band stuff. We're expected at ten."

I wasn't as sure as Buck that it would be a great idea. He and I were total strangers to Josh.

"You think it will make a difference?"

"Might help him enjoy music again."

"I don't know."

Buck let out a sigh. "I can do it alone. You've got your own problems to deal with."

My own problems? "You think I can't handle it?"

"You're out here on the steps."

"I didn't think *you* could handle seeing Josh this way."

"Me? You think I'm more fucked up than you? No way."

I snorted. I had problems, but it never occurred to me I might be in worse shape than Buck.

"You think he might remember the old stuff we used to play?"

Buck shrugged. "What are you getting at?"

"If we could trigger his memories about the songs we used to perform, maybe he could recover other memories. We might prolong his life."

"Your cup is always half full, isn't it?" Buck pulled a foiled pack of raisins from his pocket. He offered me some. When I declined, he tossed several into his mouth.

"He'll enjoy our stuff better than what the music therapist plays. Of course I'm a little rusty on my drums, but I still play a mean harmonica."

Maybe I was crazy, but I wanted our old songs to make Josh happy. I might be getting old, but I could still make a difference in people's lives.

"Let's hope we don't suck."

He clapped me on the back.

"It's worth a try."

He pulled his motorcycle key from his pocket.

"One more thing. You have heart problems, don't you?"

"Why do you think that?"

"Inside—the sweats, the wheezing. You're still pale."

"I have a broken heart."

"I'm serious."

"Ever hear of broken heart syndrome?"

Buck slapped me on the leg.

"That fits. What kind of herbs do you take?"

He commenced an herbal supplement lecture that continued until I climbed on the back of Buck's Harley and we headed home.

After he dropped me off, I entered the house, greeted Lady and stopped in front of the coffee table. I touched Emily's urn, as was my custom, then headed down the hall.

Performing oldies filled me with cautious optimism, but I had to rehearse.

In the back of my office closet, I retrieved the cracked guitar case with my forty-year-old Gibson acoustic inside. I put the acoustic away for good after Warfield fired me.

The Gibson was, like me, an antique, but unlike me, it was a true classic. Ten years earlier, with Emily's encouragement, I formed a four-piece faculty jazz band, the Milton Faculty Jazz Review. Now I had a new purpose for the guitar. I'd practice the songs The Buck Naked Band played, return to the stodgy specialized care facility with Buck and play some classic rock for Josh, Mrs. Wilcox, who thought she was still a teacher, and the other residents I hoped to get to know.

I lifted the guitar case from the closet, revealing Emily's old trunk of sixties stuff. The last time I saw the trunk was before Emily's cancer when I passed by the office and noticed her sifting through Woodstock memorabilia.

At the time, her nostalgia surprised me, since Emily rarely dwelled on the past. I let her reflect on the contents alone, a decision I now regretted. I now suspected, at the time, she sensed her health might mirror her father's fate.

Curious about what Emily looked through that day, I carried the trunk and guitar to the living room. I kicked aside an old pizza box and set the stuff down in the middle of the floor. I propped the guitar beside the rocker that once sat on her father's porch.

Lady's nose twitched and her tail wagged as I lifted the trunk's clasp and peered into the time capsule of the Woodstock generation.

How could I ever consider Emily's precious possessions just stuff? With an ache that reinforced my loss, I flipped through the Woodstock scrapbook Emily made while I was at Penn State. She pasted her original ticket and clipped magazine and newspaper articles of the event. I read every yellowed page.

She kept a festival program, a red poster that proclaimed three days of peace and music and a purple guitar pick. *Oh, Emily*. The Jimi Hendrix pick I thought I lost years ago.

I held the pick in my fist and tried to recapture the special moment when Emily gave it to me. Until I figured a place where I wouldn't lose it, I slipped the pick into my pocket.

I snatched up Buck's leather bushman's hat, identical to the one Dennis Hopper wore in *Easy Rider*. He left it with me before he shipped out to Nam, and for some reason, I never gave it back. I glanced in the mirror beside the door, set the hat on my head and made a slight adjustment. The bushman looked cool, but much cooler on Buck.

"What do you think?"

Lady wagged her tail and let out a happy bark.

I unclasped a manila envelope and discovered the picture of Buck, Josh, Emily and me, the only photo of us at Woodstock.

Buck and Josh smiled for the camera. Emily and I gazed at each other with blossoming love. Back then, we ignored the camera and the man who took the picture.

I turned the photo over and managed a smile. The inscription and the man's signature was still visible. I stared at the coffee table a moment then carried Emily to the mantel and propped the picture next to the urn.

I set the baseball on the coffee table next to the remote. "Sorry, Mick."

Lady sniffed through the trunk. I nudged her aside and retrieved a letter-sized envelope. I poured the contents into my hand: the chain with Emily's silver peace symbol she wore at Woodstock. I clamped my hand closed. My throat tightened and I began to wheeze. I fought back tears and slipped the chain around the urn.

Now I had a better idea why Emily browsed through the trunk that day. She didn't want to let go of the special memories we shared at Woodstock. For reasons not quite clear, neither did I.

I stared at the new items and couldn't stop a cry of grief. A blinding stab of pain shot through my chest. I braced myself and held onto the mantel.

Beside me, Lady whined and licked my hand. I knelt and hugged the dog. The pain subsided as I stared into her moist-brown eyes. We both missed Emily terribly.

I took a deep breath and stepped back to make a fresh evaluation of the mantel. I had to admit, with the new items, now it looked like a shrine.

I forced the painful session of examination and self-pity behind me, retrieved my guitar and took Lady out back. We sat in the shade on the backyard deck.

Unlike the house, I hadn't neglected Emily's yard. The farm girl took great pride in the plants, especially her rose garden. My biggest challenge was to keep my next door neighbor's Siamese from using the garden as his personal litter box.

Lady pawed at her favorite pillow until satisfied then sprawled and closed her eyes. A moment later, nap well under way, her hind legs twitched in hot pursuit of Old Man Simpson's cat, no doubt.

I practiced for more than an hour. I set the guitar down and inspected the string creases along my left hand's dry brittle fingertips. The skin appeared ready to crack.

Lady raised her head toward the wood fence that separated the backyard from my neighbor's. Old Man Simpson was a crotchety old buzzard, a get-off-my-lawn kind of guy. Lady didn't like him or his cat. Neither did I.

To my surprise, a teenage kid I'd never seen before stood watching over the top of the wood fence from the Simpson yard. Lady's tail thumped against the pillow.

A guitar showed through the slats in the fence. The teenager began to play the *Dueling Banjos* theme from *Deliverance*, da da da da da, da da da da da.

I chuckled, picked up my guitar and answered back, da da da da da, da da da da da.

"Not bad," the kid called out. "Wanna jam?"

"Gate's unlocked." I needed all the practice I could get.

A minute later, the baby-faced kid propped his guitar against a deck chair and petted Lady. "'Sup, blonde?"

Lady wagged her tail. She took to the teenager much better than she had to Dr. Dave.

The kid took a seat and set his guitar on one knee. The teen looked like a California surfer dude with freckles, white teeth and straw-colored hair that grew every which way. No visible tattoos or body piercings. Baggy T-shirt and jeans. At least he wasn't in low-rider shorts.

"Dude, that's some bad head gear. Not everyone can wear a hat like that."

The bushman. I set it beside me.

"Belongs to a friend of mine."

I considered telling the story of how Buck acquired the hat, but the kid seemed more interested in music.

He played a few chords on his guitar then tweaked a tuning peg and strummed again. He leaned forward and studied my guitar.

"A Gibson? Sweet."

I handed over my guitar and the teen inspected the instrument from top to bottom.

"Dude, you need new strings."

Good advice.

"You visiting Old ... Mr. Simpson?"

"Visiting? I've lived there the past five months. Where have you been?"

I'd become more reclusive than I realized.

"Old Man Simpson's my grandpa."

He didn't say grandpa with pride.

You have my deepest sympathies.

"What's the deal between you two? You bang Grandma or something? I know she ran off with a truck driver before I was born, so I'm guessing she was some kind of slut or something."

"Must have been before I bought this house."

A cheating wife would explain why Simpson was a cantankerous son-of-a-bitch from the day Emily and I moved in. Then again, a cantankerous son-of-a-bitch might explain a cheating wife.

"A skank for a grandma. Course I couldn't blame her, married to him."

The kid thumbed toward the Simpson house.

"Grandpa calls you 'professor' and a few other names I won't mention. What do your friends call you?"

I paused a moment and decided to give him the name I went by in happier times.

"You can call me Sparky."

"Sparky ... the Sparkman ... the Sparkinator."

"What's yours?"

"Heather."

"Heather." Oops. I scanned the kid more closely. I felt like an idiot, but it wasn't the first time I'd made a gender mistake.

"Dude, I am what I am. It's all good."

Heather strummed the guitar then played a few bars of Credence's "Fortunate Son." She was damn talented.

"So you like the oldies stuff?"

"I *am* an oldie."

"Want to hear something I wrote? Let me know what you think."

My guitar picking in the late sixties was the best, at least around Milton, but this girl was on another level. After she finished, I held out a fist bump. I can be current when the need crops up.

Heather returned the fist bump.

"I enrolled in an advanced music class at Milton High. Classic Rock. My old school doesn't even offer band anymore."

I'd show her classic rock. No one was more classic than Jimi. I reached into my pocket and handed her the treasured guitar pick.

"Belonged to Hendrix."

Heather giggled. "Phil Hendrix maybe. What kind of freak carries a Hendrix pick in his pocket?"

"I'm serious. I got it at Woodstock."

Heather cocked her head and gave me the once-over.

"You were at Woodstock? Now I know you're fuckin' with me. You skinny-dip in the pond? Ewwww, don't tell me. I don't want an image."

I laughed. Emily and I hadn't skinny-dipped, but Josh had.

She tossed me the pick.

"If it really belonged to Hendrix, you should put this on a mantel or something."

I smiled at the suggestion's irony and stuck the pick in my pocket. I grabbed the one I used earlier.

"How much sixties music can you play?"

"I can play the stuff you played. Simon and Garfunkel, Credence and Canned Heat. Totally underrated."

The Milton Faculty Jazz Review played *Going up the Country*, a song Canned Heat performed at Woodstock.

"Keep up if you can, freckles."

"Freckles!"

Heather grinned and more than kept up. She joined me in singing the chorus. Neither of us knew all the words, but we finished the song and exchanged a fist bump again.

Lady growled toward the fence. The golden hair stood on her neck.

Old Man Simpson peered into my backyard. He stroked the fat Siamese eyeing Emily's garden.

"What are you doing over there, Heather?"

"Jammin', Grandpa."

"Dinner's ready. Get home."

Without acknowledging my presence, the old coot headed toward his house.

"Home." Heather spit out the word.

I waved a mock salute.

"Goodbye, Grandpa Simpson."

Heather laughed and patted Lady. With obvious reluctance, she got up to leave.

I escorted her to the gate while Lady stayed and guarded the deck from Simpson's cat.

"Thanks for the jam session."

"Not much else to do in a small town like Milton. Let me know when you want to jam again." There was a lost sadness in Heather's voice. Perhaps we had something in common.

"A buddy and I made plans to visit a friend in a nursing home and play some sixties music tomorrow. Think you might like to join us?"

"Singing to geezers beats the shit out of watching Fox News with Grandpa all day. I'll ask Mom when she gets home from work."

"Your mother lives there, too?"

"Dude, you need to get out more. Mom gets off work in an hour or so. Okay if I send her over, you know, to make sure you're not a perv?"

"Sure." An hour to make my neglected house presentable? I'd do my best. I opened the gate.

"Just one thing, Sparky. Don't stare at my mom's tits. They're ginormous."

Telling a person not to stare at something was a direct invitation to the subconscious to do just that.

The screen door on the Simpson house squeaked open. Old Man

Simpson growled like a prison guard. "Heather!"

"On my way, Grandpa."

I watched our new friend head next door. I chuckled as she approached Old Man Simpson strumming the *Dueling Banjos* theme, da da da da da da da da da.

5

I stuffed unread newspapers, empty fast-food containers and junk mail into a plastic garbage bag. Cleaning now had a purpose—to impress Heather's mother. I wanted to help the teenager escape Old Man Simpson, if only for a little while, even if it meant visiting an Alzheimer's unit in a nursing home with an old geezer like me.

To mask the musty odor to which I'd grown accustomed, I lit a vanilla scented candle I found in the back of the pantry. I set the candle on the table beside the couch and stuffed the last of the visible trash into a plastic bag.

The doorbell rang. Lady barked, and I held up my hand to quiet the dog. "Behave, girl. We have company."

She sat and cocked her head as if she'd never heard the word "company." Perhaps she hadn't.

I made a quick dash to the bathroom and hid the bag of trash behind the shower curtain. I ran a comb through my hair, trying to look like a retired professor instead of an aging hippie. I checked the mirror. I needed more than a comb.

The doorbell rang again as I reached the front door. Remembering not to stare at the woman's large breasts her daughter warned me about, I recalled a technique a colleague described years ago. Stare between a person's eyebrows and they'll think you're looking them in the eye. Now seemed like the perfect time to try it.

I greeted her with my most charming smile and focused on the bridge of her nose. Even so, I couldn't help but notice her ample breasts straining against a green-silk scoop neck blouse.

"You must be Heather's mother."

The attractive mid-forties woman, with well-trimmed eyebrows, shook my hand. "Meagan. You must be Professor Ellington, my father's dear, dear friend."

We laughed as I let her in. Meagan and Heather were both teases. Fortunately, neither seemed to have inherited Old Man Simpson's personality.

Lady exhibited rare manners toward a potential new playmate. She sat beside the couch, her tail dusting the carpet.

Meagan carried herself with an air of self-assurance, surprising in a woman related to the grumpy old codger next door. "A candle, how lovely."

I hoped she didn't misinterpret the candle's purpose.

Meagan gazed around the room and focused on Emily's urn on the mantel. "Nice touch. The teal in the marble matches the curtains."

I never noticed. Was she being droll?

She brushed her forehead. "Is there something on my face? You keep staring."

"No, it's just ..."

"Heather told you not to stare at my tits, didn't she?"

Meagan set both hands on her hips. "Well, stare all you want. I paid good money for these puppies."

In spite of myself, I glanced at her cleavage. Puppies? They appeared full grown to me. "A sound investment."

"Thanks."

She tossed her purse on the couch then sat and crossed both arms.

"So you're the dirty old man who wants to date my fifteen-year-old daughter."

Blood drained from my face.

"There must be some terrible mistake. I assure you ..."

Meagan slapped her knee and laughed.

"Relax, Professor, I was just having fun with you."

Fun? That wasn't funny at all!

Meagan slipped off one shoe and massaged her foot.

"Got something to drink? Today's been a real bitch, and I still have to face my old man."

"What you would like?"

"Bourbon, if you have some, but any alcohol will do."

I needed something stronger than beer after the joke she just played. Unfortunately, I hadn't replenished my supply.

I grabbed two Budweisers from the refrigerator, returned to the room and handed her one.

"Sorry. Out of bourbon, temporarily."

Meagan popped the top and took a long gulp.

"My daughter says you play a mean guitar. How come I've never heard you?"

The woman's sense of humor and direct approach took getting used to. Maybe that's the way people acted and I'd forgotten.

"Until today, I'd given up music."

"What happened today?"

"I went to visit a friend I hadn't seen in a while. He's in an Alzheimer's unit in a specialized care facility. Josh and I were in a high school garage band with Buck Jamison. Buck and I thought he might enjoy hearing some old songs we used to play."

I popped the top on the can and guzzled my beer.

"That's the sweetest thing I've ever heard."

Her eyes misted. She grabbed a tissue from her purse and dabbed her tears.

"Of course Heather can go with you."

She patted the couch beside her. Meagan was the first woman who'd been inside my house, other than Cloe, since the funeral. I hadn't anticipated her presence would bother me, but my chest objected, sending me a twinge of pain.

Meagan's charm went beyond her brassy demeanor, wicked sense of humor and considerable cleavage. I glanced at Emily's urn on the mantel. My heart spasmed with guilt over being alone with an attractive woman.

I sat beside her and tried not to show discomfort. I breathed in the hint of a sweet flowery fragrance. Her perfume and proximity intensified my chest pain. Lady sensed my distress. She wagged her tail and panted then set a paw on my leg.

"You don't look so good."

I pressed against my sternum.

"I have chest pains sometimes. It usually only lasts a couple of minutes."

"Can I get you something? Water, a baby aspirin, some weed?" She grabbed her purse.

"Nothing, thanks." I took a deep breath.

Meagan leaned forward, showing more cleavage, and brushed a

shock of hair from my head.

"You're kind of cute, you know that?"

Her attention didn't help my discomfort. I reminded myself to look her in the eye and took a long swallow of beer.

The doorbell rang, and Lady barked.

"That's probably Heather. Sure you're okay?"

"I'm fine." With the empty beer can in one hand, I opened the door and stifled a gasp. "Cloe."

She glanced at my Budweiser. In a charcoal gray pinstriped power suit, she marched into the house. "I just thought I'd stop by and ..." She froze when she saw Meagan on the couch drinking beer. Awkward.

Meagan raised the Bud in greeting. "Hi, Cloe. How goes the ambulance chasing?"

I closed the door.

"You two know each other?"

"Dad, she's lived next door to you for months. We met one day when I came over and you were gone or didn't answer the door."

"I must have been gone."

Meagan gulped her beer. "At least once a week, your daughter comes into the Chat and Chew Diner where I work. How come you never eat there?"

The restaurant was too close to the campus I vowed never to visit.

"You're a waitress."

"Temporarily, until my father's health improves. Then Heather and I'll move back to Akron where I can resume my true calling in life."

I finished the beer and set the can on a table by the door.

"What's your life's calling?"

A smile curled from the corner of her lips.

"Cocktail waitress."

Meagan and I both laughed, while Cloe seemed increasingly uncomfortable.

"I came over to make sure your father is okay enough to hang out with Heather." Meagan smiled.

"What's wrong with your father's health?" I tried not to sound too hopeful.

"Heart attack."

Heart? I couldn't believe the bastard had a heart to attack. The grumpy old coot called the cops on Cloe's sweet sixteen birthday party and routinely filed a complaint whenever Lady barked at his miserable excuse for a cat.

"You remember, Dad. You told me about the sirens and emergency vehicles in front of the Simpson house last Christmas."

I remembered, but at the time, I stayed inside hoping they were police.

Meagan finished the beer and set the can on the table next to the couch.

"My father's a stubborn old fart. Doesn't eat right. Never exercises. You can't tell him anything."

Cloe flashed me a who-does-that-remind-you-of smirk.

"Well, I should check to make sure Heather hasn't killed him." To my shock, Meagan kissed my cheek. She whispered, "You feel better?"

I nodded, relieved she hadn't brought up my chest pain in front of Cloe. I walked her to the door and waited on the porch until she reached the front door to the Simpson house.

Cloe came outside. "You put the urn on the mantel." She answered her cell phone and moved to the end of the porch. She spoke low and secretively, attorney-like.

Lady slipped out the door and flopped down between the two wicker chairs.

I sat and scratched Lady's back. She peered up at me with the concern she often displayed toward humans. I tried to assure her with a pat on the head.

Gentle orange clouds filtered the setting sun, illuminating Cloe's hybrid parked in the driveway. On evenings like this, Emily and I sat out front and chatted with neighbors walking dogs or riding bicycles. I was a lot more social back then.

Cloe ended the call and sat beside me.

"You went to a lot of work to clean the house and impress a hot single mom with a nice rack."

"I can explain."

"I wanted you to move on with your life, but I didn't expect you to date right away."

"It wasn't what it looked like."

Cloe let out a hearty laugh.

"I know, Dad, but it's cute to see your discomfort. Did Meagan tell you she graduated from culinary school and worked as a chef in Akron? She sent in a tape to the Food Network to audition for the *Next Food Network Star* show. That's why she had her breasts enhanced."

How did Cloe get to know people so easily?

"Are you serious? There's a television network about food?"

"Don't ever lose your sense of humor."

Okay, but I'd really never heard of Food Network.

"It must be difficult to cook and have big boobs. She couldn't possibly see what she's cooking."

Cloe chuckled.

"I like her. Since you want to hook me up with Dr. Dave, you have my blessing to date Meagan."

Date? Just the word made my mouth dry and my palms clammy.

"That's not going to happen."

Cloe nodded toward the Simpson house.

"I think you just had a first date."

Cloe drummed her fingers on the chair's arm.

"Anything wrong?"

"Dad, I think it's great you're getting out, that you've reconnected with Buck and Josh, and I'm thrilled you cleaned the house, but I'm still worried about your heart. I'm glad you had Meagan over, but drinking beer?"

"One beer."

"Are you keeping a food journal like Dave said? What about exercise?"

I had to convince Cloe I'd changed.

"Come over for dinner tomorrow night and I'll cook you a heart healthy meal."

"You cook? What?"

I had no idea.

"I'll surprise you."

Cloe looked skeptical, but she nodded.

"Okay, tomorrow at seven."

I had twenty-four hours to convince my daughter I could change my eating and exercise habits and knew how to cook. I grilled steaks like Bobby Flay, but the last time I used a kitchen appliance was to heat up leftover pizza in the microwave for Lady.

Fortunately, I knew an expert cook who'd been to culinary school. I counted on Meagan knowing an easy method to prepare a healthy dinner.

Cloe checked her watch.

"I have to go.

"Let me show you a couple things I found first."

Inside, I pointed to the mantel. For a moment, I expected her to cross-examine me about spending my day lost in the past. To my relief, she picked up the picture taken at Woodstock, and her eyes filled with tears. She blinked them away and held the photo to her chest.

"I'd like to visit Josh with you sometime."

"He'd ..." I almost said, he'd like that, but I knew better. "I'd like that."

Cloe touched Emily's peace symbol necklace then ran to me and threw both arms around my neck. Her damp tears moistened the side of my face. A moment later, her cell phone rang.

She checked a text message then snapped the phone closed.

"A client. I really have to go."

"You work too hard." I walked her to her car, and she drove off.

I had a lot of work ahead if I was going to impress Cloe.

Lady followed me down the creaking wooden stairs. The basement smelled of mildew and powdered laundry soap. The dog snorted along the cracks in the cement floor then sniffed each of Emily's recycle bins I'd neglected to empty since before she died.

Lady stepped back as I removed a dozen boxes along the far wall—exercise in itself. The treadmill sat covered with junk I intended to get rid of one day—an obsolete computer printer, a broken television and stacks of old VCR movies. Everything in the basement seemed to be a product of planned obsolescence, including me.

I cleared a path, folded up the treadmill and wheeled it to the stairs. I tugged the heavy device up the stairs one muscle-straining step at a time.

Finally, I made it to the top. I leaned on the wall, gulping air. I caught my breath, wiped my brow and maneuvered the equipment into the corner of my bedroom. I unfolded the treadmill and plugged it in.

My foot stuttered as I climbed on and studied the control panel. I rubbed my hands together then gripped the wobbly handrails. The treadmill and I needed a little work to get in better condition.

Lady took a step back and barked.

"Wish me luck." In spite of my apprehension, I pressed start.

The treadmill shrieked like a little girl. Lady yelped. Her nails dug into the carpet as she dashed from the room with her tail between her legs as if the device was some kind of super vacuum cleaner. I punched the emergency stop button and hopped off.

A compressed air canister, several sprays of WD-40 and a few twists of a screwdriver gave me confidence to try again. I climbed on again, hoped for the best and pressed start.

The machine still squealed, but the noise grew less severe as I walked and the lubrication worked its way through the device. I raised the setting to stroll in the park speed. The squeaking vanished minutes later, but I couldn't help making deep sucking noises.

I hit the cool down button and walked for another minute. I didn't want to overdo it on the first day of the rest of my life.

Lady stepped into the room and wagged her tail.

In the kitchen, I opened the refrigerator stocked with my essential four b's—bread, butter, bologna and beer. Food not on Dr. Malone's approved list. I tossed Lady a slice of bologna and grabbed the keys to my BMW.

I returned home from the grocery store with enough heart healthy food to fill the refrigerator and pantry. I couldn't imagine eating tofu or the other crap I purchased, but I needed to impress Cloe. Nevertheless, I managed to pick up a bottle of my favorite analgesic, Jim Beam.

I put everything away. A behavioral change in itself. I poured a half glass of bourbon and set the bottle in the back of the pantry, behind two organic carrot juice containers that resembled liquid rust and probably tasted as bad.

I finished the drink and limited my intake to just one. I proudly demonstrated I could make changes in my behavior if properly motivated.

I plopped down on my bed. The day had been long and troubling. Tomorrow came with new challenges. After playing old songs for Josh, I had to convince Cloe I could change my behavior. With Meagan's help, I hoped I could cook a healthy meal and do just that.

♪♪♪♪♪

As night fell on Day One of Woodstock, Emily and I peered out from under the tarp and joined the crowd chanting for the rain to go away. Arlo Guthrie took the stage.

We were so close to the performers, it surprised me how young he was, how wasted as well, but when he began to play, his talent shined. He rocked *Coming into Los Angeles*. Emily and I sang along with his last song, *Amazing Grace*.

After Arlo, a clearly pregnant Joan Baez carried her guitar across the stage. Emily stuck two fingers in her mouth and let out a shrill whistle that turned heads.

Passion beamed in the singer's blue eyes. She began with a union song, "Joe Hill." Between songs, she talked about how police jailed her husband for his political beliefs. She sang an old black spiritual *Swing Low, Sweet Chariot* and closed the song saying, "Amen."

By the time Baez finished, the rain stopped. The day was over and beside me sat someone unexpectedly special. "You want to go back to our friends?"

"We'd never find them in the dark. Let's wait 'til morning." Emily took my hand. We snuggled beneath the tarp and fell asleep.

Hours later, I awoke to a glow through the canvas. I lifted the tarp. The rain had chilled the night air. The glimmer from a hundred campfires scattered throughout the thirty-five acres illuminated Emily's face.

I watched her sleep. I could get used to sharing my bed with her.

Emily awoke and touched my cheek. "I thought I dreamed you, Sparky." She drew me close, and we kissed. The gentle kiss grew into desire and passion. She ran her fingers through my hair. I kissed her neck, and she let out a soft moan.

With hunger in her eyes, the sweet farm girl draped the tarp over us. She stared into my eyes as she pulled off her top, still wet from the rain.

My eyes traveled over her smooth bare skin. I caressed her pear-shaped breasts.

Her breathing grew ragged as she tugged off my shirt. A voice of caution whispered in the back of my mind as we tossed our clothes aside. We barely knew each other.

I'd never wanted anything more than I wanted this. I had no idea how experienced Emily was, but it was clear she wanted what was about to happen as much as I did. Her fingernails slid up my leg, sending shivers everywhere she touched. Wide-eyed, with deep slow breaths, she reclined on the cardboard.

We explored each other's body; exciting new touches. My skin tingled everywhere she touched and kissed. Beneath the tarp, we were alone among a half million.

Excitement built for both of us. Emily's eyes widened as she pulled me on top. She called my name as I entered her. Gentle at first, our movements quickened. With heavy panting breaths, we moved as one.

Emily clenched my hands as we kissed. She moaned, her mouth clamped to mine. She whimpered. Her head arched back and she cried out.

I did the same. Neither of us cared whether anyone heard, or knew what we were doing. This was Woodstock.

We kissed until our breathing returned to normal. I rolled onto my back on the damp cardboard.

Covered in a fine sheet of sweat, Emily set her head in the crook of my shoulder and pressed her body against mine. She felt like she always belonged there. This wasn't my first time, but it was my first time with someone so sweet and wonderful.

"Oh, Sparky, I could get used to this." Emily let out a ragged breath. "Let's do it again."

I smiled, ran my hand along her back and stroked her smooth skin.

She softly kissed my lips. "All in one day, Sparky."

"What?"

Emily flashed a mischievous smile. "Sex, drugs and rock 'n' roll."

6

Early the next morning, I hurried next door to get some healthy dinner ideas I could prepare from Meagan. I'd never knocked on Old Man Simpson's door before. Fortunately, Heather answered. Her mother had already left for work.

I drove to the Chat and Chew and carried a spiral bound notebook inside. I hoped I wouldn't encounter anyone from the nearby campus who'd taken sides in the palace coup that resulted in my dismissal.

With the breakfast crowd, I waited until the hostess escorted me to an empty booth. I needed caffeine. I turned over the empty coffee cup and waited for Meagan.

Meagan, in a clingy red blouse, dashed through the swinging doors into the kitchen, balancing a tray of dirty dishes on one hand. She came back through, smiled at me and waved.

I held up the cup, and she brought a carafe of coffee to the booth. "You work hard."

"It's not so bad. At least I don't have to wear a uniform."

She filled the cup with the strong aromatic brew I recalled from my faculty days.

"What brings you here, Professor? Me, I hope."

"As a matter of fact, yes."

Meagan looked more than pleased.

The moment the words left my mouth, I realized I'd given her the wrong impression. I didn't know how to correct my mistake without sounding like a cad. I ignored the blunder and proceeded with my mission.

"I'd like to borrow a recipe."

Meagan burst out laughing.

"That sounds so gay!"

A woman in the next booth peered over her shoulder and checked out my appearance. She turned back and whispered something I couldn't hear to a female friend across from her.

Meagan carried the carafe to a burner behind the counter. She returned and slipped into the booth across from me.

"Why do you need a recipe?"

I tried not to glance at her cleavage.

"My cardiologist, David Malone—"

"That's dad's doctor."

Son-of-a-bitch! Having the same physician had to be the only thing Meagan's father and I had in common.

"Malone placed me on a heart healthy diet, and I'm keeping a food journal." I showed her the notebook.

She flipped through the pages. "It's empty."

I jotted down the word "breakfast" followed by "coffee."

"I want to give the program a chance, but more importantly, I need to convince Cloe I can change my nutritional intake, so I invited her to dinner tonight."

"You want to prepare a healthy meal to impress your daughter so she won't turn down that job in Virginia. Cloe stopped by the diner earlier and we chatted. Can you cook?"

"Not unless it's in a microwave container or boil-a-bag. I could use a recipe that's nutritious but simple enough for me to follow."

"I'll do you one better. I'll come over an hour ahead of time and whip up a crustless quiche, crisp salad ..." She stared off into the distance and bit her lip, contemplating a menu. "Maybe a roasted vegetable ..." She ripped a page from a notebook in her pocket and wrote down the items she'd need.

Meagan slid the list toward me. She squeezed my hand, further convincing me she misunderstood my intentions.

I liked her but didn't want to lead her on. In another life, I might have been interested, but I spent the last two years clinging to the life I had.

"You don't have to do this."

"I want to." Meagan winked. "Maybe you can do something for me sometime."

I ignored the innuendo and checked the list.

"Surprisingly, I have everything you need."

"I'm certain you do." With a smirk, she slid from the booth.

I had no idea why anyone that attractive, spirited and young would have any interest in a crusty geezer like myself. I was sixty. Old enough to be her ... older brother.

Meagan rang up a departing customer on the cash register while I drank my coffee. She returned and stood beside the booth with an order pad in her hand. She pointed at my food journal.

"If you show your journal to Cloe, coffee for breakfast won't impress her. If you're still performing later, you should have something nutritious."

The pie display on the counter drew my attention. My favorite, pecan, looked delicious, but I needed three fruit servings each day.

"I'll have a piece of apple pie with a slice of cheddar cheese on top—a fruit and a dairy selection from the food pyramid."

"Might I suggest a fruit salad and low fat cottage cheese?"

"You may suggest that, but I need to ease into nutrition, and the pie is calling."

I entered the items in the notebook below the coffee: a Granny Smith apple and a serving of fat free cheddar cheese. "Keeping a food journal isn't as difficult as I thought."

Two hours later, I waited in the wicker chair on my porch with my guitar at my feet. Down the street came the distinctive rumble of Buck's Harley. He pulled into my driveway and parked.

In a black leather jacket and white T-shirt, he climbed off the bike and removed his helmet.

I climbed down the porch steps. "Morning, Fonzie."

"Richie." Buck rubbed his knee, the one with the shrapnel. "My knee says rain."

Overhead thick clouds reminded me of Woodstock's storms.

Heather came out of her house with her guitar and flute. I introduced her to Buck, but she seemed more interested in his Harley. She ran her hands along the chrome handlebars.

"Sweet. You play an instrument?"

"Several." Buck pulled a harmonica from his leather jacket. "I'm mostly a drummer, but today I'll play a mean harmonica."

I went inside and gave Lady a dog biscuit. I slipped the Jimi Hendrix guitar pick in my pocket and grabbed Buck's hat.

Outside, I grabbed the guitar and opened the garage door. I handed the bushman to Buck.

"I'd forgotten all about this." He set the hat on his head, just so. Heather smiled at me.

"It looks better on him."

"Of course it does, kid." Buck followed me to the BMW then stopped beside Emily's white Dodge Caravan. With his mechanic's face on, he crouched and inspected the van's tires.

"When was the last time you drove this?"

I'd only driven the van once since Emily's funeral, when the battery died on the BMW. I made it a mile before I hyperventilated, pulled over and walked home.

"About six months ago."

Buck wrinkled his face.

"Check out these Firestones. They're almost flat on the bottom. If you don't use them, they'll rot off. Same goes with your dick. Sorry, kid."

He walked to the front and popped the hood.

"They're the least of your problems. Do you know where most of the oil is?"

"Saudi Arabia?"

"At the bottom of the engine." He ran a hand over his long gray ponytail. "I can understand you might find it hard to drive Emily's van, but don't let it just sit. Sell the son-of-a-bitch or give it away to someone in need."

I could never get rid of the van Emily loved so much.

Heather held up her hand.

"I'll take it."

"You old enough to drive?" Buck asked.

She shook her head.

Buck closed the hood.

"I'll come by tomorrow with my tow truck. I'll bring her to the shop and get her in shape while you decide what you want to do."

"You don't have to do that."

"What are friends for?"

Heather climbed into the BMW's backseat. Buck sat up front beside me. I drove us toward Sunrise, and rain began to fall. On the way, we talked about the songs we'd play. We hadn't rehearsed, but we'd be good enough to get a reaction from Josh.

I pulled into the lot and parked. I grabbed a black umbrella from behind the seat and my guitar.

Heather and I kept our guitars dry under the umbrella while

Buck turned his jacket collar up against the rain. Inside the lobby, I closed the umbrella and hooked it on the coatrack.

Nurse Crawford stood beside the reception desk berating Phoebe. She paused in mid-insult. She shook her head at the rainwater we dripped onto the floor.

"I'll take care of it." Phoebe appeared relieved at the interruption. She grabbed a mop from a supply closet and began to soak up the rainwater by the front door.

Nurse Crawford appeared to notice our guitars for the first time. She gave the impression she disapproved of anything that would change the facility's orderly operation.

"We just got the residents quieted down. It's not a good time for music."

Buck held out both hands.

"It's always a good time for rock 'n' roll."

Her tone softened.

"Rock 'n' roll? What kind?"

"Sixties stuff."

"Sixties?" Her face softened instantly. For a moment, she appeared to revisit a memory. "Beatles, Stones? Remind me to tell you about hitchhiking to Shea Stadium in sixty-five to hear The Beatles live. That Paul was so cute."

Phoebe froze mid-mop and stared at her. Nurse Crawford checked her watch.

"Don't start without me!"

She hurried to a closed door beside the Alzheimer's unit marked "Medical Director." She knocked and entered.

Heather shook her head.

"She was probably the original rock band groupie. I hope she doesn't throw her granny panties at us while we play."

"Good one, kid." Buck held up a hand, and Heather high-fived him.

Phoebe finished wiping up the water, put the mop away and signed us in. She entered the code to the Alzheimer's unit and followed us inside.

"Nice to see you again, Buck with a B."

"You still have my number, right?"

Josh sat in the dayroom by himself. Along the far wall, he gazed across the room with the same flat expression he wore the day before. A half dozen residents gathered in front of the television watching a rerun of *The Andy Griffith Show.*

Ms. Wilcox, wearing the same Jackie Kennedy pillbox hat, clapped as Barney Fife gave Otis a sobriety test.

"Hello, Ms. Wilcox," I said.

The former teacher glanced away from the show.

"Have you done your homework, young man?"

"I'm working on it."

Buck chuckled.

"Young man. I don't know if it's Alzheimer's or bad eyesight."

Ms. Wilcox shooed us away.

"You boys can't watch television until your homework is done." She dismissed Heather as well. "You too, sonny."

Heather looked down at her jeans, long-sleeved shirt and leather vest.

"What am I supposed to do, wear a freakin' prom dress?"

An old man in slippers and a faded blue robe shuffled up to Heather. He circled her like one might a store mannequin.

"How'd you get my vest?"

"Dude, it's mine."

Phoebe took the man's arm and led him to a chair in front of the television.

"Leave her alone, Mr. Worthington, and keep your robe cinched."

"She took my vest!"

We crossed the room, and Josh registered the same apprehension as the day before.

"Josh, this is my friend, Heather."

"Nice to meet you, Heather." He studied me with vague recognition. "Who are you?"

The question hit me like a two by four, but it shouldn't have surprised me. "Sparky. This is Buck."

"Nice to meet you, Sparky. Nice to meet you, Buck."

Buck didn't appear upset or surprised that Josh didn't remember his name. "Ready for some classic songs?"

Josh's face twisted into a grimace.

"I don't like music."

"You'll like this kind."

Heather winked at me then helped Phoebe set up chairs in the middle of the room.

Buck removed the bushman and showed it to Josh.

"You remember this?"

Josh inspected the hat for nearly a minute then handed it back. "You wore that. You had mud in your hair."

I almost shouted in triumph. He remembered! "Do you remember who gave it to Buck?"

Josh shook his head.

I handed him the old Gibson my parents bought me when we formed the band.

"Do you remember this?"

My hopes soared until he handed it back.

"It's a guitar."

I wanted to understand what triggered Josh's memory about the hat, but Heather's foot tapped impatiently. She took a seat, lifted her guitar and waved for Buck and me to join her.

Buck set the bushman on his head. "Showtime." We sat with Heather between us.

On the television, Andy and Opie strolled from the fishing hole to the whistling theme song. Phoebe shut off the television.

"Like to hear some music, everyone?"

Heather leaned toward me and whispered. "That Mr. Worthington dude keeps staring at my vest."

"I'm sure he's harmless. Consider it a fashion compliment."

Nurse Crawford came in and took a chair inside the dayroom. She wore a smile I wouldn't have thought her capable of when we arrived.

I prayed Josh would remember the song like he remembered the hat. I tuned up the Gibson by strumming a chord.

Ms. Wilcox applauded and took a seat in the front row of chairs.

"Not yet, Ms. Wilcox." Phoebe led a half dozen residents into chairs facing us.

Heather adjusted a tuning peg on her guitar.

"If we're a hit, next time I'll bring my electric and amp and we'll really crank it up."

Buck slipped the harmonica from his jacket. "I could set up my drums."

"Let's get through this first. *Homeward Bound*? To my dismay, Josh appeared as disinterested as he had with the music therapist the day before.

I hoped the Simon and Garfunkel song about longing for one's home wouldn't trigger melancholy in the residents, but the song was Josh's favorite from The Buck Naked Band days. Back then, we saved it for our encore, but no one ever asked us to play one. If Josh remembered any of our songs, it would be this one.

I kept my eye on him, waiting for his reaction. Heather and I harmonized while Buck played the harmonica. We didn't sound like Simon and Garfunkel or even Josh and me back in the day, but we were damn good for two geezers and a teenager I'd only met the day before.

A dozen more residents and staff entered the room while we played. Nurse Crawford's toe tapped to the beat, but Josh acted as disinterested as he had toward the music therapist.

We finished to enthusiastic applause. Josh applauded but didn't seem to know why. I hoped, beyond reason, the song would trigger something in him. Anything that might give hope that he'd hang onto memories a while longer. "He didn't remember at all."

Buck let out a breath. "What did you expect?"

In spite of what I knew about Alzheimer's, I wanted Josh to remember. "I wanted to make a difference in his life, if only for a while."

Buck tapped the harmonica on his hand. "Let's try another."

Heather adjusted the guitar on her lap. *"Feelin' Groovy?"*

Not appropriate for how I felt. "'59th Street Bridge Song' is the title."

"Don't be so grumpy. You sound like Grandpa."

Heather's comparison snapped me from my dejection enough to play another song. We came to the chorus and several residents sang along. Everyone seemed to feel groovy except Josh and me. He simply stared across the room.

We finished to more applause. I hung my head. "Shit."

Playing the old Buck Naked Band songs was a stupid idea. My delusion of self-importance. Maybe I wanted Josh to remember for selfish reasons. Perhaps I wanted to help Josh, and in doing so, help myself, instead of sitting at home a semi-recluse.

No. It was more than that. I wanted to help Josh fight the disease and grab a small victory over Alzheimer's. I hadn't helped Emily defeat her cancer, either.

The disease robbed Josh's memories of the oldies and music couldn't change that. He didn't have a clue who I was. Why was I even here?

Buck took off his hat and twirled it over and over in his hand like I'd seen him do years ago.

"I didn't expect him to remember, but I can't believe he didn't enjoy the music. We sounded good."

"We were awesome." Heather grabbed a flute from her vest pocket. "One more."

I planned to stop by the liquor store on the way home. I stood. "Let's go."

"I didn't get to play this." She tugged me back onto the seat. "I practiced all night. Pissed Grandpa off, too."

Buck tapped the harmonica on his hand.

"Consider it an encore."

Heather drew the flute to her lips and played the *Going up the Country* opening.

Ms. Wilcox shouted, "I love this song."

Josh bobbed his head. I couldn't believe it. My heart pounded, but in a good way.

After the flute opening, Heather and I strummed our guitars. Josh sang along, remembering every lyric as if he rehearsed. Shocked at his reaction, we continued to play, but Heather and I stopped singing and let Josh continue alone. I closed my eyes a moment and his voice sounded as smooth as back in high school.

Phoebe's mouth dropped, and several more staff members came to listen.

My eyes misted, and I struggled to play the chords. Tears even danced in Heather's eyes. Only Buck kept it together.

Josh slapped rhythm on one leg as he sang. *"You can jump in the water and stay drunk all the time."* Perhaps in his mind, he was still the lead singer in The Buck Naked Band taking Buck and me along for the ride, like he had in high school.

Heather almost missed the flute solo.

Throughout Heather's solo, Josh kept perfect time, patting his leg. On cue, he sang the next verse and never missed a word.

A man in a pinstriped suit with a red power tie stood in the doorway to the dayroom, arms folded. Who was this guy?

After the last verse, Heather left the guitar on the chair and walked toward Josh, playing the flute. Buck and I followed. We relished the joy of the moment, our small victory over a dreadful disease. Staff and residents applauded Josh when the song ended. Heather and I joined in.

Josh smiled sheepishly from all the attention.

Why would he remember a Canned Heat hit we never played

instead of songs we used to sing? "Why didn't you sing the first two songs?"

Josh shrugged. "I didn't know the words."

The expressions of Phoebe and the rest of the staff showed they sensed something significant happened during the song. Only Nurse Crawford and the man in the pinstriped suit looked unconvinced. He turned on his heel and left the dayroom.

"Any other songs you'd like to sing?" I asked.

Josh wrinkled his forehead. "Not that I remember."

As Mr. Worthington approached Heather's guitar, she snatched it off the chair then gave me a fist bump.

"Your buddy was awesome, huh? You and I couldn't even remember the words yesterday. What's with that?"

Buck took the bushman off my head.

"Josh remembered this old sixties hat."

His memory of the Canned Heat song and the recognition when he saw Buck's hat had to be some kind of a breakthrough. Was I right after all? Maybe recovering lost memories could slow the disease's progression or at least help him enjoy the time he had left.

More than ever, I regretted the time I'd neglected Josh, staying at home feeling sorry for myself while he wasted away in a place too busy to care for his needs.

I fished the Hendrix guitar pick from my pocket and showed it to Josh.

"Do you remember this? It belonged to Jimi Hendrix."

I held my breath and waited for him to answer.

Josh cocked his head.

"Who's Jimi Hendrix?"

♪♪♪♪♪

In less than five minutes, the facility's medical director destroyed my optimism over Josh singing. The doctor, the man in the pinstriped suit who observed Josh's performance, sat across a thick mahogany desk from Nurse Crawford and me while Buck stood before a spotless aquarium with large slow-moving fish.

Unlike my new cardiologist, this doctor didn't display any humor or compassion—a disgrace for someone who ran a facility with so much need for kindness and laughter.

Table lamps bathed the office in a warm glow. Soothing images hung on the walls: a painting of a waterfall and a print of piano keys that Chancellor Warfield kept in his office, too. Until now, I considered Warfield the poster boy for "if substance fails, fall back on image."

The doctor no doubt created the atmosphere to calm agitated patients and family members, but I suspected the primary purpose was to provide a soothing escape for the director.

He wound a wide red rubber band around his index fingers and explained Josh's memory of the Canned Heat song wasn't a breakthrough. With one eye on Buck, he described other Alzheimer's patients who knew song lyrics or recited poetry they memorized in school, yet they couldn't recall spouses or siblings.

Why would Josh remember a song I never heard him perform instead of the ones he sang a hundred times? The doctor didn't offer an explanation, merely a cursory attempt at compassion.

"There is no cure for Alzheimer's. No remission like cancer. At Sunrise, we try to create an atmosphere to make the resident's final journey comfortable."

Buck's face reddened. For a moment, he looked like he did in his garage when he told me how the country neglected his sergeant. He left the room and closed the door behind him.

The director wanted the residents as tranquil as the fish in the office aquarium. The facility kept them entertained with old television reruns and mind-numbing music.

I waited for Nurse Crawford to speak, but she sat as silent as the fish in the tank, as if she didn't want to voice an opinion that might contradict her boss.

The director set down the rubber band and pressed his fingertips together.

"Mr. Ellington, we deal with what you're struggling with almost every day. You're grieving over the loss of your friend. The last stage in the grieving process is acceptance. Acceptance of the inevitable is one of life's toughest challenges."

I'd had enough damn lectures about the grieving process over the past two years. Acceptance? I couldn't accept Josh wasting away in this place. I had to make a difference in what time he had left.

"If Josh can remember song lyrics, maybe he'll remember other things we think he's forgotten. Could retrieval of lost memories prolong the time he has left?"

For a moment, the doctor seemed to let his guard down as

impatience flickered across his face.

"Don't get your hopes up."

I couldn't take any more. I jumped up and smacked the top of his desk with both hands.

"Hope makes life worth living, Doctor."

He calmly held up one hand.

"Not false hope. Please calm down."

I took a deep breath and sat down. I hadn't hoped for anything since Emily died.

"How long will Josh have before even those song memories fade?"

"I'm afraid I can't even speculate."

The medical director came from behind the desk and walked me to the door.

"Mr. Ellington, please continue to visit and bring your guitar. In the long run, Josh singing the oldies won't make a difference to him, but it might to you."

That's what he thought? I came to visit my old friend not to brighten his day, but to improve mine? *Son-of-a-bitch!* I followed Nurse Crawford into the hallway.

She led me toward the lobby where Buck and Heather waited.

"The director is right, you know. You need to accept the inevitable." She glanced around to see if anyone else could hear her. "But don't give up yet."

I wouldn't give up. I accepted the inevitability of Josh's disease, but to help Josh enjoy the time he had left, I had to understand why he remembered the lyrics to *Going up the Country.*

Hat in hand, Buck stared at the bushman. He turned it over and over in his hand. "I'm sorry I wasn't much help."

"The bushman." Buck's hat triggered a memory. It wasn't the key to unlocking Josh's mind, but I had an idea what might be. I had to be sure.

I rushed to the door to the Alzheimer's unit. Nurse Crawford buzzed me through. I burst inside the unit and ran into the dayroom. No Josh.

Phoebe pointed toward the last room at the end of the hall.

"Josh is in his room, two-one-eight."

I hurried down the hall and nearly collided with an attendant pushing a food cart.

Inside a narrow, drab room, Josh sat in a chair beside the bed listening to talk radio.

"Glenn Beck, Josh? Really?" I snapped off the radio.

The tiled floor was institutional gray, the walls a dull dark-green, the color of cheese mold. On a nightstand sat the only personalized item, a picture of his bitter judgmental mother. The place needed some color and individuality, perhaps old photos or other mementoes to keep his memories alive. That could wait. I had to be sure of what I suspected.

Josh looked up with vague recognition.

"Who are you?"

"Sparky."

"Nice to meet you, Sparky."

Heather and Buck arrived in the doorway looking like I'd lost my mind.

I tried to remember all the Woodstock songs I knew. I picked one Arlo Guthrie sang the first night of the festival. I sat on the edge of the bed, strummed a chord and began to play. "*Comin' into Los Angelees ...*" I paused then strummed another chord.

Josh bobbed his head. "*Bringing in a couple of keys ...*"

Yes! My hunch was right. Josh and I smiled as we sang together. "*Don't touch my bags if you please, Mr. Customs Man.*"

I wanted to shout the news to the world. I turned to Buck and Heather.

"That's it! That's the goddamn key to helping Josh."

Heather's eyebrows bunched together.

"Dude, I'm not following."

"The key ... the key to why Josh remembered *Going Up the Country* and not The Buck Naked Band songs."

Buck held out both hands.

"So, what's the key?"

I moved my arms and feet in a victory dance.

"Woodstock!"

7

I didn't have time to focus on Josh's Woodstock breakthrough. I had to convince my daughter I'd turned my life around even if I had to use Meagan to deceive her. I wanted to make the house presentable to both.

When I finished, I rewarded myself with a glass of bourbon and returned the bottle to its hiding place in the pantry. Lady barked at a knock on the front door.

Meagan was a half hour early. In the kitchen, I fixed her a drink while she familiarized herself with the appliances and cupboards.

She took the bourbon and we clinked glasses.

"I bet this won't go in your food journal."

"Already there as iced tea."

At the kitchen table, she sipped the bourbon and swirled the liquor around the glass.

"Heather told me what you did for your friend in the nursing home. You're quite a guy."

Maybe I should tell her about the pain I caused Buck in his garage.

"No I'm not."

"Heather thinks you are. So do I."

I grew uncomfortable from her lingering gaze. Why was she interested in someone of my age and questionable temperament?

"What's with Heather ... the way she dresses?"

"Like a guy?" Meagan took a long swallow. "I think it's my daughter's way of making a statement she doesn't want to be like me, you know? That's okay. I want her to be herself, whatever that might be."

"You're a good mom."

I took a gulp and finished my drink. I wanted another, but with Cloe coming over, the second would have to wait until my daughter departed.

"Where's Heather's dad?"

"The son-of-a-bitch is none too happy I moved his daughter across state lines. Worthless slug."

Meagan finished her drink. She obviously didn't want to talk about her ex.

She set the glass in the sink.

"Most men aren't as sensitive as you."

I set my empty glass beside hers.

"You ready to get started?"

A disconcerting grin swept across her face.

"I sure am."

She threw both arms around my neck and kissed me. She ground against me and pushed me against the counter. Her open-mouthed kiss took my breath away. I hadn't been kissed like this since ... My eyes locked on Emily's urn.

Meagan's hand ran up my leg and a stabbing jolt shot across my chest. I grimaced in pain, which seemed to excite her even more. Her breathing quickened and she kissed me again. She grabbed my hand and held my palm against one of her considerable breasts.

Oblivious to my distress, she pulled me down the hall. In my bedroom, she shoved me onto the bed. She slipped out of her satin blouse and revealed a black lace bra and a peace symbol on her right breast. The irony of the peace symbol wasn't lost on me.

Weak and short of breath, the chest pain made it nearly impossible to move. My breathing grew short and ragged, which Meagan mistook for passion.

She crawled on top of me, unbuckled my belt and kissed me. I began to hyperventilate. I tried to ask her to stop, but the words came out of my mouth as squeaks and groans.

"Oh, Sparky."

Face flushed with passion, Meagan pinned down my wrists then let go.

"Are you all right?"

I couldn't answer but managed to shake my head "no."

"Your heart?"

I nodded.

"Oh, my God!" Meagan leaped off the bed. "I could've killed you."

"I'll ... I'll be okay."

She snatched her blouse, covered her chest and backed to the doorway. Meagan's look of horror changed as comprehension swept over her face. She peered down the hall. Her face flushed with irritation.

"It's her, isn't it?"

If there was evidence I hadn't moved on with my life, my current situation was proof.

"Goddamnit. She's been gone how long? Two years? You're thinking your wife is in the next room, and you were about to cheat on her. Let me make this easy for you, Sparky Ellington. I won't be the other woman to a ghost."

Meagan slipped into her blouse, left the room and bolted down the hall to the kitchen.

I lay in bed trying to recover from the encounter. Lady stood in the corner wagging her tail, her mouth open, practically smiling.

"A lot of help you were, Lassie."

A minute later, the chest pain eased and my breathing returned to near normal. I sat on the edge of the bed and made it to my feet.

In the kitchen, Meagan stood with her back to me, slicing celery for the salad on a chopping board.

"Perhaps I gave you the wrong impression."

She spun and pointed the knife at me. "If you don't want your balls to be a quiche garnish, don't say another word."

I held up both hands and backed away.

Meagan grabbed a head of lettuce. Holding my gaze, she smacked it on the counter. She ripped out the core and threw it into the trash.

"Can I help?"

She tossed me a package of low fat Swiss cheese.

"Get grating. Two cups."

While I grated, she finished making the salad then set two salad bowls into the freezer. She gathered the cheese, a pint container of egg substitute, a bunch of spinach and began to prepare the quiche.

In minutes, Meagan slid the heart healthy spinach quiche into the oven. She checked her watch. "I need a saucepan."

I wasn't sure what a saucepan even looked like and was afraid to ask. With her back to me, I slipped my phone from my pocket and Googled saucepan. Several images popped up and I found the appropriate pan in my cupboard.

Meagan filled it half full of water.

"I'll blanche the broccoli then drizzle the dish with extra virgin olive oil. I'll place it in a bowl in the microwave and set the timer for sixty seconds. When the oven buzzer goes off, remove the quiche and let it cool while you serve the salad."

A knock sounded at the door and Lady barked.

"Shit!" I checked the clock. Meagan's premature arrival had been a disaster. Now Cloe's early arrival jeopardized my carefully planned meal. I might as well confess and face her disappointment in me like a man.

Meagan remained calm.

"You'll have to stall while I finish."

Another knock.

"Give me five minutes. I'll slip out the back door and leave through the gate."

When she grabbed me by the shirt collar, I didn't know what to expect.

Meagan kissed me on the lips. She wiped lipstick from my mouth and dismissed me with a wave.

"Go. Stall."

Did the unexpected kiss mean she forgave me? Like Ricky Ricardo in an *I Love Lucy* episode, I hurried to the front door. I paused and sucked in a deep breath. I stepped onto the porch and hugged Cloe.

"You okay, Dad? You look a little flushed."

"That's what working over a hot stove will do. The meal's not quite ready. Why don't you have a before-dinner smoke."

"I've decided to quit ... again."

"One more for old time's sake wouldn't hurt." I kept myself between Cloe and the front door.

"I can't believe you're suggesting I light up." Cloe sat in the chair and lit a Winston.

Inside, Lady barked and scratched at the front door. I let her onto the porch.

Lady let out a low growl. The fur stood on her neck. I managed to grab the dog's collar before she bolted into the yard.

Simpson's cat was using a tree well in my yard as a litter box again. For a moment, I considered letting Lady loose, but that might interfere with the evening. "Quiet, girl."

I sat beside Cloe while Lady tugged and tried to break free. The Siamese finished his business and pawed the ground in a halfhearted attempt to bury what he deposited. He strolled home, flicking his tail, his work of irritating Lady and me complete.

Cloe took a drag on her cigarette and leaned back in the chair.

"I can't talk to your doctor about your medical status."

"Oh?"

My daughter smiled.

"David ... Dr. Malone called last night and asked me to dinner. It would be unethical for us to discuss your condition over a three-course meal."

Cloe deserved romance in her life. She and my doc might make a great couple, but what would a relationship mean to her plans to move to Arlington?

The gate opened. Meagan.

I jumped to my feet. "Let's go inside."

"Can I finish my cigarette?"

"You shouldn't smoke."

Cloe took a long hard drag then crushed the cigarette. As always, she field-stripped the butt, pocketed the filter then followed Lady and me inside.

I hurried to the kitchen as the timer to the stove went off. Perfect! I slid the quiche from the oven and set the dish to cool on a cast iron trivet Meagan must have found in the recesses of one of the cupboards.

I checked the broccoli in the microwave, removed the salad from the refrigerator and grabbed the chilled bowls from the freezer. Like a well-choreographed Fred Astaire dance, I spun and faced my daughter with the salad in one hand, the bowls in the other.

Cloe stared like she didn't know me.

I set the salad in the center of the table, a bowl on each plate and pulled out a chair for her.

Wide-eyed, Cloe sat and picked up a cloth napkin I hadn't seen in years intricately folded in the shape of a rose. "Dad, when did you learn about chilling salad bowls, making quiche and this?" She held up the napkin.

I sat across from my daughter, snapped open the napkin and grinned. "How did I ever manage before the Internet?"

I avoided asking Cloe about the job offer during dinner. We talked about Josh remembering Woodstock songs. She promised to visit and see for herself.

Cloe cleaned off the table, raving about the meal she thought I prepared. I rinsed the dishes and placed them in the dishwasher, normally a monthly task for me. She thought everything tasted perfect. The quiche was light and flaky. She found it hard to believe the rich custard-like filling didn't contain heavy cream. It had "just the right amount of spinach."

She handed me the last plate. "Did you blanche the broccoli?"

Blanche? Meagan mentioned something about blanching, but I didn't have a clue how one blanched food. I hoped she wouldn't ask how I did that. "Sure did."

I snatched the notebook from a magnetic clip on the side of the refrigerator and showed her my food journal.

Cloe raised an eyebrow.

"Coffee, a Granny Smith apple and fat free cheddar cheese for breakfast."

"Breakfast is the most important meal of the day. Eating jump-starts one's metabolism."

"Dad, I'm so proud of you."

I looked away. I couldn't let her see my guilt over my deception. I'd do anything to help my daughter evaluate the job offer without considering my health.

Lady followed us down the hall to my bedroom. I showed her the old treadmill along the far wall. The dog took one glance at the treadmill and backed into the hallway.

"Diet is only half the battle for a healthy heart." I couldn't tell my daughter the only real exercise the treadmill provided was the effort to haul the damn thing up the stairs from the basement.

"I can't believe how seriously you're taking your health."

"You know what they say, if you don't take care of your health, who will?"

On the way to the kitchen, Cloe stopped at the entrance to my home office. She went in and studied the whiteboard I didn't want her to see. Her name was on the board.

Cloe gasped.

"I'm one of your life stressors? Son-of-a-bitch!"

"If you turned down a job you wanted because of concerns over my health, I'd never forgive myself."

Cloe's eyes misted.

"After tonight's dinner, the food journal, the treadmill and this list—everything shows me you're dealing with problems instead of ignoring them like you have the past two years. Whether or not I decide to accept the job, your health won't be an issue, okay?"

"Fair enough."

I grabbed the eraser and wiped Cloe's name off the board. The remaining items wouldn't be so easy to remove.

We returned to the living room, and Cloe looked wistfully at her mother's urn on the mantel.

"I never realized how many other tough breaks you've had the last few years, but even if you deal with everything on the list, you need something more, Dad. You need to find a purpose in life without mom."

"Is that how you dealt with losing her?"

"You may think I work too many hours, but it beats sitting at home thinking about what I've lost."

That's how I lived the past two years.

Cloe touched the urn then gently held the peace symbol necklace in her hand.

"I think I've created a shrine, haven't I?"

"Mom wouldn't want to be a constant reminder to you of what you've lost."

"My brain tells me to let go, but my heart holds me back." My heart was broken in more ways than one.

"Mom's not in that urn. She's somewhere else."

Our memories were there. I hung my head and fought back tears I didn't want to shed in front of Cloe.

"Dad, letting go doesn't mean you don't love her anymore." Cloe placed a hand on my shoulder. "I think she'd want her ashes scattered someplace that meant something to the two of you."

Emily's ashes were my only connection to the life we had. Could I start each day without seeing her in the living room? Could I leave the house and not say goodbye?

"Mom loved the ocean, the trips we used to take as a family. I remember Cape Cod, that lighthouse in Maine, the cruise we took."

I didn't know if I could do it, but I knew the perfect spot. My recent dreams, Josh's memories of the old songs, Emily's trunk of memorabilia—all of that made me realize how important the festival was to Emily and me.

"Woodstock."

Cloe smiled. "I never tired of Mom describing the day you two met and fell in love at Yasgur's farm. How you were interested in her friend Crystal at first, the prunes, the rain, the music, how you left the festival. She remembered every detail. The event changed both your lives."

I slumped down in the rocker and buried my head in my hands. I hadn't just kept her ashes on display for two years, I'd kept her bottled inside until my heart weakened.

Emily fought against the cancer until the end with courage I'd never possess. She wouldn't want me to give up and let my heart wither away.

I swallowed a lump in my throat and walked to the mantel. I began to wheeze as I picked up the urn as if for the first time. Was it possible? Could I let her go? Could I take her back to where we met? Could I scatter Emily's ashes among the green fields that hosted an era's musical giants along with a half million idealistic young Americans convinced of our ability to change the world? Her ashes, her spirit would drift across the fields she knew growing up, the fields where the ghosts of Janice Joplin and Jimi Hendrix walked.

"You'll go with me?" I wiped away a tear I didn't know I'd shed.

"I was afraid you wouldn't ask." Cloe threw both arms around me. "When would we leave?"

Soon. Before I changed my mind. "Saturday."

"This Saturday?" Cloe checked her cell phone. "That sounds perfect."

I walked Cloe to her car.

She kissed my cheek. "You're doing the right thing."

"I know."

Letting Emily go was the right thing to do, but it wouldn't be easy. I waved as Cloe drove off.

♪♪♪♪

The morning of Day Two of Woodstock, I awoke naked beneath the tarp. I stared into Emily's innocent, sleeping face. It was cold and there was mud all around. Nothing mattered except being with her.

My windbreaker half covered her naked body as she slept on the cardboard that had partially sunk into the soft, watery mud. Desire stirred within me. I ran a hand up her side and cupped her breast.

Emily's eyes flickered open. She kissed me then appeared to realize neither of us had clothes on. Her expression changed from joyous to something I couldn't read.

"I don't even know your last name."

"Ellington."

Emily shook my hand. "Nice to meet you, Mr. Ellington." Sarcasm dripped with each word. She pulled on her soggy shirt and slipped into mud-spattered jeans.

"You must think I'm a slut."

"I don't think that at all." What happened to the sweet girl from a few hours ago?

Uncomfortable being the only person naked, I hurried into my wet jeans and shivered, the denim cold against my skin.

Emily tossed off the tarp. Dawn's purple glow peeked over the empty stage. "Crystal must be worried." She scrambled to her feet and dropped the tarp over me.

I finished dressing. Emily's flowered panties lay beside my windbreaker. I stuffed them in my pocket and climbed out of our makeshift tent.

Desperate to find out what was wrong, I went after her. I stepped over sleeping couples on my way up the hill's slippery slope. "Emily, wait."

She didn't wait. What came over her? Anger? Guilt? Remorse? Would I ever understand girls?

My tennis shoes slipped on the gooey muck as I tried to catch up, but Emily strode more agilely through mud than me. Halfway up the hill, I caught up. "Emily, what's wrong?"

We stood beside a couple lying on a blanket, both bare from the waist up. The man lit a joint, and the couple watched our conversation.

I clutched Emily's hand and didn't want to let go until I understood what troubled her. I tried to lead Emily away, but she dug her heels in the mud. "You came here to get laid and got what you wanted, right?"

I got more than I wanted. It wasn't just sex. We made love, but I couldn't use the "L" word with someone I only met a few hours ago. She'd think I was a complete dork. Could a person fall in love in less than a day, or did that only happen in nineteenth century literature?

She shook off my hand and crossed both arms. "Well?"

Buck once told me I'd fall for the first girl I slept with. That hadn't happened. Not with the first or the second, but with Emily, I felt something I'd never experienced before. Were my feelings a Woodstock glow of joy and peace, or something deeper?

Emily wasn't a hippie committed to free love. She was a seventeen-year-old farm girl. I didn't have a clue about how she felt about me and what happened between us.

"I don't know what to say."

Emily's eyes narrowed with disgust, and I didn't know why. She turned and made her way up the hill.

The man offered me a hit on the joint. "Hey, man, don't sweat it. You got laid."

The girl beside him took the joint without covering her breasts and took a toke. "Tell her you love her, you know?"

I tried not to stare at her breasts. "We just met."

"She wants to hear you care." She took another hit and held the joint toward me. "I can see you do."

"I do. I really do. Emily, wait."

The mud grabbed my shoe as I went after her. I lost my balance and fell to my hands and knees in the soft clinging sludge. I pulled myself up, wiped both hands on my already filthy jeans and hurried after Emily.

By the time I caught up, she'd arrived at the area where we left our friends the day before. Crystal sat alone on the side of the hill. Where were Buck and Josh?

Crystal scrambled to her feet with a sleeping bag draped over her shoulders. Mud streaked her hair and wet clothes. Missing one of her sandals, she hardly resembled the girl who caught my eye.

She hugged Emily and began to cry. "This festival sucks. I'm soaked. I haven't slept all night. I could barely see the stage."

Crystal's stomach growled. "Where's the food you went after?"

I reached into my jacket pocket. I handed her the cold hot dog and Emily's panties dropped to the ground.

Crystal rolled her eyes. "Are you kidding me?"

Emily grabbed the panties, stuffed them in her jeans pocket and shot me a scorching glare.

A smirk crossed Crystal's face. "Stan won't be happy."

Stan? "Who's Stan?"

Emily's face flushed and Crystal flashed a self-satisfied grin. Stan must be a boyfriend Emily apparently forgot to mention while describing her life on the farm. Maybe I should be pissed at Emily.

Crystal unwrapped the cold dog, took a deep breath and devoured it in three bites. "Emily," her hand covered a silent belch, "your parents are expecting you."

"You can't go."

"I can't?" Emily set one hand on her hip. "Why not?"

"Because if you leave, we'll never see each other again."

Crystal threw the hot dog wrapper at me. "Fuck you. I bet she doesn't even know your name."

Emily shot her friend a look. "It's Sparky. Sparky Ellington."

"You ditched me for this skinny runt?"

Runt! "Where are my friends?"

"Like I care. Your friend Josh is sweet, but Buck ..." Crystal shook her head. "Buck was okay until he dropped acid."

LSD? "You sure he took acid?"

"You calling me a liar?" Her voice rose an octave. "He tried to bite me."

Buck wouldn't bite anyone. I was reasonably sure he wouldn't, even on LSD.

"So where is he?"

Crystal pointed up the hill where people stood outside a large tent.

"The freak-out tent."

Had Buck overdosed? Was he on a bad trip? I had to find out and make sure he was okay.

Crystal tried to fold up the sleeping bag. The wet slippery bag wouldn't cooperate. She finally gave up, threw it to the ground and kicked the bag with her bare foot. "Fuck it. I'll leave the damn thing. Emily, we have to go."

Emily chewed on her lip. Apparently, people didn't often say no to Crystal.

I pleaded with her. "Please stay."

"Why, Sparky?"

Because I think I'm falling for you, but I can't bring myself to say the words. I led her away from Crystal.

"I don't want what happened to be just a one-time special moment, a precious memory I look back on when I get old and you're living on a farm somewhere ... with Stan."

Emily's eyes misted as she softly touched my cheek.

"If what happened between us was merely a moment, then I'll

regret I came to Woodstock."

"Then don't go. Let's see what happens the rest of the weekend."

Emily's lower lip quivered. She threw both arms around me and kissed my cheek.

"Go check on your friend."

"Don't leave until I get back."

"Emily, don't listen to him," Crystal shouted.

I held her hand a moment, then let go and gazed up at the tent. I had to make sure Buck was okay. What about Josh? Would Emily be here when I returned? Who was this Stan guy and how did Emily feel about him? I had so many questions, but before I found any answers, a loud beeping sound came from nearby.

8

The incessant beep of a truck backing into my driveway jolted me awake. My eyes glazed over, trying to focus on the alarm clock I hadn't paid attention to in months. 6:30 a.m.?

Lady barked and jumped down from my bed, wagging her tail. I stumbled into my slippers and a robe. I left her inside and hurried out the front door to discover the source of the racket.

Buck's tow truck sat backed into the drive. I'd forgotten Buck's offer to tow Emily's Dodge Caravan to his garage.

In gray coveralls, he hopped down from the cab. "Top of the mornin' to you, Sunshine. How about opening the garage?"

Barely conscious, I entered a code on the keypad by my garage, and the door rumbled open.

Buck crawled beneath the back of the Caravan and hooked the winch to the van. He slid out, got to his feet and wiped both hands on his coveralls. He circled the Dodge, inspecting the vehicle.

"How 'bout a cup of coffee?" I could certainly use one.

"If it's decaf. Do you want to know what caffeine will do to you?"

"Absolutely, but wait until after I have a couple of cups before you tell me."

Inside, Lady greeted Buck like a long lost friend. I found a jar of instant decaf coffee in the cupboard. I fixed Buck a cup and brewed a pot of the real stuff for me. "Give me a few minutes."

I stood under a hot, soothing shower and washed away my fatigue. In the kitchen, I poured myself a cup of coffee and joined Buck in the living room.

With Lady at his side, he stood in front of the mantel. He set his cup beside the urn and stared at the picture of the four of us at Woodstock.

I cleared my throat.

Buck wiped his eyes. "I'm sorry I wasn't at her service." The tears and quivering voice reminded me of the vulnerability below the surface of his bravado.

"This weekend, Cloe and I are taking Emily's ashes to Bethel to scatter them at the festival site."

"That's perfect. The place where you met ..." His voice broke, and he covered his eyes. "Where you'll say goodbye."

"Would you go with us on Saturday?"

"I don't deserve this."

I fought back my own tears.

"Of course you do."

"Man, it'd be an honor."

He threw both arms around me and gave me a hug. Blinking rapidly, he stepped back. He wore a sheepish expression that he'd shown his vulnerability.

Buck's cell phone rang. He smiled. "Hey, baby ... on a call." He checked his watch and made a jack off gesture with one hand.

"Sparky ..." Buck nodded to me. "Ashley says 'hey.'"

"'Hey' to Ashley." I sounded like someone in Mayberry.

"I won't be long, baby. Keep your motor running. Go ahead and start without me, just don't finish until I get there." Buck ended the call and grinned. "Looks like I left something turned on when I drove off this morning."

Outside, he checked the winch then yanked open the door to the tow truck.

"Thanks again for asking me to go back to Woodstock with you. Remember that shop where I bought the prunes?"

"Sure."

"We sat on a bench while Josh called his old lady. You said the trip wouldn't be our last roadtrip. Took forty years, but turns out we'll make one more."

Buck started to climb into the cab of the truck. With one hand on the wheel, he paused then hopped out and approached the van.

"Everything okay?"

"I should have her up and running by day's end. Let's take the van to Woodstock."

"What's wrong with the BMW?"

Buck checked out my car.

"This little thing? It's a half-day's drive to Bethel. We'd be more comfortable in the van and it would be more like a roadtrip back in the day."

Maybe. Had the last few days given me enough courage to get behind the wheel of Emily's van?

"You might have to do most of the driving."

"No problem. One more thing, and don't say no until you hear me out."

He walked to the front of the van and held up both hands, framing the hood. "Let me paint a peace symbol on the front."

"No way."

"We're driving to Woodstock in a van. Without a peace symbol, it just wouldn't feel right."

"A peace symbol." I trusted Buck to tow the van and work on the vehicle's mechanical needs, but I couldn't trust him to paint a peace symbol. I pictured some flamboyant psychedelic symbol with flames shooting out the sides.

"I had one on my old VW, remember? Come on. I've got all the equipment at the shop. If you want, when we get back, I'll repaint the whole thing good as new." Buck's eyes sparkled as he described how he could recreate the peace symbol he'd painted on his old VW. I began to weaken.

"It would have to be subtle."

"You don't think I can be subtle?" His forehead wrinkled into a wounded expression. "Man, that really hurts."

"Okay, you can paint the peace symbol, but don't get carried away."

Buck held up one hand and high-fived me.

"This will be awesome."

I was just played.

He climbed into the van and searched above the driver's visor and found the extra key. He shook his head.

"This is the first place a thief would look. You want it to get stolen?"

"At least the oil would have circulated through the engine."

Buck inserted the key, shifted the transmission into neutral and hurried to the tow truck before I could change my mind. He climbed inside and started the truck. He gazed off in the distance as a look of melancholy swept over him.

"It's a shame Josh can't go with us."

"Damn shame." Buck drove off. There might be a way.

I spent most of the day trying to make sense out of Josh remembering Woodstock songs. Did something happen at Woodstock that imprinted itself on his brain, or was it the magic of Woodstock?

I called two colleagues I knew from Milton College. One had a father die of Alzheimer's and one had written an article on Alzheimer's and cognitive therapy. Neither offered great insight into Josh's situation. They both suggested the Internet.

Four and a half million Americans had the disease and the number grew every year. New evidence suggested a link between Alzheimer's and heart disease. I stared at the search engine and scrolled through Web sites until a name jumped out from the monitor.

A Pennsylvania physician wrote a paper on the connection several years earlier. The author was my cardiologist and Cloe's new squeeze.

I finally tracked down Dr. Dave just after five in the same outdoor lounge where he'd explained my heart condition to me. I waited on a bench while he spoke to a woman who dabbed her eyes with a tissue.

When he finished, she walked past me and nodded, then left the lounge through the door.

The doctor stood beside me. "What's up?"

I explained what happened at Sunrise and questioned whether Josh remembering Woodstock songs was some kind of breakthrough.

His expression gave me the answer. He sat beside me. "I've heard of similar examples with Alzheimer's patients. It's not a breakthrough. I'm sorry."

I closed my eyes and tried to shut out the disappointment of hearing the doctor's opinion. I desperately wanted Josh's memory of Woodstock songs to mean something for his sake, and for mine. I couldn't face him drifting further away day by day, but that was the disease's inevitable consequence.

The painful reality was no amount of desperation or hope or wishing something to be true would change the medical reality.

Dr. Dave stated what the Sunrise medical director had said, but in a much nicer manner. I barely listened. I wanted a drink.

I rose from the bench.

"Thanks for taking the time to talk about this."

"Your face shows the same I-need-a-drink to deal with life's disappointments look I first saw in the ER."

Was I that transparent?

"Confronting emotional pain isn't easy. It's why people bury the hurt inside until ... until it's too late. Don't do that, Mr. Ellington."

I headed for the door then stopped before leaving.

"Then what's the point?"

"Did your friend enjoy singing the songs?"

I nodded.

"Then that's the point. You made his day. Make as many days enjoyable for your friend as you can. Maybe ..." He ran a hand over his five o'clock shadow. "Maybe we should do that to all our friends, every day."

Was that it? Was that all it meant.

"Thanks for your time."

"Good luck, Mr. Ellington."

In spite of my disappointment, I liked Dave. He cared and showed compassion even when he delivered devastating news.

"Call me Sparky."

By the time I arrived home, I still wanted a drink. I decided to allow myself one after dinner.

I fed Lady, and since I hadn't eaten all day, I made myself a salad. I opened a bottle of ranch dressing and drizzled it over the greens. I had to admit the improvised meal tasted good. Maybe I could get used to eating healthy. I entered the items in my food journal, like I was supposed to, then fixed a glass of bourbon.

I took Lady outside and eased my tired body into a porch chair. Lady lounged at my feet while I tried not to think about food journals, treadmills and life stressor lists. I wanted a drink, just one.

I sipped the alcohol, but it didn't feel the same. I set the glass down then bolted upright when the screen door slammed at the Simpson house. Lady scrambled to her feet and stood on the edge of the porch. Her tail wagged against my arm.

Next door, Meagan paced then slumped down on the porch swing and buried her head in her hands. She'd no doubt had an argument with her old man. Who wouldn't?

Instinct told me to mind my own business, but thanks to her, Cloe thought I'd taken control of my health. I picked up the half-full glass of bourbon and led Lady across the moist lawn to the Simpson house.

Meagan's head snapped up as we stepped onto the porch. She brushed her hair from her eyes. The porch light revealed wrinkles on her forehead I hadn't noticed before. Stress.

"You okay?"

"Hell no." She petted Lady, who set her nose against Meagan's leg.

Through an open window, a television blared. From the sounds of gunfire and a car chase, I guessed Simpson was inside watching a "Dirty Harry" movie.

"Anything I can do?"

Her voice cracked.

"Something I have to work out myself."

At least I offered. "Come on, Lady. Let's go."

"I'm sorry, Sparky. Right now, I'm kind of pissed at the entire male gender. Self-absorbed, son-of-a-bitch!"

"Your dad?"

Meagan managed a smile. "He *is* a self-absorbed son-of-a-bitch, but I meant my ex. The bastard got a judge to schedule a custody hearing the day after tomorrow. My lawyer called to inform me the judge turned down our request for a postponement due to my father's health."

"Too bad Cloe's not licensed in Ohio. Do you have a good attorney?"

I gave her the bourbon. She needed the booze more than I did.

"A real ball-buster."

She downed the bourbon in one long gulp and handed the glass back.

"I'm not worried about the hearing. My ex has no chance of gaining joint custody. He's only doing this because he's apparently decided making my life miserable is his lot in life."

"He is a self-absorbed son-of-a-bitch."

She let out a sigh. "I don't want to take Heather. Being the center of a custody dispute wouldn't be good for her, but I'm concerned about leaving her and Dad alone."

The kind, generous woman uprooted her life in Akron to care for her miserable, ungrateful old man. Meagan was a dedicated daughter and a caring mother, and in a short time, offered friendship when I needed friends. I took a deep breath and rubbed my palms on my slacks.

"I'll keep an eye on Heather and your old ... father."

Meagan cocked her head.

"Are you serious?"

"Heather, where's your mom?" Old Man Simpson barked over the sound of the television. "Get me a beer."

"Get it yourself, Grandpa." A door slammed inside the house.

Meagan burst out laughing.

"Sparky, you sure you want to watch over those two?"

"I wouldn't need to spend the night, would I? I mean, I'm next door. Heather could call if she needed anything."

"Sure, but it's still a lot to ask."

"After what you did for me last night, I owe you."

She flashed a flirtatious smile.

"Are you referring to the dinner, or your near-death experience in the bedroom?"

I hoped she'd never mention our brief romantic encounter again.

"Dinner."

"I'm not sure how long I'll be gone. Up to two days. If you're serious, I plan to leave around one tomorrow." She took my hands in hers. "You sure you want to do this?"

I couldn't imagine how Meagan and Heather put up with that grumpy old coot, but I could be on call for a day or two.

"I'm sure."

"I'll leave you a list of emergency numbers."

In the front window, Simpson's cat sat on the windowsill and hissed at Lady and me.

The fur rose on Lady's neck. She lunged for the window, and I pulled her back by the collar. "This isn't our house, girl."

Meagan followed Lady and me to the porch steps.

"About last night, I shouldn't have come on to you like that. It was pretty insensitive of me not to realize you haven't let go yet."

"I'm working on it."

She kissed me on the cheek.

"Good luck with that. I mean it. I don't want to put any pressure on you, but if you ever want to try again, let me know."

Since I'd neglected Lady, I took her for a walk then returned home and went to bed. It didn't take long to fall asleep.

♪♪♪♪

I hoped I'd talked Emily into staying at least until I returned from checking on Buck. I neared the crest of the hill and tried not to think I might never see her again or discover her feelings about me and this Stan guy.

I encouraged Buck and Josh to come to Woodstock. I had a responsibility to them.

At the top of the hill, a shirtless hippie in a red bandana slid down the slick mud on a slice of cardboard like sledding on snow. He whipped past me and tumbled off. Covered in milk-chocolate colored soupy mud, he leaped up, pumped a fist in the air and shouted, "Right on!"

Another person followed, and soon a line formed for the new sport of the day.

I made my way toward the freak-out station that looked like an old circus tent. A handmade sign hung by the front entrance: "Bad Trips Here."

I recognized Josh's style of guitar playing from a picnic table beside the tent. He was in the middle of an Arlo Guthrie song, surrounded by a dozen people, mostly hot-looking girls. With a doobie hanging from his mouth, he sang, *"Comin' into Los Angelees ..."*

Two young women brushed past me and hurried toward him. Words bubbled from a pretty Asian girl. "He's amazing. This guy knows every song played so far."

In four years of high school, I never heard a girl refer to Josh as amazing. Good for him. I left Josh to his fans and went to find Buck.

I entered a chaotic first aid station specializing in treating drug overdoses. The place smelled of antiseptic and body odor. A woman wearing a badge that read "Nurse Sanderson" appeared to be in charge.

Uncertain what I'd find when I located Buck, I made my way through the crowded tent where volunteers and medical staff tended to overdoses, people who stared into the sun in a drug-induced haze, or others who cut their feet stepping on broken glass or soda can pull tabs.

Holy crap! Buck cowered on a canvas cot, his eyes glazed over. He sat with both arms around his knees rocking. A young man in a peace symbol shirt tried to keep him calm.

Buck's gaze focused on me as I approached, but I felt certain he didn't know me.

He lowered his voice. "There's a gremlin on your shoulder."

"No there's not." I knew a little about LSD. I hoped the young man could assure me the drug wouldn't have any lasting effects.

Buck stared at Nurse Sanderson and whispered, "Her head spun around and wouldn't stop." He clamped his eyes shut and looked at her again. "See?"

The volunteer patted Buck on the leg. "If this happened earlier, doctors would have shot him up with Thorazine, but we learned from the Hog Farm folks it's best just to talk people through the trip. He's a lot better. Just talk calmly to him and he'll be good as new in a couple of hours."

I let out a sigh of relief. I sat with Buck until he no longer showed signs of hallucinations. He reclined on the cot and closed his eyes.

It would be some time before he recovered and I could return to Emily. The staff and volunteers needed help. I went up to Nurse Sanderson. "Anything I can do?"

She pointed to a table with gauze, bandages and antiseptic.

"Think you can take care of cut feet?"

"Not my favorite body part, but I'll do my best."

"Any sign of infection, let me take a look."

I inspected the supplies on the table. How hard could this be? Cut feet? With one eye on Buck, I sat on a metal folding chair and waved my first patient over.

A two-hundred-pound hippie in jeans and a vest sat in a chair across from me and took a bloody rag from his foot.

I poured water onto a towel. I wiped away most of the blood and exposed a two-inch slice of skin not too deep.

The big man ran a hand over his forehead.

"Will this hurt?"

"Probably, since I've never done this before."

He laughed.

"Good one. Damn, you weren't kidding." He clamped his eyes shut as I swabbed the cut with alcohol.

The activity kept me from obsessing about whether Emily would be there when I went down the hill. I kept an eye on Buck as my first aid skills improved, but I tired of handling feet.

A couple of hours later, Buck woke and watched me play doctor. During a break in patients, he came over and sniffed the air. "You smell like my dad's old work boots."

I held my hands toward him.

Buck wrinkled his nose and waved a hand in front of his face.

I washed my hands then wiped them with alcohol and dried them with a clean towel.

"You okay?"

He ran a hand over the stubble on his face.

"I'm never gonna touch that shit again. I don't think I can handle drugs."

"You really saw a gremlin on my shoulder?"

He shrugged.

"Guess I mistook it for that chip you usually carry around."

I laughed.

"You've always been an adrenaline junkie. You were a health nut when you played football."

His jaw tightened.

"Yeah, well, I don't play football anymore."

"I can't believe you dropped acid."

Buck shrugged.

"Josh tried it and enjoyed the hell out of the trip. It looked like the thing to do."

"Josh dropped acid?"

"Can you believe it? Where is the little douchebag?"

"Last I checked, he was outside giving a concert to several enchanted groupies."

"Our boy is growing up. How'd things go with that cute hippie chick?"

"Emily." I grinned.

"You hound." He gave me a playful punch in the arm. "Get back to her. I'm okay now, but I think I'll help here awhile. Least I can do after acting like such a turd."

A gangly teenage girl in jeans and a bikini top entered the tent. As she limped toward us, Buck grabbed the bottle of alcohol and pretended to drink.

The girl laughed and sat across from him.

"Are you a doctor?"

Buck grinned and held her hand.

"Yes, I am."

She showed him a cut between two of her toes.

"Think I'll need stitches?"

Buck flashed the white-toothed grin girls always seemed to fall for.

"I'll have you in stitches in no time. Did you hear the one about the traveling salesman and the farmer's daughter?"

The girl laughed and slapped his knee, leaving her hand there. I left the tent knowing Buck would be just fine.

9

I opened my eyes and Lady pawed my arm. I glanced at the clock. I slept until after nine!

I let her into the backyard and climbed into a hot shower. In clean clothes, I let Lady in and fixed a bowl of oatmeal. I entered it into the journal. Dave and Cloe would be pleased.

The rumble of a motorcycle came from the front of the house. I opened the door.

Buck climbed off his Harley.

"What do you say we go to lunch?"

"I just had breakfast."

"We should take Josh. I'm sure they'd let him leave on a pass or something. It would be good for him."

"That's a great idea. Give me a few minutes. There's something I want to find."

In my bedroom closet, I rummaged through a box of hundreds of pictures Emily and I always planned to organize into albums. I wasn't even sure I kept the one I was searching for. To my surprise, I found the photo and stuck it into my pocket.

I climbed on the back of Buck's motorcycle. He drove less eventfully than he had the first ride.

At Sunrise, I paused and looked over the plants. The shrub I'd watered was green and healthy.

Buck held the door open. "You coming?"

We signed in, and a volunteer buzzed us through. Phoebe glanced up from the nurses' station. She took off her glasses and smiled at Buck.

He leaned over the counter and checked her out.

"Damn, girl, I bet you look good naked."

Phoebe giggled and blushed.

"Josh is in his room."

"So who do I have to sleep with to get a pass to take Josh to lunch."

"Nurse Crawford." Phoebe laughed. "If you promise not to get into trouble, I'll take care of it."

Buck winked at Phoebe and followed me down the hall.

"I don't get it. Your girlfriend, Ashley, is a very attractive—"

"Very attractive? Do you have to talk like you're stuck in the sixties? Ashley's 'all that.'"

"Okay, she's all that. So why flirt with Phoebe?"

"Flirt. Change is hard, isn't it?" Buck laughed until he snorted. "I get what you're saying, Sparky, but just because I've hung a work of art on a wall at home doesn't mean I can't admire a painting in a museum. Besides, under all that business casual attire, Phoebe's one hot package. My guess, a package no one's unwrapped in a while."

"Why jeopardize a good thing with Ashley?"

"Sparky, my man, what I'm about to say never applied to you because you had Emily. For the rest of us poor saps, life is a constant battle between a man's heart and his dick. " He slapped me on the back as we entered Josh's room. " And a man's heart never wins."

Josh sat in a chair beside his bed. He tugged on a string that had unraveled from the cuff of his green sweatshirt. He didn't look up when we stepped into the room.

Buck lost his bluster. He set a hand on Josh's shoulder.

"Hey, buddy."

Josh studied Buck's face.

"Who are you?"

"Buck … Milton High, all-state … Buck Naked Band." Buck gazed around at the bare walls and drab furnishings with a sour twist on his mouth.

Josh registered a flicker of recognition.

"Remember me? I'm Sparky."

He held out his hand.

"Nice to meet you, Sparky."

I pulled the picture from my pocket and handed it to Josh. Would he remember?

He stared at the black and white photo and clamped his eyes

shut, clearly trying to reclaim a memory. Josh opened his eyes and a broad smile swept across his face as he studied the picture.

"That's my dog, Buttons. Can I keep it?"

I set the photo in the frame on the nightstand, partially covering his mother's picture.

A young Hispanic aide left the food cart outside the door. He set a tray on a table beside the bed. Green beans, gray meatloaf cut into half-inch squares, mashed potatoes with brown paste-like gravy and a dinner roll, no butter. One plastic spork.

Buck wrinkled his nose.

"Man, I ate better in the slammer."

The aide shrugged.

"Dude, I don't cook the stuff. I just deliver, you know what I'm sayin'?" He left and pushed the cart down the hall.

Buck popped a green bean into his mouth then spit it on the floor.

"He can't eat this shit. No wonder people don't get better with food like this."

"Josh, Buck and I want to take you to a restaurant."

"Can I have a hamburger?"

"Whatever you want."

We stopped at the nurses' station, and Phoebe handed me a leave slip. She wrote down the time in a logbook.

"Just one hour. No caffeine and, of course, no booze."

"Never touch the stuff." Buck registered mock offense.

At the entrance to the dayroom, Mrs. Wilcox, without her fifties hat, appeared lost.

"Where's your hat, Mrs. Wilcox?" I asked.

She gazed through me with a blank stare.

"Mr. Ellington." Phoebe shook her head. "She's having a bad day."

The change in the former teacher made me realize how Alzheimer's relentlessly erodes a person's memories. I had to help Josh preserve his memories as long as possible.

With more than a little reluctance, Phoebe buzzed us through.

"I might lose my job if you get into trouble."

Buck held out both hands.

"What, do we look like troublemakers?"

Phoebe blushed again.

"*You* do."

I stuffed the pass into my pocket as we stepped onto the street. For a moment, we were the three amigos in high school with a hall pass, looking to get into trouble.

Josh gazed around at the shops near the facility as if seeing them for the first time. He probably was.

Buck clapped him on the back.

"You look better already, my friend."

I pointed down the sidewalk.

"The Chat and Chew is a couple blocks away. I think you'll like this waitress I know."

Buck nudged Josh in the ribs.

"The way he said 'you'll like' makes it sound like the waitress has a nice rack. You still a boob man?"

Josh smiled. He walked between us, more hesitant than in the old days, like a foreigner in a big city for the first time. When something caught his eye in a thrift shop, he stopped, ran a hand along the glass and smiled at the display of tie-dyed shirts. Halfway to our destination, he stopped at the window of a travel agency and studied posters of exotic destinations. Seeing the joy already from our excursion, I vowed to take him some place special next time.

At the busy diner, we slipped into the last available booth. Josh and Buck sat across from me. I looked around and let out a sigh of relief when I didn't recognize anyone from the college.

"I bet that's your waitress." Buck nodded toward Meagan.

In snug tan slacks and a plain white blouse, she paced behind the counter. She talked on a cell phone and rubbed her furrowed brow. She snapped the phone closed then smiled at me. Meagan brought menus to the booth and set place settings in front of us.

I took a menu. "You okay?"

"Not looking forward to confronting my ex." She handed me a key. "I forgot to leave this with you last night."

I stuck Meagan's house key into my pocket. I intended to explain about the key, but Buck's knowing smile told me he'd never believe my explanation.

I introduced her to my two friends.

"Sparky's told me all about you," Meagan said to Josh.

Buck cleared his throat. "Did he tell you about me?"

Meagan sized him up. "I think I'd have remembered you coming up in conversation."

"I'm Buck."

"You must be Buck Naked."

"Not at the moment." Buck grinned.

Meagan politely chuckled but didn't seem as charmed by Buck as Phoebe. For a reason unclear to me, I took some pleasure from her reaction.

She snatched an order pad from her belt.

"What will you boys have?"

"A hamburger." Josh tapped a picture on the menu. "Like this one."

She glanced where he pointed.

"A cheeseburger, curly fries platter. You got it."

Buck ordered a gluten-free meal, then shook a finger at me.

"You should go gluten free, too. How's your prostate?"

"Fine. Thanks for asking." I collected the menus and handed them to Meagan. "A chef salad."

"That will look good in your food journal." Meagan wrote down the order. "Before I forget, I lost an earring at your place."

I hadn't found anything.

"Where do you think you lost it?

Meagan raised an eyebrow. *Oh, the bedroom.*

My face flushed. I ignored Buck when his mouth dropped open.

"I'll search when I get home."

"Thanks. I'll leave you boys and your prostates. I'll be back with the orders in a few."

As she walked away, I leaned across the table and smacked Buck's arm.

"How's your prostate? Why'd you embarrass me like that?"

"Because I can?" He ruffled my hair. "Let me give you a tip for finding that earring. She probably lost it making a one eighty under the sheets."

Buck stared at Meagan's ass.

"Sparky's got himself a girlfriend."

"She's not my girlfriend."

Buck cocked his head.

"Something wrong with a hot woman interested in you?"

"It's been a long time since someone other than Emily was interested."

"Come on. College girls never hit on you?"

From time to time. "Sure. That's one disadvantage of teaching college."

"Disadvantage? Sounds like one of the perks." Buck nudged Josh. "Hear that? Our friend has cold feet."

Buck checked out Meagan as she disappeared into the kitchen.

"You know a good cure for cold feet?"

I guessed his answer.

"A hot woman?"

Buck held out both hands.

"There's hope for you yet."

Josh laughed. "Sparky has cold feet."

During the meal, he smiled a lot. I hadn't seen much smiling at the assisted living home. He initiated conversation and even laughed at Buck's humor. This mini-roadtrip was good for him, for Buck and for me.

Josh finished his burger and shifted uncomfortably. "I need to pee."

Buck sighed. "I'll go with him. I know what it's like to pee on one's self. Wouldn't want that to happen."

My two friends left for the restroom as Meagan came from the kitchen with her purse. She stopped by the booth and handed me a list of emergency numbers.

"My boss said I could leave early. With any luck I'll be back within twenty-four hours."

"Don't worry about Heather or your dad. I'm next door."

"He wasn't feeling well this morning."

"I'll check on him when I get home."

"You're so sweet."

As Buck returned, she kissed me on the cheek. With a wave of her well-manicured fingers, she took off.

Buck slipped into the booth.

"Where's Josh?"

Dread smacked me in the face. I jumped to my feet. Lightheaded, I held onto the table as adrenaline surged through my veins.

Buck's eyes widened with alarm.

"He left as I washed my hands. He couldn't have gone far."

I tried not to panic. I scanned the restaurant.

"Josh could be any place. He has Alzheimer's!"

My cell phone rang. Cloe. My daughter's timing couldn't be worse.

While Buck bolted from the booth in search of Josh, I took a deep breath, hoping Cloe wouldn't hear the panic in my voice.

"Hi, sweetie."

"Dad. I'm at Sunrise. You need to bring Josh back right away."

"Why? We have a pass. Josh wants dessert." I hurried through the restaurant searching each booth and table as Buck rushed outside and scanned up and down the street. I had to stall until we found him.

"Just do it, Dad." She hung up.

This can't be happening. Where was Josh?

I hurried into the men's room. Empty. When a woman approached, I paused outside the ladies' room door. She gave me a cautious look.

I tried to remain calm as if nothing was wrong.

"Would you go in and check whether a man is inside?"

She took a step back.

"I don't think I want to do that."

"Then would you wait while I go inside?"

She put a hand up and backed away with a shudder into the dining room.

The door opened. Josh came out of the ladies' room. "I got lost."

I let out a giant sigh of relief. I considered explaining to the woman but didn't want to embarrass Josh. I led him to the cash register, paid the tab and went outside.

Where was Buck? I checked my watch as we waited outside the entrance to the restaurant.

Buck sprinted from around the building and skidded to a stop in front of us. He let out a deep breath. He bent over and sucked in gulps of air.

"You scared us, man."

Josh's eyes glistened as he ran a hand over the stubble on his chin.

"I was scared, too."

♪♪♪♪♪

Cloe waited on the steps of the Sunrise facility, appearing as grim as she'd sounded on the phone. Her face softened when she saw Josh.

"Hello, Josh. I'm Cloe. Can I give you a hug?"

He held out both arms, and Cloe hugged him.

She smiled at Buck.

"It's been a long time."

Buck hugged her.

"You're as pretty as your mother."

"Ohhh. I wish we were meeting under more pleasant circumstances." She led us inside.

"What's this about?" We approached the Alzheimer's unit.

Before she answered, the door opened and the reason stared me in the face.

I last saw Josh's mother at Emily's funeral. The fact she brought Josh suggested she possessed some decency. I'd always be grateful, but her face retained the judgmental puritanical expression I remembered from high school.

Buck spoke so only I could hear. "God help us all."

With the compassion of a gargoyle, the diminutive, stoop-shouldered woman hurried to her son's side, her cane tapping on the tile.

"Joshua, are you alright?"

"I got lost."

"Lost?" She shot me a scowl I remembered well.

The medical director stood beside Phoebe at the nurses' station. This must be serious to prompt him to come out of his office. Clearly frustrated by the tension in his facility, he gestured down the hall. "Perhaps if we go to my office."

My daughter stepped forward, taking charge as attorneys do. "As you can see, Mrs. Channing, your son is fine."

The old woman snatched a hankie from her pocket. "What's that on your face? Mustard?" She wiped a brown dot from Josh's chin and shot me another angry glare.

"The doctors at Sunrise have my son on a strict diet."

"Strictly crap." Buck chuckled.

Mrs. Channing looked ready to beat Buck over the head with her cane.

Josh's joy at the restaurant vanished now that he'd returned to the facility. Or maybe his mother's presence caused the darkened mood.

"My father meant well." Cloe hadn't given up diffusing the situation.

Josh's mother rapped her cane on the cold, hard tile.

"Who are you people? Why did you take my son?"

"We're Josh's high school friends. This is Buck Jamison. I'm

Walter Ellington. Sparky."

Her pasty white face paled even more.

"I remember you now." She let out a sarcastic laugh and held Josh's arm. "You two haven't changed at all, always getting my boy into trouble. You were bad, bad boys."

I forced myself to remain calm.

"That was a long time ago."

She took Josh's hand and closed her eyes.

"God, in his infinite mercy, has taken Joshua's memory to wipe away past sins."

She blamed Buck and me for Josh's Alzheimer's. That's why everyone acted like we kidnapped him.

Buck's face approached the color of a Coke can.

"I don't know what your son told you about the old days, but he never did any sinning when I was around."

Mrs. Channing's voice sputtered with indignation.

"He ... he didn't need to tell me. You three were obsessed with sex, drugs and rock 'n' roll."

Buck held out both hands.

"It was the sixties."

Phoebe covered her mouth, hiding laughter.

Buck looked at me, appearing confused as to why the old woman couldn't grasp his logic. "It *was* the sixties."

"When my son went off to Penn State, I found marijuana in his closet and ... and pornography." Her eyes narrowed into slits as she scowled at Buck. "Joshua told me you gave them to him."

"Me?" Buck shrugged. "The pot was probably mine, but if you found porn, you can bet the stuff was Sparky's."

I felt my face flush.

This time, Cloe hid a smile with her hand.

"He accumulated quite a collection of Penthouse Magazines in high school." Buck's voice trailed off, as he appeared to realize he wasn't helping the discussion. "Not a collection, really ... never mind."

Mrs. Channing stepped toward me, as if I possessed more sense than Buck.

"Can't you two just leave my son in peace?"

Peace? So he could die alone without friends?

"Did anyone tell you about the songs Josh can sing? He knows the words to every Woodstock song."

"Woodstock!" She shrieked the word. She pressed her hands together in prayer and closed her eyes, as well as her mind. "You tempted him with talk of drugs and fornication."

"We didn't tempt Josh." Buck's hand trembled. For a moment, I thought he might lose it. "Your son came up with the idea of the roadtrip. We went for the music. The sex and drugs were an unexpected bonus."

Buck clapped Josh on the arm. "Sorry, man." He headed for the exit, and Phoebe let him out.

"Woodstock was Satan's work." Josh's mother pointed the cane at me. "The music you played is the devil's music. Why doesn't he remember the hymns he learned in church?"

I couldn't explain why Josh remembered Woodstock songs and not others, but clearly, the three days in August of sixty-nine affected him in a way I hadn't appreciated at the time.

Josh clamped his eyes shut, growing agitated by the confrontation. He clenched both hands and pounded the sides of his head.

"See what you've done? Come, Joshua. I'll take you to your room."

She shot me a cold dead glare then led Josh away.

I could prove the music at Woodstock wasn't the devil's music and didn't need my guitar. Joan Baez, Emily's favorite, sang the spiritual *Swing Low, Sweet Chariot* a capella. Her voice was the instrument.

"*Swing low, sweet chariot.* Sing with me, Josh!"

Josh stopped. His mouth opened, but his mother led him away.

Desperate, I tried the next verse as they walked away. "*Comin' for to carry me home. Swing low, sweet chariot ...*" Sing, Josh! Show her how wrong she is.

With her face lit with bitter triumph, Josh's mother led Josh into his drab, dreary room.

"*Comin' for to carry me home.*" I wiped away tears of frustration. I failed my friend, not for the first time, but surely the last.

Was there anyone in the room besides me who might stand up to the woman and do what was best for Josh?

Phoebe couldn't hold my gaze.

The medical director retreated to the safety of his office.

Cloe grasped my arm.

"Dad, it's over."

"It's not over!" I couldn't let that woman control what was left of Josh's life any longer.

How many coherent months, weeks or days did he have left? How much longer would he be able to enjoy a meal with friends or a song he recalled? I'd do whatever it took to extend his enjoyment of life as long as possible.

A painful stab shot through my chest, but I couldn't let Cloe see my discomfort.

"That woman has no right to keep Josh from enjoying the one thing he's grasping to hold onto."

"Unfortunately, she has every right." Her voice filled with lawyerly resignation. Cloe led me toward the exit door. "Josh's mother has power of attorney."

10

The Cheshire cat-like triumphant grin of Mrs. Channing, as she led her son into his room, shattered my optimism about improving Josh's quality of life in the time remaining. What could I do?

I paced the facility's parking lot, trying to control my frustration and my breathing. I fought the urge to double over, to ease my discomfort, but I had to conceal my throbbing chest pain from Cloe and Buck.

Red-faced, Buck straddled his Harley while my daughter explained the law's intricacies that allowed Josh's mother to control what her son could do, who he could see, even what he might eat.

She finished, and I shook my head. "What's lawful isn't always what's just."

"Dad, don't quote some sixties radical to me."

I stopped pacing. I hadn't quoted a sixties radical.

"Your mother used to say that, or have you forgotten?"

"That's not fair."

I closed my eyes and pictured Josh's drab room and his dreary existence.

"I need to walk."

"Sure you don't want a ride, man?" Buck slipped on his helmet.

"I have to work this out on my own."

"Don't do anything stupid, Dad."

Her tone meant, "Don't get drunk." I wanted a drink, but I knew this time I wouldn't stop at one.

I left Sunrise behind and set off down the street at a brisk pace. Perhaps exercise would work off my hostility toward Josh's mother and ease my throbbing heart.

In spite of Cloe's legal explanation, I couldn't accept letting Josh's mother determine what was best for him. My options were limited. However, I wouldn't let the law take away my friend's freedom to experience life, if only for a few months, weeks or even days, no matter what cost I might pay.

During our freshman year, on a day I'd never forget, a drunken driver blew through a stoplight on a blustery November morning and slammed into Josh's father in a crosswalk, killing him instantly.

Always a religious woman, Josh's mother survived by turning to God. In the months and years after the tragedy, however, she used her faith as a club to control her son and keep him close so she wouldn't lose him like she lost her husband. She never let go.

Buck and I and music kept Josh sane throughout high school, but when we went to Penn State, his mother smothered him with guilt. She convinced him of her failing health. He went home for a semester and never returned.

With Buck in Nam, Josh and my parents in Milton and Emily in New York, I found myself hundreds of miles from people I cared about the most. On my own, I focused on academics. Four years later, I graduated with honors, but without the idealism and passion for life I had embraced at Woodstock.

I stepped off the curb. A red Camaro swerved around me, tires squealing, horn blasting. The car missed me by less than two feet.

The startled driver stuck his middle finger out the window. "Watch where you're going, old man!"

I staggered backward and almost fell. Old man? Maybe I'd become one and just hadn't realized it.

Shaken by the experience, I took a deep breath and crossed the street. A Frisbee skidded along the sidewalk and landed at my feet. I grabbed it and tossed the Frisbee to a waiting young couple who waved their thanks.

The well-manicured greenbelt and ivy-covered brick buildings made me realize I'd stepped onto the campus of Milton College, something I vowed never to do again. My mouth grew dry and a wave of queasiness surged from my gut.

I loved instilling an appreciation of literature in young people, but I couldn't imagine working under Chancellor Warfield again, even if the board now supported me. I decided to e-mail the bean counter when I got home and reject his offer before I changed my mind.

The afternoon sun cast long shadows across the green grass of the campus. I had to get home and check on Heather and Old Man Simpson, but not yet. I set off toward the other side of town to a school with more pleasant memories.

Half an hour later, I stood in front of Milton High, a place I'd avoided the past two years, like so many others. Josh, Buck and I graduated from the school—Class of sixty-nine. Emily taught history for fifteen years here before she accepted the position of vice principal and two years later, principal.

A plaque on the side of the administration building read "Goodbye, Emily Ellington." I swallowed hard as I read the message below, Emily's favorite Gandhi quote: "Live as if you were to die tomorrow. Learn as if you were to live forever."

As a teacher and administrator, Emily fought for her students with the same fervor she used when demonstrating against the Vietnam War. In nineteen eighty, at a Milton College demonstration commemorating the tenth anniversary when National Guardsmen gunned down four unarmed students at Kent State, police arrested Emily for failure to disperse. She wore the arrest like a badge of honor.

Emily never lost the commitment to peace we both possessed at Woodstock. She didn't have to quote Gandhi. She lived the principles of nonviolence and civil disobedience. She wasn't afraid to stand up to injustice, even if it meant extreme action. I never possessed her courage.

A man came out of the administration building struggling to carry a cardboard box stuffed with books. He stopped behind a rusted-out sedan in the parking lot. Balancing the box on the car's bumper, he unlocked the trunk. The box fell and the books tumbled onto the hot pavement.

I went to help and realized I knew the man, Bob Windsor, the bartender at The Library.

Windsor set the box in the trunk as I helped him gather up the books.

"Thanks, Professor. Glad to see you're okay. I called the hospital the day after that trucker coldcocked you, but they said you hadn't been admitted. You're one tough dude."

"Hardly." Toughness had nothing to do with checking myself out of the hospital. Stubbornness maybe.

I picked up two more books. Both dealt with English literature.

"You work here?"

Windsor cocked his head.

"I teach English. Did you think bartending was my full-time job?"

"Tending bar is an honorable profession." I set the books into the box.

"It is, but I like teaching better."

I handed him two more books that dealt with education in the twenty-first century.

"What made you become a teacher?"

He placed the last of the books in the box and slammed the trunk. The latch didn't lock. He slammed the trunk twice more before it closed.

"You did."

Me? I prided myself in teaching students, but until now, I never thought I inspired anyone to emulate me.

Windsor unlocked the driver's door.

"I took two classes from you. I joined a study group where five of us met weekly and discussed your lectures at The Library over drinks."

"My apologies to your liver."

"That's when I realized I wanted to teach, something you clearly excelled at."

"Something at which you clearly excelled," I corrected.

Windsor laughed and checked his watch.

"I'm late for the job that pays. Can I give you a lift to The Library? You look like you could use a drink."

"That's my normal look. Thanks anyway."

The young man yanked the door open. The hinges made a metal on metal squeal. He climbed behind the wheel and slammed the door closed. He pumped the gas. The starter made a grinding sound much like Buck's old Volkswagen did on our roadtrip. The car finally started, and the tailpipe belched a blue smoke cloud. Windsor peered through the open window.

"You know a good mechanic who can keep her running until I pay off my student loans?"

"Buck's Garage in Lawrenceville. Tell Buck Sparky sent you."

"Who's Sparky?"

Windsor caught on and laughed again.

"I'll do that."

He waved and drove off. The shocks hit bottom as he pulled out of the lot. More blue smoke belched from the car as he chugged away.

Before I could reflect on the unexpected insight into my teaching abilities, my cell phone rang. I didn't recognize the number.

"Sparky." Heather's voice choked with panic. "Grandpa's dying!"

♫♫♫♫♫

The buzzing drone of cicadas filled the warm June twilight. I bounded up the Simpson house porch steps and rang the doorbell. For Heather's sake, I hoped the old man wasn't dying. The front door opened. I wanted to leave.

"Well if it isn't the turd police. My cat crap in your yard again?" The porch light illuminated a thin white T-shirt stuck to Simpson's skeletal frame. If he managed to get up and answer the door, he couldn't be dying. However, Heather made the right decision to call.

Simpson's hair didn't appear to have been washed in days, and his sunken face needed a shave. Except for his gaunt build, he looked a lot like I did the night Shrek put me in the hospital. I hadn't seen him this close up in months and the deterioration shocked me. Seeing how heart disease ravaged his body gave me further reasons to fix mine.

His Siamese cat weaved between Simpson's legs then hissed and raked my shoe with its claw.

"Well?"

I took a step back from the damned cat.

"Meagan asked me to check on Heather."

"My granddaughter don't need checking up on. She's got me."

"Can I talk to her?"

"She's doing homework." He started to close the door.

I placed my hand on the door and kept it from closing.

"It won't take long."

The old man's eyes narrowed with contempt.

"Get the hell off my porch."

Cantankerous as always, Simpson couldn't be that sick, could he?

"Meagan has enough on her mind. If she calls and I haven't checked up on Heather, it'll make things worse for her. You wouldn't want that."

Simpson looked like he'd throw me off the porch if he had the strength. His face reddened, and his breathing grew labored. He called over his shoulder.

"Heather, Old Man Ellington's here to see you."

I choked back laughter. I'd never encountered anyone who referred to me as Old Man Ellington. Maybe I'd just never heard.

"I've got it, Grandpa."

Heather appeared behind him and shot me a wait-here look. She grabbed his arm and led him away. His shuffling gate made me realize how sick he might really be.

The cat sat in the doorway, tail swishing, and stared as if I was a mouse he needed to chase.

I hissed, and the cat took off. Just as I suspected. *Coward*.

Heather reappeared, stepped onto the porch and closed the front door behind her. Her voice quivered, and she bit her lip as if she thought her grandpa might die any minute.

"I got Grandpa to lie down. Before I called, I dialed his doctor, but I only reached the answering service."

I checked my watch. Dr. Dave was probably on his date with Cloe.

"Take a deep breath and tell me what happened."

Heather dropped to the porch swing and hugged both arms as she rocked.

"Grandpa's had trouble breathing since Mom left this morning. Sometimes, he stops talking and just stares across the room. Creeps me out."

I considered calling 911 but didn't want to overreact for Heather's sake and Meagan's.

The last thing I wanted was to disturb my daughter's date with my doctor, but I didn't have any choice. I grabbed my cell phone and dialed Cloe's number.

She answered right away.

"You okay, Dad? Have you been drinking?"

"Fine and no. Is the doctor in?"

Cloe chuckled. "David and I just arrived at *Chez Nous*."

Milton's finest, pricey restaurant but a place a cardiologist could afford. Nice move, Doc.

"I need to talk to him a minute."

"Dad, are you sure—"

"Cloe."

Dr. Dave came on the line.

"Something wrong, Mr. Ellington?"

"It's Simpson, my neighbor. He's one of your patients."

I couldn't remember the old coot's first name. I'd called him Old Man Simpson since I first met him.

"What seems to be the problem?"

"His daughter is out of town. His granddaughter is worried, says he's been short of breath and drifts in and out."

"Do you know how to take a pulse?"

"I took a CPR class a few years ..."

Why did I admit that? If Simpson's life depended on CPR from me, I didn't like his chances.

"Maybe I should call 911."

"Take his pulse and tell me the color of his skin, particularly around his eyes."

"I need to take his pulse," I said to Heather.

She hurried to the door and held it open.

I followed Heather inside. Apparently, Simpson hadn't made any changes in décor since the late seventies—avocado green walls, rust-colored shag carpet and a blue couch frayed at the legs (obviously the cat's favorite scratching post).

Heather led me down the hall and pointed into a bedroom. The old man lay on the near side of a king-sized bed as if waiting for his wife to return one day and reclaim the other half. Letters lay scattered at the foot of the bed.

"Why the hell are you here?" Simpson struggled to sit up.

"I'm going to check your pulse."

"Like hell you are."

I handed him the phone and waited for the doctor to run interference.

Simpson scowled but brought the phone to his ear and listened. A moment later, he handed the phone back. Disgust twisted his face as he held out a bony wrist.

"Get on with it."

I laid the cell phone on the nightstand between an open box with more letters and a thirty-year-old photograph of Simpson, the wife who left him and Meagan as a teenager. The three, all smiles, stood in front of the Grand Canyon, perhaps the last time the old man smiled about anything.

I gripped his wrist and located his pulse. I checked the sweep second hand of my watch and counted the heartbeats. Fifty-six beats per minute. I knew a marathon runner at Penn State with a pulse that low, but Simpson was no athlete.

I picked up the phone.

"Fifty-six."

"How's his breathing?"

I stepped away from the bed and lowered my voice.

"Shallow, and his color is a bit pasty ... even for him."

"Has he eaten?"

Heather stood inside the doorway, looking grateful for my presence.

"Has he eaten?" I asked her.

"A couple of doughnuts for breakfast, but he puked that up."

Doughnuts? Really? Where was *his* food journal?

"Nothing since he vomited his breakfast. Why does he get to eat doughnuts?"

Dr. Dave ignored my question. "He's probably dehydrated, and his blood sugar might be low. Can he keep fluids down?"

I repeated the question to Heather.

"He had a beer an hour ago and kept that down."

A beer! Beer and doughnuts? "Does he have any more beer?" I asked Heather.

"I'll go get one." She dashed from the room.

"Cloe and I are on our way," Dr. Dave said. "Any sign of discomfort or chest pain?"

I studied Simpson's features.

"Are you in pain?

"Yup. Ever since you knocked on my door you've been a big pain in my ass."

Heather rushed into the room, unscrewed the cap on the bottle and handed the beer to me.

I chugged a long swallow.

Heather's mouth dropped.

"Dude. I thought you wanted the beer for Grandpa."

"He's sick. He shouldn't have alcohol." I swallowed another gulp and set the bottle on the nightstand beside a tissue box.

Simpson's eyes glazed over, and he stared across the room.

"That's what he did before." Heather shivered.

I leaned closer to make sure he was still breathing. His eyes closed, but his chest continued to rise and fall. For the first time, it occurred to me the man might actually be dying. I lowered my voice into the phone.

"I think you should get here as quickly as possible."

"We're ten minutes away. I'll have an ambulance meet me. Let me know if he gets worse."

I kept an eye on Simpson, as if staring would keep him alive. I swallowed a long gulp of beer.

"The doctor's on his way."

Simpson's Siamese jumped on the bed and hissed at me. I shooed the beast off the bed and knocked a letter on the floor. I picked up the yellowed paper and noticed the date—nineteen sixty-nine, the year I fell in love with Emily.

I set the letter with the others in the box on the nightstand.

"Maybe he read something that upset him."

She pulled me aside and lowered her voice so her grandpa couldn't hear.

"He reads a different one every night."

"What are they?"

"Love letters Grandpa and Grandma wrote each other when they were ... courtin'."

I finished the beer, set the bottle into a trash can beside the bed and stared at the letter collection. I saw Simpson from a different perspective.

He hung onto those cherished letters like I clung to mementoes of my life with Emily. Maybe the memories and words of love in the letters kept my neighbor alive, or they might be killing him. Simpson couldn't let go of the past any more than me.

Heather's voice quivered with desperation. "Tell me he's going to be okay."

"He'll be fine."

She wiped tears from her eyes.

"You're just saying that."

"Why don't you wait on the porch for Cloe and Dr. Malone."

She wiped her eyes, scooped up the cat and left the room.

I pulled up a chair and sat beside the bed. The knowledge that Simpson read old love letters from a wife who left him fifteen years ago conflicted with everything I thought I knew about the man. Fifteen years was a long time for the old geezer not to have experienced a woman's love. No wonder he was such a crotchety bastard the entire time I'd known him.

Simpson's eyes blinked open.

"You're still here? Where's Heather?"

"She's waiting for Dr. Malone. He's on his way."

I hoped the doctor arrived soon. If Simpson died, I didn't want his last words to be spoken to me.

"I've got shoes older than Dr. Malone. What good's he going to do?"

A wracking cough shook his body. Spittle dripped from his mouth.

I handed him the box of tissues.

He wiped his mouth and balled the tissue in his hand.

"I'm not ... I'm not going to make it, am I?" He sank into the pillow and closed his eyes.

"You'll be fine. You're too mean to die."

A smile flickered across his face.

"Can I do anything?" *Other than CPR.*

Simpson took a ragged breath. He licked dry lips.

"If I ... don't make it ... will you do me a favor?"

A favor? He no doubt wanted me to look after Heather and Meagan.

"If I die ... would you ..." He began to cough. "Would you ... take care of ..." He coughed again. "...my cat?"

Son-of-a-bitch! His damn evil cat? The beast would terrorize Lady and my house, but I couldn't deny a dying man's last request.

"Of course."

A smile swept over Simpson's face, and he chuckled. His voice sounded as strong as ever.

"Gotcha."

I couldn't help but laugh.

"You old coot."

He laughed.

"Arrogant bastard."

Heather, Dr. Malone and Cloe burst into the room and stared at Simpson and me.

With the two of us laughing, they looked at each other as if we'd lost our minds.

I rose from the chair as the doctor took a stethoscope from his black bag.

"I think I'll drink another one of your beers, Simpson. Tastes better knowing you paid for it."

"You owe me, Ellington."

I stood between Heather and Cloe and checked out Cloe's outfit. She wore a red silk dress I'd never seen, lower cut than I thought she should wear on a first date, but a refreshing change from her usual attire of blue or gray business suits. She must like this guy.

Dr. Dave tended to the old man, and I glanced at the box of love letters on the nightstand. Simpson and I weren't so different after all.

11

After stabilizing my neighbor's condition in the emergency room, the hospital transferred Simpson to the cardiac unit for observation. I tried to keep Heather calm in the waiting room, down the hall from her grandfather. In spite of his grumpy demeanor and the frustrations I'd seen her display toward him, her behavior at the house convinced me she loved the old coot.

The clock passed midnight as Heather sorted through tattered magazines on a table beside her. She settled on watching television where an infomercial spokesperson rambled on about how everyone needed to juice beets and pickles.

I sat beside her on a hard plastic chair that probably would leave a bruise on my butt, leaning my head against the wall and closing my eyes to rest.

♪♪♪♪♪

With Buck back to his old self, I stepped outside. Down the hill on the stage, John Sebastian performed a solo acoustic version of *Darlin' Be Home Soon.*

"Sparky." Josh set down the guitar. He kissed a pretty hippie girl then ran toward me. "When did you get here?"

"In the middle of *Coming into Los Angeles.*" Josh was a little too into himself, but I cut him some slack. Because of his controlling mother, he never received this kind of attention from girls.

"How's Buck?" He lit a cigarette and winked to a braless hippie girl who smiled at him as she strolled past.

"I think he's learned his lesson about messing with drugs." I gestured toward the tent. "He's playing doctor now, something you should consider. Would be good practice for when you become a real sawbones."

Josh took a long drag.

"I should probably quit smoking if I'm going to be a doc, don't you think?"

"Probably. So you dropped acid?"

"Pushing boundaries, my friend."

He took another drag from the cigarette and gazed toward the long line at a bank of pay phones.

"I better call Mom."

"No, you shouldn't."

"She thinks we're coming home today."

"Why would she think that?" He probably told her that when he called from Monticello.

Josh ran a hand through his red hair.

"I know Mom's controlling and manipulative, but I'm all she has."

I'd spent the last three years trying to get him to stand up to her. I hoped Woodstock would strengthen his resolve. The trip might have helped his confidence with the ladies, but he was still under his mother's domination.

"Do what you have to do."

Josh held out both hands in frustration.

"Her health isn't the best. I don't know how long she has left. It's not like she'll control my life forever."

The hot girl waved to Josh and held up the guitar.

"Play another song, huh, baby?"

"Be right there." He gave me a nudge.

"Come on. She has a twin sister and they have a tent in the woods. Let's get laid. Oh and if she asks, we're juniors at Penn State."

"Are you serious?"

"She's a sophomore at Vassar, and 'freshman' means we just graduated from high school."

"We did just graduate from high school."

Josh crushed the cigarette beneath his shoe.

"Come on. Let me introduce you to her sister."

"Can't. I have to go check on Emily."

Josh cocked his head.

"Who's Emily?"

Who's Emily? I'd had enough of the new self-indulgent version of my friend. I started down the hill.

"Later, Josh."

♫♫♫♫♫

I jumped up from my chair and paced the cardiac waiting room. Disappointment toward Josh waned as the images of the dream faded. I grabbed the remote and punched the mute button, silencing the infomercial on the television in the corner.

Loosening the kinks in my stiff neck, I rolled my head, making a sound like popping bubble wrap.

Heather stared at me with an open magazine on her lap.

"Dude, what's a freak-out tent? You mumbled in your sleep."

"A first aid station where they treated people with drug overdoses at Woodstock."

"Shut up!" She tossed the magazine on a table beside the chair. "You really were at Woodstock! I thought you were bullshitting me about that."

"I don't bullshit."

"Sure you do."

I smiled and sagged into the chair beside her.

"How's Grandpa Simpson?"

I loved calling him that. The reference sounded more respectful than Old Man Simpson. We were far from friends, but we'd shared a moment. With our focus on the women we loved in our past, we shared much more.

"The doctor's in with him now."

Just after one, the elevator chimed, and Meagan stepped off heels clicking across the tile. She spotted us and waved. Heather and I rose as she rushed into the room.

Meagan hugged her daughter then squeezed my hand.

"Thanks for being there when I couldn't."

"Sparky was the man. He kept me from totally losing it." Heather patted me on the back.

"What about the hearing tomorrow?"

"All the crap he put me through to get to the hearing, the bastard ... I'm sorry, 'your father' ... asked for a freakin' postponement! The judge got pissed. My attorney filed a motion to dismiss and bottom line, you and I can live anywhere we want."

Heather let out a huge breath of relief.

"Super."

"Thanks for waiting with Heather." Meagan checked her watch. "You should go home and get some sleep."

"I'd like to hear what Dr. Malone says before I leave."

Meagan snorted laughter.

"Seriously?"

"Mom, Sparky and Grandpa have become tight since you've been gone."

Meagan stared at me as if I'd grown a second nose.

"I haven't been gone that long."

I shrugged.

"We're neighbors."

Dr. Dave stepped into the waiting room carrying the suit coat he wore on his date with Cloe. Tired wrinkles around both eyes showed me a little irritation his evening hadn't turned out the way he had hoped.

Meagan touched her fingertips to her lips.

"Another heart attack?"

Dr. Dave shook his head.

"Your father had an episode of low blood sugar, which affected his breathing and lucidity. So far we've regulated his sugar level and BP. If we keep the numbers stable, he can go home tomorrow."

"Thank God." Meagan gave her daughter a comforting hug.

"I'll be back for rounds in the morning." He shook Meagan's hand and left.

Meagan sagged into a chair.

"I think I'll stay until morning."

"I'd like to stay, too." Heather squeezed her mother's hand and sat beside her.

Earlier, I felt Simpson's medical episode originated from his consumption of doughnuts and beer. Now I suspected another cause.

"Can I have a minute alone with him before I leave?"

Meagan caressed my arm.

"After what you've done? Of course."

I entered Simpson's dimly lit room that smelled of lemony antiseptic. Four rows of wavy lines beeped on a heart monitor behind the bed. A plastic bag hung from a hook beside the bed and dripped a clear fluid into a tube connected to the old man's wrist. I might turn into Simpson if I didn't change my ways.

Eyes closed, he appeared to be asleep. Before I could decide whether to leave, Simpson opened his lids.

"Don't you have anything better to do?"

I sat in the chair beside the bed.

"Your doctor says you're going to live."

"What does that quack know?" He grabbed a paper cup on a tray beside the bed and took a sip of water. "Heather says you've started sniffing 'round my daughter."

"I'm not ready for a relationship."

"What are you waiting for?"

Good question.

"Sometimes with people like you and me, it takes a while to get over the pain of separation from the women we loved."

"We're not talking about me." His face reddened to the color of a ripe tomato. "We're talking about you and my daughter."

"I met Meagan a couple of days ago. Might be too early to call you 'Dad.'"

Simpson coughed. He finished the water, crumpled the cup and threw it at me.

Time to get serious.

"I won't say anything to Meagan or Heather, or even Dr. Malone, but you don't fool me. You're not as sick as you let on."

"I'm dying, dumb-ass."

"No, you're not."

I didn't know what the lines on the heart monitor meant, but the blood pressure read one hundred nineteen over seventy-three. For someone with an episode of low blood pressure, the numbers looked almost normal to me.

"You want Meagan and Heather to think you're dying so they'll keep living with you."

Simpson gazed toward the window.

"I preferred it when you and I were mortal enemies."

"Why don't you ask them to stay? Heather likes her school better, and Meagan has a job here. They could save on rent and your daughter could open that restaurant she's always wanted."

"They wouldn't want to move in permanently, even if I wanted them to—which I don't. Me and my cat got along just fine without them."

"You and your cat are both miserable alone. You'll never know unless you ask."

Simpson held my gaze. In that brief moment, I knew he'd at least consider my suggestion.

The chair legs scraped the tile as I stood. I'd had my say. The rest was up to him. I almost suggested he get rid of his collection of love letters, but I'd save that message for another chat. One thing at a time.

At the door, I glanced back at my neighbor.

"Get some rest, old man."

"You think you're pretty smart don't you, Ellington?"

I couldn't help but smile.

"Sometimes."

"Arrogant bastard."

"Old coot."

♫♫♫♫♫

Lady greeted me with slobbers. I let her outside and headed for my office. I stared at the five remaining items on the whiteboard.

With the eraser, I wiped the word "career" off the board. The position no longer held the same importance to me. The satisfaction of watching Warfield grovel when he offered my position back was enough to make me realize I didn't need his damn job. Childish and petulant perhaps, but I looked forward to turning down his offer in an impersonal e-mail, the perfect revenge.

I erased Buck's name from the board as well. We'd reentered each other's lives and would stay connected.

Broken heart syndrome and two names remained, Josh and Emily. I hadn't done enough to improve Josh's existence in the time he had left, and I had no idea how I'd deal with letting Emily go.

I let Lady inside. In my bedroom, I tossed off my shoes and collapsed onto the bed.

Lady sniffed the shoe the Simpson cat clawed, and she let out a loud bark.

I patted the bed and she climbed up and dropped beside me, eyeing the doorway and me with equal vigilance.

In spite of my exhaustion from a long and trying day, I couldn't sleep. My restless mind drifted to two old people I struggled to understand, Josh's mother and Grandpa Simpson. There might be hope for Simpson, but I wished I felt the same about Mrs. Channing. I had to find a way to work things out with her, for Josh's sake.

I welcomed a good long sleep. The last thing I needed was another dream about Woodstock.

♪♪♪♪

I made my way down the hill, approached the spot where we'd left our sleeping bags and stumbled to a halt. I did a three-sixty searching for Emily and Crystal. A sickening feeling that I might never see her again swept over me.

Maybe they decided to stay and went for food and water. Perhaps they went to call their parents or use the Porta John. Maybe ...

"Are you Sparky?" A girl in a red T-shirt handed me a handwritten note.

I flinched when I took the note, as if the paper was a knife that cut deep. Though I could guess what the note said, I sank down to the ground and read.

I'm sorry, Sparky, but I had to go home. I hope you'll understand. You made Woodstock a moment I'll never forget. Have a wonderful life. Emily.

A wonderful life? "Son-of-a-bitch!" I crumpled the note and flung the paper as far as I could.

Everyone around me grooved to Santana's Latin soul music on stage, but I barely paid attention. I sat and picked at the wet matted grass in front of me. With quick shallow breaths, I tried to understand why she took off and just left a one-paragraph note.

Apparently, what happened between us didn't mean as much to Emily as it had to me. Had I misread her signals, her body language, the tenderness in her eyes, her touch? Did I mean so little she could just walk away and wish me a wonderful life?

People nearby passed around a bottle of red wine. I held out my hand, grabbed it and took a long swallow, then another.

Josh plopped down beside me. He grabbed the wine, took a sip and wiped his mouth with the back of one hand.

"You okay? You look like you did that time your favorite goldfish died."

"Don't you have a tent you should be in?"

"She gave me a rain check." He took a long swallow. "Guess I got a little too into myself back there, huh?"

He handed me the bottle then dug through his sleeping bag and pulled out a soggy paper sack. He reached inside and held out a handful of prunes.

"Hungry?"

"Not that hungry." I took a final swig of wine and passed the bottle to the girl who gave me Emily's note.

Josh finished the prunes as rain fell. He hunched over and turned his collar against the shower.

"I forgot Emily was the girl who went with you in search of eats. Crystal kept whining about you two not coming back. How did that go?"

"I thought ..." I almost admitted to Josh I'd fallen for her. "I thought it went great, until I got back and read a note that said she and Crystal were going home to Bethel."

"Chicks."

The newly crowned expert on girls lit a cigarette and cupped it from the rain.

"Even if Emily stayed, you and I'll be at Penn State the next four years and she'll be in New York."

A long-distance relationship wouldn't be easy, but if Emily cared about me the way I cared about her, we could make it work.

I flinched when thunder rumbled overhead. The warm rain fell in sheets, and the performers hurried from the stage. Roadies scrambled to remove and cover the vast network of electrical devices.

Josh took a long drag from the cigarette.

"You need to go after her."

"Get real. I have no idea where she lives. I don't even know Emily's last name."

He crushed out the cigarette.

"What *do* you know?"

"She lives on a farm outside of Bethel. Probably one of a thousand. Crystal's parents own a bar in town. I'd never find her."

Josh shouted over the storm's growing fury.

"You gotta go, man. You need to be sure how she feels about you and how you feel about her."

I was sure about my feelings for Emily. I'd fallen for her bad, but if she cared about me, she'd have stayed.

"I'd miss Credence."

I wanted to see them perform more than any other.

"Then you miss Credence."

"You need to go after her."

A girl's voice came from behind us—the girl who handed me the note.

"She was upset, made me promise to give the note to you and you just threw it away like it was garbage."

I pictured Emily's dimpled smile. Had she cried?

"How upset?"

"Upset, okay?"

The girl flinched as lightning flashed and thunder cracked like wood splitting.

The announcer pleaded with those on the metal scaffolding around the stage to get down. A half-dozen people scrambled down. The last man got caught up as wind buffeted the scaffolding and lightning crackled. To my relief, people on the ground climbed up and helped the man down while a half million chanted, "No rain. No rain. No rain."

Unstable after several gulps of wine on an empty stomach, I struggled to my feet. Emboldened, I was determined to do something I could never have anticipated—leave Woodstock.

Josh finished the prunes and got to his feet.

"I'll go with you a ways."

The rain made footing treacherous. We made our way through the crowd and struggled up the muddy slope. I slipped and fell, and Josh helped me to my feet. I wiped my hands on my windbreaker.

We stopped at the downed fence we'd stepped over when we first arrived. I hesitated. What was I doing? I'd known Emily less than a day, a few hours really. Josh, Buck and I planned this roadtrip for months and now I planned to walk away from the festival.

"This is crazy, man."

"You have to do this."

"If Buck was here—"

"If Buck saw in your eyes what I see, how you feel about this girl, he'd tell you to go after her, too."

"You think?"

"If you don't try to find Emily," Josh clapped a hand on my shoulder, "you'll regret it the rest of your life."

I wiped rain from my eyes and glanced back at the hundreds of thousands and the empty stage. The once-green fields and brightly colored tie-dyed shirts now melded into a sea of gray, soupy mud.

I took a deep breath and stepped across the downed fence. At the road, I glanced back and waved.

Josh waved back and shouted over the din of the pounding rain. "Go find Emily."

Through the steady downpour, I walked away from Woodstock determined to see this through. No matter how illogical or impractical my quest might be, I had to find out how Emily felt about me.

I followed the twisting line of side-by-side cars that led away from Yasgur's farm. I stepped into a puddle, and my shoe sank in thick sucking mud. I pulled and my foot came out of the shoe, which I reached down and fetched with my hand. I stumbled. Soaked, literally from head to toe, I laced back up and continued my slog in the rain and through the mud.

12

The next morning, Lady and I stood on the sidewalk in front of the modest house where Josh grew up. We proceeded up the driveway. I hoped the hostile old woman wouldn't slam the door in my face.

I had to get through to Mrs. Channing and discuss what was best for her son, for his well-being and hers. Somewhere inside decades of bitter pain lived a caring mother who used to bake the best chocolate chip cookies, a wife who doted on her husband and son, a woman who found peace in religion, not bitterness.

I checked my appearance in the reflection of the partially open front window. Hair combed to minimize its length, I wore casual slacks and a sport shirt, doing my best to hide my aging hippie appearance. I looked more like a college professor than I had since Warfield gave me the boot.

Lady's eyes sparkled, excited by a new destination. She wagged her tail as I rang the doorbell. A "No Solicitors" sign hung in the window. Did people still go door-to-door selling vacuum cleaners and magazines like they did when I was a kid? Or was the old woman a recluse sending a message to everyone who came to the door?

Footsteps and the tap of a cane on a wood floor sounded through the open window. A lock unlatched, followed by another. The door opened six inches, secured by a thick brass chain.

"Good morning, Mrs. Channing, it's ... Sparky Ellington."

Josh's mother glared at me then looked at my dog. She didn't appear to approve of either of us.

Lady gazed up at me with a look that asked why we hadn't gone inside already.

"I'd like to talk to you about Josh."

"We have nothing to talk about." She closed and locked the door.

I had to keep her talking. Over time, I could win her over.

"I'm sorry about yesterday. We should have asked your permission before we took Josh out for a hamburger. I'm sorry for any mistakes I've made in the past that may have upset you."

The door opened, the chain still secure.

"I'm not so old I can't see through you. You want something."

"I came by to say I'm sorry and seek forgiveness."

"Repent, then and turn to God, so your sins may be wiped out ... Acts three nineteen."

"To err is human, to forgive divine. Alexander Pope."

Nice comeback, but I regretted it as soon as the words left my mouth. I hadn't come to win a theological debate.

"Just go." The old woman closed the door.

"Could you spare some water for my dog?"

Lady wagged her tail, looking hopeful. The door opened a crack, and Lady panted as if on cue.

"I suppose."

I flashed Lady a thumbs-up as Mrs. Channing headed to the kitchen.

She returned, removed the chain and set a cereal bowl half full of water on top of a faded welcome mat.

Lady lapped up the water in seconds. I didn't have much time.

"Do you think I could have some water? It's a long walk home."

The old woman sighed.

I handed her the empty dish.

She opened the door and let Lady and me inside. A small victory.

Josh's high school graduation picture hung on the far wall, above a table displaying a track trophy and several cross country medals he won in high school. A half-dozen frames held pictures of Josh through the years. Two candles burned on both sides of the photos. This was a shrine.

I didn't see any pictures of Josh's father. Apparently, she'd moved on from that tragedy.

Mrs. Channing returned and handed me a glass of tap water, no ice. "Thank you for attending my wife's funeral and bringing Josh. I should've thanked you before now."

Her eyes narrowed with contempt.

"Don't pretend to be nice. Leave my son alone. Let him go in peace. Don't fear death, Mr. Ellington."

The woman didn't fear death. She feared life, life alone. Broken heart syndrome stared back at me.

"Yesterday I tried to get Josh to remember a song from the first night at Woodstock, *Swing Low, Sweet Chariot*. I'm certain he remembers it. That song is a spiritual."

"That song is a *Negro* spiritual."

Reasoning with this woman had been a hopeless dream. My contrition didn't budge her. I considered mentioning Arlo Guthrie sang *Amazing Grace* on Day One, but she'd no doubt come up with a reason not to respect that hymn as well. I couldn't think of anything to warm her cold, intolerant heart. I finished the water and handed her the glass.

Her voice was firm and final.

"I've instructed the nursing home not to allow you, or your drug-addled friend, Buck What's His Name, to visit my son."

Disappointed but not defeated, I tugged Lady's leash toward the front door.

"Your son might be approaching the end, but he still has time to enjoy life."

"Time? Don't lecture me about time. I'm eighty-eight and I'll outlive my son. Only the Bible can lead the way."

I stepped outside with Lady.

"I, too, know something about time." I didn't have enough of it with Emily. "There's a time to be born, a time to die, a time to plant, a time to reap, a time to kill, a time to heal, a time to laugh and a time to weep. It's not time yet to weep for Josh."

She lifted her chin with a smug look on her face.

"Impressive, Mr. Ellington. Ecclesiastes, chapter three, verse one."

"The Byrds, nineteen sixty-five."

♪♪♪♪♪

Lady and I headed home. I reflected on Mrs. Channing's mean spirit and abusive cruelty. Her behavior, even more than the Alzheimer's, robbed her son of joy. She was hastening his deterioration and his death. I wouldn't let that happen.

The law was on her side. No one could prevent her from ruining the time Josh had left. No one except me, as long as I had the guts to accept the consequences.

We returned home, and I gave Lady a well-deserved dog biscuit. She performed her role to get Josh's mother to talk to me to perfection. I failed.

I fixed a glass of bourbon. I left the booze on the counter when I remembered I had a drive ahead of me. I entered my office and stared at Josh's and Emily's names on the whiteboard. I had a plan to get Josh's name off. It wouldn't be easy or lawful.

The sixties taught me when a law wasn't just, a person had a responsibility to challenge the law and do the right thing. My plan would be an act of civil disobedience that would make Emily proud.

♪♪♪♪♪

I arrived at Buck's Garage in Lawrenceville just before six. I dreaded seeing his idea of a subtle peace symbol.

A light was on over the bay. At the front of the van, Buck removed a paint respirator from his face, waved me over and stood back for my inspection.

To my surprise, he had painted a simple understated peace symbol less than three feet in diameter. He blended different shades of blue that gave the image a three-dimensional quality. I stepped back, totally impressed.

Buck wiped sweat from his brow.

"Tell the truth. You expected the worst, didn't you?"

He set the respirator on the table. His friendly expression changed as he opened the passenger door and grabbed a yellow sheet of paper from the glove compartment. His jaw clenched as he held up a five-year-old flyer announcing an upcoming gig for the Milton Faculty Jazz Review.

"You and Josh formed another band? Milton Faculty Jazz Review. Bet you wore blue blazers with gold script on the pocket that read 'MFers.'"

His face reddened, and he slammed the door.

"Buck, that was fifteen years ago."

With his back to me, Buck reached into a cigar box on the workbench and removed a joint.

"What the hell!" I couldn't believe Buck still smoked grass. "How long have you been using?"

Buck shrugged.

"Since eighth grade, I guess."

"I mean lately."

He lit the cigarette, took a hit and let out a slow puff of smoke.

"What's with you?"

"You shouldn't do drugs."

"Pot's not a drug, really."

The discussion of drugs seemed to have tempered his anger about our faculty band. A couple of hits later, his face softened into a mellow expression.

"Don't tell me grass leads to harder drugs, man. Smokin' weed didn't get me using coke or H." Buck took another puff and offered me a hit.

I shook my head.

"I thought you were a health nut."

"Eating healthy doesn't mean a person is a nut. Knowingly eating crap seems kind of nutty to me. Besides, weed isn't bad for you. It's available by prescription in several states."

"Not this one."

"Not counting grass, I've been sober for ten years. Technically, marijuana is a drug, but that's just the government talking. It's an herb. Weed is better for you than booze. If your liver could talk, man, it would tell you the same thing."

Mellowed out from the joint, he led me to the refrigerator where a recycled grocery bag sat on top.

"I decided to do a better job bringing along eats than our last trip to Woodstock."

Prunes.

"This time, I got plenty of stuff." He began to unload the bag, "Granola, raisins—"

"Raisins are like miniature prunes."

" ... macadamia nuts, wasabi peas, chips, doughnuts, Ding Dongs ..."

"Now you're talking." I gave him a fist bump.

"I'll have the van finished in time for tomorrow. What time do we leave?"

"Depends."

With a depends-on-what look, Buck carried two folding chairs to the open entrance of the garage. We sat and enjoyed cooler air than in the garage. I told him about my unsuccessful visit with

Josh's mother.

"If his old man hadn't been killed, or his old lady wasn't such a religious freak, Josh would have made something of his life, you know? No offense, but he was smarter than you."

I couldn't agree more.

The streetlight blinked on and a bug zapper with its purple hue crackled as another mosquito bit the dust.

I surprised Buck when I grabbed the joint and took a hit.

"I think we should take him with us."

Buck's mouth dropped.

"Man, if the old witch has power of attorney, wouldn't that be like kidnapping?"

"Custodial interference." I took another puff and handed the joint to Buck. "Mrs. Channing will press charges."

Buck shrugged.

"So what. We've got to take him with us. We'll make the roadtrip a weekend we'll never forget."

Josh would, but Buck's words matched the thoughts I'd wrestled with the past twenty-four hours. Recreating the original roadtrip would be a great experience for Josh, like singing Woodstock songs.

Buck stared at the joint.

"The lunch at the Chat and Chew was probably the best hour he's had in years. Our buddy laughed, Sparky. You think he laughs at the home?" He blinked away tears welling in his eyes. "If Josh is going to check out soon, he needs this one final flash of enjoyment like we experienced at Woodstock."

I didn't need convincing, but I played devil's advocate for Buck's sake.

"By the time we return, he won't even remember this weekend."

Buck jumped to his feet.

"But, man, he will have lived it. We all check out eventually. Life's not about how long we live but what we do while we're here. Don't back out now."

"I won't back out. I'll do this, but I can't involve you and Cloe."

"You're joking."

"You two will have to drive to Bethel and wait for us. If the cops stop me before we get there, I don't want you and Cloe to get in trouble. You could get busted for a felony."

"What are you talking about?"

"I've never been arrested. Cloe will plea bargain me to

community service, but with your priors, the consequences would be worse for you."

"Are you shittin' me? You grew up in the sixties and never got arrested? Man, you have to place your life on the line from time to time or you ain't living."

He took a final toke then twisted the paper so the final flakes of marijuana floated away from the garage.

Buck leaned forward. His eyes bored into mine.

"Listen, Sparky. This is it, man. This really will be the last roadtrip for the three amigos. You know that, don't you? I won't miss the adventure with you guys, no matter what the risk."

"You sure?"

"Definitely sure."

Bringing Josh back to Woodstock was the right thing to do for him. The trip would benefit Buck and was right for me as well. For my well-being, for my heart health.

From an early age, I planned out my life and accomplished what I wanted, but there was emptiness in my heart where satisfaction should reside. Maybe I needed a dose of spontaneity, even uncertainty. Except the time I left Woodstock to find Emily, this might be the first time I took a real chance in life.

"I had to be sure." I held up my hand and Buck high-fived me. "I can't involve Cloe."

"You're right. She'd get disbarred or something." Buck nodded. "Got a plan?"

"I've never kidnapped anyone before."

He puffed his chest out with pride. "I have."

What? I couldn't believe it. "Care to explain?"

"In Nam."

He hurried to the workbench and grabbed a scratch pad and pen from a drawer. He returned and drew a rectangle and lines that formed a map.

"What's that?"

"The nursing home."

He drew arrows to one side of the building then drew the two hallways leading from the nurses' station.

"There's only one emergency exit in this hallway. Josh is in the other hallway. If we open the exit door from the outside, the breach will trigger an alarm. They don't use the silent kind, because if someone gets out, they need to know right away before they get too far."

"How do you know all this? You've only been there a couple of times."

"I have a photographic memory."

"Of course you do."

Buck chuckled.

"I do when it comes to shit like this."

"Makes sense, but I thought we should go in quietly."

"We wouldn't make it past the nurses' station. Creating a diversion is the way to go. We'll coordinate by cell phone. I'll open the rear door and set off the alarm. The big problem is getting the code to get into the unit. Maybe I could sweet talk Phoebe to tell me over a little pillow talk."

"You'd sleep with Phoebe to get the code?"

"Sometimes you gotta be willing to take a bullet for the team."

"Thanks for offering to make the *sacrifice,* but it won't be necessary. I know the code. I watched Phoebe. The whole time we went there, the code never changed."

"You sly dog. You didn't just pull this idea out of your ass. You thought it through some time ago."

Buck grinned and slapped my palm.

"I figure you'll get no more than five minutes to get to Josh's room, convince him to go with us, grab his stuff and get the hell out."

"Five minutes isn't a lot of time.

"What happens if Josh doesn't want to go?"

"That's his choice to make, not his mother's. If he doesn't want to come with me, we go to plan B, which is you, me and Cloe drive to Woodstock and scatter Emily's ashes."

"What time do we do this tomorrow?"

Phoebe's shift started at eight and I didn't want her blamed in any way.

"Early. No later than seven."

Buck checked his watch and adjusted the time.

"I'm thinking we should plan the break earlier, say O six hundred."

"Six o'clock."

"Okay, you weren't in the military, you hippie draft dodger; yeah, O six hundred means six in the morning. We'll rendezvous at your house at o five thirty. The earlier we get in and out of Sunrise with the package, the better chances the mission will succeed."

I chuckled at Buck's use of military lingo.

"Copy that."

"Smart ass." Buck laughed. "This will be the best roadtrip ever."

"Or we could wind up in prison."

"Man, you're such a downer."

He stepped inside the bay and plucked another joint from the special box. He lit it, went to the front of the van and studied the peace symbol.

"With a roadtrip of such epic proportions, this peace symbol doesn't do the occasion justice. I think I'll jazz her up some."

"Don't even think it."

"But man, this is once in a lifetime. This looks fine for you, me and Cloe, but if we recreate the original roadtrip with Emily along, we need something more than just this puny peace symbol."

I didn't want to draw attention to ourselves if the police came after us. "If you don't like it, I'll give you a brand new paint job. I assume your favorite color is beige."

"No, Buck. The peace symbol you painted is good enough."

Buck let out a sigh. He took a hit, inhaling and slowly letting it out.

"Okay, you win."

"Good. One more thing." I nodded to the joint in his hand. "No grass in the van. I don't want to add to any possible charges against us."

As if taking an oath, Buck held up his hand with the joint in his fingers.

"Absolutely not."

"Then everything's settled." Settled? Hardly. In less than twelve hours, my life would become more unsettled than ever.

Make as many days enjoyable for your friend as you can, Dr. Dave suggested. That's exactly what I intended by recreating our original roadtrip.

13

I returned home from Buck's garage confident of our ability to spring Josh from Sunrise. With attention to detail usually reserved for preparing a lesson plan, I made a list of everything needed to liberate Josh, recreate our original roadtrip and bring Emily's ashes to her final resting place. I memorized each task then ripped the list into pieces.

Lady watched, with dog curiosity, as I flushed the bits of paper down the toilet. "I'm just being careful, girl. No paper trail."

She followed along, tail wagging as I gathered up two emergency sleeping bags I hoped we wouldn't have to use. I added an overnight bag with a second set of clothes and placed everything next to the front door. I turned around, and the dog stood wagging her tail, her leash hanging from her mouth.

What to do with Lady for the weekend wasn't on the list I flushed. "We might get arrested."

Lady dropped the leash, let out a bark and showed the golden retriever smile I knew so well. This one said she didn't care about the risks any more than Buck or I.

"Okay." I patted the side of her neck. "You can come with us."

I grabbed an empty cardboard box from the garage and removed everything from the mantel. I carried the urn to the rocking chair that used to sit on the front porch of Emily's family's farmhouse. I sat with the urn in the crook of my arm and rocked.

It wasn't even close. I didn't need Emily's ashes to remind me of what we had. I set the urn beside the chair and closed my eyes, hoping I would dream about Woodstock.

♪♪♪♪♪

Sheets of rain continued as I struggled along the muddy road. A Chevrolet Corvair came from behind. To my relief, the driver stopped beside me, climbed out and offered a ride.

I climbed in back, sitting atop wet blankets and a soggy sleeping bag. We drove off, weaving around abandoned cars.

The woman in the front passenger seat ignored me. The couple's body language told me they disagreed about leaving the festival. I couldn't tell which of them wanted to escape the rain, mud and event's rotting garbage smells or who preferred to tough it out to experience the music and atmosphere of joy.

I endured ten minutes of uncomfortable silence, but at least I dried a little. They dropped me off in the center of Bethel. I thanked them, and they drove away.

I had no idea where Emily lived, so I focused on Crystal. Her family owned a bar in a town half the size of Milton. How many could there be?

Rain fell as hard as ever. I crossed the street to a restaurant with a sign that advertised the best barbeque in Sullivan County. An old man came out and sat beneath an overhang on a bench beside the door. He lit a cigarette and waved to me. I stepped out of the rain, at least for a moment. He glanced at me then went inside and returned with a towel and a hot cup of coffee.

I wiped my face and drank half of the steaming brew in one gulp. I described Emily to the old man, but he didn't know her. I mentioned Crystal.

The man scratched his head. He thought Crystal might be last year's homecoming queen. Her parents owned a tavern on the outskirts of town called The Old Schoolhouse, because in the old days the building housed Bethel's only school. He gave me directions.

I thanked the man, stepped into the rain and stuffed both hands into my Penn State windbreaker. At the end of the block, I hitched a ride with a local who knew the tavern. He dropped me off and flashed a peace symbol as he drove away.

I gathered a measure of hope and hurried to the front door. I wiped my feet and entered.

A cue ball cracked on a table in a back room, and a man in coveralls groaned and slapped a bill onto the table. Johnny Cash sang about a boy named Sue from a jukebox beside the front door.

A dozen patrons scrutinized me as I crossed the room, my sockless shoe squeaking on the wood floor. Rainwater dripped from my soaked clothes as I approached the bar and a cautious-looking bartender.

Red baskets of peanuts atop the counter and each table might as well have been Josh's mother's delicious warm apple pie. I hadn't eaten all day.

A broad-shouldered customer with a duck-tailed crew cut sat on a barstool, chatting with the bartender. He checked me out with a sneer, finished his beer and ordered another.

I didn't want any trouble.

"I'm looking for Crystal."

Crew cut-man hopped off the stool and shoved me.

"What do you want to see Crystal about, Longhair? Want to sell her drugs?"

I wouldn't take crap from the town bully. I didn't care if he was six inches taller with the calloused hands of someone who spent too much time in a weight room. I'd barely slept or eaten in twenty-four hours. Tired and wet, I was on a mission. I got in his face and waited for him to make the next move.

The bully stared back, and the bar quieted.

Apparently, I'd called the man's bluff. He cleared his throat.

"Crystal's my sister."

"I just want to ask her about her friend, Emily."

"Emily Baker?"

He grabbed his beer and took a long swallow.

Emily Baker. My heart raced with anticipation.

"Short, dark hair, thin, cute, hippie-looking."

Crew cut-man laughed.

"Emily Baker's a hick country girl. She's skinny all right and has a butch haircut. I think she's a lesbian."

"I don't think so."

"Oh you don't?" The man raised an eyebrow. "Hear that everyone? Sounds like the hippie nailed Emily."

Crystal came through the kitchen doors. Her blonde hair shimmered in the bar light. Makeup highlighted her blue eyes and perfect complexion.

"Darrell, what's all the racket?" She froze. "Sparky."

Darrell sized me up. "Oh yeah, you're definitely a Sparky."

He dismissed me with a derisive wave and climbed back onto

the barstool. He gulped the beer and grabbed a handful of peanuts.

"Don't mind Darrell. He's my neanderthal brother."

Crystal led me to a booth in the corner.

"Buck's not with you, is he?"

"Just me."

"Is he alright?"

Why had she asked about Buck?

"Buck's okay, but I doubt he'll try drugs any time soon."

I sat across from her, swallowed some peanuts and relished the salty taste. I devoured a handful in seconds.

"You want something to eat?"

"I need to talk to Emily. I hope you'll tell me how to get to her place."

"You left Woodstock, in this weather. Why do you want to talk to her?"

"To tell Emily ..." It seemed everyone in the bar had paused to listen, but I didn't care. I was wet, tired and needed to talk to Emily. "I love her."

Crystal let out a snort of dismissive laughter.

"You just met her yesterday."

Darrell cackled to the bartender.

"Emily Baker? Now I know this guy's on drugs."

"Just tell me how I can get to Emily's."

Crystal leaned across the table and thumped my chest with a manicured nail.

"Don't hurt her. Emily likes you. She likes you a lot."

"Then why did she leave?"

Crystal looked away, appearing to decide how much to explain.

"Her daddy's sick, okay?"

There was sick, and there was sick.

"What's wrong with him?"

"Not for me to say."

"Tell me where she lives."

"You'd never find the place."

She slid from the booth and held out one hand. "Darrell, give me your keys."

"Hell, no. You're not driving in this weather."

He signaled the bartender for another beer.

Crystal kept her hand out.

"You can't drive him to the Bakers'. You're wasted."

"I wouldn't take that filthy freak across the street to a hospital if he was dying and I was stone cold sober."

I looked down at my clothes and laughed. Crystal's brother described me accurately.

His eyes narrowed into slits.

"You laughing at me, hippie freak?"

"I'm laughing at myself."

"Sure you are." Darrell jumped off the barstool with both fists clenched. He took a menacing step toward me.

"I'll take him." A man rose from a table in the corner, his chair scraping the wood floor. He left a tip alongside an empty plate and grabbed a cowboy hat from the table.

Darrell groaned. He relaxed his hands and sat back on the stool.

"You serious, Hawk?"

"Shut up, fool." The man set the cowboy hat on his head. He came to my booth and held out his hand. "Leroy Hawkins."

I stood and shook his hand.

"Sparky Ellington."

He gestured to the door.

"Wait." Crystal led me a few feet away. "Emily just turned seventeen."

"So?"

"Her mama was in a car accident four years ago that left her in a wheelchair. Emily's brother's in Nam. Now her daddy's sick. Got the picture?"

The *picture* helped me better understand why Emily left Woodstock.

"I didn't come back to complicate her life."

"You will if you tell her you love her."

"Who's Stan?"

She held my gaze but didn't answer.

Hawkins held the door open for me.

"Stan is Emily Baker's fiancé."

Fiancé? The word stabbed at my heart. Was that why Emily left Woodstock?

Hawkins drove his truck to the edge of town while I tried not to think about Emily being engaged. Wipers struggled to slap rain from the windshield as he turned onto a winding road.

After a series of forks in the road I never would have been able to navigate, he pulled up to a mailbox. A cinder drive led to a two-story farmhouse and a weathered red barn. Hawkins pointed to the house.

"The Bakers are good folks. They've had plenty of tough breaks. Don't add to their burden."

I wouldn't cause problems for Emily or her family.

"I won't. Thanks for the ride." I shook the man's hand and climbed out. "Mr. Hawkins, is Stan a good guy?"

"Stan's a punk ass." Hawkins put the truck in gear and drove off.

In the steady drizzle, I slogged down the muddy drive toward the farmhouse, emboldened by his characterization of Emily's fiancé as a punk.

A grain silo rose from behind the barn. An empty corral, a henhouse and a chicken pen stood in front of cornfields waving in the breeze and rain. A wheelchair ramp ran alongside the front steps.

A man in a Mets cap sat in a rocking chair on the porch. He watched me approach through the pelting rain. An olive-green Army blanket was neatly tucked over his lap and around both legs.

I stopped at the foot of the steps and shielded my eyes from the rain.

"Mr. Baker?"

The man dropped the blanket beside the chair. Face gaunt, he struggled to his feet. He held onto the railing and climbed down the steps. With a farmer's calloused hands, he shook my hand with a surprisingly strong grip.

"Ben. Ben Baker."

"I'm Walter Ellington from Milton, Pennsylvania. Is Emily here?"

He studied my slovenly appearance, and I worried he might order me off his land. I wanted to explain I usually made a better first impression.

He nodded toward the house.

"She's inside."

I climbed the steps behind him and noticed the bald head beneath his cap. The loss of hair and thin frame probably resulted from chemotherapy treatments.

On the porch, a flutter of queasiness surged through my stomach. How could I ask Emily to return to Woodstock with me after knowing about her mother's disability and seeing her father's serious illness?

We wiped our feet on a mat and stepped into a mudroom with a washing machine and a dryer. Ben hung his hat on a metal hook above a ceramic sink. He removed his boots and set them on a rubber mat by the door. "Better take off your shoes so you won't track up my wife's floor."

I removed my muddy sneakers, humiliated by my appearance. With one bare foot, I followed Emily's father into the kitchen. The sweet scent of freshly baked bread made me lightheaded. The aroma of simmering potatoes and bacon overwhelmed me. I'd never smelled a room so wonderful.

The farm, and now the country kitchen, reminded me of something out of *Life* magazine. The cabinets were painted white. Red checked curtains framed the porch window. A braided rug covered the wood floor beneath a round pine kitchen table. Through the open door to a living room, a grandfather clock chimed.

In a wheelchair, Emily's mother, gray hair in a ponytail, sat slicing vegetables on a cutting board propped on top of her chair. Her eyes widened as she scrutinized my wet, muddy clothes. She glanced at my bare foot and stifled a laugh.

"You must be Sparky."

Apparently, Emily had mentioned me.

"Yes, ma'am." I smoothed my wet hair but realized I couldn't do anything to improve my appearance. Water dripped off my clothes onto the wood floor. "I'm sorry."

"It's only water. I'm Kathleen. You can call me Katy." She set the cutting board on the table. Her soft smile reminded me of Emily. "You look starved. Let me get you some hot soup."

I inhaled the soup's bacon and potato aroma.

"That would be wonderful, ma'am, but that can wait."

"Guess it can." Emily's mother wheeled her chair to the edge of the kitchen and called her daughter through the open doorway. "Emily."

Footsteps pounded down the stairs.

"Momma, is Daddy alright?" Emily stepped into the room. She looked as wonderful as I pictured her while slogging through the mud toward Bethel. In a red flannel shirt and jeans, she radiated a country girl image. A smile flickered across her face.

"Sparky."

Then her lips moved, but I didn't hear any words, just a ringing telephone. The phone rang a second time, and Emily and the farmhouse dissolved into vapor.

♫♫♫♫

"No!" I bolted upright in the rocking chair. I reached for the faded image of Emily in her parents' kitchen and tumbled to the floor.

Lady whined and licked my face as my phone rang a third time.

I pulled myself to my feet and reassured Lady as Cloe's voice came on the answering machine. "Hi, Dad. Calling to check what time you'll be by tomorrow. I'm going out tonight, so I might be in late. Looking forward to the trip. Love you."

Emily's image in the farmhouse kitchen returned so vividly I couldn't move. Lady licked my hand, helping me leave the dream world behind. On unsteady legs, I gripped the chair until I regained enough strength to stand.

I carried the urn to the mantel. Lady kept an eye on me as I deleted the message from Cloe. I ignored my guilt about deceiving her. I had no choice. I couldn't tell her my plans and wouldn't jeopardize her career for my selfish needs.

Lady followed me to the bedroom. The clock on the nightstand read nine thirty. Buck would be by in eight hours. I needed a restful, dreamless sleep. Tomorrow would be a challenging day.

Sleep didn't come. I lay in bed and relived the day I met Emily's parents. I remembered the joyful expression on Emily's face before her temper flared. I never expected her angry reaction.

I fidgeted so much, trying to get comfortable, Lady hopped off the bed and retreated to her blanket in the corner. At three thirty, I gave up the battle and rolled out of bed. My footsteps echoed down the wood floor hallway, something I only noticed late at night or early in the morning.

In the kitchen, I fixed a pot of coffee and some heart-healthy oatmeal. After the warm breakfast, I showered and dressed then stepped outside.

Lady and I waited for Buck on the porch in the cool morning air. I sat in the chair and patted her as she lay beside me. A purple hint of dawn peaked over the Simpson house as I closed my eyes, just for a moment.

14

Emily rushed past her mother and threw both arms around me. With a passionate kiss, she displayed the emotion I hoped for while trudging through the rain and mud. Her heart beat against mine. I held her tight as if we were the only ones in the room.

Without warning, she stiffened and let go. Emily stepped back, clearly uncomfortable with this display of affection in front of her parents, but something more ominous hid beneath the frosty glare.

"If you came to ask me to go back to Woodstock, you've wasted your time."

The rejection snapped like a bullwhip. Had I come all this way and made a dreadful mistake?

Emily's mother's eyes filled with sympathy. She grabbed her daughter's hand.

"Your friend's soaked and hungry. Get him some of your brother's clothes to wear while we wash these."

"Mama."

Emily looked like she preferred I turn around and leave. What had I done to cause this reaction?

"Go!"

Her mother sent Emily on her way with a wave.

Emily shook her head, left the room and climbed the stairs.

Emily had ripped out my heart and fed it to the farm animals. Hopefully the hurt, confusion and disappointment didn't show.

"Thank you for your hospitality, Mrs. Baker, but I think I've made a terrible mistake. Sorry for any inconvenience I may have caused."

"Nonsense. You need a hot shower, a change of clothes and some warm food. Then you and Emily can sort this out."

Mrs. Baker pointed past the kitchen entryway.

"Bathroom's at the top of the stairs. There are fresh towels. Ethan's clothes might be a bit large, but they're clean and dry."

I climbed the stairs. I'd made a complete fool of myself. I wished I never left Woodstock.

In the bathroom, I stared at my unrecognizable reflection. I hadn't shaved or showered in two days. Mud streaked my clothes, hair and face. I couldn't believe Emily's mother offered hospitality to such a freak.

A drawer slammed in the next room. I stepped into the hall and peered through the open doorway of a young man's bedroom. Athletic trophies for football and track covered shelves along the far wall. 4-H ribbons pinned to a bulletin board above a wood desk contrasted with two very cool Rolling Stones posters. I entered the room that held the faint smell of mothballs and aftershave.

Emily wiped a tear from her cheek. She set a pair of jeans, a belt, a stack of colored T-shirts and socks on the bed.

"Don't flatter yourself, I always cry when I'm ticked off."

Why was she mad at me? I left Woodstock to find out whether the future held anything for us, and I received an emotional kick in the balls. I should be angry. Not her.

She opened another dresser drawer.

"You've a choice, boxers or briefs." She brushed past me and pounded down the stairs.

I didn't understand her behavior. Of course, I hadn't understood girls since maybe third grade. I gritted my teeth and snatched up the clean clothes.

In the bathroom, I closed the door and turned on the shower and stood under the hot soothing spray. I shampooed my hair and ran soap over my body. Mud and grime washed down the drain, but frustration couldn't be washed away so easily.

As I stood in the tub drying my face, Emily pulled open the shower curtain, glaring at my eyes and ignoring my naked body.

"Why did you leave Woodstock and come here?"

I wrapped the towel around my waist. Recovering my modesty, I whispered, "I came for two reasons. One, to ask you to return to Woodstock with me."

"Forget it." She folded both arms. "I told you I'm not going back."

"I had to ask."

Her hardened exterior softened.

"You came a long way. It's at least five miles to Yasgur's farm."

Frustration over her behavior spilled out.

"You should've given me your phone number. I could've called and saved us both some grief. Come to think of it, you might have mentioned your last name, too, before we slept together."

"Well, now you've got a farmer's daughter story to tell your friends."

Emily's face flushed. She grabbed a bar of soap from the sink and threw it at me.

I ducked, and the soap flew past my head and landed in the tub with a loud clatter. My wet feet slid on the cold tile. I braced myself against the wall and managed to hang onto the towel.

Emily laughed then covered her mouth with concern.

"Oh my God, I threw something. I'm so sorry."

"Gandhi would be ashamed."

Emily managed a slight smile.

"What's the other reason you came here?"

"Doesn't matter now."

I opened the bathroom door, and to her surprise, I gently nudged her into the hallway.

The clothes were two sizes too big, but the belt kept the pants up. The athletic socks, soft and warm, fit well. I glanced in the mirror. Though I'd been emotionally pummeled by a five-foot-two seventeen year old, at least I looked more presentable to her parents. I carried my wet clothes downstairs and followed the aroma of fresh bread and hot soup.

In the kitchen, Emily avoided eye contact as she set the table.

Her mother held her hands toward my wet clothes.

"I'll take care of those."

"Thanks, Mrs. Baker, but I'll do it."

In the mudroom, I tossed the clothes in the washer and measured out the detergent. I set the dial to start and returned to the kitchen.

Emily looked surprised I knew how to wash clothes. She filled two bowls with soup then went outside, banging the screen door behind her.

Mrs. Baker waited for my reaction to the lunch. I buttered the fresh warm bread and took a bite. Delicious. I tried the comforting soup, thick warm and slightly salty from the bits of bacon. I'd never tasted anything so wonderful. The food soothed my empty stomach. I covered my mouth and stifled a burp.

Mrs. Baker smiled, wheeled her chair to the table and joined me in the meal. Although Ethan and I had little in common, I sensed I reminded her and her husband of their son whose life was in danger every day in Nam.

She asked about my life in Pennsylvania. She was easy to talk to.

I told her about Milton, the decision to attend Penn State instead of Milton College and my teaching plans after graduation. I explained the roadtrip to Woodstock was a sendoff for Buck before he left for the Army.

She blinked away misty eyes and gazed toward the door.

I never should have talked about the service.

After the meal, I set the bowl and plate into the sink and peered through the open window. The rain had finally stopped. A sliver of sun sliced through thick gray clouds casting an amazing rainbow that arched from the cornfields to the barn. Mr. Baker sat rocking on the porch, watching Emily as she raked hay in the barn stalls.

I thanked Mrs. Baker for the wonderful meal, put on my shoes in the mudroom and went outside.

The rain had cooled the afternoon air. I sat in a wicker chair beside Mr. Baker and asked him about the farm.

While Emily did her chores, he described with pride the four generations of Bakers who farmed the land. He bragged about crops and animals he raised, the awards his kid won, the neighbors he cared for and those with whom he occasionally feuded.

He described the land with reverence then looked me in the eye and spoke with pride about his two kids. After the war, Ethan planned to become a pilot, not one of those crop duster kinds but a commercial airline pilot.

Emily wanted to be a teacher, which surprised me, what with her lack of communication skills.

It sounded like the family farm might end with Mr. Baker's generation. It was a shame, too, because the chickens scratching through the mud in their coop, the white wood fences outlining green pastures and a fruit orchard behind the red barn—it all reminded me of a travel calendar. I understood why Emily might not want to leave such a place.

"It took guts to leave your friends in search of a girl you just met.

You must really care for my daughter."

"I do. I did. I don't know." I ran a hand through my hair in frustration.

"Emily told her mama she felt bad she left Woodstock without explaining to you. She's glad you came all this way."

Glad?

"She has a funny way of showing it."

He wiped a smile from his face.

"Women have a certain way of making men act foolish. That's not always bad. They get us to do things we wouldn't ordinarily have the courage to do."

The farmer's country wisdom made sense. He'd been married most of his life, so he knew women a whole lot better than I did.

"It's hard for me to think of Emily as a young woman. When did that happen? My daughter's stubborn like her mama, but stubborn is another word for courage. Stubbornness helped Katy recover from the car accident when most people might have given up. Emily has the same courage, same pigheadedness. Don't give up if you care about her."

In the barn, Emily wrestled a hay bale onto a cart. The hippie turned country girl wasn't afraid to work and get her hands dirty.

I rose.

"I should go help."

Ben grabbed my arm and pulled me down into the chair.

"I think it might be best for you to let her work off some of what's ailing her."

He stopped rocking, and his face grew serious.

"Did you come to ask Emily to go back to Woodstock with you?"

"I did, but she said no, very emphatically."

"That keeps me from having to put my foot down. You seem like a fine young man, son, but Emily just turned seventeen. It's one thing to give permission for her to join Crystal camping out with half a million strangers. It's quite another to let her to go off and spend the weekend with a dang fool like you."

I laughed. I *was* a dang fool.

"If she's only seventeen, why is she engaged to marry Stan?"

"I suspect Stan thinks they'll marry someday, but I don't remember my daughter ever saying so. Katy and I are friends with his parents. Their farm is just down the road. They went to school together. Guess most everyone 'round here expects they'll end up married someday. Maybe they will, but," he cleared his throat, "she's never kissed Stan in front of us the way she kissed you."

Good. Mr. Hawkins called Stan a punk.

"Is he good enough for her?"

Mr. Baker ran a hand over his chin.

"Stan's like a lot of farm boys his age. He drives too fast, drinks too much, gets into fights too quick, but I suspect he'll settle down once he has responsibilities of his own."

Emily dusted off her hands and approached the house. She plucked a daisy from flowers growing along the steps, reminding me of the flower painted on the side of her cheek when we first met. She stuck the daisy in her hair. She might not be a hippie, but she was more than a farm girl.

She climbed the steps.

"Daddy, where's your blanket?"

"Doesn't matter. I'm going inside." Her father rose on unsteady legs and braced himself with the chair. "It *is* a little chilly out here." He winked at me. The screen door squeaked as he shot me a nod of encouragement and went inside.

Emily leaned against the porch railing. A bead of sweat slid down the corner of her forehead. On her, it looked good.

She picked hay off her flannel shirt as if searching for what she might say.

"I'm sorry you came all this way."

"Guess I misread your feelings about us."

"You didn't misread anything, but I have other responsibilities."

She avoided my gaze and brushed the last of the hay from her shirt.

"What's the point getting all worked up? After Woodstock, you're off to Penn State and I'm staying here in New York."

"Penn State's not so far."

"From this farm," Emily said with a wistful smile, "it's a million miles."

"That why you're going to marry Stan, to be a farmer's wife?"

She smacked the porch railing.

"Son-of-a-bitch. Who said I'm going to marry Stan?"

"Apparently everybody around here, including Stan."

Emily faced the cinder drive that lead away from the farmhouse.

"In small towns, everyone thinks they know what you're going to do before you know it."

Hardly the denial I hoped for. I stood beside her, gripped the porch railing and gazed over the farm.

"Your father said you want to be a teacher."

Emily shrugged.

"What I want isn't always that important."

"So you'll stay on the farm and care for your parents like they took care of you all your life."

"Something wrong with that?" Emily's eyes glistened and a tear slid down her face.

I hadn't come all this way to get Emily to question her values, and I hadn't come to make her cry. I wrapped both arms around her.

She buried her face against my chest. Emily finally stopped crying, threw her arms around my neck and kissed me with the same passion she had at Woodstock.

The kiss ended, and Emily stared into my eyes.

"I can't go back to Woodstock with you. Daddy wouldn't let me. I've always been his little girl, but since Ethan left for Vietnam, they're even more protective than before."

Damn. I wanted to spend more time with Emily. I also hoped she'd return and we could experience the music together and share the communal spirit of half a million. These could be precious moments we might always remember.

"Will you write me?" Emily pressed her body against mine and nuzzled my neck. She ran a finger across my cheek. For the first time since I arrived, Emily flashed the smile and dimple that made me pay more attention to her than the music I came for.

"I've seen you naked, twice. I think that qualifies us as pen pals."

I wanted much more than to be her pen pal. Was that all she wanted?

"I'll write."

I'd write. She'd write back. Over time, the distance would prove too much. Letters would become less frequent until we both chocked up our brief encounter to a one-time summer fling.

"I'm still mad at you." She stepped back and crossed her arms.

I could accept the disappointment of returning alone to Woodstock, but I couldn't go without understanding her anger.

"What did I do? Is it because I went to check on Buck and left you and Crystal?"

"Guys are so stupid."

I held out both arms. What had I done?

Emily's eyes narrowed.

"You told Darryl we slept together."

"I did no such thing."

I recalled my conversation with Crystal's brother. Guess I had. "I ... I might have implied it. So that's why you're mad."

She groaned.

"I could care less what Darryl thinks about me. He's an idiot."

"Are you going to tell me?"

She cocked her head.

"You told Crystal why you left Woodstock."

What did I say?

"Son-of-a-bitch, Sparky. You told my best friend how you felt about me before you told me!"

Was that all? Her unexpected reaction reminded me that in spite of her kindness, caring and so many wonderful traits I'd only begun to know, Emily *was* just seventeen.

"Crystal called you?"

Emily rolled her eyes. "Duh, that's what best friends do. By now, everyone in Bethel knows how you feel about me, except my parents."

"I didn't think Crystal would tell me where you lived unless I told her why I left Woodstock."

"So tell *me*. I need to hear you say it."

Emily set both hands on her hips.

"Well?"

Her eyes widened as I took her hands in mine. I prepared to tell Emily I loved her in a way that took my breath away and made it difficult to sleep. I wanted to find out whether she felt the same. It didn't matter we'd only met the day before. I loved her more than anything or anyone.

"Emily, I—"

The screen door squeaked open.

Emily stepped away from me, and I let go of her hands as her mother wheeled her chair onto the porch.

"Your clothes are dry." Mrs. Baker appeared to recognize she interrupted a moment. "I think I forgot something inside."

"It's okay, Mama."

I looked at Emily. The opportunity to share my feelings about her evaporated like the smoke-filled soap bubble at the festival.

"I better go change."

Inside, I climbed the stairs and changed into my clothes, except for the comfortable pair of Ethan's socks. I folded his clothes and left them on the bed in his room.

A notepad lay on his desk. I printed my address on a sheet of paper for Emily. I wrote Ethan a note, thanking him for the use of his clothes and for his service to the country. I went downstairs and stepped into the kitchen. The phone rang in the mudroom.

Mr. Baker answered and called to Emily.

"Stan's on the line."

I froze beside the kitchen table.

Outside, Emily let out an exaggerated sigh.

"Tell him to call back, Daddy. I'm kind of busy with something."

He set the phone down. The screen door opened, and Mr. Baker joined Emily on the porch.

"He sounds mad."

"Gosh, imagine that."

I ran a hand through my hair, trying to shake the guilt over eavesdropping, but I wanted to hear what she'd say to her fiancé.

The porch screen door opened, and Emily stepped into the mudroom. She cleared her throat and picked up the phone.

"I thought you went hunting." She listened for half a minute. Her voice rose with bitter contempt. "Yes it's true ... because it's none of your business ... I'm my own person and always will be."

She slammed the receiver down. Emily stepped onto the porch and banged the screen door closed.

"Idiot."

I pumped my arms in a silent victory dance. I waited another minute then stepped onto the porch. The three Bakers gazed in different directions.

"Thank you all for your hospitality."

I shook Mr. Baker's hand.

He tugged a set of keys from a pocket and nodded toward the pickup.

"I'll take you to Bethel and as close to Yasgur's farm as I can get."

"You don't have to do that."

He pointed to the darkening sky and grinned.

"I doubt if you'd find your way to town much less to Woodstock."

Mrs. Baker squeezed my hand, drew me closer and kissed my cheek.

I took Emily's soft hand and led her down the porch away from her parents. I kissed her, and we hugged. I whispered in her ear, "Come back with me."

She glanced at her parents. Her eyes misted.

"I can't." She gave me a quick kiss on the cheek and turned her back.

For a moment, I held out hope she might change her mind and come with me. Finally, I swallowed my despair. I left Emily on the porch, followed her father to the pickup and climbed inside.

♪♪♪♪♪

I snapped awake at a noise that sounded like Emily's van. I checked my watch. O five thirty. Buck was right on time.

The image of Emily's family remained imprinted. Unfortunately, I never got to meet Ethan. Six months after I left him a note on his desk, he died in an ambush outside of Saigon.

A year later, Emily went to college in Albany. We wrote each other, sometimes every day. The distance, if anything, made us closer.

The Bakers owned the family farm for four generations, but Ben sold off half of the land to set up an account for his daughter's college costs. Emily didn't know until years later. By then, she couldn't do anything about the decision. Her father valued her future more than his past.

While Emily was at college, her father battled cancer with the stubborn determination inherent in all the Bakers. Sapped of energy, Ben Baker never let Emily see how ill he'd become. Six months after she graduated, the cancer finally won. In a way, he defeated the disease by lasting until he watched his daughter graduate and marry a man who loved her so.

Katy Baker died in her sleep three years later. Doctors said it was a heart attack, but now I knew she died of a broken heart.

I finally met Stan. Crystal introduced us at Emily's funeral. We shook hands and held our gaze a moment. Stan did settle down. He bought what remained of the Baker farm in the mid-seventies and married a Bethel girl, a sturdy woman who bore him six kids before he turned thirty.

The van pulled into the driveway. The security light blinked on and illuminated the passenger side. I jumped to my feet. My friend had painted more than a peace symbol on the hood.

I hurried down the porch steps with Lady close behind. Emily's conservative white van resembled a sixteen-foot peacock. Buck painted the top half a bright canary yellow. The bottom half contained psychedelic swirls of purples, blues and reds from the front bumper to the rear.

In green slacks and a jungle camouflage sweatshirt, Buck hopped out like John Wayne in *The Green Berets*. He held up both hands. "I know what you're going to say."

"It's unbelievable." I stared with disbelief.

"That wasn't my first guess."

I stepped back and took it all in.

"What, you didn't have time to install purple fluorescents underneath?"

"That wouldn't be authentic. I went for the sixties look."

"Really? I thought you went for the I've-just-kidnapped-an-Alzheimer's-patient look."

Buck contemplated his work.

"I guess I got carried away a little. After you left, I smoked more weed and got high."

"You were high *before* I left."

Lady sniffed the tires while I circled the van in awe. At the front, he'd enhanced the peace symbol. It had grown in color and dimension. The driver's side appeared as gaudy as the passenger's side. The paint job was truly a work of art, but a psychedelic Dodge Caravan would attract attention we didn't need.

"What were you thinking?"

"That Emily would want the van with psychedelics."

"What about what I wanted?"

Buck waved derisively.

"It's always about you."

"What's with your camouflage?"

"Me?" Buck laughed at my black slacks and black long-sleeve T-shirt. "You're dressed like a cat burglar. Where's your ski mask?"

I opened the side door to the van and peered inside. I expected to see love beads hanging from the ceiling. Instead, an ice chest and two boxes of food and supplies sat behind the passenger seat.

"Tell me there's no dope in the van, or I'll call the whole thing off."

"There's no dope in the van. I know I got carried away, but I kept thinking this was our last roadtrip. We gotta go out in style, man."

"It'll look terrific in the police photos."

"Now that's what I'm talking about!" Buck grabbed a radio from the supply box.

"What's that?"

"Fuzz scanner." He opened the passenger door and set the scanner inside the glove compartment. "Time's a wasting, Sparky. You're jeopardizing the mission."

I'm jeopardizing the mission? What about the psychedelic van? Our carefully planned undertaking was about to explode in our faces. However, I learned from Emily life was about taking risks. Not helping Josh would be the biggest risk of all.

I led Lady inside, grabbed an empty travel bag from beside the door then returned to the van and climbed behind the wheel. I started the engine and gripped the steering wheel, my hands cold and clammy, my heart thumping. The van contained too many memories of summer vacations to places like Cape Cod and Atlantic City.

Buck checked his watch.

"Man, we don't have time for you to get in touch with your feelings."

"You better drive." I climbed out, and we switched seats.

The sky brightened into a purple glow above the trees as we drove off. I grew increasingly nervous while Buck's face flushed with excitement as if on a rescue mission.

He parked in the nursing home's rear employee parking lot. I wiped sweaty palms on my pants. My throat was dry, but I was determined to carry through with the plan.

Buck clapped me on the shoulder.

"We can do this. You go around front. I'll open the emergency door and trigger the alarm. I'll tape the latch so the alarm continues even after the nurse closes the door. Remember, you'll have maybe five minutes to get in and out with Josh. I'll wait out front with the engine running."

The metal emergency door appeared impenetrable. The plan that looked so good on paper while smoking a joint now seemed fraught with complications.

"How will you get the door open?"

Buck flashed a Jack Nicholson-evil grin and removed a three-inch manicure set from his shirt pocket. He unsnapped the latch, revealing tools never intended for this purpose.

"Let's rock 'n' roll, Professor."

I let out a long breath. I carried the travel bag to the front of the building. I climbed the steps, went inside and stood beside the locked door to the Alzheimer's unit. My heart hammered, as I waited for the alarm to cause confusion.

The pulsing sound finally came. My hands shook as I punched in the code and held my breath. The door clicked open and I hurried inside the unit. I ran past the empty nurses' station and down the hall toward Josh's room.

Josh stood in the doorway to his room in gray sweats. He looked confused like the other residents who'd awakened from the alarm. He wrinkled his brow.

"Who are you?"

"Good morning, Josh. I'm Sparky. Remember me?"

Josh rubbed his forehead.

"You ... you took me for a hamburger. What's going on?"

"Probably a drill."

"It's probably a drill," Josh called out to a man across the hall.

The old man shuffled into his room.

I tried to appear calm. The sweep hand on the wall clock seemed to move at twice its normal speed.

"Would you like to take a trip with me and Buck?"

"For a hamburger?"

"Farther than that. We might be gone a couple of days."

Josh peered into the safety of his room.

The alarm stopped. I clutched at my chest. That wasn't part of the plan.

I checked my watch. Only a minute and a half had transpired. Cold sweat dripped down my back. What went wrong? Would the nurses return?

I fought to remain calm and keep Josh from seeing the panic that threatened to overwhelm me.

"I'll bring my guitar. We can sing some old songs. I'm bringing my dog, Lady, too."

"Can I bring Buttons?"

"I'm afraid not."

The alarm went on again. How much time did we have left?

"What do you say? You want to come along?"

"Where would we go?"

"Woodstock."

To my surprise, Josh registered a flicker.

"Woodstock. Have I been there before?"

"We all have."

"Okay. Let's go."

I went into the room, picked out clothes for him to wear and tossed them into the travel bag. "All set?"

"Wait. I need this." He grabbed the picture of Buttons I gave him.

At the nurses' station, I peered down the hall. A nurse on a cell phone paced in front of the emergency exit. She appeared frantic, as if trying to figure out why the alarm hadn't stopped.

I punched in the number to unlock the door. Josh and I slipped out of the unit.

Outside, I gazed up and down the street. The van was nowhere in sight. I led Josh down the steps and reached for my phone to call Buck.

"Where do you think you're going?"

I spun and faced Nurse Crawford. She approached from the parking lot, calmly smoking a cigarette.

"We're going to a restaurant," Josh said.

Had she called the police? Where was Buck? I forced myself to remain cool.

"An excursion for the weekend."

With the alarm still pulsing, she coolly took a long puff.

"I suppose you've considered the consequences."

I nodded.

"I know you think I'm a cold, heartless bitch."

"No, I—"

"Most people do." She took another puff and blew a plume of smoke into the cool morning air. "I sought out work with Alzheimer's patients because people like your friend Josh need understanding, but it's hard to see them arrive and ..." She lowered her voice. "Die. Over the years, a person builds up a wall or goes crazy."

Emily's van turned the corner, tires squealing. Buck pulled up and let the engine idle. He shouted through the open window.

"Sorry I'm late."

Josh inspected the van's psychedelic paint job, but Nurse Crawford barely seemed to pay attention.

"Patients come to Sunrise because family members can no

longer care for them, and you think you can take care of him for a weekend."

"This wasn't an easy decision. I'm doing what I think is best for Josh."

"I know that. That's why I haven't called the police. Mr. Ellington, in nearly every case I've worked, to the family, death comes as a relief. In this case, however, Josh's mother seems a bit too anxious."

To my utter amazement, Nurse Crawford seemed to feel the same about Josh's mother.

She climbed the steps. Beside the front door, she crushed out the cigarette and kicked the butt into the bushes.

"After the excitement dies down, I'll order a head count. You've got an hour before that happens. Of course, if you tell anyone about seeing me this morning, I'll deny it."

"Of course. Thanks."

"You may not thank me when the shit hits the fan. Believe me. It will." She pulled open the front door and went inside.

Buck hopped from the driver's seat and slid open the side door.

"She call the cops?"

"She gave us an hour."

He patted Josh on the back.

"Hello, buddy, it's me, Buck."

"Nice to meet you, Buck." Josh ran a hand along the psychedelic design. "Cool van."

"See, he loves the paint job." Buck pumped his fist.

The alarm grew silent as Buck helped Josh into the van.

"They found the tape."

I climbed in beside Josh, in the second row of seats.

"Go, go."

Buck slammed the side door, sprinted to the driver's door and climbed in. We sped off, tires squealing like we'd robbed a Brinks truck.

I leaned forward and shook Buck's shoulder.

"Slow down."

"Faster!" Josh's face glowed like someone on an adventure ride at an amusement park. He probably hadn't ridden in a car in a long time.

The van slowed while my heart raced. In spite of the last hour's chaos, for the first time in two years, stress hadn't caused chest pain.

The hardest part of the plan had succeeded. The second hardest would be telling my daughter I deceived her for her career's sake.

I pulled out my cell phone, hoping Cloe was still asleep. To my relief, I reached her voice mail.

"Change of plans. You'll have to drive and meet us in Bethel. I plan to scatter the ashes at dawn Sunday morning. Hope you can make it. Sorry for the last minute change." I snapped the phone shut before she could pick up.

Seconds later, my phone rang. I let Cloe's call roll to voice mail. She'd be livid when she found out what we'd done.

Buck parked on the street in front of my house. I tried not to appear nervous around Josh as I opened the side door.

"How you doing?"

"I have to pee."

I led him inside where Lady greeted us, wagging her tail. Josh petted her.

"Josh, this is Lady."

"Nice to meet you, Lady."

I showed him the bathroom and changed out of my cat burglar clothes and into jeans and a denim shirt.

I stepped into my office and grabbed an eraser. I was confident I'd confront each remaining item by the end of the weekend. I wiped the whiteboard clean. A former poker player, I was going all in.

I snapped the leash to Lady's collar and lifted the urn off the mantel. Regret hit me like a punch from Shrek. I buried the emotion, set the urn in the box with other memorabilia and grabbed the guitar.

Josh came out of the bathroom.

"There's a bag of garbage behind the shower curtain."

I'd forgotten about the garbage I stashed the night Meagan first visited. I handed him the Gibson.

"Would you carry this for me?" With the box in one hand and the leash in the other, I stepped outside with Josh.

The morning sky was a dull gray. Meagan, Heather and Grandpa Simpson stood beside the van as Buck described how he painted the psychedelics. The flashy van had drawn the attention I feared.

Heather ran a hand along a purple swirl on the front fender.

"Awesome van, Sparky." She handed me her flute. "You'll need this if you play *Going Up the Country*."

"Thanks." I set the box with Emily's urn behind the passenger seat and laid the flute inside.

Buck helped Josh into the third row of seats and buckled his seat belt.

A car turned onto the street. Buck rose up and bumped his head on the roof of the van.

I couldn't help but laugh as the car drove past.

"Getting a little jumpy are we, Buck?"

Buck rubbed his head and chuckled.

"So the man who couldn't drive the getaway car is now the voice of calm."

I high-fived him.

"Whatever happens, happens, my friend."

Lady climbed into the back row, and I let go of the leash. She sat beside Josh and panted with impatience.

Meagan led me away from the others, into my front yard.

"Buck said you don't have permission to take Josh. You know you'll end up in jail. You think this is a wise decision?"

Inside the van, with Lady beside him watching, Josh strummed the guitar trying to play chords.

Any lingering doubts vanished.

"It may not be wise, but taking Josh is the *right* thing to do."

Buck removed his camouflage shirt, reached in the van and slipped into a red tie-dyed shirt and his bushman hat. He showed the Scout Dog tattoo on his arm to Grandpa Simpson who raised his T-shirt, revealing bony ribs and his own military tattoo. The two veterans clapped each other on the back.

A blue Miata screeched to a stop behind the van. To my surprise, Cloe, with her hair disheveled, hopped out of the passenger door clearly surprised by the presence of so many people and the psychedelic paint job of Emily's van. Gone was the attorney look. Now she just seemed like a daughter worried about her father.

"What's this all about?"

Dr. Dave climbed from the Miata. In casual clothes and clean-shaven, he appeared uncomfortable. I knew why my daughter was up so early. She hadn't been alone.

Cloe peered in the van.

"You just took him, didn't you?"

"I couldn't involve you."

Cloe's voice sputtered.

"You're damn right I can't be involved. If you bring him back now—"

"We're taking your mother's ashes to Woodstock."

Buck pumped his fist. "Roadtrip, roadtrip."

"Roadtrip," Josh repeated.

"Only Mrs. Channing can grant permission for Josh to come along. You remember what happened when you took him to lunch? Dad, this is kidnapping."

"I like 'custodial interference' better."

"It's nothing to joke about." Cloe held out both hands in frustration. "This is crazy. Josh has Alzheimer's, Buck has ..." She glanced at Buck and paused as if searching for the right words to use.

Buck tipped his hat and completed the sentence, "...his own demons."

"You have a heart condition."

She faced the new man in her life, the one with whom she was now sleeping. Her words dripped with desperation.

"Would you talk some sense into your patient? If he won't consider the legal arguments, tell him about the health risks."

Dr. Malone rubbed his chin. "Actually, your father is dealing with the issues that led to his condition."

Cloe turned her back and tapped her foot. A moment later, she spun and held out both hands.

"Are you serious? Six months in prison won't do his heart any good."

He reached for Cloe's hand. "Babe ..."

Babe? When did my daughter become the doctor's babe?

He held Cloe's hand.

"Your father's confronting the issues that led to his condition. He's taking his wife's ashes to scatter at a place that meant a lot to the both of them. He's gotten in touch with his friend Buck who he hasn't seen in years, and he's dealing with Josh's Alzheimer's."

Cloe wasn't happy with her new boyfriend or her old man. Her shoulders sagged.

"They'll throw you in jail, Dad. There's not much I'll be able to do about it."

I repeated something Emily said after she was arrested at the peace demonstration: "Sometimes you need to take risks in life."

From the box of memorabilia I'd set in the van, I removed Emily's peace symbol necklace she wore to Woodstock. I placed the precious keepsake in Cloe's hand and closed her fist around it.

"Your mother would want you to have this."

Tears welled in Cloe's eyes, and her anger vanished. "Dad, I ..." She threw both arms around me and whispered, "I hope you make it. I really do."

For a moment, she wasn't a worried daughter or attorney concerned about her client's actions. She was my shy little girl with blonde pigtails and her mother's eyes. I kissed her cheek.

"I hope to see you tomorrow morning when we scatter your mother's ashes."

"Don't count on me being there. I'll stay here and see if I can work something out to keep you and Buck out of jail. Maybe I can reason with Josh's mother."

"Good luck with that." I gave her a final hug then went to say goodbye to Heather and Meagan.

"Dude." Heather slapped my palm. "A roadtrip to Woodstock in a psychedelic van. It's like you're taking a journey in a freakin' time machine."

For the first time, I appreciated Buck's paint job. Perhaps we were about to enter a time machine, one that would take me, Buck and Josh back to nineteen sixty-nine.

Meagan kissed me a little more passionately than the sendoff called for. I didn't understand her interest, but I let her have her way with me. She wiped lipstick from my lips.

"Be careful, Sparky."

Grandpa Simpson flashed me a stay-off-my-lawn sneer that softened into a grin of acceptance. For the first time, he shook my hand.

"Stay one step ahead of the law."

"We'll do our best." I checked my watch. A half hour remained until Nurse Crawford ordered the head count. I held my hand out so Buck would toss me the keys.

"I can drive."

"I'm driving. You and Josh ride in back."

Buck lifted the urn from the box and opened the passenger door. He set the urn on the seat. He secured it with the seat belt and closed the door.

"Emily's riding shotgun."

16

The midmorning sun burnt away the earlier gloomy haze as we hit the interstate north to Scranton. With Buck driving a couple miles under the speed limit, Emily's urn in the front passenger seat and Josh happy in back petting Lady, for the first time in more than two years, the van didn't remind me of what I'd lost.

Josh held the picture of Buttons in one hand and peered out the window. The wide-eyed look of wonder on his face confirmed the virtue of our mission.

I hoped the nursing home would conclude Josh slipped out the door during the confusion of the pulsing alarm. With Nurse Crawford sympathetic, we might actually make it to Bethel, scatter Emily's ashes and return to Milton without drawing attention to ourselves.

I grabbed the guitar from the backseat. I strummed a few chords of *Darlin' Be Home Soon*, the song I heard standing outside the freak-out tent, watching Josh impress the young ladies.

Josh swayed in time to the music. I sang the first verse and he joined me, sounding almost like John Sebastian. Buck snatched his harmonica from his pocket and played along one-handed as he drove.

Before I could play another, Josh's foot tapped the floorboard. He leaned forward in the seat. "I gotta pee."

"We should gas up." Buck turned off at the next exit and found a station with a minimart at the corner. He pulled up to the pumps and shut off the engine. To my relief, the few people pumping gas paid no attention to our dazzling van.

I handed Buck my credit card and slid open the side door. I grabbed Lady's collapsible dog dish and a bottle of water from the cooler. I clipped the leash to her collar and led her and Josh to the restrooms at the side of the minimart. Josh went inside. I found Lady a patch of grass in the landscaping next to the building. After she peed, I emptied the bottle into the dish.

She lapped up the water as a Pennsylvania State Patrol car turned into the station. My throat tightened with a sickening sense of doom.

The officer pulled up behind Emily's van, no doubt running the license plate. A moment later, the patrol car parked near the entrance to the minimart.

A female officer stepped from the car, wearing dark aviator glasses and a crisp gray uniform that probably could stand on its own. She studied our psychedelic van too long for my comfort before she went inside the store.

I clamped a hand over my heart—chest pain for the first time since we sped away from the Sunrise Assisted Living Center. I poked my head in the restroom. "Need any help in there?"

A beer-bellied biker with rattlesnake skin cowboy boots pushed through the door. He gave me a wide berth and muttered, "Damn old fairies." Before I could explain, he hopped onto a Harley and started the bike. He flipped me the bird and rode off burning rubber.

Josh came out singing *Darlin' Be Home Soon* and watched the man ride away. "He didn't like that song."

I tried not to display a sense of urgency as I led Josh and Lady to the van. I helped them into the backseat while Buck finished gassing up.

The police officer came out of the minimart. I began to wheeze as she headed for the van.

Buck climbed into the driver's seat. He tossed me a bottle of water.

"Get a grip and try not to look like we just robbed a bank. Remember, we're on a roadtrip." He flashed a commanding expression. "Guys, let me do all the talking."

The officer reached the open door of the van. "Nice van. What are you fellows up to?"

"Roadtrip!" Josh bellowed, eliciting a red-faced frown from Buck.

She peered at Josh over the top of her sunglasses.

"Where to?"

"Florida," Buck quickly answered.

The officer pointed down the freeway in the direction from where we'd come.

"Florida's that way."

I wiped sweat from my brow. I drank a gulp of water and tried not to wheeze.

The officer slipped off her sunglasses and studied my face.

"You don't look so good. You boys haven't been drinking, have you?"

Buck shook his head.

"I don't drink. Neither does my friend in the backseat, but this one," he pointed to me, "drinks like every night's Mardi Gras, but it's early, even for him."

I suspected any minute the officer would grab her Taser and put me spread-eagle against the side of the van.

She stuffed the glasses into her shirt pocket.

"License and registration, please."

Buck handed over his license and gestured toward me.

"It's his van."

He reached into the glove compartment for the registration. The officer moved toward the passenger door and peered into the open glove box.

"Is that a police scanner?"

"I guess." Buck handed her the registration.

She glanced at Emily's urn in the passenger seat.

"That what I think it is?"

Buck nodded. He jerked a thumb in my direction then mouthed *his wife.*

The officer checked the registration then turned her attention to me.

"You're Walter Ellington?"

Buck shot me a silent but clear warning. *Don't say anything stupid.*

"I'm Walter Ellington, Officer."

I gave her my address to demonstrate my honesty and cooperation and handed over my license, without her asking.

"What's with the scanner, Mr. Ellington?" She studied the license like the fat bouncer had our senior year of high school when Buck, Josh and I used fake IDs to get into a frat party.

Why did Buck stash the damn thing in the glove box? Scanners weren't illegal, but the device aroused the officer's suspicion, as if the psychedelic paint job wasn't enough.

"My daughter's a fireman ... firewoman ... fireperson. I like to listen occasionally when she's on her shift. Guess I worry too much."

Apparently sensing my discomfort, Lady stood on the seat behind me and wagged her tail.

I glanced over my shoulder. Smart dog. I gave her a silent command she mastered as a pup. Lady hopped out of the backseat and licked the officer's hand.

For the first time since she approached us, the woman's posture relaxed. She petted Lady and looked at us with greater understanding, as if anyone with such a sweet dog must be okay. She handed Buck the registration.

"Drive careful. Florida's a long trip."

"Roadtrip!" Josh called.

The officer ignored Josh and my own suspicious behavior and gave Lady a final pat. She slipped on her sunglasses, tipped the visor of her cap and headed to her patrol car.

My heart hammered. I closed the side door, helped Lady into the backseat and buckled my belt.

"Go, go, go!"

Buck started the van and laughed as he drove off.

"To think I worried Josh might give us away. Nice touch about your daughter, the *firewoman ... fireperson*. Very smooth."

We reentered the interstate heading north to Scranton. Before my racing heart returned to normal, my cell phone rang. I braced myself, hoping it wouldn't be bad news.

"Morning, Cloe."

"Sunrise called. I'm there now, along with the police—two uniforms and a detective. An aide spotted you leaving with Josh."

"Damn!"

"They sent a car to your house. They'll find the BMW in the garage and search for mom's van."

They'll search for a beige van, not a psychedelic one. Maybe Buck's paint job would buy us enough time to reach New York.

"Josh's mother arrived a minute ago and nearly collapsed when they told her you were involved. She doesn't like you very much."

"We go way back."

"She comes across as a caring mother concerned for her son's welfare."

"Give her enough time and her true nature will come out."

"We don't have a lot of time."

In the rear seat, Josh petted Lady. He gazed out the window like a kid on his way to Disneyland.

"Tell her Josh is enjoying himself, and he'll be back late tomorrow."

"Dad, you're not thinking clearly."

I hadn't been this clear about anything for two years.

"Work your legal magic."

"There's no magic about the law. I'll do my best to give you more time to come to your senses."

She ended the call.

"Sup?" Buck gazed at me in the rearview mirror.

"They know we took Josh. What do you want to do?"

I searched Buck's face for evidence he might want to turn back and give up our increasingly improbable quest.

"Let's jam." Buck snatched up the harmonica. Driving with one hand, he played the blues.

Josh swayed in the seat.

"I like this kind of music."

I tried to put the conversation with Cloe behind me and picked up the guitar. I'd barely begun to join in when my cell rang again.

"Dad, things just got worse."

Worse?

"Did they issue a shoot to kill order?"

"Not funny. The DA showed up. The media hungry, political opportunist Henry Culpepper. He's blown the situation totally out of proportion. He's turned the dayroom into a command center. They've given me one opportunity to talk you into surrendering Josh. You've got two hours to avoid jail time."

I unfolded a map from the supply box and studied our route. Even if we pushed it, we'd never make New York by the two-hour deadline. Culpepper's influence would end at the border.

"Can you get us more time?"

"Are you listening to me?" Desperation flowed from her voice. "In two hours, they'll put out an APB. That's—"

"I know what an APB is. We watched *CHiPS* when you were a kid."

"They'll arrest you and Buck."

"Would you repeat that?" I held the phone so Buck could hear.

"I said you and Buck will be arrested."

Buck and I knew the risk of jail before we finalized the plan to bring Josh along on the roadtrip. The actions of his mother and the cops weren't unexpected, but the addition of the ambitious media magnet Henry Culpepper meant our roadtrip might reach a perfect storm of bad luck.

"Culpepper's waving me over. Gotta go." Cloe hung up.

Buck glanced at me in the rearview mirror.

"Culpepper's a tool. Fuck him."

"You willing to play this out?"

"We knew what we were getting into. Don't chicken out now, Nancy."

Josh leaned forward in the seat, his brow wrinkled with concern. "Who's Nancy?"

I smiled reassurance and set the guitar on my knee.

"How about some music? We're still on a roadtrip aren't we?"

Josh grinned. "Roadtrip!"

For the next half hour, we played Woodstock songs by The Who and Jefferson Airplane. Like all the others, Josh remembered every word. After "White Rabbit," he yawned and mentioned he was tired. With one arm on Lady, he laid his head back and soon fell asleep.

I offered to drive, but Buck wouldn't hear of it. In spite of the threat of arrest, I grew groggy from a lack of sleep. I reclined the seat and closed my eyes.

♪♪♪♪♪

I sat in the passenger seat of Mr. Baker's pickup as he prepared to drive me from his farm to the Woodstock festival.

Emily—obviously trying to hold it together—and her mother waited beside the pickup as the sun dipped behind the barn. Mrs. Baker peered at me through the driver's window.

"I'm so glad we had the opportunity to meet, Sparky. Good luck at college." She glanced at Emily. "And with everything."

"Thanks, Mrs. Baker."

She patted her husband's hand through the open window and something unsaid passed between them. She turned to Emily.

"Why don't you go with them?"

"Really?"

"The boy came all this way." Mrs. Baker reached up and hugged her daughter.

Emily kissed her mother's cheek then ran to the passenger door. "Do you mind?"

Mind? "Of course not." I hopped out and let her sit between her father and me. I climbed in and waved to her mother as we drove off down the muddy drive.

Stone faced, Emily avoided looking at me, as if doing so would trigger emotions she didn't want to display in front of her father, or maybe I merely read feelings into her expression I wanted her to have. In any event, the three of us didn't speak on the drive to town.

We passed the "Welcome to Bethel" sign and drove by The Old Schoolhouse Crystal's parents owned. I remembered Crystal imploring me not to hurt Emily. She hadn't said anything about Emily breaking my heart.

Emily's face softened as we left Bethel. She held my hand. Tears danced as we looked in each other's eyes.

Mr. Baker turned on the headlights and weaved the pickup through the parked cars. A quarter of a mile from the festival, abandoned cars blocked the road. Mr. Baker pulled the truck over and let the engine idle.

I reached across Emily and shook her father's hand.

"Thanks for the lift, Mr. Baker." With a sinking sense of loss, I let go of Emily's hand and climbed out.

Mr. Baker nudged his daughter.

"Aren't you at least going to get out and say goodbye?"

She nodded and climbed from the truck.

Rock music blasted from past the trees as we stood beside the road. A soft breeze stirred the grass at our feet. Emily brushed a wisp of hair from her face.

I held her hand, but words failed to come. I didn't know if I'd ever see her again and didn't know how to say goodbye.

Her father put the truck in gear and turned the pickup around, I assumed to give us a moment of privacy. He pulled alongside us, facing toward Bethel.

"Enjoy the rest of the weekend, you two. See you Monday, Emily."

I stared in disbelief.

Emily's mouth dropped open. She clutched the driver's door.

"Daddy, what's going on?"

"We trust you. Now, don't be a dang fool. Go with the boy. Enjoy yourselves."

He pointed a steady finger at me.

"You take care of my girl, Son."

I placed my arm around Emily's shoulder.

"I will, Mr. Baker."

"But, Daddy, what will Mama say?"

Ben's eyes glistened as he smiled.

"It was your mama's idea."

Emily glanced at me then her father.

"Are you sure you and Mama will be okay?"

"Sweetie, your mama and I appreciate all you do for us, but you've reached a point in life where you need to consider what's best for you, not for me, your mama or your brother."

He nodded toward me, "Or even this one. You hear?"

Emily wiped a tear from her face.

"Yes, Daddy."

Her father set his jaw. I could see how difficult it was for him to let go of his only daughter. He removed his hat and ran a hand over his bald head, reminding me of his battle with cancer.

"Now go."

Emily's eyes misted as she waved goodbye to her father. We watched until the taillights disappeared into the dark night.

I swallowed a lump in my throat, touched by her parents' gesture of trust in Emily and me.

"You okay?"

Emily managed a smile and gave me a kiss. Hand in hand, we headed toward the jazzy rock music playing from the giant speakers. The distinct sound was Sly and the Family Stone.

At the edge of Yasgur's farm, she stopped and cocked her head.

"I wasn't very nice to you."

"No, you weren't."

"I can't believe you left the festival and came all the way in the rain and mud just for me."

"You're worth a little mud."

Emily beamed. We made our way through the campsites and woods. At the crest of the hill, we gazed over the amphitheater. The place appeared as if we'd never left. An orange glow of marijuana smoke hovered over the blue stage lights that bathed Sly and the Family Stone.

I smiled at Emily.

"I didn't get around to telling you the second reason why I left Woodstock to find you."

Emily knew the reason. She knew what I was about to say. Still, she bit her lower lip and waited for me to say the words.

On stage, Sly Stone sang "I Want to Take you Higher." He implored everyone with "Higher," and the crowd answered, "Higher."

The chant went back and forth between the stage and the crowd, but I barely heard it as I took a deep breath. I gazed into her brown doe eyes.

"I left Woodstock because I couldn't go back to Pennsylvania without telling you how I feel. I love you, Emily."

I held Emily's shoulders and kissed her. Although she was only seventeen and I had just turned eighteen, the moment felt like it might last a lifetime.

♫♫♫♫♫

I opened my eyes. I sat in the psychedelic van on the road somewhere in northern Pennsylvania. I clamped my eyes closed to retain the moment when Emily and I knew we loved each other, but the image vanished like a wisp of smoke.

Behind me, Josh slept, snoring softly. Lady lay beside him. She looked up as if telling me she intended to watch over him, like the good therapy dog she was.

"Good dog." I faced the front. A cigarette dangled from Buck's lips as he drove. I sniffed the air and realized the cigarette was a joint. Oh, hell no!

"Where'd you get the weed?"

"In the glove compartment behind the scanner. Who'd have thought Emily kept a stash in her van." Buck chuckled.

"I don't think so." Emily hadn't smoked grass after Woodstock, as far as I knew. Buck brought the weed after assuring me he hadn't. I tried to control my temper for Josh's sake.

"Okay, the shit's mine." Buck waved the smoke out the window.

Glove compartment!

"That cop looked in the glove compartment. We could've been busted for dope!"

Buck let out a hearty laugh and slapped the dash.

"You dumb-ass. We're on the run for kidnapping and you're worried about a little possession charge." He offered me the joint.

He was right. We faced bigger problems. I grabbed the joint and took a toke. I leaned back in the seat. I smoked half the joint and began to relax. Smoking weed wasn't the issue—honesty was.

"Before we left to pick up Josh, I asked if you'd brought grass and you said no."

"Actually, you asked if there was any grass in *the van*. At the time, I had the stash in my pocket. Don't be so uptight."

Buck had been less than truthful, but I admired his carefree attitude I'd never been able to master. I took another hit and handed him the joint.

He finished the joint and tossed the tiny end of the cigarette out the window.

"Nice van." A girl's voice shouted through the open driver's window.

Buck slapped the outside of the driver's door.

"Thanks, I did it myself."

"You're very talented."

I leaned forward and peered out the driver's window. Two girls in a red convertible kept pace alongside us. The driver was pretty with dark skin and hair and the passenger a hot-looking redhead wearing a black tank top.

The redhead brushed her windswept hair from her eyes.

"Got any beer?"

Buck glanced at me over his shoulder.

"There's a six-pack in the cooler."

"Buck, they're in their mid-twenties."

"That makes them about seven years older than we were at Woodstock. What's your point?"

I wasn't sure. I pulled cold cans of beer from the cooler's icy water.

"I didn't think you drank."

"I don't, but in times like this, alcohol can be used as tools of the trade, if you know what I mean."

I had no idea what he meant.

Buck grabbed the beer and held it out the window.

"Happen to have an extra six-pack. Can you catch?"

"Just a sec." The redhead took off her top and revealed a tiny black-lace bra. She held out her T-shirt as the convertible edged closer to the van.

Buck leaned out the window, extended his arm and dropped the six-pack into the girl's waiting shirt. She caught the beer and set the cans on the floor. She faced Buck and cupped her breasts. Laughing, she slipped into her top as the driver flashed a peace symbol and sped away.

Buck honked the van's horn and waved.

"Well, that was disappointing."

"What?"

"It's only common courtesy when a man gives a woman a six-pack on the highway that she flash her breasts."

I searched through the cooler. That was the extent of our beer.

"Why'd you give away our only beer?"

"Because it was fun? By the way, I hope your neck feels better."

"My neck?"

"I thought you might pull some ligaments when you leaned forward to watch that girl take off her top."

I laughed, pulled a Coke from the cooler and took a long swallow.

"What did Ashley say when you told her you were going away for the weekend."

He rubbed his chin, then slid his cell phone from his pocket and dialed.

"Hey, babe. I forgot to tell you, I'll be gone for a few days ... New York. You sound breathless. You working out?"

Buck stiffened in the seat.

"You're banging Tony?" He tugged on his ponytail. "It's not the same thing."

He snapped the cell phone shut and smacked his fist on the steering wheel.

"She cheated on me! She's cheating on me as we speak. Son-of-a-bitch!"

"Sorry." I felt bad for Buck, but he was hardly the poster boy for fidelity. "It probably doesn't mean anything to her."

"It'll take time to recover from this. There are other women, but damn, I'll never find another mechanic as good as Tony .... Hey, I don't make up the rules."

I laughed at Buck's way of looking at life.

"Never get involved with a stripper, Sparky."

"Maybe you should date women your own age."

"In my teens I used to date *older* women, including Miss

Flanders."

"You dated the typing teacher?"

"Not in a dinner and a movie kind of way, if you know what I'm saying." He gazed out the driver's window. "I haven't nailed someone my age since Crystal at Woodstock."

"You and Crystal?" I couldn't believe I just learned this tidbit for the first time. I was certain Emily never knew.

"We hooked up before my acid trip while Josh was off skinny-dipping in the pond and you were romancing the future Mrs. Ellington."

Buck glanced over his shoulder at me. His eyes widened in shock.

"You and Emily did it that night, too, didn't you?"

I never told Josh or Buck, but now I couldn't help but smile.

"You slut!" Buck laughed. "She was only seventeen."

"So was Crystal." Now I understood why the day I left Woodstock and stepped into her parents' bar, Crystal asked about Buck. That wasn't the only time, either.

"Crystal asked about you at Emily's funeral."

Buck appeared pleased by the news.

"Crystal asked about me? Home come you never told me?"

"When would I have told you?" My cell phone rang. "Hi, Cloe."

"Dad, if you let Josh go now, they won't press charges."

"We're not letting him go. Not yet."

"Okay, Culpepper offered a final deal. This is the best I can do. You can take Josh to your destination as long as you're back tomorrow morning."

Since she hadn't mentioned where we were headed, I knew Culpepper was listening to the call.

"I'll consider the deal if that weasel Culpepper will shave off his ridiculous porn star moustache."

"Dad."

"This plan is okay with Josh's mom?"

"She just wants her son back."

I covered the microphone on the phone.

"How long 'til we reach Bethel?"

Buck checked his watch.

"If we stay on the interstate, six hours. Would get us in by midafternoon."

I uncovered the microphone.

"We can be back by this time tomorrow."

"The DA's office insists on getting this in writing."

My bullshit radar went on high alert.

"Tell the twerp it's the twenty-first century. I'll send him a text."

"Culpepper and Mrs. Channing want a written agreement, in case anything goes wrong. I'll meet you in Scranton. You can sign the papers and be on your way." Her voice had an edge, different from the earlier calls. Guilt perhaps?

"I thought Culpepper was being a jerk."

Cloe hesitated.

"Henry Culpepper is a reasonable person."

Reasonable? "Pompous media whore" had always been her favorite expression to describe the DA. I covered the microphone.

"Cloe must be setting us up so we avoid jail time."

"You think she'd sell us out?"

I had to find out. I uncovered the speaker.

"We're past Scranton. I'll call you later to arrange a place to meet."

I terminated the call before she could object.

"I can't believe it."

"Cloe's doing what she thinks is best for you and me. Culpepper gets a little time on the nightly news and we get probation."

"What about him?" I thumbed toward Josh, peacefully asleep in the backseat. "What does he get?"

I studied the map again. I spotted a little town Emily and I passed through several years earlier. Titusville was right on the Pennsylvania-New York border. I handed the map to Buck and pointed to the spot.

"I'll call Cloe and tell her we'll wait for her there."

My daughter would no doubt do anything to keep Buck and me out of jail. The situation was bound to get worse. With Culpepper involved, it was only a matter of time before the media pounced on the "kidnapping" of an Alzheimer's patient and a grieving elderly mother. I just hoped Cloe wouldn't be too mad when she realized I double-crossed her.

Buck glanced at me in the rearview mirror.

"Once we're there, then what?"

"We're going to need some binoculars."

16

Ipulled Buck's camouflage shirt over mine and slipped his binoculars around my neck. I left Buck, Josh and Lady with the van, at the bottom of the hill on the New York side of the border. I climbed the hill and stuck to the shoulder of the road.

The midday sun beat down from a cloudless sky. Sweat dripped into my eyes. My quads ached and my breathing labored as I climbed. I should've spent more time on the treadmill.

At the crest of the hill, I limped through ankle-high grass. I collapsed in the shadows of a tree and gulped air. Minutes later, my breathing returned enough oxygen to my brain so I could continue with the plan. I focused the binoculars on a greasy spoon diner, Sandy's Roadhouse, where Emily and I enjoyed an excellent breakfast while passing through Titusville several years before.

I hoped my suspicions proved groundless and Cloe wasn't setting us up to end the roadtrip. I found it difficult to believe she'd work with Henry Culpepper, the unscrupulous DA she always ridiculed.

A young man stepped from the diner with a backpack slung over his shoulders. He reached the road and held out a thumb. Several cars passed him by. He headed up the road and climbed the hill in our direction.

I glanced over my shoulder. At the bottom of the hill, Josh led Lady through a field of dry grass beside the van. Buck sat in the open side door smoking. Had to be a joint. How much weed did he have?

I focused the binoculars on a car approaching the diner. Cloe's hybrid pulled into the parking lot. In dark sunglasses, she climbed from her car. She scanned the lot, no doubt searching for Emily's van.

Cloe leaned against her car and lit a cigarette. Damn, I thought she quit!

The hitchhiker passed by without seeing me. I waited until he was far enough away, pulled out my cell and called Cloe. Cloe dropped the cigarette and crushed it under her shoe. She answered with irritation in her voice. "Dad, where are you?"

"In the diner."

"You said to meet in the parking lot." She peered in a window. "You're inside?"

I ignored the guilt over my deceit and stuck to the plan.

"I'm in the men's room. The van doesn't have a toilet."

"Where are Buck and Josh?"

"Buck went to gas up. Why?"

Cloe checked her watch.

"It might reassure Josh's mother if I could report he's okay."

"Josh is great. They'll get here after I call and give them the okay everything's on the up- and-up."

Cloe turned her back to me and gazed down the road.

"Why wouldn't it be?"

"Find an empty booth and I'll meet you in a couple of minutes."

I ended the call and waited for her reaction.

Cloe stuffed the phone in her pocket and hurried into the diner.

A media van with satellite antennae pulled into the diner's parking lot. My heart sank. I refocused the binoculars and glimpsed Cloe inside the restaurant gesturing to a waitress at the window, apparently trying to describe me.

Seconds later, on her cell, she burst into the parking lot. A line of black cars sped toward the diner. She snapped her phone closed and ran toward the vehicles, holding up a hand for them to stop.

Too late.

A camera crew pointed their camera at three patrol cars and an unmarked black SUV. The caravan turned into the lot and skidded to a stop behind Cloe, kicking up a cloud of dust. Six officers with assault rifles burst from the three patrol cars. In black combat gear, they took orders from a sergeant.

The SWAT team set up as Henry Culpepper calmly climbed from the SUV. He straightened a dark-blue suit, which must be miserable on a hot June day. A fuzzy caterpillar-like line of hair snuggled under his nose. He hadn't taken me up on my negotiation demands to shave off the ridiculous moustache.

The well-drilled SWAT team approached the diner's front door. Like a scene from a movie, two members busted through the door. With a reporter and camera operator documenting the assault, the team burst inside, determined to take down a sixty-year-old retired professor with a bad heart. I felt bad I deceived Cloe, but I couldn't help but chuckle.

Cloe argued with the DA. Although I was disappointed she'd gone along with a plan to return Josh to Sunrise, I hoped she'd slap the son-of-a-bitch enough to leave a mark for the six o'clock news.

Culpepper and Cloe gestured wildly as they went nose-to-nose. Snippets of their shrill voices made their way up the hill. The DA turned away with a derisive wave and approached the police sergeant, who emerged from the diner and shook his head.

A cook in a white hat and greasy apron stepped past the broken diner door. He tried to get the sergeant's attention. He gave up and pleaded his case to Culpepper. The DA ignored the cook and tried to lay the best possible spin on the failed operation to the reporter.

Cloe walked to the edge of the lot. She shielded her eyes and peered toward the top of the hill in my direction.

She couldn't see me in the shadows. Although pleased I outsmarted "the Man," I regretted placing Cloe in such a difficult position.

I stood and waved the binoculars over my head. Just as quickly, I disappeared down the hill toward the van where Buck sat talking to the young hitchhiker.

The return trip inflamed different leg muscles than the climb. Halfway down, my cell rang. I bent over, massaged my leg and answered.

"Dad, I know you saw what happened. That was your last chance to come out of this without going to jail. You're out of Culpepper's jurisdiction, but not out of his plans. You've crossed state lines. Now the feds can get involved. Before long, the FBI, New York state police and local jurisdictions will all search for you. This has gotten completely out of hand."

"I noticed that when the SWAT team broke down the diner's front door."

"I didn't know they'd be involved."

"I know you were only trying to keep us out of jail, but we're determined to see this through. We didn't kidnap Josh."

Cloe let out a sigh.

"I know."

"Tell me they don't know where we're headed."

"They don't know the destination, but you should turn off your cell phone. They can track those things."

"I figured as much."

"One more thing. They have a pretty good description of the psychedelic paint job from a cop at a gas station."

"Cloe, if we make it to 'our destination,' I hope you'll join us."

"Dad, you'll never make it."

"I have to try."

I shut off the phone and made my way down the hill. The front and back of both legs ached. I stumbled as I neared the bottom of the hill. I almost fell but made it to the van.

Lady sat in the grass in the shade of the van. She barked and wagged her tail.

Buck looked up at me. "You okay?"

"Peachy."

He gestured to the young hitchhiker.

"This is Lincoln Holmes. Lincoln, this is my friend Sparky."

Lincoln shook my hand and grinned.

"What kind of a name is Sparky? What did you do, burn down your parents' house or something?"

I glared at Buck.

"You told him?"

Lincoln's eyes widened.

"Dude, I was joking. If you're a firebug, I can catch a ride with someone else."

"I'm not an arsonist, and I didn't burn down my parents' house."

Buck chuckled.

"I told Lincoln we'd give him a lift."

I led Buck away and told him about the SWAT team assault at the diner. I nodded toward Lincoln. "We don't need any more complications."

"Sparky, we're on a roadtrip. We can't leave him by the side of the road. Didn't you learn anything at Woodstock about taking care of your brothers and sisters? Besides, he's a child of God."

"A child of God. What the hell are you talking about?"

"Woodstock!" Buck sighed then began to sing the Joni Mitchell song Crosby, Stills, Nash & Young had popularized.

"Well, I came upon a child of God, he was walkin' along the road, and I asked him tell me where are you goin', this he told me—

"Yeah, yeah, he's going down to Yasgur's farm to join in a rock 'n' roll band."

Buck held out both hands, imploring me with a don't-you-get-it look.

"The rock 'n' roll band. That's us, man—you, me and Josh—The Buck Naked Band. We're headed back to the garden. Can you dig it? It's a sign from God, I tell you. We gotta take him."

I scanned the road in both directions, hoping the young man might catch a ride from someone else. There were no sign of approaching cars.

"I haven't picked up a hitchhiker since my college days."

"Man, that's nothing to be proud of."

For all we knew, Lincoln might be a crazed killer. Maybe he carried a gun or knife in the backpack.

"What if he's wanted—?"

"Wanted by the Man? Sparky, *we're* wanted by the Man."

Buck laughed and clapped me on the shoulder.

We stood beside the van's open door. I studied the map.

"We have to stay off the interstate and state roads to avoid the state police, and we need to avoid as many towns and cities—"

"I'm so proud." Buck wiped away a fake tear. "You might have a future in industrial espionage or organized crime."

A county sheriff's patrol car sped past the van, a reminder our slim odds of eluding the cops once Culpepper notified his New York peers.

Lincoln peered over my shoulder.

"You guys need to stay away from the cops? I know back roads that ain't even on your map."

"He's a child of God, I tell you." Buck beamed.

Lincoln stared at Buck as if he was some kind of religious fanatic.

"Hate to disappoint you, but I'm a child of Shaniqua and Frank, the married mailman. I sure could use a lift north. Ever been to Bethel?"

"I'm telling you, Sparky, it's a sign from God." Buck held up both hands. "I bet Lincoln means 'fate' or 'destiny' or something. Am I right?"

The young man shook his head.

"Nah. I think it means overpriced luxury car."

I chuckled and had to admit Lincoln's knowledge of back roads might be our best chance to make it to Bethel.

"Okay, let's go."

I helped Lady and Josh into the backseat. Lincoln sat behind Buck in the center row of seats beside me. I closed the side door.

Buck plugged the police scanner into the outlet and hit the power switch.

"I knew we'd need this."

He eased onto the road. A quarter-mile later, Lincoln pointed to a cluster of mailboxes. "There."

Buck turned onto a rutted dirt road. He slowed, but the van still shuddered along the baked, rutted surface.

Lincoln lowered his voice so only I could hear.

"You some kind of cult?"

"Cult?" Why'd he think that?

"The driver keeps talking about child of God shit, and the dude in back acts kind of spacey."

"Josh has Alzheimer's and Buck was in Nam."

Lincoln nodded understanding.

"Okay. Everything's cool. So where you dudes headed?"

"Florida," Josh answered. "Roadtrip."

I shrugged. "It's best you don't know."

Lincoln gazed at the boxes.

"You guys got any coke?"

"Diet."

"Dude." Lincoln laughed. "I'm not talkin' about soda."

Josh leaned forward in the rear seat.

"I'm thirsty. Can I have a soda?"

I rummaged into the cooler.

"You like Coke, Josh?"

"They only let me have soda without caffeine. Caffeine's not good for me."

"You got that right, Josh," Buck called from the driver's seat. "Give him a bottle of pomegranate white tea."

"One can won't hurt." I popped the top and handed the Coke to Josh.

Lady sniffed the can, and Josh took a long swallow.

"Coke! I like Coke. Hope you brought a lot."

"Careful, Josh." Buck laughed. "You'll turn into a cokehead."

Josh took a long swallow.

"What's a cokehead?"

Lincoln sniffed the air.

"I know you got weed. I smelled it when I walked up."

Buck caught my eye in the rearview mirror.

"We're out of weed, man."

"Out of weed, out of weed," Josh called.

Lincoln gestured toward Josh.

"Is he going to do this all the way?"

Buck turned down the volume on the scanner.

"Lincoln, you should stay away from coke. It could lead to the hard stuff."

I chuckled.

"Buck, coke is the hard stuff."

"Like you'd know. The hard stuff is heroin. Stay away from that shit. H can cause brain damage. Good thing I got off heroin before that happened."

He turned to me and let out an over-the-top, maniacal giggle.

"What's with the guitar and harmonica? You guys a sixties band?"

Buck nodded.

"Mostly sixties stuff."

"No, dude, I mean you guys are *in* your sixties, right?"

I snorted laughter. We might be old, but we could still rock. I snatched the guitar and strummed a few chords from a Credence song, *Green River*.

Josh joined in. Like the other Woodstock songs, he never missed a word. Halfway through, Lincoln tapped his toe to the music.

Buck slowed the van. "There's a fork in the road."

"I should sit up front." Lincoln appeared as if he'd heard enough sixties music. He started to climb between the two front seats and froze as he spotted Emily's urn. "Shit, man, what's that?"

Buck laughed. "That's Emily. Unbuckle the belt and hold her on your lap."

"Dude, I'll stay where I am." He peered over Buck's shoulder and gave directions.

Josh and I sang Jefferson Airplane and Joe Cocker songs for an hour while Lincoln directed Buck through the New York backcountry. He helped us avoid towns and cops.

Josh sang and gazed at the green countryside. He seemed to enjoy the roadtrip as I hoped he would, but I grew increasingly concerned Buck assumed too much of the responsibility to get us to Bethel. After all, the roadtrip was my idea.

A couple of times he wiped sweat from his brow. I worried about his fragile emotions. As the afternoon wore on, he gripped the wheel tighter and grew disturbingly quiet.

We passed a sign that read "100 miles to Bethel." Josh asked for a hamburger. Lincoln mentioned a roadside diner less than a mile away. Buck could use a break, so I insisted we head there.

The diner sat alongside a well-maintained but deserted park with thick ash and maple trees. Willows danced along the edge of a pond. Buck parked behind a clump of trees at the back of the pond. No one could spot the van from the road.

Lady and Josh climbed out and walked to the water's edge where a handful of ducks lazily floated in the midday sun. I carried the urn and set Emily on a picnic table.

Buck set the cooler beside the urn.

"You have a ways to go to heal, don't you?"

Maybe I did. "I didn't want to leave her in the van."

"Right." Buck smiled but couldn't hide the dark circles under his eyes.

"You okay?"

"Peachy." He grabbed raisins and a bottle of pomegranate white tea from the cooler. "I don't want any greasy diner food."

I was determined to drive the final hundred miles to Bethel. Lincoln grabbed his cell phone, and we headed toward the diner.

Lincoln surfed the Internet on his phone as we crossed the park.

"What did we do before 4G, huh?" He froze and grabbed my arm. His eyes bored through me.

"Tell me you and Buck aren't kidnappers."

"Technically, maybe."

Outside the diner, Lincoln read aloud a breaking news story.

"Alzheimer's patient kidnapped in Milton, Pennsylvania. Authorities continue the search for a psychedelic van and two men, Walter Ellington and Buck Jamison, in connection with the abduction. 'These are two desperate individuals,' said District Attorney Henry Culpepper."

"Let me explain."

"You can drop me off right here."

I'd grown fond of the hitchhiker in the couple of hours he spent with us. I didn't want him to think he joined up with some kind of aging Manson Family members.

"In sixty-nine, Josh, Buck and I drove to Woodstock where I met the girl I would marry, Emily. We're going back to spread her ashes. Josh has been in a nursing home because of Alzheimer's. His mother doesn't like us so we took him without permission. We didn't kidnap him."

Lincoln clipped the phone to his belt.

"Dude, I believe you, but if *the Man* is after you for kidnapping, we need to go our separate ways. I can't afford to be an accessory. I got a couple outstanding warrants. You see—"

"You don't have to explain."

"I'm not a bad guy."

"Neither are we." I clapped him on the back, and we went inside.

The only customer was an old man asleep at a corner table. A bored teenage girl stood behind the counter painting her nails. The cook cleaned a sizzling grill. An old television hung from metal brackets in the corner. The sound was muted, but text of the audio scrolled along the bottom of the screen.

We ordered enough burgers and fries for Lincoln, Josh, Lady and me then waited at a plastic table that wobbled with one leg shorter than the others. A "Breaking News" banner flashed on the screen followed by a headline that read "Alzheimer's Patient Kidnapped."

Tightness clamped over my chest. First, news on the Internet, now CNN. I'd underestimated Culpepper's ability to manipulate the media into covering a non-story. To my relief, neither the cook nor the girl behind the counter paid any attention to the broadcast.

A four-year-old Milton College ID photo of me appeared on the screen. Fortunately, that image, clean-shaven, shorthaired and enjoying life, barely resembled my current appearance.

The gum-chewing counter girl blew on her nails then pointed a remote to the television. "You guys wanna listen?"

Before I could answer no, the sound came on.

My image disappeared, replaced by an old mug shot of Buck that made him look like a drug-crazed mutant. The voiceover described Buck Jamison as a former felon. Why didn't they describe him as a Vietnam vet?

Lincoln lowered his voice. "Man, I'm surprised they haven't linked you to al-Qaeda."

The network showed a live shot from Milton. A female reporter stood beside Josh's mother, in front of her house.

"Mrs. Channing, why would someone want to kidnap your son?"

The old woman thumped her cane on the driveway.

"It's the devil's work. Sweet Jesus, pray for me."

The reporter quickly cut her off and faced the camera.

"As you can see, Josh Channing's mother is understandably upset. We've received unconfirmed reports the two suspects were headed to Florida with the victim, but as I said, this is unconfirmed."

Josh isn't a victim. The media could manipulate public opinion, and now I feared the public as much as I feared the cops.

The reporter held a hand over one ear.

"I understand we're switching to a report where the kidnapping occurred."

"Guys, your order's up." The teenage girl set two brown paper bags on the counter.

I tried not to look like a wanted felon. My hand shook as I peeled a twenty from my wallet. The bill almost stuck to my sweaty palm.

Thankfully, Lincoln took the money, paid the girl and grabbed the sacks of food.

"Let's go."

I couldn't move. On the television, a young male reporter in front of Sunrise stood alongside Henry Culpepper and Cloe. She looked so professional in her blue suit and pretty, like her mother.

Phoebe and Nurse Crawford stood in the background, reminding me of the staff's dedication. Conspicuous by his absence was the facility's medical director. The reporter didn't appear intimidated by Culpepper.

"I understand you had one of the kidnappers cornered, is that right?"

Culpepper smoothed his caterpillar moustache.

"The fact that they made it into New York shows how desperate these two criminals are. We won't give up until Josh Channing is safely home ... at the home."

After the stumble, Culpepper deftly shifted into a campaign stump speech about keeping the state safe, presumably from desperate criminals like Buck and me.

Cloe interrupted Culpepper.

"Walter Ellington and Buck Jamison aren't kidnappers. The media has incorrectly portrayed this incident as an abduction. In spite of what the district attorney asserts, the facts don't support his theories."

Culpepper smirked as the reporter questioned Cloe.

"A witness says Walter Ellington, your client and father, broke into Sunrise Assisted Living Center. Assisted by Buck Jamison, they set off an alarm and left with the victim, Josh Channing."

Cloe maintained her composure.

"There is no victim. My father and Mr. Jamison have been friends with Josh Channing since high school. They became concerned over Josh's long-term mental health, so they took him away for a simple weekend getaway."

"They're not going to *get away* with it."

Culpepper appeared pleased by his feeble attempt at humor.

The reporter faced the camera.

"Cloe Ellington paints a far different story about Josh Channing's disappearance. We'll be right back." The picture dissolved into a commercial.

The teenage counter girl turned to the cook.

"They didn't kidnap him at all."

Sweat dripped down the center of my back as I pictured a SWAT team bursting through the door. I led Lincoln outside. "Don't say anything about the media attention until I have a chance to break the news to Buck."

Lady, off the leash, wandered along the pond's grassy bank. Her nose shot into the air and she sprinted toward me. She sniffed the paper sacks and trotted beside Lincoln and me.

I took out Lady's burger and fed her as we walked.

At the picnic table, Lincoln sat next to Josh and handed him a hamburger and fries then bit into his own.

Buck ignored the greasy diner food and studied my face. "Something wrong?"

I took a bite from my burger, but no longer felt hungry.

"The media's running with the story."

"We're a fucking story?"

"We might not make it, Buck."

His face softened. He nodded toward Josh's broad grin as he fed a French fry to Lady. "Man, we've already made it." He held up his palm. "*C'est la vie* said the old folks ..."

I couldn't help but smile. I slapped Buck's palm. "Goes to show you never can tell."

"Man, you old dudes are crazy."

Lincoln finished his burger and gave his fries to Josh.

"I gotta hit the road."

"What?" Buck asked.

"You've got enough problems." Lincoln grabbed his backpack and the map from the van. He spread out the map and drew the best route to Bethel in pen then wished us luck.

Josh looked confused as Lincoln slipped into his backpack. "Why you leaving?"

"I've got to, my man." Lincoln hugged Josh then walked around the table and gave Buck and me man hugs. "You dudes take care of my friend Josh."

I asked Josh to wait with Lady. Buck and I walked Lincoln down the gravel drive toward the park turnoff. We reached the road and shook hands.

"You dudes did the right thing for Josh. I hope you make it."

Lincoln hitched up his backpack and walked down the road. He held up his thumb as a pickup approached.

Buck smiled at me as we headed toward the van.

"We'll see him again."

"What makes you say that?"

Buck slapped me on the shoulder.

"A child of God."

I didn't think he was a child of God, but we were a hundred miles from Bethel. We wouldn't have made it this far if we hadn't given Lincoln a lift. It was painful to admit what I felt.

"Buck, we'll never make it to Bethel."

He gave a halfhearted shrug.

"I know."

We returned to our spot in the park. Josh sat at the edge of the pond beside Lady. He gazed into the reflection of the afternoon sun on the calm water.

I stopped beside the van.

"You did a nice job with the psychedelics."

"Have you decided what color you want me to paint her when we get back?"

"I like it just the way it is." Emily would, too.

Buck pulled a joint from his pocket and lit the cigarette. He took a hit and handed it to me.

"I bet Cloe can still work something out with Culpepper."

"Want me to call her?"

Buck shrugged.

"It's your call."

I took a hit and handed the joint back. We shared the joint in silence, but when we finished, I didn't feel any better about giving up our quest so close to our destination.

We approached the picnic table as Josh wiped his face with the back of one hand. He held the photo of his dog and gazed at me through teary eyes.

"Buttons is dead, isn't she?"

A knot constricted my throat. I exchanged a look with Buck then nodded.

"Why do dogs have to die, Sparky?" Josh's eyes glistened. "Is she in heaven?"

"Yes, Josh. Buttons is in heaven."

"I miss her." He petted Lady, who licked his hand. "I never sang a song when she died."

"A song?"

Josh's forehead wrinkled as he searched his memory.

"After someone dies, people get together with friends and sing songs, don't they?"

"A funeral. Yes, people sing at funerals."

"I went to a funeral once. A man's picture was on a table up front. My mom cried."

Buck and I attended as well. I cursed the terrible disease that robbed Josh of precious moments and made him retain painful memories of his father's funeral.

"I don't remember a funeral for Buttons." Josh's voice caught. He cleared his throat.

"Could we have a funeral now? I have a picture of Buttons and two friends with me. I know a funeral song."

"Of course we can."

Buck's eyes shimmered. He slumped down at the end of the picnic table and buried his head in both hands.

Josh climbed to his feet and propped the picture of Buttons against Emily's urn. He sat across from Buck and began a song Arlo Guthrie sang on Day One of Woodstock, a perfect funeral song. *"Amazing grace, how sweet the sound, that saved a wretch like me. I once was lost, but now I'm found, was blind, but now I see."*

A chill swept over me as I considered what the lyrics meant about Josh and the roadtrip's effects on him. I couldn't give up now.

By the time the song ended, Buck wiped away tears with a diner napkin.

"Buck, I can't give up, not now, not when we're so close."

If I'd learned anything in my sixty years, standing up for one's beliefs, regardless of the consequences, wasn't limited to young people.

"I'll call Cloe if you'd like to turn yourself in."

"Now you're insulting me. I'm coming with you."

We tossed the remnants of our meal into the trash can beside the table and headed for the van. I grabbed Emily's urn and held out my hand for the keys.

"Let me drive. You're tired."

"Maybe I am, but with all the publicity, you need me to drive more than ever." Buck slid behind the wheel.

I considered arguing, but Buck was right. I secured the urn in the front seat and helped Josh and Lady into the back.

Josh stared out the window with a dejected look, still thinking of Buttons, no doubt.

Lady rested her nose on Josh's leg. He petted her head.

"You're a good dog."

I settled into my seat behind Buck and closed the side door.

Buck turned on the police scanner. We left the park, pulled onto the dirt road and headed north. It would be dark by the time we reached Bethel. If we reached Bethel.

Since Josh still looked depressed, I grabbed my guitar.

"How about some music?"

He shook his head and stared at his hands.

"I miss Buttons. I miss my mom, too."

Buck slapped the steering wheel.

"You gotta be joking."

Maybe Josh didn't miss the controlling, judgmental person his mother had become. Perhaps he missed the mother she used to be before the death of his father.

"Would you like to call her?"

Buck glanced over his shoulder at me.

"You should put the kibosh on that idea. You shouldn't use your phone. Besides, he might say something that would give us away."

"We have to take the chance. Right now, Josh needs his mother."

Buck ran a hand over his face.

"You're right."

The woman lived in the same house, so I hoped she kept the

same phone number. I dialed the number I remembered growing up. When the familiar shrill voice came on the line, I handed Josh my cell phone.

"Hi, Mom ... Me, Josh." He smiled. "Good ... yes ... We're on a roadtrip ..." Josh continued to stroke Lady. "Mom, where's Buttons? Sparky said she's in heaven." As he listened, his eyes widened, and a smile spread across his face.

Josh set the phone on his lap and grinned.

"Buttons is in the backyard. She's under a tree. She isn't dead."

Josh listened to his mother then looked at me again.

"Where are we? Oh yeah, now I remember. We're in Florida."

Buck chuckled.

"Nice one, Josh."

Joy faded from Josh's face. His forehead narrowed.

"Don't call me Joshua. My name is Josh. No, Mom." His jaw tightened. "I think I should go now." He handed me the phone, and I terminated the call.

Josh stared at his clenched fists.

"Sometimes she makes me so mad."

I gently shook his arm until he looked me in the eyes.

"Listen to me. Your mom loves you. Maybe she loves you a bit too much, but she loves you nonetheless. Understand?"

"I guess."

Josh pulled the picture of Buttons from his pocket, and smiled. In his mind, Buttons wasn't dead. She was in a backyard he vaguely remembered, asleep beneath an oak tree we helped his father plant when the three of us were just boys.

Happy again, Josh gazed out the window as late afternoon shadows fell over the tree-lined road.

"Where are we going now?"

As the police scanner chattered, Buck met my gaze in the rearview mirror.

"Back to the garden, my friend. Back to the garden."

17

Evening shadows covered the lightly traveled back roads of upstate New York farmland. Buck followed the directions Lincoln drew on the map. He seemed to sense patrol cars before they appeared.

I sat behind Buck with growing optimism. I flashed him a thumbs-up as we passed a sign that read "50 miles to Bethel." Against all the odds, we might be able to make it before the cops closed in.

Josh and Lady stared out the window at the picturesque red barns and green fields of corn while Buck kept turning the dial on the scanner, listening to the various law enforcement channels. The device didn't help us evade detection as much as his military training and instincts, and as dusk fell, his ability to navigate without headlights.

With the scanner adding little information, Buck lowered the volume and turned on the radio. "Maybe the news has forgotten about us."

He found a news talk station fielding questions about the disappearance of Josh Channing. No surprise to me, talk radio latched onto the story exploiting the issue of gray rights. The host, with all of life's answers summarized in sound bites, ranted to each caller. Buck and I should be sent to prison, waterboarded or both. To the host's irritation, most of the callers sympathized with us.

The next caller sounded disturbingly familiar. "I hitched a ride with these dudes today. You've got them all wrong. They're alright."

"Shit, it's Lincoln." Buck turned up the volume.

Skepticism dripped from the host's voice. "I bet you were also the second shooter on the grassy knoll."

Lincoln described our van inside and out then detailed the three of us until the host became convinced. "I know where they're headed and why."

"No!" Buck smacked the dash with his hand.

"They're headed to Bethel. They're going to the site where Woodstock was held to spread the ashes of Sparky's wife."

"Holy shit. Bethel will be crawling with cops when we get there." Buck snapped off the radio. He rounded a bend on the gravel road, drove a hundred yards and came to a stop with the engine idling.

"Just one more obstacle, Buck. Lincoln meant well."

"Forget that." He nodded to a cluster of trees half-a-football-field-distance away. "There."

I squinted but saw nothing to merit concern.

Buck put the van in reverse and backed up.

Beneath the clump of trees, headlights blinked on a vehicle I hadn't seen. A patrol car? How had Buck spotted the car?

Buck cranked the steering wheel. He made a tight turn and kicked up gravel. We sped away in the darkness.

In the side mirror, the patrol car raced in pursuit, lights flashing.

"Buck, you'll never outrun them."

"Hold on, everyone." Buck sped up as we approached the turn. He ignored the turnoff and plowed straight ahead.

I held onto the passenger seat in front of me. The van drove off the road and slammed into rows of corn. The van bounced and bucked through the cornfield. We were doing forty! Cornstalks lashed the windshield and scraped the sides of the van like fingernails on a chalkboard. In the backseat, Lady and Josh looked as scared as I felt.

Buck weaved through the cornfield, smacked a row of corn and nearly came to a stop. He gunned the accelerator and plowed on.

I hoped Buck knew what he was doing. I stared out the windshield as leaves and ears of corn slapped against the front bumper.

"Do you know where you're going?"

"To the other side."

"Think the cops followed?"

His face wrinkled.

"Want me to stop and check?"

Lady barked as a tall figure appeared in front of us. Before I could shout a warning, the van slammed into the man. He hit the windshield with a loud crack of glass. He tumbled and bounced over the van.

"Shit." Buck slammed on the brakes. The van fishtailed through the corn. We skidded to a stop.

"What happened?"

"You hit something." *Someone.*

Buck tried to open the driver's door. He shoved with his shoulder, but the cornstalks kept the door closed.

My heart thumped in my chest. I slid the side door open and dashed from the van in search of the person we hit. Buck climbed out and hurried to the back of the van while I searched through the corn.

Lady leaped from the van, a golden blur. She sprinted past Buck.

"Lady!" Buck worked his way through the corn behind the van.

Before going after Lady, I made my way to the front of the van and inspected the three-foot crack in the windshield. A patch of red flannel stuck to the windshield wiper. I swatted specks of circling gnats and hurried to the open side door.

"You okay?" I asked Josh.

He nodded.

"Your dog ran away."

"I'll find her."

A crackle of dried leaves came from behind the van. Buck stepped out, his face a twist of agony. In his arms was a body in a red flannel shirt and jeans. Oh my God. Where were the head ... and feet?

Buck leaned against the van and dropped the body.

Lady bounded from behind the van carrying something in her mouth. She dropped the head at Buck's feet and wagged her tail.

"No!" Buck slumped to the ground beside the rear bumper.

I looked closer at the head Lady dropped. What the hell? A white pillowcase covered the head. No, the head *was* a white pillowcase. Someone drew big eyes and a snarling mouth with a marker and stuffed the head with straw. Straw stuck out the bottom of the jeans where the feet should be. I bent over, unable to hold back nervous laughter.

"You killed a scarecrow."

Buck wasn't laughing. Arms clutched across his chest and sweat slid down his face.

"I decapitated him, man."

I grabbed the scarecrow and tossed it over the row of corn.

"No you didn't." I climbed inside the van, reached over the front seat and turned on the headlights. With the area around us partially illuminated, I hurried back.

Buck didn't look any better.

"We can't go on. The gooks will be waiting for us."

Gooks? The cocky confidence Buck displayed the past few days was gone. His face showed the same tortured expression he had in Buck's Garage when he explained why he hadn't attended Emily's funeral. He looked worse this time. Far worse.

I had no idea how to talk him through this. I almost wished the cops would find us and help, but there was no one, only me.

"There are no gooks, Buck."

Wild-eyed, he gripped my wrist and squeezed.

"I didn't say gooks. I said cops. The cops will be waiting for us in Bethel. Lincoln gave away our position. It's all over, Sergeant."

Lady whined as I knelt beside Buck.

"Remember the freak-out tent at Woodstock?"

Sweat dripped down his face.

"Yeah. I was at Woodstock. The guys don't believe me." He pushed me away, balled his hands into fists and clamped his eyes shut.

"The head. The head."

"It's made of straw." I looked around but couldn't find the scarecrow's head. "Buck, the freak-out tent. The feelings you had were temporary. The effects faded away. This, too, will pass."

Buck pointed to the row of corn and shrieked, "They're out there. We're surrounded. We're gonna die!"

I struggled to remain composed. "We're in New York, Buck. We're on our way to Woodstock."

He blinked several times then seemed to notice me for the first time. "Woodstock. Freak-out tent. Breathe."

"That's right. Take deep breaths."

Buck sucked in a ragged gulp of air. His voice broke.

"Sparky. I can't do this. The head ... the head."

"I'll be right back."

I squeezed his hand and hurried to the open door of the van.

"You okay, Josh?" I grabbed a roll of paper towels from the supply box and a bottle of water from the cooler.

"I'm okay, Sparky." I didn't have time to celebrate Josh

remembering my name.

Buck's head snapped toward me as I returned. "Sergeant?"

I gave Lady the silent command she responded to with the patrolwoman at the gas station. This time she ignored the command and crawled beneath the van. "Lady."

I hoped Buck could get through this. I knelt beside him and blotted his damp forehead with the paper towels. I unscrewed the cap and gave him the bottle.

Lady crawled from beneath the van and dropped the scarecrow's head beside Buck.

"No!" Buck shrieked and clamped his eyes shut.

Lady licked Buck's hand and wagged her tail. She gazed into his troubled face then lay down with her head in his lap.

"Check this out." I pulled straw from the head and placed a handful in Buck's hand.

Buck's eyes opened. He crumpled the straw and stared at the pillowcase head.

"A scarecrow?"

"That's right."

His troubled expression softened as Buck focused on Lady. His hands trembled as he petted her. His breathing gradually grew close to normal. He spoke to Lady in a whisper.

"It's a fucking scarecrow."

Buck gulped half the bottle. He drank the rest and stared over my shoulder.

Josh stood beside the open door. He bit his lip.

"You okay?"

Buck nodded.

"I'll take care of you." Josh ripped off a paper towel and blotted Buck's face. "A nurse did this for me once. It helped."

Buck managed a smile. He threw both arms around Josh and gave him a warm hug.

Convinced the worst was over, I leaned against the side of the van. I closed my eyes and choked back a sob.

I was responsible for Buck's meltdown. Concerned only with my own troubles, I took an Alzheimer's patient from a specialized care facility and placed a troubled Vietnam vet with horrific war experiences in nerve-racking situations that nearly broke him.

Buck held up a hand, and Josh and I helped him to his feet. Buck, far from recuperated, braced himself against the side of the van.

"You probably guessed this has happened before. You don't know what it's like to be haunted by the past."

Lately I did, but my dreams about Woodstock brought a mix of joy and loss. Buck's were filled with unimaginable horror.

His troubled eyes bored through me.

"The ambush happened on a quiet night like this."

"You don't have to tell me."

"Actually, I do." He pointed to Lady. "Hey, Josh. Take Lady back to the van. Be there in a second."

While Josh and Lady climbed in the van, Buck, in a near whisper, described the ambush of his patrol near Da Nang. The Viet Cong hid in elephant grass the height of the corn. A mortar round knocked half the unit off their feet. Buck was one of the lucky ones. He suffered a shrapnel wound to his knee. His sergeant's head rolled against Buck's leg, spewing blood. Buck survived the attack, but the image of his sergeant's severed head never left.

Buck shivered. "I've only told one other person what happened that night, a shrink. He wasn't much help."

If an Army psychiatrist couldn't help, what good could I do? Buck couldn't take any more pressure. I couldn't imagine how he'd react if the cops arrested us for kidnapping.

"We should turn ourselves in."

"Hell, no!" He grabbed me by the shirt and slammed me against the side of the van. "You chicken shit. We can't end this now."

Buck smacked the van and left a fist-sized dent.

"The odds were stacked against a couple of fuckups like us from the beginning." He lowered his voice. "If we don't try to help Josh enjoy the last part of his life, then we might as well spend the rest of our time on earth sitting on a porch somewhere, letting the world pass us by instead of grabbing life by the balls and holding on for all it's worth."

Buck's anger was oddly reassuring, certainly preferable to the near catatonic state minutes earlier. We both wanted to see this through. Though we'd be arrested in Bethel if we made it that far, neither of us wanted to just give up. "Let's do this."

"I'm with you." With a sheepish smile, he pointed to the dent he'd left. "I can fix that."

"I know you can."

"The keys are in the ignition. I think you'd better drive."

Good idea.

"One more thing." Buck appeared to struggle to find the right words. "Thanks for talking me through my ... panic attack." His voice quivered. "More important, for getting back in touch after all these years, inviting me on this trip and giving me the honor of being there when you ..." He cleared his throat. "When you say goodbye to Emily."

Through misty eyes, I gave Buck another hug.

He turned and kicked the scarecrow's head like it was a soccer ball. "Fuckin' scarecrow." He climbed in through the side door.

I walked around the van and pushed through a row of corn. I pried the door open and pulled myself onto the driver's seat. I glanced at Emily's urn in the seat beside me. She'd have been proud we made it this far and happy the three of us had become friends again.

I adjusted the seat and both side mirrors. I tweaked the rearview mirror.

Behind the front passenger seat, Buck groaned.

"You're not taking a driving test. Let's go."

I clenched the steering wheel when a siren sounded in the distance.

"Relax, man." Buck shook my shoulder. "They're headed in the other direction."

"How can you tell?"

He shrugged and glanced at Josh.

"Keep an eye out for *the Man*."

Josh peered out the window.

"What man?"

"Police man." Buck smiled.

I drove through the cornfield far slower than Buck had. Eventually we emerged into an eight-foot wide break between fields. I mentally flipped a coin, turned right and headed down the dirt path. A moment later, we reached a grassy clearing. A small farmhouse sat with a light on inside. I shut off the van's headlights.

"There." Buck pointed to a dirt road that led from the farmhouse.

A quarter-mile later, I pulled the van to the side of the road.

"Any idea where we are?"

Buck grabbed a flashlight from the supply box. His hand shook as he studied the map.

"If there's a fork a click ahead—"

"A click. I'm supposed to know what a click is."

Buck smiled.

"A thousand meters. Take the left one."

I inched the van forward, trying to stay on the road. I held no aspirations I could elude cops as well as Buck had. Even if we reached Bethel, cops from several jurisdictions would be waiting.

Buck grabbed a Coke from the cooler and handed the can to Josh.

"Here, cokehead."

Josh popped the top.

"Thanks."

Buck grabbed another and held the cold can against his forehead.

"I could use a beer."

"You gave our only six-pack away, remember? Besides, you shouldn't drink."

"It's just beer. There's more alcohol in cough syrup."

"But you don't drink twelve ounces of cough syrup at one time."

"Not anymore." Buck set the map between the two front seats. "Too bad we don't know anyone in Bethel who could hide us out 'til morning."

"Crystal."

"You're toying with my emotions. She still lives in Bethel?"

"Did last time I saw her, two years ago."

"At this speed, she probably won't be alive by the time we get there."

I ignored the rebuke.

"She owns a bar at the north edge of town. She bought The Old Schoolhouse from her parents and renamed the place Crystal's. Unfortunately, we'll enter from the south, but if we can reach the bar, I'm sure she'll hide us out."

Actually, I doubted Crystal would want to offer refuge to anyone wanted by the cops, but she might be our only option.

Buck spotted the fork in the road. While he navigated, I managed to stick to Lincoln's directions and avoid all but the smallest towns. For the next two hours, we didn't spot a single patrol car, but as we drew closer to Bethel, the scanner chirped with activity.

We finally reached a "Welcome to Bethel" sign. I felt a sense of accomplishment and a sense of dread.

The town didn't look like what I expected or remembered. Cars filled the streets and noisy revelers appeared to celebrate some kind of festival. Less than five thousand people lived in the quiet town, but that many seemed to be walking along the sidewalks going in and out of shops.

Our van crawled through the heavy traffic. I couldn't help but notice several vans and cars with psychedelic paint jobs. Half the people in town wore tie-dyed clothes.

"Any idea what the hell's up?"

"Check it out." Buck pointed down the street.

Ahead, a state patrol car with red and blue flashing lights had pulled over a psychedelic VW bus, vintage sixties. The officer parked in front of the VW, climbed out and approached the longhaired driver.

"They're looking for us." I gripped the wheel when we neared the officer and fought to control my rising panic.

As we passed the officer, he noticed our paint job and shouted.

"Stop this vehicle." He lunged for our door handle.

I stomped down on the accelerator. The van swerved around the line of cars ahead and missed the patrol car by inches.

Buck laughed.

"If I'd used thicker paint, you would have hit it."

I checked the passenger side mirror. The cop who ordered me to stop climbed into his patrol car, but at least a dozen people blocked him from pursuing us for the moment.

We faced a stalled line of cars half a block long. I glanced back at the officer and didn't hesitate. I drove onto the sidewalk and smashed into a trash can, crunching the metal like a cheap beer can. Vegetables and garbage flew into the air, but I kept going. A drink container landed on our hood and brown soda splattered the windshield.

"Wahoo," Buck shouted. "That's what I'm talking about!"

Soda slid across the cracked windshield. I turned on the wipers, pushed the washer fluid button, but only managed to smear the brown liquid over the glass. I could barely see out.

Ahead, Starbucks customers at outdoor tables scattered like chickens in a storm. I spotted a gap in traffic and bounced off the sidewalk into slow-moving traffic.

"Hold on." My adrenaline surged as I smashed down on the accelerator again. Tires squealed as we turned the corner. We fishtailed into oncoming traffic and raced head on toward a Hummer.

I fought for control and jerked the steering wheel. The van

swerved into the right lane. I took quick glances both ways and blew past a stop sign. We narrowly missed an SUV blasting its horn.

A block later, I pulled into a residential street. We skidded to a stop in the middle of the road. I let the engine idle and caught my breath. Blood pounded in my temples, but to my surprise—no chest pain.

In the back of the van, Lady stood and panted. A broad grin covered Josh's face.

Buck snorted with laughter.

"That was the best, my friend. I think you added unlawful flight, resisting arrest, endangerment and reckless driving to the charges you face. You'll do more jail time than me!" He high-fived me.

My improvised flight apparently helped Buck regain his normal brashness.

I pressed the windshield washer and the wipers cleared my view. The cops would have already radioed our position. We had minutes.

I grinned at Buck.

"You forgot speeding." I smashed down on the accelerator. Two blocks later, doing sixty, we approached our destination, Crystal's.

"Hold on." I turned and squealed the tires. The van scraped bottom as we bounced into the parking lot.

Cars jammed the lot, but I made my own space, skidding to a stop behind a dumpster at the backdoor of the bar. I let out a deep breath, shut off the engine and pried my fingers from the steering wheel.

"That was fun," Josh called from the back.

Buck slid open the side door and hopped out.

"We made it."

"To Bethel."

We'd outsmarted Henry Culpepper and eluded police in two states, but we still had a ways to go to accomplish what we came for.

I climbed from the van and loosened a bulb above the rear door of the bar, darkening the area around the vehicle.

Buck chuckled.

"Nicely done, Mr. Bond."

"Next time, you drive."

Josh climbed from the van holding Lady's leash and his picture of Buttons in his other hand.

I unbuckled Emily's urn. For the first time all day, reality hit. We just might make it to the site and scatter her ashes in the morning.

Maybe in my heart, I wanted the cops to stop us so I wouldn't have to do this frightful thing. Letting go wasn't as simple as I thought.

Buck frowned.

"You coming?"

I nodded and carried the urn to the front door.

More than the name had changed. Noisy and crowded, the bar retained the country-western theme, but the poolroom was now a dance floor with a stage and sound system for live music.

The bar, like the entire town, was busier than I expected for a small town on Saturday night. Half the crowd appeared to be in their early twenties. The rest were closer to our age, most dressed in sixties chic.

We made our way through the boisterous beer-guzzling crowd. To my relief, no one paid any attention to us, the urn or Lady.

"Sparky!"

Crystal stood behind the bar, waving. Like most people our age, she'd gained a few pounds over the years, but that only added more curves. She kept her attention-grabbing smile and glistening shoulder-length blonde hair.

In a low-cut peasant blouse, she fought her way through the crowd and threw both arms around me.

"I can't believe you made it."

I hugged her back.

"Your story's all over the news."

Crystal bent down and petted Lady, who acted nervous by all the noise. "You must be Lady. If you could talk, I bet you'd tell quite a story."

She sized Buck up with a smile of approval.

"Hi, Buck."

"Crystal, you're prettier than a cherry snow cone on a hot summer's day."

"You sweet talking man."

Buck admired her cleavage then surprised me when he gazed into her eyes and planted a lingering kiss on her lips.

Crystal's face flushed after the kiss. She smiled at Josh. Her brassy attitude mellowed.

"Hello, Josh." She kissed him on the cheek. "I'm Crystal."

"Nice to meet you, Crystal."

"I have to show you something." Crystal took my arm and led us through the crowd.

Behind the stage hung dozens of band posters, groups that had played Crystal's over the years. She pointed to a freshly printed psychedelic poster in the dead center that read "Buck Naked Band, Sparky Ellington, Josh Channing and Buck Jamison."

On the adjacent wall, a glossy blue banner ran the length of the room. *Go, Sparky, Go!*

Two aging hippies, Woodstock Nation members like Buck and me, approached the banner. One took out a pen and signed his name. He handed the pen to his friend, who signed just below then faced the crowd. He raised a fist and shouted, "Solidarity!"

I looked closer. Hundreds had signed the banner. I was speechless. The crowds in town came because of us?

"I don't know what to say."

"Sparky at a loss for words? Mark down the date and time for posterity." Buck clapped me on the back.

Crystal took my hand.

"Thousands of people descended on Bethel to cheer you on. Since everyone heard on the radio you were headed this way and why, people poured into town. They want to see you make it. It's like your quest to accomplish something important, something relevant became theirs ... ours."

I couldn't believe our roadtrip garnered all this attention. Lincoln gave away our destination, but instead of cops waiting to arrest us, a few thousand former freaks—that looked like the three of us— packed the town and complicated the police search.

"Thanks, Lincoln."

"Who's Lincoln?" Crystal asked.

Buck smiled.

"A child of God."

We made it this far, but if the cops spotted Emily's van, our luck wouldn't hold.

"I parked by the backdoor."

"People have been talking about your psychedelic van." Crystal sized Buck up again. "I bet you were responsible."

"I'm not just a mechanic, I'm an artist."

Crystal smirked.

"Don't remember you being that talented."

"You'd better jog your memory." Buck grinned. "I've still got plenty of talent in me."

The sexual tension between the two was obvious, even to Josh, who smiled at Buck.

Crystal waved toward the end of the bar.

"I'll have my brother take care of the van. Darrell!"

Her brother climbed off a barstool. The bully was now a balding overweight barfly, but he still appeared as if he could snap a man half his age in two.

Darrell, with his well-fed belly, greeted me like I was a kid brother returning from war.

"Sparky Ellington. It's great to see you again." He thrust out his chin. "Go ahead, give me a sock in the jaw, I deserve it."

"I'll do it." Buck gave him a fake punch to the face. "Sparky told me about you."

Darrell pointed one finger at his temple and cocked his thumb.

"I was a tool in those days."

"Weren't we all?" I gave him the van keys. "I parked a psychedelic Dodge Caravan by your backdoor. Don't want too many people to notice."

"Say no more. Got a tarp in the storeroom should keep her from prying eyes."

He made his way through the crowd and disappeared into the kitchen.

Two state patrol officers came in the front door. They showed flyers to people who appeared mostly disinterested.

"This way." Crystal led us into the kitchen. Lady sniffed food scraps and crumpled paper towels that littered the tile floor. We dodged busy waitresses carrying food to customers on copper platters. A harried-looking cook paid us no attention as he flipped burgers and grilled onions. My stomach rumbled from the hot food smells.

Crystal filled a bowl with water from a deep stainless steel sink. She carried the bowl toward an office by the backdoor.

Buck lowered his voice.

"I've got dibs on Crystal."

We entered the cramped office, and Crystal closed the door. An Army blanket covered a small couch that sagged in the middle. Forms, invoices and empty paper cups covered a metal desk.

"Forgive the mess." Crystal set the bowl on the floor, and Lady lapped up the water. She finished her drink and jumped on the couch. Josh sat beside her.

Crystal slipped into a chair behind the desk. She glanced at the urn, grabbed a tissue from a drawer and dabbed teary eyes.

"Emily Baker Ellington, the kindest person I ever knew. Can I hold her a minute?"

I handed her the urn.

Crystal cradled Emily's urn in her arm and closed her eyes. For a moment, she appeared lost with memories of Emily. She opened her eyes, set the urn on the desk and blew her nose.

"Can I go with you when you scatter her ashes?"

"Of course."

Crystal dropped the tissue into a trash can behind her, blinked her eyes and regained her composure.

"You boys want to tell me how you became America's most wanted?"

I skipped the part about the fight at The Library and my heart condition. I began with our visit to Josh at Sunrise and the discovery of his ability to recall Woodstock song lyrics.

Buck told most of the story of our roadtrip. With his usual drama and theatrics, he kept Crystal laughing. She was still a hot-looking woman, and Buck noticed.

He ended by telling how I eluded the state police with my Bond-like driving skills.

"Sparky thought you might hide us out until morning when we leave to scatter Emily's ashes."

"You bet. We have plenty of food. There's this couch and a couple of cots in a storage room down the hall. A lot better accommodations than at Yasgur's farm, right? In the morning, we'll take my SUV. The cops will never know."

It looked like we might actually pull this off. I glanced at the urn with more than a little regret.

"I don't know how to thank you."

"I have an idea. Josh really remembers every song sung at Woodstock?"

"Every one we've played so far."

"I know lots of songs." Josh smiled proudly.

"You still play?" Crystal asked me.

"Guitar's in the van."

Crystal came from behind the desk and grabbed my hands.

"I'd be honored if the three of you would play some of the old songs for the crowd. They'd go wild."

The last thing I wanted, with the cops going door to door with flyers, was to draw attention to ourselves.

"We can't risk the attention."

"Darrell and some of his lowlife friends can act as lookouts. If a cop so much as gets within a block of the place, we'll hustle you off the stage and out of sight."

Buck rubbed both hands together.

"Come on, Sparky. What's a roadtrip for a garage band without a gig?"

"Buck ..."

"Let's ask Josh."

We all looked toward the couch. Singing with friends in a van, or in front of a couple dozen people in a nursing home, was one thing, but if we went through with this crazy idea, we'd be on stage in front of hundreds—something we'd never done, even in high school.

Josh cocked his head.

"What?"

I sat beside him.

"You, Buck and I used to be in a rock band in high school."

Josh's eyes widened.

"Were we good?"

"I think so."

Buck smacked me on the back of the head.

"We were damn good!"

"Crystal has invited us to sing on stage later. There will be lots of people."

"Lots?" Josh wrinkled his forehead and petted Lady as if asking her for advice. Then he smiled.

"Whatever you decide is okay with me, Sparky."

I was indebted to Crystal. She offered to hide us out and drive us to the site to scatter Emily's ashes, but all we had to do was stay put until morning. I ran both hands through my hair in frustration.

"It's not worth the risk," I said.

The room grew quiet. Buck let out a sigh.

"You're right." He seemed willing to give up an opportunity we thought had passed us by forty years ago.

Crystal nodded.

"It was selfish of me to ask. What was I thinking?"

I looked at Emily's urn and wondered what she'd think.

"Guess a couple of songs wouldn't hurt."

Buck whooped with delight.

"Now that's what I'm talking about."

He hugged Crystal and kept one arm around her waist.

She took his hand and pulled his arm tightly around her.

"Don't start something you can't finish."

Buck grinned.

"I've always been known as a good finisher."

Crystal bellowed with laughter then stared at Buck. Their eyes revealed something I never expected, feelings that went beyond mere flirtation. The emotions went back years ago to that first day at Woodstock.

Buck looked at Crystal differently than he did Ashley or the other younger women I'd known him to hook up with. He gazed at her like ... like I used to look at Emily.

Holding Buck's hand, Crystal flung open the door to her office. She shouted over the din of waitresses barking out orders and food sizzling.

"Ladies and gentlemen, by popular demand, tonight and tonight only, the final performance of ... The Buck Naked Band!"

18

The breathless anticipation of performing in front of so many people kept me from worrying about cops and feds who wanted to throw Buck and me in jail for kidnapping. I had an even bigger concern than jail. In the morning, I'd say goodbye to Emily.

We sat on a weathered picnic table in the rear of the kitchen—the bar's employee lounge. Crystal prepared a plate of heart healthy sandwiches for Buck and me and burgers for Josh and Lady.

While we ate, Buck and I decided we could manage no more than three songs. The three of us discussed what to include in our playlist. We settled on *Coming into Los Angeles* and *Going up the Country*, the first where Josh displayed his amazing Woodstock memory.

Buck insisted we needed an encore song. Though I doubted the crowd would demand one, we agreed on Credence's *Green River*. Now we needed to rehearse.

Crystal retrieved my guitar and Heather's flute from the van. Two hours wouldn't be enough to shake off four decades of rust, but we had to try. I didn't want us to embarrass ourselves or the artists whose songs we'd perform.

She introduced us to the lead guitarist of her regular Saturday night band, Commotion. Perhaps the gray in our hair made the early-twenties rocker take pity on us. He offered to loan me an electric guitar and back us up on keyboard. We needed all the help we could get.

I hadn't played electric in years, but Buck tried to reassure me by comparing it to riding a bike or sex, two interests I'd taken to with little training. The Commotion guitarist showed me his Fender electric, and I grew comfortable with the instrument in minutes.

With an extra pair of drumsticks from Commotion, we retreated to Crystal's office to rehearse. Buck grabbed a stool from the kitchen and used the desktop as a drum set. He and I both messed up several times as we ran through the three songs. I hoped the mistakes were nerves and not an erosion of our skills. Josh, however, nailed every line, tempo and beat.

Crystal, mostly making eyes at Buck, sat in while we ran through the songs a second time. I checked my watch when we finished. We had an hour before Commotion took a break and we'd perform.

Buck massaged my tense shoulders.

"Relax, man. It's just a gig."

"Relax? We've had forty years between gigs." What were we thinking? I wasn't a rocker. I was an ex-college professor. "Let's run through the set again."

"I think you guys sound terrific." Crystal winked at Buck. "You want to help me check out those cots in the storage room and make sure they're okay to sleep on?"

"There's such a thing as overpracticing."

Buck dropped the sticks on the desk. He took Crystal's hand and followed her out the door. I suspected Crystal was about to become our band's first official groupie since the sixties.

Josh and I rehearsed the songs again. When we finished, Lady lifted her paw. Josh shook her paw and smiled at me.

"Thanks for the roadtrip, Sparky."

I swallowed a lump in my throat. Joy danced in Josh's eyes, so different from the look I first saw in Sunrise. In spite of everything that went wrong on the trip, taking him along was the right thing to do, regardless of the ultimate outcome.

I hugged Josh. "I'm so glad you came with us."

"Break it up you two."

Darrell staggered into the office, carrying a mug of beer and a paper sack. I hoped the beer was for me. Lady sniffed the bag as if it contained dog biscuits. No such luck for either of us.

He drank half the beer in one gulp then picked up the drumsticks.

"Where's Buck?" I hesitated, and he shook his head. "I might have guessed. Crystal's always had a soft heart for stray dogs and hard-luck stories."

Buck might be a hard-luck story, but he'd turned his life around.

"Lady's no stray, and Buck's a terrific guy."

"Didn't mean nothin'. It's just ... Crystal's always helped me whenever I fucked up. Now I look out for her."

Crystal could make her own decisions. After all, she successfully owned and managed a bar. Still, I didn't want to argue with the person who helped conceal Emily's van and would provide security against the cops during our performance.

He turned one of the folding chairs around, set one foot up and guzzled more beer.

"My life didn't turn out like I expected back in high school. I played quarterback and could dunk a basketball. Girls thought I was someone special," he took another swallow, "back then."

I couldn't deny a flicker of sympathy for Darrell.

"I'm on disability because of my back. I've been married three times, have two kids. One's in the slammer, the other's in rehab. Being a fuckup runs in the family."

His voice began to tremble, "And I don't want Crystal to mess up her life."

Giving Buck a tumble didn't seem like the disaster Darrell thought it might be.

He finished his beer and turned the chair around. "Guess I've always been an overprotective big brother." He tossed me the sack. "I thought if you didn't sound good, you might look the part."

I removed three matching bright yellow tie-dyed short-sleeve shirts. "Crystal's" was stenciled in purple on the back.

"Really?"

"It would mean a lot to ... Crystal."

I didn't care for Crystal's brother, or trust him. Mostly though, I felt sorry for the man, bitter that life hadn't turned out the way he planned. Life didn't always turn out the way people hoped, but not everyone became so disillusioned.

"Well, break a leg." Darrell left and didn't close the office door.

The din of kitchen activity didn't keep the buzz of bar patrons from coming through the kitchen door. Holy crap. Could we pull this off?

My hands shook as I closed the office door and tried not to picture how many people would hear us perform. At most, the Milton Faculty Jazz Review played before a few dozen at a time, mostly friends, family and fellow faculty members. I took a deep breath and tried to ignore the task ahead.

Josh and I tried on our shirts as I struggled with the certainty I'd soon make a fool of myself in front of hundreds. As if sensing my concern, Lady nuzzled my hand. I stroked her neck, giving her my undivided attention for the first time since we left Milton. I'd taken her completely for granted.

Lady was a comfort to Emily in her final days and my only companion the past two years. Hours earlier, she knew what Buck needed most when I wasn't sure myself. Most of all, she'd taken to Josh, giving him the comfort and affection he'd lacked in his life for a long time.

I bent down and gave Lady a long overdue hug.

"I'm so glad I brought you along. What would we have done without you, girl?"

Lady licked my face, then gazed at me with her familiar smile.

Buck and Crystal returned to the office, holding hands. I pretended not to notice her tousled hair and flushed face.

With the bushman tilted on his head just right, Buck looked renewed and energized. He appeared as if he could take the stage at the Rock and Roll Hall of Fame and not be nervous. He checked me out and frowned.

"You look awful."

"Nerves."

"No, the shirt."

"A present from Darrell." I tossed him his shirt. "If Josh and are I wearing these, so are you."

He looked away and tightened his jaw. He regained his composure and changed into the shirt. "Bitchin'."

Crystal smoothed the shirt, running her hands tenderly over Buck's chest.

"Darrell's not into fashion, but at least you look like a group."

"Yeah." Buck studied the fabric. "A hippie bowling team."

"They'll love you."

The more she talked about our performance, the queasier I became.

"This place has never been filled like tonight. Capacity is two hundred, but there's twice that."

Buck seemed like he'd have preferred thousands.

"Word must have spread we made it to Bethel. It's almost like we're the Stones or something. I think Commotion is about to take a break. You ready?"

"We have another fifteen minutes."

"This isn't a college schedule, Professor. Welcome to the real world." Buck cocked his head. "You look like you're about to puke."

"I'm about to make an idiot of myself in front of hundreds."

"You're a college professor. I'm sure it's happened before."

I managed to chuckle, but I grew dizzy as a wave of apprehension hit me. I held onto the desk.

"Sparky, it's a bar. People cheer anything. You shouldn't waste time worrying we might fuck up." Buck grabbed his drumsticks.

"But—"

"Enjoy the moment, man, or it'll be over before you know it. It's why we took Josh, right, so he could enjoy moments ... special times ... like this. Same goes for you and me. Now man up. You ready, Josh?"

"Ready for what?"

I fought a fluttery empty feeling in my gut with a deep breath. I patted Lady and wiped sweaty palms on her fur.

"I won't be long, girl." The last time I said those words to her, I ended up in the hospital.

I nearly hyperventilated as we made our way through the boisterous fans that grew more energized as we neared the stage. The enthusiastic reception was for the notoriety we'd gained in our successful flight from *the Man*, not for our musical abilities.

The man who signed the *Go, Sparky, Go* banner and shouted "Solidarity," clapped me on the back. "We're with you, Sparky."

My heart pounded faster, but in a good way. Except for in high school when I still thought anything was possible, I never imagined performing at a concert.

We stepped onto the stage, and the cheers grew louder. The Buck Naked Band poster on the wall gave me a sense we might actually belong on stage. I took my position at one of the mikes and gazed over the half-young, half-geezer audience. People dressed in sixties garb packed the dance floor and spilled into the main bar. If the cops arrived, we'd have plenty of time before they made it through everyone.

The Commotion lead guitarist handed me the electric guitar, retreated to the keyboard and smiled encouragement.

I slipped the Fender over my shoulder with trembling hands and told myself I could do this.

Buck stepped behind me.

"Suck it up, Ellington. It's showtime."

I had to laugh. To my relief, Josh didn't appear intimidated by the number of people or the level of their enthusiasm. Buck sat on a stool behind the drums, shoulders back, chest out and sporting the playful grin of a seasoned performer.

Even with our lame yellow tie-dyed shirts, we could do this. Josh still sang well. Six months ago, I was still a damn good guitar player until Warfield fired me. Buck was an underrated drummer, though I wished he'd rehearsed with us a little longer instead of nailing Crystal.

Buck was right about special moments. On stage in front of so many supporters was truly special. I smiled at Josh then nodded to Buck.

"Enjoy the moment!"

Looking sixties cool in the bushman, Buck spoke into the drummer's mike, "I'm Buck ... Naked."

The crowd hooted and laughed. Buck held the drumsticks over his head and shouted, "We're The Buck Naked Band!"

I flashed a peace symbol then sucked in a deep breath.

Buck rapped the sticks together, "One, two ..."

Josh never missed a beat.

Comin' in from London from over the Pole, flyin' in a big airliner ..." Confident he'd shine, I focused on the guitar, not wanting to miss any chords. Amps magnified the slightest mistake. The Commotion keyboard player made the three of us sound better than I hoped.

I joined in the chorus.

"Don't touch my bags if you please, Mister Customs Man ..."

To my relief, everyone dug our performance. Perhaps we didn't deserve our fifteen minutes of fame, but the music brought back special memories for the people our age, especially charter members of Woodstock Nation.

Josh performed like a seasoned artist. The musical talent he displayed when we were just kids was still evident in spite of the Alzheimer's. He didn't merely know the words. From some recess of his memories, he captured how Woodstock's top acts gave their heart and soul to their performances. The crowd wouldn't believe Alzheimer's robbed most of his long-term memories except Woodstock music.

Sweat flew from Buck's hair with each beat of the drum. He

rocked the drums like he'd practiced for days.

I'd never forget this moment with my two best friends. The day proved something I wouldn't have recognized if we hadn't recreated the roadtrip. Age didn't matter. Every day was full of endless potential, if I just allowed myself to be receptive to life's possibilities. Even without Emily, I now realized life was worth living after all.

The song ended, and the bar erupted with enthusiastic cheers, whistles, even a cowbell. People in front high-fived each other. Darrell stood in front of the kitchen door and flashed a thumbs-up.

I wiped sweat from my brow with the heel of my hand while Josh gazed over the crowd with a blank emotionless stare. I stood beside him and shouted to be heard.

"How you doing?"

Before he answered, a pair of black-lace thong panties landed at his feet.

His brows furrowed.

"Why did someone throw underwear?"

I tossed the thong to Buck.

"Probably a gift for him."

Buck twirled the panties around his finger and shouted, "Thanks, Sparky!"

"You're Sparky?" Josh looked like he'd never seen me before.

A sickening feeling dropped in my gut. Josh's vague expression and the question reminded me, in spite of his singing excellence, that Josh wasn't a rock star. He was just a regular guy who suffered from a dreadful disease.

"Yes, I'm Sparky."

"Nice to meet you, Sparky."

The crowd grew impatient and called for more, but I didn't think we should continue.

Buck shouted, "*Going up the Country!*"

Josh scratched his head.

"We're going to sing?"

"Do you want to?"

Josh gazed over the bar and nodded.

Against my better judgment, I removed the flute from my back pocket. *Enjoy the moment, Josh.* I moved back to my microphone and played the flute.

Josh's eyes cleared, and his head bobbed in time to the music. As usual, Woodstock music transformed him. He came in at just the right moment.

"I'm goin' up the country, baby, don't you wanna go ..."

The cheering almost drowned out his voice. Josh nailed the chorus.

"All this fussin' and fightin' ..." Then his face went blank. For the first time since I discovered his amazing Woodstock ability, Josh didn't remember the words.

I jumped in and finished the verse into my mike, *"... man, you know I sure can't stay."*

No one seemed to notice my part hadn't been planned. I did my best to keep going as Buck and the Commotion keyboard player fed off the crowd's electric vibe.

Josh missed more lines, but no one appeared to notice he forgot words. No one but me.

The song ended, and I hurried to his side.

Everyone hollered for more, but Josh looked confused and upset.

"I ... I couldn't remember."

"That's okay. It's been a long day. I almost forgot, too."

The devastating disease had advanced, as I knew it inevitably would.

Oblivious to Josh's stumble, Buck played to the audience like always. I got his attention and made a slashing motion to my neck. He raised the sticks in a triumphant gesture and joined Josh and me at the front of the stage.

We acknowledged the Commotion member. I stood between Buck and Josh and clasped their hands. For the last time, The Buck Naked Band took a bow.

We climbed off the stage, and Buck set a hand on my shoulder.

"We're coming back for the encore, right?"

"No, encore, Buck."

"I get it. We walk off stage and they cheer for more."

Crystal led us through the jubilant bar. Dozens patted us on the back as the crowd chanted, "Buck Naked ... Buck Naked ..."

Behind the bar, Darrell smiled and opened the kitchen door. Crystal took the thong panties from Buck and dropped them on the floor.

Josh went in the kitchen, followed by Crystal and Buck. Wondering how best to handle Josh's deteriorating condition, I entered the kitchen. A chill shot up my spine.

Four uniformed sheriff's deputies and three men in identical blue suits stood waiting.

Buck acted cooler than anyone in the room. He shot me an expression of regret.

"What a kick in the balls."

Lady barked in the closed office in back. Josh's eyes darted around as if looking for answers.

I tried to help. "Josh, it's okay—"

"Don't talk to him." A lantern-jawed suit half my age flashed his badge. "Mr. Ellington, you're under arrest. You have the right to remain silent ..." He continued to read me my rights.

Buck's head dropped as another suit read him *his* rights.

Crystal cast a suspicious eye at her brother.

"Darrell, what's going on?"

A man in a suit, with the compassion of a sack of rocks, grabbed Josh by the arm.

"Come with me."

"Do I know you?" Josh tried to shake the man's grip. "I don't want to go. I want my picture of Buttons."

"Picture of buttons?" The man led Josh toward the back door. "We'll get you all the buttons you need."

Josh shook off the man's grip but looked lost like he didn't know where to go. He clenched both hands to his face with a look of wide-eyed panic, and I could do nothing about it.

Crystal appealed to one deputy.

"Ricky, how did you get in here?"

The deputy avoided Crystal but glanced at her brother.

She spun and faced Darrell, eyes glaring with disgust. "You double-crossing son-of-a-bitch!"

Darrell held up both hands and backed into the wall beside the kitchen door. "I had to do what's best, Crystal. You wouldn't. They might have pulled your license."

He shot me a cold look of disgust.

"These two losers are wanted for kidnapping."

Losers! I lunged and drove Crystal's bitter fat brother into the wall. The kitchen door frame shattered. I leaned back and slammed my fist into his face. Cartilage cracked. Blood flowed from his nose like thick strawberry jam.

"You the man, Sparky!" Buck shouted as a deputy cuffed and dragged him out the backdoor.

Two deputies wrestled me off Darrell, who cowered against the wall with both arms protecting his head from further assault. The knuckles on my hand throbbed, but the pain was worth it. I broke the bastard's nose. I lunged and tried to throw one more punch, but a deputy swept my feet out from under me.

My face cracked against the floor. Blood gushed from a split lip. I had to stop getting into barroom brawls.

A deputy with a cocky smirk yanked my hands behind my back and cuffed me.

"You're a feisty old bastard."

I worried how the sudden end to the roadtrip would affect Josh's deteriorating condition and Buck's fragile psyche. I spit blood onto the floor.

"I want to speak to my lawyer. Her name is Cloe Ellington."

Lady barked louder than ever as someone stepped inside the kitchen and stood over me. My reflection glistened in the man's spit-shined Italian dress shoes inches from my face.

"Sorry, Professor." The man's voice had a familiar self-righteous quality. "I'm afraid your daughter isn't here, but I am."

Two deputies wrestled me to my feet. I sucked in gulps of air and stared into the face of the last person I wanted to see. I couldn't take my eyes off the triumphant expression and porn star moustache of Pennsylvania District Attorney Henry Culpepper.

19

This was all my fault. I stared at the floorboard in the backseat of a Sullivan County Sheriff's patrol car, consumed by a dull ache of guilt.

Would Buck suffer another meltdown? Would Josh withdraw into a shell? Would the premature end to the roadtrip hasten the progression of his Alzheimer's? Where were Emily's ashes? So many questions.

Two deputies drove me to the police station in Middleton. I barely paid attention as a deputy fingerprinted and booked me. The arrest didn't bother me nearly as much as being separated from my friends. Even worse was witnessing the advance of Josh's Alzheimer's as he struggled to remember all the words to a Woodstock song.

After my mug shot, a deputy let me make a phone call. I flexed my swollen knuckles from the fist that flattened Crystal's brother and called Cloe's cell. I reached her voice mail. Damn!

I left a message about the arrest and the station's phone number. I wasn't the only father who called his daughter from jail. It just felt that way.

A deputy led me down the hall and locked me in an interrogation room. I sat with my head in my hands and tried to imagine something good coming from this. This was it. Our roadtrip ended in failure.

Jail wouldn't be a new experience for Buck, but I'd seen Josh's confusion and panic in Crystal's kitchen. He'd be better off in his dull dreary room at Sunrise with his mother calling all the shots.

The door opened. The detective who read me my rights in Crystal's kitchen came in and smiled.

"Professor Ellington, I'm Nathan Briggs, a detective with the Pennsylvania State Police."

I rubbed a hand over my forehead. I wasn't up to playing an interrogation game.

"Mr. Ellington."

He snatched a recorder from his suit coat pocket and set it on the table.

"At this point in our investigation, we're unclear whether a crime was committed in the disappearance of Josh Channing. If you don't help us piece this together, we'll base our findings on incomplete information. Do you mind if I record this interview?"

I'd always been able to talk myself out of trouble, but Cloe would advise against speaking to a detective without an attorney present.

"As you mentioned before, anything I say can be used against me in a court of law, so let's postpone the interview until I talk to my daughter."

Red-faced, Briggs jammed the recorder into his pocket and scraped the chair back against the cold tile.

"Come with me."

I just wanted to be left alone.

"Mr. Ellington, this will be easier for both of us if you cooperate."

With a halfhearted shrug, I went along as the detective led me down the hall into a dimly lit room. He pointed to one of two chairs that faced a window. I assumed it was a two-way mirror.

"Take a seat."

I accepted the offered chair, and he sat beside me.

On the other side of the two-way mirror, Josh sat in an interrogation room similar to the one I just left. He stared into space with both hands flat on the table. A uniformed Sullivan County Deputy Sheriff stood in the corner while another detective paced the room.

It broke my heart. Josh looked nearly catatonic. Worse than at the nursing home. All the joy and delight he displayed on the roadtrip had vanished, and I was to blame.

"You're interrogating an Alzheimer's patient?"

"We didn't interrogate him. We asked him what happened. You'll want to hear what he told us earlier."

Briggs pressed a buzzer beside the window.

"Okay, Sawyer, ready when you are. Repeat the last few questions you asked him." The detective sat beside me. A confident grin creased his granite jaw.

Sawyer stood beside Josh.

"We'll take you home to your mother in the morning."

Before the Alzheimer's, Josh would have preferred a night in jail.

Josh spoke in a monotone.

"I want to see my friends."

Sawyer glanced toward Briggs and me.

"First, I want to ask you to repeat what you said earlier."

Josh looked confused by the question. "I want to see my friends."

The detective clenched his jaw. "Earlier."

"I want to see my friends ... earlier."

Sawyer smacked the desk then paced the room.

Beside me, Briggs snickered.

The detective pulled up a chair and tried to act like Josh's best friend, but I doubted whether Sawyer had ever dealt with an Alzheimer's patient.

"Let me ask again. How did Mr. Ellington and Mr. Jamison treat you?"

"Who's Mr. Ellington?"

Sawyer took a deep breath. "How did Sparky and Buck treat you?"

"I got this new shirt to wear." Josh tugged on the sleeve of his yellow tie-dyed shirt. "They gave me hamburgers and fries."

"What else did Buck and Sparky feed you?"

"That's all, just hamburgers and fries."

"You cheap, heartless bastards." Briggs spat out the words.

"That's all he wanted," I explained.

Sawyer asked a follow-up question.

"Did they get you to try something you'd never had before?"

Josh nodded. "Coke."

I chuckled, though I knew the transcript of Josh's interview wouldn't reflect any humor.

Briggs's lip curled in disgust.

"Something funny?"

"It was Diet Coke, you moron. He's not talking about drugs."

Briggs didn't believe me, or didn't want to.

Sawyer looked pleased with himself.

"Who gave you coke?"

"Sparky."

"When they gave you coke, what did Mr. Jamison ... Buck call you?"

"A cokehead."

I didn't like where the conversation was headed. The questions weren't funny anymore.

"Tell your colleague to ask if it was Diet Coke."

Briggs held up one hand. "Wait."

Sawyer flashed Briggs and me a smile.

"Josh, in the van, after they gave you coke, did they run out of anything?"

"You'll like this answer." Briggs smiled.

Josh cocked his head, searching his memory.

"They were out of weed."

"Weed?" Sawyer smiled into our room again.

"Diet weed, I suppose." Briggs flashed a malicious grin.

I could explain Josh merely repeated what he heard Buck say to Lincoln, but I wouldn't throw either of them under the bus.

Briggs shook his head.

"Culpepper will love this. You gave cocaine and marijuana to an Alzheimer's patient."

"No, we didn't."

"We found traces of marijuana in the glove compartment. We'll have to wait for lab results on any cocaine. Care to explain?"

I'd had enough of the detectives' manipulation of an Alzheimer's patient to manufacture evidence against me.

"I need to talk to my lawyer."

"Innocent men don't lawyer up." Briggs stepped into the hallway and returned with Ricky, the deputy Crystal spoke to in the kitchen.

"Get this bum out of my sight, Deputy."

Ricky led me down a narrow corridor with gray walls and a cement floor. We stopped outside a noisy cell.

"Crystal asked me to tell you she has your dog, but Culpepper took your wife's urn."

That bastard took Emily's ashes! "Son-of-a-bitch." I banged my fist against the cell door.

"Hey, knock that shit off, old man." A hulking steroid-freak, with a ZZ Top beard and a snake tattoo on his arm, looked to be in charge of a half-dozen unruly inmates.

The deputy removed a key from his belt.

"I wanted to stash you in a holding cell, but they decided making you uncomfortable was a good strategy."

"Thanks for trying, good cop."

"If you get into an altercation in there, I can take you to your own cell."

"So to ensure my safety, all I need to do is pick a fight with one of your Saturday night regulars?"

"You broke Darrell's nose. My dad went to school with that bully. I enjoyed watching you make him bleed."

He unlocked the door, and I stepped inside. Ricky clipped the key to his belt.

"Hey, Snake, watch out for this one. About an hour ago he broke Darrell Thompson's nose."

The door locked behind me with a clank of finality I'd never forget. Green-chipped paint covered the walls. A toilet with no seat sat in one corner. The cement floor had a drain in the center, to facilitate washing away bodily fluids, no doubt. The cell reeked of sweat, vomit and men's desperation.

Snake got in my face. His breath smelled like the back of the patrol car. The men in the cell appeared to enjoy my discomfort.

He grabbed the sleeve of my yellow tie-dyed shirt and sneered. Buck's camouflage shirt might have given me more cell cred.

"I can't believe an old fuck like you broke Darrell's nose."

I offered my swollen fist as proof.

"Only one other person I know has smacked him around ... me."

"My man." I held up one hand, hoping he'd high-five me, but he ignored the gesture.

"My name's Bruno. Friends call me Snake."

Apparently, Bruno hadn't been tough enough sounding.

"My name's Walter. My friends call me Sparky."

Everyone in the cell burst out laughing.

Snake silenced the outburst with a glare.

"Why do people call you Sparky?"

I barely hesitated.

"I burned down my old man's tool shed."

"Arson. That what got you here?"

"Nah. Kidnapping."

"You didn't kidnap no kid, did you?"

I wanted to come across tougher than a retired college professor. I spit on the floor.

"The dude was my age."

"Kidnapping could get you ten to life."

Snake pointed out each person in the cell. "This here's Larceny, that's DUI, Meth, AA—Aggravated Assault, Grand Theft Auto. The guy on the bench is Armed Robbery."

"Nice to meet you fellas, but there's more." I pointed out my swollen lip and bruised knuckle. "Assault, resisting arrest, illegal flight, endangerment, possession and … speeding. Took cops from two states and the FBI to finally get us."

Snake looked impressed. He gave me a good-natured slap on the back that nearly knocked me off my feet.

"You get the prize, Sparky."

I didn't want any jail cell prizes. I'd established a measure of credibility and just wanted to be left alone.

Snake led me to an eight-foot metal bench bolted to the wall. He kicked Armed Robbery in the ass. The man bellowed, rolled off the bench and crawled to the corner. Snake gestured to the bench.

"Your prize."

I couldn't say no. I'd no doubt claim the bench until someone more impressively sinister came in. I'd barely slept in the last twenty-four hours. I lay down and cradled my hands behind my head. I closed my eyes and tried to tune out the noise and smells of my surroundings.

The day stated with a roadtrip I'd never forget and ended with overwhelming despair. The trip had been a stupid idea from a self-indulgent old man who thought he had solutions to everyone else's problems.

Josh and Buck would be better off if I never reconnected with them. I'd be better off with my mantel shrine and bourbon. In spite of my self-pity, I became drowsy. I soon drifted off and dreamed of a much better day than this one.

♪♪♪♪♪

Emily and I returned to Woodstock and picked our way through the crowd illuminated only by the glow of campfires and the blue lights from the stage. We'd never find Josh and Buck until daylight, if then, so we found a spot on the side of the hill and enjoyed the performance of The Who.

As much as I loved the music, the experience wasn't nearly as satisfying as wrapping my arms around Emily again and feeling her against me.

Emily's eyes glistened from the glow of a nearby campfire.

"Even when I was mad at you, you made me feel special knowing you left Woodstock to find me."

"It was Josh's idea."

"Are you serious?" She stiffened and sat upright. "You would have just stayed!"

I was on dangerous ground here.

"Of course I'd have gone to find you. Josh merely gave me the nudge I needed."

Emily's face softened. She nestled her head against my shoulder.

"It sounds silly, but you've changed my life."

We'd only known each other two days, but I felt the same about her.

Her eyes shimmered as she held my face.

"We'll make it work when you go off to Penn State. Won't we?"

"Not a doubt in my mind."

Emily kissed me.

"I love you, Sparky."

I told her I loved her then held her in my arms. We fell asleep on the cool damp grass, holding each other. We awoke the same way to a cloudy gray dawn with Jefferson Airplane's Grace Slick telling everyone good morning. Emily and I wiped sleep from our eyes while the group played their psychedelic San Francisco rock I found hard to appreciate so early in the morning.

Hand in hand, we searched for Josh and Buck. The morning light illuminated the accumulation of muddy trash. Day One's sweet smell of pastureland was replaced by the stench of wet manure and man-made garbage.

Heavy clouds hung overhead. Yet another storm on the way.

Near the woods, members of the Hog Farm passed out granola in Dixie Cups. Emily made a face.

"Looks like something we'd feed our animals." She took a bite. "But much better."

Emily and I ate the granola and made our way toward the pond. Guys and girls bathed with soap or just skinny-dipped in the murky water. I never imagined I'd see so many naked women.

Emily smiled.

"It's about equality. Women saying if the guys can get naked, so can we."

"I'm all for that."

Emily giggled.

"You going in?"

"I showered at your place."

Emily blushed.

"I was there, remember?"

"That's right. You tossed me the soap."

Emily laughed as we made our way toward the stage. The two days of rain had soaked the ground and swept water downhill toward the stage, making the area around it a gooey brown soup. We stopped at the edge of the slime.

Joe Cocker, with his white soul sound, sang "With a Little Help From My Friends." Emily squeezed my hand.

"I meant to ask why you and Josh are going to Penn State when you live in a college town."

"The easy decision would be to stay at home. The right thing is usually hard."

Emily cocked her head.

"You're not talking about what I should do after I graduate next year, are you?"

"Nope."

I wouldn't presume to tell Emily what to do. Whether she stayed on the farm or went away to college to become a teacher, I knew her well enough by now to know she'd make the right decision without any prodding from me.

Cocker finished the song as rain fell once again. Roadies began to dismantle the stage's electrical works. Most people covered their heads or dashed toward the woods for cover, but Emily and I raised our arms and welcomed the warm shower.

"Sparky." The voice sounded like Buck's.

Buck and Josh walked toward us. They both looked worse than Emily and me, particularly Buck. Covered with mud, he must have participated in, if not mastered, the mudslides down the hill.

As they approached, jolting thunder rolled over the festival.

♪♪♪♪♪

The metallic clank of the cell door opening jolted me awake. I bolted upright on the cold metal bench in the dimly lit cell. Half the men snored, curled on the cement floor. I groaned from the ache of lying on the cold slab.

A deputy led Buck inside the cell. My friend's calm appearance offered a small measure of relief, but I still worried about Josh and Lady.

At least Buck somehow ditched the tie-dyed for his camouflage shirt. How had he pulled that off?

Snake got in Buck's face like he'd done to me.

I leaped to my feet and grabbed a kink in my back. "He's with me, Snake." I winced and sat back on the hard bench.

"Okay, that's cool." Snake held up both hands. "Any friend of Sparky's is a friend of mine."

Buck's mouth dropped open.

"You part of his kidnapping gang?" Snake led him to the bench.

"Gang. Yes, I'm second in command. Now the cops want to pin a cocaine charge on us. Did you know that?" Buck sat beside me.

"Yup."

Snake crossed the room to pee in the toilet while I rolled my head, trying to ease the stiffness in my neck.

"I fucked up big time, Buck."

He looked at me as if I was crazy.

"We knew this might happen before we left but, man, we got to perform on the biggest stage of our lives, like we were something again, you know?"

"You think that was worth getting arrested?"

"This isn't as bad as it seems."

I nearly exploded.

"We've been arrested for kidnapping! Ten to life, Buck." With our cellmates stirring, I forced myself to lower my voice and regain my jailhouse cool. "Now they're trying to manufacture drug evidence against us."

"They won't find cocaine. Possession of trace amounts of weed, come on. All this little shit will go away. Cloe will take care of the kidnapping charge."

"Culpepper won't let us off so easy."

His political career might depend on making an example of us. Buck likely faced prison time. Even if Cloe got him off on probation, he'd already lost Ashley and his lead mechanic.

"How can you remain so calm?"

"Haven't you ever heard if life hands you lemons, make margaritas? My friend, you've missed the big picture."

I jumped to my feet.

"The big picture?"

"We're famous. We were on CNN."

"As kidnappers!"

"I bet we're on *Letterman* by the end of the week."

Buck tugged on my arm, and I sat.

I didn't want fame. I wouldn't exploit Josh anymore than I already had.

"Sparky, everyone will want to know about the miracle of Josh remembering Woodstock songs. How we made it to Bethel. How we took the stage and kicked ass, all thanks to you."

"Thanks to me?" I gazed around at the sleeping thieves and cutthroats. "Buck, we're in jail!"

"You're tired. Get some rest. It's after two." Buck stepped over Armed Robbery, walked to the cell door and peered down the hallway. "You'll feel better in the morning."

No, I wouldn't.

Something gnawed at me since I met up with Buck at his garage. This might be as good a time as any to ask.

"Can I ask you one more thing?"

"You can ask me anything, man."

"Years ago when you got off drugs in St. Louis and checked out of rehab, why didn't you call me for help? Why call Emily?"

Buck let out a deep breath.

"You changed over the years. Emily kept that sweet innocent compassion she had since we met. I knew she wouldn't ask why I needed it. She just asked how much. That's how she was. Always."

"I know."

I swallowed a lump in my throat. When would I get Emily's ashes back? When would I see Josh or Lady?

I leaned my head back and closed my eyes. To my surprise, I grew sleepy.

♪♪♪♪♪

I opened my eyes. Buck, Josh, Emily and I sat in the middle of the amphitheater. The storm had passed. It was Sunday night. The last scheduled day of the festival. Josh and Buck shared a joint while the four of us dug Crosby, Stills, Nash & Young on stage.

Stephen Stills spoke into the mike and said the group was

scared shitless. Then they sang "Suite: Judy Blue Eyes" with their unmistakable and unique harmonies.

As night turned into Monday morning, people began to pack up and leave, but we stayed. Jimi Hendrix, the best guitar player ever, had yet to perform.

With so many people gone, we made our way closer and found a spot fifty yards from the stage. Emily began to pick dried mud from Buck's hair but gave up the hopeless task.

Hendrix took the stage and made music from the electric guitar I never imagined possible. He closed the two-hour set with *Hey Joe*, but *The Star Spangled Banner* made an impression I'd never forget.

The amazing performance ended. I reluctantly got to my feet and helped Emily up.

Woodstock was officially over. A sudden feeling of finality swept over me. I didn't know when I'd see Emily again.

We made our way up the hill. Emily placed my arm around her waist and leaned close. We trudged through the layer of trash in silence. Halfway up the hill, Buck tripped over a sleeping bag and a Polaroid camera tumbled out.

Buck picked up the camera and gazed around to see who might have left it.

I peered over his shoulder.

"Any pictures left?"

"Two." Buck wiped away mud. A whirring sound came from the camera and a picture slid out the front.

"One."

We all laughed when the photo developed a close-up of Buck's mud streaked hair.

Emily took the camera.

"Let's get someone to take a picture of the four of us."

Rotting garbage lay everywhere. There wasn't a decent backdrop for a photo. I pointed to the stage where roadies worked to take down equipment.

"Let's get a picture on stage."

"You're the smartest boyfriend ever!"

Emily grabbed my hand. We slogged through the slippery mud and climbed on stage. I couldn't believe I stood where the greats performed the past three days.

Buck gazed out over the nearly deserted amphitheater and talked into an imaginary microphone.

"And now, the superstars you've waited for, The Buck Naked Band."

I called to a group of people at the back of the stage.

"Excuse me. Would one of you take a picture for us?"

Emily held up the camera.

A tall black man with an Afro, in jeans and a white shirt with fringe on the sleeves, turned and faced us.

"I'll do it."

Holy crap. Jimi Hendrix.

Josh whispered.

"Jimi Freakin' Hendrix."

Jimi approached with a smile.

Buck looked like he might pee his pants.

"Mr. Hendrix, you were terrific."

"My old man is Mr. Hendrix. You all can call me Jimi."

Emily gave him the camera.

"We should take your picture."

"You all don't need a picture of me, Foxy Lady."

Emily giggled like a little girl.

With his back to the amphitheater, Jimi positioned us on the stage. He looked through the viewfinder then peered over the camera toward Buck.

"Big guy, do something with your hair. You're getting your picture taken, Son."

Josh had bathed in the pond, but Buck's long hair hadn't been washed in three days and was covered in streaks of mud. He ran his fingers through his hair and tried to make himself presentable.

"Hey, Luther." Jimi shouted to a roadie wrapping a coil of cable. "Give the big guy your hat. Looks like shit on you anyway. Besides, it's a white guy's hat."

"Say what?" The roadie dropped the speaker wire he'd unplugged from an amp and removed his bushman. "This ain't no white guy's hat, Jimi."

"It is now." Jimi grabbed the hat and tossed the bushman to Buck. "Keep it, my man. A gift from Jimi."

Buck stared at the hat as if it was a thousand dollar bill. He set the bushman on his head and tucked his hair beneath the brim. He looked cool.

Jimi peered through the camera and positioned us closer together.

Emily squeezed my hand. I gazed into her dimpled face as she smiled at me.

Jimi snapped the picture. We stood beside the legend and watched the photo develop. Perfect.

He removed a pen from his pocket and turned the photo over.

"You got names?"

"I'm Emily, this is Josh, Buck and Sparky. They're The Buck Naked Band."

Jimi laughed, wrote on the back and handed the photo to Emily. She read aloud.

"Best of luck and success to The Buck Naked Band and Foxy Lady, Emily." Emily blushed. "Jimi Hendrix."

Jimi lit a Salem Menthol cigarette.

"What did The Buck Naked Band think of *The Star Spangled Banner*?"

Josh cleared his throat.

"It was an anthem for a country at war. You made the guitar sound like jets making strafing runs. Unreal."

"You know your music, Son." Jimi shook Josh's hand.

Jimi checked me out then nodded toward Emily.

"This your lady?"

Emily slipped her arm in mine.

"I'm definitely his lady, and he's my man."

"You're a lucky guy. Mind if I give your lady a kiss goodbye?"

It wasn't my decision to make. Emily's eyes widened. She slowly nodded.

I tried to think of a nice way to tell Jimi Hendrix not to get too carried away.

"Sure."

Jimi crushed his cigarette under his boot. He held Emily's shoulders and gave her a gentle kiss that lasted longer than I hoped. I clenched my teeth and tried to hide a twinge of jealousy. The kiss finally ended, and he gave her a hug.

Emily's face flushed. She'd just kissed a superstar.

Jimi reached into his pocket.

"A token of my appreciation."

He placed something in her palm. He closed her fist and kissed her hand.

Emily smiled her dimpled smile at him.

"Thanks for taking our picture ... Jimi."

"Goodbye, Emily." He rejoined his friends.

Emily held trembling fingertips to her face.

"Oh my God! Oh my God! I kissed Jimi Hendrix. Wait 'til I tell Crystal."

Josh clapped me on the shoulder and grinned.

"Good luck with that."

Buck elbowed me in the ribs. "Can I kiss her, too?"

"No."

"Might be the only way to get her to forget kissing Jimi Hendrix."

"I'll do that myself, but thanks for offering."

I took Emily's hand. We all climbed off the stage and walked away.

Emily clutched the photo in one hand and held out the other.

"I want to give you something."

She'd already given me her heart. I didn't need anything more.

She placed the guitar pick Jimi Hendrix gave her into my hand.

"Jimi Hendrix gave that to you."

Emily smiled and showed her dimple.

"What's mine is yours."

I'd treasure the gift always, like I'd always treasure Emily.

We made our way through the garbage, crossing what once had been green rolling hills of Yasgur's farm. Josh glanced at the stage and his voice broke.

"I'll never forget this place."

Emily would return to her farm. Buck would go to boot camp. Josh and I would head off to Penn State. I didn't know when we would be together again. An idea popped into my mind.

"Let's make a vow and shake on it."

I offered my right hand and placed Emily's on top of mine. Josh set a hand on Emily's and Buck placed his on top of Josh's. We repeated the sequence. With eight hands together, I nodded toward the stage.

"Let's promise each other one day we'll come back to Woodstock."

We looked at each other and shouted, "Woodstock!"

I held Emily's hand, and the four of us climbed the hill. A pledge to return would ensure everything we experienced the past three days—the music, the joy, the communal spirit, a belief we could accomplish anything if we set our minds to it—would live in us.

At the top of the hill, I looked back toward the stage. No one spoke. The melancholy look on my friends' faces reflected our sorrow over the end of an event we'd never forget.

I had to make sure the pledge was more than words. Whatever changes life brought or how long it might take to accomplish, no matter what, I'd make sure we kept the promise we made to each other. One day, the four of us would return to Woodstock.

20

How could I have forgotten that pledge? Had I changed so much, like Buck said, that the promise we made never came to mind?

Awake on the cold hard bench in the Sullivan County jail cell, I sat and buried my head in my hands, disgusted with myself. Making sure we came back was my responsibility. It was too late for Emily. I failed us all.

Buck slept on the floor beside the bench. I whispered, "Emily, I'm sorry. I made such a mess of everything."

Snake stepped over sleeping inmates, crossed the room and set one foot on the bench.

"Got a good lawyer?"

I arched my back and stretched. Stiff from lying on cold metal, my spine popped like a string of firecrackers going off.

"The best. My daughter."

"I got a kid. Lives in Syracuse with his mama."

He tugged a photo from his pocket of a boy in a hockey uniform and a pretty, young woman with Cloe's smile.

"Has his daddy's eyes. You see him much?"

Snake stuffed the picture into his pocket and sat beside me.

"Not as much as I'd like. Josie thinks I'm a bad influence on Cody. She's probably right. Look around."

"What did they bust you for?"

"I work construction. They pay up Friday after work. I get drunk, get in fights, get tossed in the can. I agree to pay restitution and they let me out in time to go to work Monday mornings. Guess I'm kind of in a rut."

I could empathize. I'd been in a rut for two years.

Footsteps sounded down the hallway. Two deputies arrived at the door.

"Ellington and Jamison."

"Next Friday, why don't you go visit your boy instead of the bar?" I shook Buck awake.

"Don't think my old lady would like me showing up on her doorstep." Snake stroked his beard. "I'm behind on child support."

"Give her what you can. Show her you're trying. Pay a little each week instead of drinking your money away."

One of the deputies shouted.

"Come on, Ellington."

Snake walked a sleepy-eyed Buck and me to the cell door.

"You're a cool dude. Too cool to be in here."

"So are you, Snake." I shook his thick calloused hand.

A smile curled from the corner of his mouth.

"Call me, Bruno."

The two deputies escorted Buck and me through a maze of corridors. They locked us in an opulent conference room with marble floors and a mahogany table with thick leather chairs. A wall clock with Roman numerals read six fifteen.

A glass-framed document hung beside the closed door. The text contained a quote I vaguely recalled: "As long as I have a choice, I will stay in a country where political liberty, toleration and equality for all citizens before the law are the rule." *Albert Einstein.*

Buck ran a hand over the expensive table.

"Why do you think they brought us here? It's a good sign, right?"

"Even a condemned man gets a last meal."

He smacked the table.

"I thought your glass is always half full."

I peered through blinds covering windows that stretched the length of the room. A CNN satellite truck was set up in the parking lot. A reporter with a microphone searched for a backdrop. A dozen other media members gathered near the front door. Behind the media stood at least a hundred people in sixties clothes carrying signs. One read "Free The Buck Naked Band," another "Go, Sparky, Go!"

"This might be your answer."

"You think Culpepper plans to parade us in front of a bunch of reporters like we're the catch of the day?" Buck asked. He ignored the leather chairs and hopped onto the edge of the tabletop.

The door opened, and my heart fluttered. David, carrying his black bag, and Cloe with her briefcase, entered. She handed the briefcase to the doctor then ran and wrapped both arms around me.

"Are you okay?"

I hugged my daughter. Tears leaked through my closed eyes.

"I'm sorry, Cloe. I should've listened to you. I never should have taken Josh."

"You did what you thought was right. I'm proud of you."

Cloe caressed my cheek with the palm of her hand.

"Maybe it wasn't exactly legal, but you did the right thing for Josh."

What made her change her mind?

Buck hopped off the table and hugged Cloe.

David set Cloe's briefcase and his black bag on the table. He examined my swollen lip then palpated the bruise on my knuckle.

"Your hand doesn't appear fractured, but we should get an X-ray. In my professional opinion, I'd say you were in another fight."

"Wasn't much of a fight." Buck clapped me on the back. "Sparky busted the guy's nose."

Cloe shook her head. "Dad!"

David removed the stethoscope from his bag and listened to my heart. He listened to my lungs while I took deep breaths.

"What about cardiac pain?"

"Not one." We dodged cops in two states and sang live in front of hundreds. I punched out a jerk and broke his nose, was wrestled to the floor by deputies and thrown in a jail cell. Even during the car chase through Bethel, I had no chest pains.

"Everything sounds okay." David stepped toward Buck. "What about you?"

Buck held up both hands.

"Back off, sawbones."

Cloe took my hands in hers.

"You're both getting out of here."

"You posted bail?"

"I'm getting the charges dropped."

Her words echoed like a timpani drum. Charges dropped? All of them?

Buck pumped his fist into the air.

"I told your old man you'd take care of this. He worries too much."

Cloe opened the briefcase.

"The DA's reviewing the paperwork now."

"Culpepper?" I asked.

"Bailey Houston, the Sullivan County DA."

Cloe removed a paper from the briefcase and handed me the document.

"This is a copy."

My eyes blurred from the tiny print, but I recognized Mrs. Channing's notarized signature at the bottom. I handed the paper to Buck to read.

"Josh's mother signed this?"

"She signed over temporary power of attorney to you, Dad."

"To me?" Had I heard right? "Why would that self-righteous old shrew do that?"

"Dad, she's not an old shrew. She's stubborn and set in her ways like ... like you. She's self-righteous, but religion helped her through some tough times, the sudden loss of her husband and the gradual loss of her son."

Cloe's understanding attitude made me wish I'd been more tolerant of Josh's mother.

"You're a miracle worker, Cloe."

"I had nothing to do with her decision to grant power of attorney. You did."

Me? "What did I do?"

"You let Josh call his mother. I spent two hours in her kitchen trying to talk some sense into the woman. Nothing worked. I almost gave up. Then Josh called. While they spoke, tears rolled down her cheeks. After the call, she asked me to wait in the other room while she prayed. She returned a different woman. You know what convinced her you were a good person after all these years?"

Buck shrugged. He didn't have any idea either.

"What?"

"You told Josh his dog, Buttons, was in heaven. All these years Mrs. Channing thought you were an atheist."

"Halleluiah, Jesus!" Buck thrust both hands into the air.

"Josh can go with you wherever he wants." Cloe beamed.

The door opened. Damn. It wasn't Josh. Where was he? How was he?

A silver-haired man in his mid-sixties, wearing a tailored

pinstriped suit, came in with Emily's ashes. He handed me the urn.

I clutched the urn against my chest and slumped down into a leather chair. I rocked in the chair as relief swept through me. I'd almost lost her to Culpepper. With her back, how could I scatter her ashes and let Emily go?

Cloe shook the man's hand.

"Dad, this is Mr. Houston, the Sullivan County DA I told you about."

"Walter Ellington." He shook my hand. "I've reviewed the paperwork and everything is in order. Sorry for the inconvenience."

Buck pumped the man's hand.

"You're all right, Houston!"

The DA smiled and ran his fingers over the lapel of his suit.

"Don't let the threads fool you. I'm a charter member of Woodstock Nation. To this day, I can't hear a Janice Joplin song without tearing up. Wish I could've seen your performance last night."

"What performance?" Cloe cocked her head.

"The Buck Naked Band on stage at Crystal's in Bethel," Houston explained.

Buck pumped his fist.

"We kicked it, and … Crystal recorded the performance. We're going to open a Web site and sell downloads, *The Buck Naked Band Live at Crystal's.*

What was he talking about?

"Why didn't you tell me?"

"When? You weren't in any mood to discuss a financial enterprise after we stepped off the stage last night."

With all our undeserved publicity, the idea made sense.

"Proceeds will go to the Alzheimer's Foundation, right?"

"Oh, sure, sure." Buck winked at Cloe.

"What happens now?" I asked.

Houston smiled.

"You're free to go."

The room grew still as the reality of our impending release sank in. The roadtrip, with all its twists and turns, was about to take the final leg. No more cops or Culpepper to stop us.

How could I ever thank my daughter for what she'd done for me.

"Cloe …" My voice caught, and I broke down. I clutched Emily's urn to my chest and tried to stop a tsunami of emotions.

Tears slid down my face as I sorted through the guilt over the pain I caused Buck and Josh, my deception of Cloe and my loss of Emily. I reached a hand to Cloe for comfort though I hadn't been there when she needed me.

Cloe knelt beside me. She wrapped her arms around my shoulders and cried with me. She grabbed tissues from her briefcase, dried her eyes and handed me several tissues.

I sobbed against her shoulder. I wiped my eyes but couldn't stop the tears. I let out the grief welling inside for two years. I went through several tissues until I finally dried my eyes.

Tears shimmered in Buck's eyes. He smiled and broke an awkward moment for me. He tapped his hands on the conference room table like he played the bongos and sang the Richie Havens song we heard when we first arrived at Woodstock.

"*Freedom ... freedom ... freedom, oh freedom.* Come on Sparky, we're free, man."

I managed to smile and sang along with Buck. "*Freedom ... freedom ... freedom, oh freedom.*"

My daughter laughed.

"Let's go."

I rose on unsteady legs as the door opened. Our celebration screeched to a halt.

Henry Culpepper stepped into the room with a not-so-fast look on his face.

"Hate to spoil the party."

Buck nudged the Sullivan County DA.

"Houston, we have a problem."

Culpepper wore a three-piece suit perfect for a media interview. He appeared much shorter than he had on television and the last time I saw him. Of course, then I was face down on the floor of Crystal's kitchen and blood flowed from my lip while deputy sheriffs stood over me.

I clung tightly to Emily's urn and forced myself to remain calm while Cloe handed him the power of attorney.

Culpepper's eyebrows narrowed like two caterpillars ready to battle as he read the document. It took only seconds to regain his smug composure.

"The abduction occurred before Mrs. Channing granted power of attorney. Your clients still kidnapped Josh Channing from the Sunrise facility, and the people of Pennsylvania intend to press charges."

The knuckles of Buck's clenched fists turned white. I shot him a chillout-look. *Let Cloe take care of this.* How ironic I could reason with a construction worker who drank too much and spent weekends in jail, but I wouldn't even try to reason with Culpepper.

"I assumed you might say something like that."

Cloe removed another paper from her briefcase and handed the document to Culpepper.

"This is your copy of a letter from Mrs. Channing stating had she known all the facts, she would have granted power of attorney *before* my father, Mr. Jamison and Mr. Channing left for a weekend getaway to New York."

Without reading the letter, Culpepper stuffed it into his pocket. He peered through the blinds toward the throng of reporters and straightened his tie.

I held my tongue as a Samuel Butler quote that perfectly described the man came to mind: "The truest characters of ignorance are vanity and pride and arrogance."

Culpepper's pride seemed shaken, but he faced us and crossed both arms, giving his best Mussolini pose.

"There are still a number of other charges pending—possession of marijuana, illegal flight ..."

"Don't forget speeding," I added.

District Attorney Houston stepped forward.

"Those occurred within my jurisdiction, Mr. Culpepper. Sullivan County has dropped all charges, including an assault complaint filed and withdrawn by one Darrell Thompson."

Culpepper took another look out the window at the media circus that waited, as if imagining what might have been.

"I might consider a plea bargain."

Buck sneered.

"Fuck your plea deal."

"No plea bargain," Cloe insisted. "All charges get dropped or I go out to the parking lot and explain to those reporters how you pursued a case against a Lawrenceville businessman and decorated veteran and a retired Milton College professor with permission to take an Alzheimer's patient back to Woodstock."

Culpepper let out a ragged sigh of resignation.

"You win, Ms. Ellington. This time." He locked eyes with me. "I watched my grandfather die of Alzheimer's, Mr. Ellington. He was a brilliant and kind ..." He cleared his throat. "The point is, back then there wasn't a specialized Alzheimer's facility like Sunrise. Caring for my grandfather almost destroyed my family. What you did for your friend, however well intentioned, was ill-advised, ill-conceived and dangerous." Culpepper left the room, followed by the Sullivan County DA.

Taking Josh without permission might have been ill-conceived, but we had no choice. The roadtrip allowed him to experience one glorious day. I'd do it again.

At least now I better understood Culpepper's motives. His vendetta had been personal, but not against me.

Buck's lip curled in disgust.

"I saw that."

"What?" I asked.

"That flicker of sympathy in your eyes for Culpepper. That son-of-a-bitch is still a tool. Don't be a damn weenie. You know what they say. Anger's the best medicine, right doc?"

I chuckled.

"*Laughter* is the best medicine."

"In academia maybe. Not the real world."

I clapped Buck on the back.

"Let's go get Josh."

Buck's eyes twinkled as he stepped into the hallway and sang, "*Freedom ... freedom ... freedom ... oh, freedom!*"

The sheriff's office processed our release and returned our personal items including my cell phone, Heather's flute, my guitar and the bushman Buck set on his head.

I handed the guitar to David and carried Emily's ashes down the hall toward the lobby, anxious to see for myself that Josh was all right.

"I didn't know you were a decorated veteran," I said to Buck.

"You didn't? I got decorated after the battle for Da Nang." He rolled up the sleeve of his camouflage shirt and showed me the Scout Dog tattoo on his arm. "Impressive decoration, don't you think?"

Cloe stopped before opening the lobby door.

"Dad, I've decided not to take that job in Virginia."

"Because of him?" I nodded toward the handsome doctor, who looked positively giddy about the news.

"If you're concerned about my health, the chest pains are gone."

I could overcome broken heart syndrome, but my broken heart

over losing Emily would never entirely heal.

"My decision had nothing to do with David or you. I love my life in Milton and being a defense attorney, but I learned from you the last few days there's more to life than my career." She took David's hand and smiled.

The doctor held the door open for us.

"You have more people waiting for you, Mr. Ellington."

"Sparky, remember?" *Not "Dad." Not yet.*

We stepped into the lobby. In the middle of the room, Crystal held Lady on the leash.

Lady spotted me and tugged away from Crystal's grip. The leash trailed behind her as she sprinted toward me, nails clicking on the tile floor.

I handed the urn to Cloe. Lady leaped into my arms and nearly knocked me over. I hugged her and buried my face in her golden fur. "I'm so sorry I left you alone again, girl."

Lady licked my face. Laughing, I made her stop and set her down. Her eyes danced. She smiled the familiar golden retriever smile.

Buck held out his arms, and Crystal ran to him. He picked her up and twirled her around in a long passionate kiss. The embrace ended, and he gazed into Crystal's eyes with more tenderness than I'd seen him display toward Ashley or any woman I ever remembered. Crystal's expression showed she felt the same about him.

With one arm around Buck, she squeezed my hand.

"I'm so sorry Darrell turned you in."

"It wasn't your fault." I kissed her cheek. "Thanks for looking after Lady and for everything you've done for us."

I picked up the end of the leash. Lady stared across the room and wagged her tail.

My new neighbors, Heather and Meagan, rose from chairs beside the entrance. They smiled and hurried toward us.

I hugged Heather, who wore a Free The Buck Naked Band T-shirt. I handed her the flute.

"I'm glad you're here."

"A police station?" The teenager laughed. "You don't think I came to see you, do you? I have a chance to check out where Woodstock was held."

Meagan threw both arms around my neck. Her lips melted into mine. The woman's interest in me was inexplicable. She was gorgeous, smart, a caring mother and a fabulous cook, and I had to admit, a terrific kisser.

She rubbed my chin with the palm of her hand.

"You need a shave, sweetie."

Was I her sweetie? I didn't know what might happen between us, but I'd come to realize unknown surprises made for an intriguing future.

The door we'd just come through opened behind me.

Detective Briggs and Sawyer led Josh into the lobby.

With Alzheimer's deteriorating his memory, I didn't think Josh would recognize me, but he grinned.

"Sparky!"

Buck and I exchanged hugs with our friend.

"You all right?" I asked. "Did they treat you okay?"

"They wouldn't let me have a hamburger, but they gave me Coke."

I smiled at Detective Briggs.

"They gave you Coke, huh."

With a don't-give-a-shit shrug, Briggs, followed by Sawyer, disappeared behind the door.

The glow faded from Josh's face.

"I lost something, but I don't remember what it was. I think a picture ..."

Crystal slid a photo from her pocket and handed it to Josh.

"My dog!" Josh studied the old black-and-white picture of Buttons. "Her name is ..." His face twisted clearly searching his memory. "She's asleep under a tree in my backyard."

Cloe blinked moist eyes.

"I have to sign Josh's release." She carried her briefcase to the counter.

I almost burst with pride as I watched my daughter. She displayed her mother's idealism tempered with her own pragmatism. Cloe had reasoned with Josh's mom, gone nose-to-nose with Culpepper and managed to get all our considerable charges dismissed. She was stubborn, like Emily and her old man. Unfortunately, she dealt with the grief of losing her mother without my help.

I had been self-indulgent far too long. After Emily died, I messed up my life and the lives of those close to me. My mistakes even jeopardized my health.

Buck clapped Josh on the shoulder.

"Ready to resume our roadtrip?"

"Roadtrip?" Josh looked confused then his eyes widened with understanding. "Roadtrip, yeah!"

For me, the roadtrip didn't begin when the psychedelic van left Milton. My journey started the day Emily passed away. I took the wrong route at times, became stuck frequently, but now with the help of Cloe and friends old and new, I regained my bearings. I just needed to take the final step.

I tugged on Lady's leash and led Buck across the room toward the entrance where the others couldn't hear.

"I don't know if I can go through with this, letting Emily go."

Buck let out a deep breath.

"I dreamed about Woodstock last night in the jail cell."

"Really? How does that—"

"Let me finish. The Buck Naked Band performed at Woodstock. Everyone loved us. I woke up and remembered being on the stage for real—Jimi Hendrix taking our picture, giving me this."

He took off the bushman and studied it a moment before setting it back on his head.

"Before we left Woodstock, we made a vow to each other that one day we'd all come back. I'd forgotten about the pledge until my dream."

"It's my fault we never made it back. Now it's too late."

"What are you talking about?" Buck put his arm around my shoulders, called Josh over and did the same to him. He nodded to Emily's urn in my arms.

"It's not too late."

Heather, Meagan and Crystal joined us. David and Cloe, holding hands, did as well. My daughter held up her briefcase.

"All set. We're free to go. You okay, Dad?"

Surrounded by family and friends, I managed to nod. Buck opened the door, and I clutched Emily's urn to my chest. We stepped into the breezy morning air outside the police station.

We would return to Woodstock after forty years.

21

Gray, ragged clouds above threatened rain. Maybe showers would postpone our quiet ceremony, and I'd get to hold onto Emily a little while longer.

Buck sucked in a deep breath.

"I love the smell of freedom in the morning."

"Come on, Mandela." Crystal followed him toward the media gathered in the parking lot, along with a hundred or more dressed like us in the sixties.

Buck glanced back at me.

"You don't mind do you?"

"Be my guest." I had no interest in fielding questions from strangers.

The crowd cheered, and reporters with microphones and recorders hurried toward us and shouted questions.

I glanced around, looking for an exit, embarrassed by all the attention. I held Emily close and acknowledged the supporters with a wave. I appreciated everyone who clogged Bethel and kept the cops from arresting us—until Darrell turned us in—but now all I wanted was to gather my courage to scatter Emily's ashes with family and friends.

Cloe and David went in search of their car while Buck eased into the celebrity role. He raised a hand and silenced the questions. He brushed a shock of windblown hair from his brow and smiled like a politician about to announce a run for the White House.

Buck occupied the reporters as the rest of us moved toward the crowd.

"I'm Buck Jamison. Before I take any questions, I want to say a few words about ... Emily."

I froze and stopped to listen to what Buck would say.

"I guess you're here because of our roadtrip back to Woodstock, but you may not know about the woman whose ashes we brought with us. Full of joy and kindness, Emily wasn't a hippie, she was a local farmer's daughter."

I tuned out Buck's words and pictured that first day walking hand in hand with the cute girl in the rose-colored glasses who smiled and said, "I'm Emily." I remembered how her parents, Ben and Katy, welcomed me into their home. I recalled our surprise when Ben drove us back to Yasgur's farm and left us for the weekend. I pictured our Woodstock photo, special not for who took it but for the frozen moment in time.

Applause from the crowd interrupted thoughts of my past. Buck spoke of the present.

"Woodstock Nation may be aging, but as long as we continue to care about this world we live in, we'll be, as Dylan said, *forever young*. Unfortunately, there are still wars we must end, peace to be made ..." His voice trembled as he looked at Josh standing beside me. " ... and songs to be sung."

The parking lot grew quiet as Buck cleared his throat. I didn't think he could continue and couldn't let him crash and burn in front of so many people. As I stepped forward to help, he glanced up and smiled at the reporters. "If you have any questions."

I blew a breath of relief and tugged on the leash. Lady and I, Josh, Heather and Meagan disappeared into the crowd as Buck answered a question about how to order "The Buck Naked Band Live at Crystal's" download.

Well-wishers patted my back and called out words of encouragement to Josh and me. We searched the lot for Emily's van until Heather let out a shrill whistle. "Over here."

Near the fenced exit, the teenager shook her head.

"Dude, is that the same van you drove off in?"

It took a second to make sure. Mud covered the tires and dust dulled the psychedelic paint job. A three-foot crack slivered across the windshield. Dried soda smeared the hood. Two ears of corn were wedged in the grill and withered lettuce pieces clung to the nicked and scratched front bumper.

I removed the vegetable road kill and opened the side door.

Lady and Josh climbed into the backseat. Meagan and Heather took the seat in the middle. I slid the door closed and pulled myself into the passenger seat. With the urn on my lap, I closed the door and blocked out the buzz in the lot. The familiar surroundings of Emily's van provided comfort after the night in jail.

I didn't want to think about letting Emily go. I turned on my cell phone to check for messages. Cloe left most of the voice mails, but one phone number, left minutes earlier, piqued my curiosity.

"Professor Ellington, this is Dr. Warfield. Please ignore yesterday's voice mail. I was under a lot of stress fielding questions from the press and ... well, in spite of the notoriety of your actions, according to the latest news, things worked out after all. I wanted to let you know the offer to return to Milton College still stands. Please call me when you get back. Don't even bother to listen to my previous message."

As Buck would say, what a tool.

Heather leaned forward in the seat.

"So, Sparky, you never told me much about Woodstock. Did you meet anyone famous?"

Before I could tell her about Jimi Hendrix, the van's side door slid open. Buck and Crystal gave each other a deep, lingering kiss.

"Ewwww," Heather shuddered watching the two sixty year olds locked in a passionate embrace. "Sparky, make them stop."

After the kiss, Buck helped Crystal into the middle seat beside Meagan. He walked around the front, climbed into the driver's seat and held out a hand.

I slapped the keys into his palm.

"That didn't take long."

"Like with women, always leave reporters wanting more."

Crystal tugged on Buck's gray ponytail.

"How many?"

Buck chewed on his lower lip.

"How many what?"

"Women." Crystal raised an eyebrow while Meagan and Heather exchanged grins.

Buck shot me a look of cold panic.

I held up both hands. *You're on your own.*

Crystal burst out laughing and playfully slapped his shoulder.

"I was just teasing."

Buck let out a halfhearted laugh. "Yeah, that was funny." He removed a lighter and a joint from his camouflage shirt pocket. He lit the joint and took a long hit.

For the past twenty-four hours, marijuana appeared in Buck's hands as if by magic.

"We're in a police station parking lot. Where did you get that?"

"The universe provides." He offered me a hit.

I nodded toward Heather.

"We have a teenager in the car."

"Where are my manners?" Buck turned toward the middle seat and held out the joint to Heather.

"Buck," I shouted.

"Oh you mean ... Got it. Hey kid, don't do drugs."

Heather winked at me.

"Okay. I won't."

Cloe, with David in the passenger seat, drove her hybrid alongside the van. She tapped her horn and waved.

The final leg of our roadtrip was about to begin. With the joint hanging from his mouth, Buck turned the key. The van coughed and didn't start, much like his old Volkswagen back in the day. He patted the dash and tried again.

"We're almost there, girl."

The engine rumbled to life.

"Roadtrip," Josh called from the backseat. Beside him, Lady let out a happy bark.

Heather pointed to the cracked windshield.

"So, Sparkinator, what happened to the windshield?"

I hoped the question wouldn't freak Buck out. Now wasn't the time for him to revisit the cornfield meltdown.

"I decapitated a scarecrow." Buck held out a closed hand, and I returned his fist bump.

We drove away from the police station. My lingering worries faded that Culpepper might run up and wave some kind of document to throw our butts back in jail. Still, I checked the side mirror. Dozens of cars and a media van fell in line behind Cloe and followed us. My plan to scatter Emily's ashes in a quiet personal moment vanished.

The pastoral scenery took my mind off what I'd come to do. Not much had changed since my first visit to upstate New York—green rolling hills, quaint farms with wood barns painted red.

A chill shivered up my arms when we turned onto the highway Josh, Buck and I had hiked the final miles to the festival. We reached

Bethel and took the same road where I slogged through the mud and rain in search of a girl whose last name I didn't know.

Blocks from the site, Buck pulled up behind a media truck and shut off the ignition. Parked cars packed both sides of the road. A festive crowd strolled the road, now transformed into a giant street fair.

A dark-haired girl, who couldn't have been more than seventeen, danced past the window. With a daisy painted on her face, she blew bubbles from a plastic ring and disappeared out of view. For a moment, I thought I'd seen Emily's apparition, but nearly everyone was dressed like it was nineteen sixty-nine.

People poured from our car caravan and joined the festivities. I stepped from the van and opened the side door. After everyone climbed out, I clipped the leash to Lady and handed it to Josh. I retrieved two mementoes from the box behind the front seat and stuffed them into my pocket.

Like a state fair midway, food and vendor booths were set up along the road. Crosby, Stills, Nash & Young's song *Woodstock* blasted from speakers up ahead. The images reminded me of the song's lyrics. "Everywhere, a song and a celebration," I said to Buck.

"We should get a percentage." He pointed to a booth selling Woodstock shirts.

Next to the vendor, a black street musician sat playing an acoustic guitar. Heather pulled the flute from her pocket and jammed as he played a bluesy version of The Mamas and The Papas' *California Dreamin*."

Cloe and David approached.

"Where to, Dad?"

Where were the woods, the pond, the natural amphitheater? Almost everything had changed, except the sea of heads and tie-dyed shirts.

"I'm not sure."

Heather stopped playing the flute.

"Dude, you know about the monument where the stage used to be, right?"

That would be perfect.

Heather dropped a bill in the musician's guitar case.

"Max Yasgur sold off most of the farm to developers. We've got to check out the museum before we leave."

A museum? I couldn't believe how much she knew about this

place. I smiled and gestured down the road.

"Lead the way, tour guide."

I ignored people who nudged each other and pointed toward Emily's urn. Dozens followed us.

Heather and Meagan walked ahead with Josh and Lady, who sniffed everyone within reach.

Cloe and David held hands, their arms swinging up and down like pre-teens. I didn't wish them the same joyous life Emily and I had together. I hoped they'd find their own special happiness.

Rock music played from unseen speakers as we continued down the road. Mothers pushed babies in strollers. Wind nudged a red balloon across a gray matted sky. A young couple shared a container of popcorn, and like during Woodstock, a breeze carried the unmistakable sweet aroma of marijuana.

Buck draped an arm around Crystal's shoulders as he walked beside me.

"It's not the same, is it, Sparky?"

Ahead, Heather played the flute while a little boy, not much more than six, danced to the music.

"It is for her."

In spite of my initial disappointment that so many had joined us, I knew Emily would love to return with people enjoying a Woodstock experience.

When Crystal bought a Coke for Josh from a vendor, Buck took me aside. He handed me the keys to Emily's van. As if confiding a deep secret, he spoke in a conspiratorial voice.

"I won't be driving back to Pennsylvania with you."

"Why not?"

"Crystal and I need to mix The Buck Naked Band music she recorded. She can help set up a Web site so we can sell downloads. And ... and the bar—"

"So, staying is a financial decision."

We both knew his answer was complete bullshit.

Buck grinned.

"Okay, you got me."

I wanted to hear him say the real reason he decided to stay. I'd waited since high school for him to admit he fell for someone.

"You'll probably think this is crazy talk coming from someone as cynical about women as me, but I think ... I want to find out if there's something between the two of us, something Crystal and I left at

Woodstock forty years ago."

"Not crazy talk at all."

He rubbed the stubble on his chin.

"I didn't go search for her like you did Emily. Back then, it never occurred to me. Now I'm thinking maybe I should have. Who knows if things might have turned out differently."

"Who knows. What about the garage?"

"I called Tony. Says he can handle the place for a week or two. After banging Ashley, I think he owes me. Don't you?"

"And after a couple of weeks?"

Buck shrugged. "Not sure. I've never made plans that far in advance." He gave a playful punch to my shoulder and hurried after Crystal. He wrapped an arm around her waist and kissed her neck. He whispered something in her ear, and she giggled like she was seventeen again.

I had no idea what the future held, but the unknown made life interesting.

Meagan watched her daughter trying on hats from a vendor. I caught up.

Heather picked up a pink baseball cap with psychedelic swirls and set it on her head just so.

"What do you think, Sparky?"

"Sweet." Surprisingly girly, in a good way.

While Heather paid the man, Meagan walked beside me.

"How you doing, neighbor? I mean really."

"I'm okay."

She gave me a skeptical tilt of the head. Meagan rescued me from talking about my feelings when she changed the subject.

"Dad asked us to move in with him permanently."

The old coot listened to my advice after all.

After an uncomfortable pause while I tried to figure out what I should say, Meagan brushed a fleck of marijuana from my yellow tie-dyed shirt.

"A couple months ago, a restaurant closed near campus. It needs a lot of work, but I thought a classy bistro would be perfect for faculty and students. Maybe you could give me your read on the community, help me connect with people who—"

"Yes, I'm a people person."

Meagan laughed.

"You've lived in Milton all your life."

"Sixty years." Before this went any further, I wanted to make sure she knew my age.

Meagan touched my arm. Her hand lingered.

"I know how old you are. You were at Woodstock. I can do the math."

"Of course I'll help, but what does Heather think about staying in Milton?"

Meagan laughed.

"She and Dad will have to work things out, but she loves the school and living in a town where everything seems to be within walking distance. She likes the neighborhood ... and our neighbor."

"What about you?"

A smile swept across her face.

"I like our neighbor, too."

We walked a moment in silence. I glanced down at her hand. Before I could decide whether to hold her hand, someone called to me from behind.

"Mr. Ellington."

I turned and faced two uniformed cops. My heart threatened to explode from my chest.

A young officer, who didn't look old enough to shave, stepped forward. A brass nameplate read "Cooper."

In the past twenty-four hours, I'd become familiar with the equipment clipped to a police officer's belt. This one had a gun, handcuffs and a Taser.

"You're Walter Ellington?" Officer Cooper asked.

Cold sweat trickled down my back.

"I am."

Beside me, Meagan tugged my arm.

"Maybe I should get Cloe."

I expected the officers to arrest Buck and me on some trumped-up charge. I gazed around for help, but across the road, my attorney was planting a lip lock on my doctor.

The young officer glanced back at his impatient-looking partner, who checked his watch.

"I just wanted to say I'm glad you made it back."

The comment was the last thing I expected.

"My father passed away three months ago. He was at Woodstock. I'm sure he didn't tell me everything, but he always said next to the birth of his son, Woodstock was the best experience of his life. He was a good man, my dad." He held out his hand.

I shook the young officer's hand.

"I'm sure he was."

Heather ran up and skidded to a stop. She checked out the cop and caught her breath.

"We're here, Sparky."

"Where?"

Heather pointed ahead to a gravel path that led away from the road.

"The monument's down there."

I gathered my courage.

Officer Cooper tipped his cap then headed down the road with his partner. He shot a quick glance back and flashed me a peace symbol.

No one in our group spoke as we made our way down the gravel path. Each crunching step brought me closer to letting go.

Dozens of people followed, respectfully quiet. The path ended with several hundred gathered to watch. The crowd parted and revealed the Woodstock monument.

The cast-iron and concrete sculpture looked like a large tabletop plaque. The monument faced a white fence with green fields beyond. The far end of the plaque was a replica of the red Woodstock poster Emily kept in her trunk—a white peace dove perched on the neck of a guitar. Below were the words "peace and music" and the sculptor's name, Wayne Saward. The plaque listed the festival dates and the performers I remembered so vividly from my recent dreams.

I stopped at the base of the monument, between Josh and Cloe, still holding David's hand. Buck, Crystal, Heather and Meagan stood on both sides in a half circle facing the monument.

The wind brushed the green grass. In the distance came a rumble of thunder. If the storm broke, I hoped the rain wouldn't be like the first time we were here.

The crowd quieted, and Cloe gently touched my arm.

"You should say something."

Buck nodded encouragement.

I hadn't planned to talk. I wasn't sure what I might say to those who knew Emily and the hundreds who didn't, but saying a few words felt like the appropriate thing to do.

"We gather today at this special monument to peace, love and music to say goodbye to ..." I struggled to control a quiver in my voice. " ... a wonderful wife ... a caring mother, a devoted antiwar activist, a dedicated teacher, a principal with principles and," I swallowed hard, "the love of my life."

I wanted to say more, to let everyone realize how special Emily was, but the words caught in my throat.

I took a deep breath and tightly clutched Emily's urn that I'd selfishly kept on display for two years. For a moment, there weren't hundreds of people around, just the familiar green fields beyond the white fence.

Emily's peace symbol necklace hung around my daughter's neck. I hadn't noticed. Cloe reminded me so much of her mother. She grieved alone when Emily died, without my comfort. I squeezed Cloe's hand.

She kissed my cheek, comforting me.

"It's time, Dad."

From my pocket, I removed the two items I retrieved from the box in the van. On the monument I set the picture Jimi Hendrix took.

A gust of wind tossed the photo into the air. The picture fluttered and landed face down beside the monument.

Cloe snatched up the photo and read the inscription.

"Jimi Hendrix. Dad, you and mom never told me."

Meagan showed the inscription to her daughter.

Heather's eyes grew round. "Holy shit!" She covered her mouth. "Sorry."

I smiled, took Heather's hand and placed the Jimi Hendrix guitar pick into her palm. A talented musician and a softy at heart, I knew Heather would cherish the pick always.

"It really *did* belong to Jimi Hendrix."

She kissed my cheek then showed the pick to her mother.

The rain held off, but the wind swirled around us. I breathed in a deep breath and told myself I could do this. I froze. I couldn't move or talk. Panic overwhelmed me, and I began to wheeze.

Lady nuzzled my hand. She licked my palm. The dog's gentleness provided comfort as she had for Josh and Buck when they needed it on the roadtrip. I patted her neck as my breathing returned to normal. "Thank you, girl."

Lady wagged her tail and smiled at me as she so often had.

My hand trembled as I removed the top of the urn. I took a deep breath.

I gently tossed Emily's ashes toward the monument. The wind lifted the ashes past the white fence and across the green grassy fields.

I closed my eyes and pictured Emily the day we met, the young farm girl with the flower painted on her face, the dimpled smile that captured my heart. I saw her red-faced embarrassment the day she backed her car into mine and her exhausted but joyous face the day Cloe was born. I remembered her in a different hospital two years ago, the day she weakly squeezed my hand one last time and in a whisper told me it was time for her to let go.

Josh tugged on my sleeve.

"Is this a funeral?"

He didn't remember Emily's funeral. I blinked away tears and nodded.

"Could I sing?"

"*Amazing Grace?*"

Josh shook his head.

"I remember another song. It's like a ... prayer."

"Then we'd all love to hear it."

In his soft tenor voice, Josh began a song Joan Baez sang at Woodstock.

"*Swing low, sweet chariot, coming for to carry me home. Swing low, sweet chariot, coming for to carry me home.*"

As he continued, I scattered more ashes and swallowed a lump in my throat. The ashes blew across the field that had once been Yasgur's farm.

Cloe dabbed her eyes with a tissue. She leaned against the new man in her life.

Buck hated funerals, but he looked like he'd survive the ceremony. He wiped away a tear. Crystal's lower lip quivered as she patted his hand.

Josh's voice sounded almost as pure and mellow as back in high school.

"*I looked over yonder and what did I see, coming for to carry me home. A band of angels coming after me, coming for to carry me home.*"

He forgot a few words in the chorus, but Buck and I joined in. So did most of the crowd.

While hundreds sang along, Josh remembered the rest. To me, he wasn't singing about angels who welcomed Emily. He was singing about the band of angels that would come for him in the near future, as they eventually would for us all.

I'd be with him until the end. Before that time came, I'd make peace with his mother, as I had with my neighbor next door, who struggled to survive the loss of a woman he loved. I'd make sure Josh's final journey would be a peaceful one.

Angels would one day come for me, but I wasn't ready to go. Not yet. Not for a long time. The roadtrip reaffirmed how much I had to live for—family, old friends and new ones. I even had my health.

Perhaps I'd finish the novel about the college professor I started, or write about our return to Woodstock. I might even accept Warfield's offer. There were lessons I could teach young people— and not just about literature.

I'd embrace the future as she'd want me to. I'd welcome the good days and tackle the tough ones, the way Emily lived her life. One day, I'd see Emily again. Until then, she'd be in my thoughts, my dreams, my unbroken heart.

I gathered the courage to whisper the two words I dreaded saying since the roadtrip began. Now the words comforted me. I hoped they did the same for her. "Goodbye, Emily."

Woodstock Trivia

1. What Oscar winning film director worked as an editor on the 1970 documentary Woodstock?

2. Which performer famously informed the crowd. "The New York State Thoroughfare is closed, man. Isn't that far out?"

3. Which act, known for its long concerts, had to end their performance during the fifth song when their amps overloaded?

4. Which came first, the Woodstock Music Festival or the Woodstock character in Charles Schultz's Peanuts cartoon strip?

5. When political activist Abbie Hoffman climbed on stage and interrupted a performance, what Woodstock perform knocked him off the stage with his guitar?

For answers and more Woodstock trivia, visit the author's website at www.mjmurphy.com